"In the tradition of John Grisham, Craig Parshall brings together his legal talents and his imagination to produce a very exciting book. *The Resurrection File* has action, adventure, and very good courtroom scenes. The characters are real. The dialogue is compelling. The story situations keep the reader riveted and—it's a cliché, but I will repeat it—'I couldn't put it down.'"

Ted Baehr, *publisher of* MOVIEGUIDE®, *(website:www.movieguide.org) and Chairman of the Christian Film & Television Commission*

"Craig Parshall is both a successful lawyer and a gifted novelist. His newest book, *The Resurrection File,* is a spellbinding story of spiritual, political, and legal intrigue that will keep you on the edge of your seat. Don't miss it!"

Jerry Falwell, *Chancellor, Liberty University, Lynchburg, Virginia*

"Craig Parshall has written a gripping book that is a must-read. Few authors have the experience and ability to write with such conviction and realism. You will not want to miss this book."

Jay Alan Sekulow, *Chief Counsel, The American Center for Law and Justice*

"Intriguing and intense, *The Resurrection File* pulls you in with complex characters and a breathtaking pace. It keeps you in with its undercurrent of eternal truth. Woven throughout are hot topics—terrorism, the endless Arab-Israeli conflict, and questions of 'fundamental fanaticism.' But ultimately, it's the people you will remember. Craig Parshall's first novel is a winner that will satisfy your soul and mind."

Janet Chismar, *News & Culture senior editor,* Crosswalk.com

"Craig Parshall is not only a brilliant lawyer currently practicing in the Washington, D.C., area, he is an excellent fiction writer. *The Resurrection File* is one of the most fascinating books I have read in years. It is powerful."

Tim LaHaye, *educator, minister, and coauthor of the bestselling* LEFT BEHIND® *series*

"If you are captivated by the work of John Grisham, you are really going to love *The Resurrection File.* It's not a good book to start reading if you need to sleep, because you won't get any. A very compelling read it is."

Tim Wildmon, *author, vice president of the American Family Association, and host of American Family Radio*

The Resurrection File

CRAIG PARSHALL

HARVEST HOUSE™ PUBLISHERS
EUGENE, OREGON

All Scripture quotations are taken from the New American Standard Bible ®, © 1960, 1962, 1963, 1968, 1971, 1972, 1973, 1975, 1977, 1995 by The Lockman Foundation. Used by permission.

The following Scripture quotations in this book are not identified in the text:
page 184 John 20:2; Luke 24:11; Matthew 28:17; John 20:5; 20:6-7

Cover by Left Coast Design, Portland, Oregon

Cover Photo by Tayeko/Photonica

This novel is a work of fiction. Names, characters, places, and incidents are either the product of the author's imagination or are used fictitiously. It is the intent of the author and publisher that all events, locales, organizations, and persons portrayed herein be viewed as fictitious.

THE RESURRECTION FILE

Published by Harvest House Publishers
Eugene, Oregon 97402

Library of Congress Cataloging-in-Publication Data
Parshall, Craig, 1950–
The resurrection file / Craig Parshall.
p. cm.
ISBN 0-7369-0847-1
1. Clergy—fiction. I. Title.
PS3616.A77 R47 2002
813'.54—dc21 2001043634

Printed in the United States of America.

05 06 07 08 09 10 /BC-CF/ 10 9

To my wife, Janet, who followed
in the footsteps of the Gospel women.
Like them, she hurried to this doubting man
many years ago, brimming with
extraordinary news about the tomb.

Acknowledgments

Much appreciation is owed to my administrative assistant, Marilyn Clifton. Her typing, editing, research, and constructive suggestions were invaluable, including her input as a member of the U.S. Marine Corps. Sharon Donehey's help in managing the office and interacting with editors was truly helpful, particularly as we approached deadlines.

My wife, Janet, was as always a source of inspiration, who also gave me the benefit of her pragmatic eye. So much of us is "between the lines" of these pages—the mountains and valleys that mark the pursuit of justice, the land of Israel, the archaeology of the Bible, the frontier where the gospel meets public policy, the influence of the media, and both the primacy of truth and the power of love.

I must also thank my now-adult children, Sarah, Rebekah, Samuel, and Joseph, for their love of the bedtime stories I invented for them as children. As an eager (but discerning!) audience, they taught me the interpersonal connection that can come with storytelling. (And now that Allison and Matthew have married into the Parshall family, I look forward to a whole new generation of rapt listeners, yet to be born!)

And, of course, a very special note of thanks is due to Harvest House Publishers: to Terry Glaspey and Carolyn McCready, for taking a chance on a new novelist, and for their unbounded support and encouragement in the creative process; and to Paul Gossard, for his superb suggestions in the final edit of the book.

1

Monroeville, Virginia
In the Near Future

WILL CHAMBERS WAS LATE AGAIN. For the last year or so the forty-year-old attorney had been getting to his law office late almost every day. This morning his head felt like it had been pressed in a trash compactor. Coping with a hangover was part of Chambers' daily routine. Today, like most days, he was recovering from his liquid diet of Jack Daniels. He had spent the last night in the usual manner—sitting alone in the great room of his empty, half-restored pre–Civil War mansion, listening to music, and drinking himself numb. He would drink until things hurt a little less for a while—and his personal demons were a little more fuzzy and a little less distracting. And he would fall asleep in his chair with his golden retriever lying next to him on the floor. Then, about two or three in the morning, he would awaken, stumble up the winding staircase, and fall into bed. Clarence, his big dog, would pad up the stairs close behind and bound onto the bed next to him.

This morning, amid the hammering inside his head, Chambers suddenly remembered that he had to be in court. He was grabbing around his cluttered office trying to locate his case file when Betty, his secretary, yelled for him around the corner. Chambers walked into her area. A lit cigarette was hanging out of Betty's mouth.

"Will," she said in an exasperated voice, "You've got to get going. You're going to be late for court." Will took two fingers and snatched the cigarette from her lips, crushing it out on a message pad at her desk.

"This is a non-smoking office, Betty," he said. "Geez, you know that."

Betty's eyes narrowed. "You're going to be late for court. Have a nice day."

The lawyer looked at his watch and saw that he might not make it to the central Virginia federal court on time. He stopped for a split second to examine the framed photograph of his wife that was prominently displayed on his bookshelf. He stared at the pretty face in the photograph, then carefully placed it back on the shelf. For a moment, he felt the old buried sorrow clawing once again to the surface. A noise outside jolted him back, and he grabbed his briefcase, picked up his suit coat, and dashed down the stairs, his almost shoulder-length hair flying wildly behind him.

When Will reached the street below he crossed it at a run, heading to his red-and-white 1957 Corvette convertible. There was a yellow parking ticket stuck underneath the windshield wiper, which he didn't bother to retrieve. He leaped into the driver's seat, tossing the briefcase to the seat next to him, and in one continuous motion started the car and wheeled it around in a half circle, cutting off a tour bus driver.

By the time Will had swung his car around by the front of his building, Betty had bolted out of the front door. She was waving the case file above her head that Will Chambers had forgotten. Will slowed his car down and motioned for her to toss it into the moving Corvette. With a lunge, she threw the thick brown folder onto the passenger seat. Will waved at her without looking back as he gunned the engine and accelerated out of sight, the yellow parking ticket flapping wildly underneath the windshield wiper.

2

WHILE WILL CHAMBERS WAS MOTORING on the Interstate toward federal court in north-central Virginia, a small panel truck with a lone driver was heading toward New York City from across the river. The white vehicle bore only a sparse message in black lettering that read "Pay Load Truck Rentals."

The truck was nearing the New Jersey border, heading for the George Washington bridge into Manhattan. Traffic was jammed to a crawl that morning during the tail end of rush hour.

Several years had passed since the attack on the World Trade Towers. Renovation and construction at ground zero was nearly complete. Gritty New Yorkers, refusing to succumb to a bunker mentality, had returned to daily life.

But memory had been altered. Like a flag raised and lowered in daily salute, the images of destruction had continued to speak a warning and a resolve.

Then one day last year, a van had pulled up in front of the New York Stock Exchange. Two Middle Eastern men in the van bowed their heads in prayer. Then they shouted something. That was when the driver touched his sweaty thumb to a homemade plastic button connected to a wire that disappeared into the back of the truck.

And then he pushed down, causing the van to evaporate in a blast that rocked Wall Street. In the months that followed, it became clear that the prime suspect was Abdul el Alibahd, a rising leader in a Syria-based terrorist network. But the FBI was still lacking clear evidence linking him to the Wall Street bombing. For a while, magazines and television news programs carried Alibahd's face—bearded, deeply lined, expressionless, with black turban and tinted sunglasses.

So once again, New Yorkers had to shake off the dust, mourn their dead, clear the rubble, and carry on.

But this particular morning, thirteen months after the Wall Street attack, normalcy seemed to reign, at least for a while. Cars and trucks inched along toward the bridge into the city. In the middle of the traffic was the white rental truck.

A New Jersey state trooper sat in his parked squad car, watching the snaking line of vehicles. Officer Ezer Nabib took off his wide-brimmed trooper's hat and scratched his head, then smoothed his hair back.

Nabib, a Sufi Muslim, had only been on the state patrol a few months when the Wall Street bombing took place. He resented the fact that those claiming that they were serving Allah had, again, committed unspeakable acts of slaughter. None of the other troopers said anything. They didn't have to. Nabib felt it in their eyes, and their grim silence said it all.

The trooper eyed the tide of snarled traffic. Then he heard the code number of his squad over the dispatch. He picked up the receiver.

"Officer Nabib here."

The female voice at the other end started talking. "We've got a suspect vehicle, a rental truck heading toward the river, plates are JM435X. Here's the VIN..."

Nabib jotted down the VIN in his daybook. Then he asked, "Suspect for what? I think I see our vehicle here in the traffic jam, heading for NYC."

The radio dispatcher was silent.

"Copy, please," Nabib continued. "Suspect for what? I've got no probable cause for a stop. Do you have some warrants outstanding? Is this a stolen vehicle? What's the deal? Advise."

"Proceed with extreme caution."

"Please identify yourself, dispatcher," Nabib shot back. "Annie, is that you?"

The other voice said, "Follow the vehicle with extreme caution."

Nabib slammed his squad car into gear and swooped into the safety lane, pulling up to a few car lengths behind the truck.

"Track the vehicle and then apprehend on the other side of the river," the voice said.

"That's New York," Nabib countered. "I suggest we call NYPD right away. I can't arrest over there."

"Apprehend on the other side. Secure the vehicle. But use extreme caution. It may be carrying very dangerous contraband."

"Request to speak to the barracks commander," Nabib countered nervously.

But that was when the communication ceased. Nabib pushed the call button on his handset. Nothing.

As the trooper followed the truck across the bridge, he snatched his cell phone and quickly punched in the number for headquarters. A familiar voice announced, "State Patrol..."

But before the trooper could talk, the cell phone indicated low battery. Then it blinked off completely.

Nabib tossed it aside in disgust. The truck was exiting the bridge on the other end, heading into New York City. The trooper switched on his lights and siren and pulled up next to it. He glanced into the cab and motioned the driver over.

Nabib quickly exited the squad car, wishing he could have called for back-up. The driver, who looked Middle Eastern, produced a license that identified him as "Rahji Ajadi."

After frisking the driver and finding no weapons, the trooper ordered him to the rear of the truck. "Open it slowly," Nabib instructed him. The trooper had already un-holstered his side arm.

The driver rolled up the door, and the trooper peered in cautiously. A tarp covered something long and large.

"Lift up the canvas," Nabib ordered.

He stared at the sleek metal that was unveiled, then gestured at the driver to pull back more of the tarp so he could get a better look. Then the trooper saw the familiar symbol on the side of the gleaming steel. His knees almost buckled.

Nabib snapped up his head and pointed his weapon at Ajadi.

"Out of the truck," the trooper screamed, "on the ground now! Now, get down now, spread them on the ground or I blow your head off!"

Ajadi dropped to the pavement like a weight was tied to him.

Nabib scrambled back with his revolver trained on the driver.

A whirling sound of high-speed rotor blades sucking and slicing the air made the trooper look up. Three U.S. Army helicopters were sweeping down to his location, as a chorus of car horns was beginning to rise in angry confusion along New York harbor.

3

WILL CHAMBERS WHEELED UP TO THE FEDERAL court building for the Central District of Virginia and roared down into the underground parking garage. He grabbed his briefcase, stuffed the file into it, and started walking at a fast clip toward the front doors of the courthouse. He could see the huge figure of his client, William "Tiny" Heftland, pacing out front, waiting for him.

Heftland was wearing bright-red suspenders, a white shirt, and a tie. He stood six-foot-four and weighed about two hundred and seventy pounds. Back when he had worked as a beat cop with the D.C. police, and later in the Middle East in the security force of the State Department he had been in mean, lean, fighting shape at two hundred and twenty pounds—most of it muscle. But after a permanent knee injury, problems with his supervisor and, ultimately, a discharge from government work, he was on his own now as a private investigator, cruising around in his black Cadillac, filling up on cheeseburgers and shakes, mostly doing surveillance in divorce cases and serving process. The years had caught up with him.

"Hey, good buddy," Heftland called out to Chambers as he saw him coming. "Man, did you hear about that truck they stopped in New York?"

Will, in his mad dash to the courthouse, hadn't turned on the radio and didn't have a clue what Tiny was talking about. And frankly, he didn't care. He did not respond to the big private eye until he was two inches from his sweaty bulk.

"Don't give me the 'good buddy' treatment," Will said. "Why haven't you paid your bill? You still owe me five thousand dollars from the last case I handled for you. And you still haven't paid the retainer for this one yet."

"Yeah, okay, I was going to be talking to you about that. First of all, I'm good for the money."

"Is that it?" Will asked. "That's your best shot—you're *good* for the money?"

"Hey, we're not going to break up a wonderful friendship over something like money, are we?" Heftland quipped as they entered the court building.

"I'm waiting for the '*second* of all.' You said '*first* of all.' So where is the 'second of all'...?" Will asked as they both climbed up the stairs at a fast clip.

"Okay, second of all, I just sent you a really great case the other day. This Reverend Angus MacCameron guy, who is being sued in federal court in D.C. I mean sued *big time.* Guess who the attorney is on the other side? Just guess? J-Fox Sherman himself—head legal terrorist with that real blitzkrieg-type law firm in D.C. The name escapes me. But a really big-time law firm."

"Get to the point, Tiny," Will said, panting a little as they topped the marble stairs to the second floor. Tiny was breathing heavily, trying to keep up.

"Okay, so anyway, Reverend MacCameron hires me to do some P.I. work on the lawsuit for him—some investigative stuff—to check out the plaintiff who is suing him in the lawsuit, this Herr-Doktor type with like a dozen different PhD degrees. The plaintiff who is going after MacCameron is this Dr. Albert Reichstad guy—nice name, huh? So I am right in the inside loop on this case. And get this—the Right Reverend asks me for a recommendation on legal counsel to defend him. So I sent him your way. I said you were like the genius of the American legal system as far as I was concerned. So, the way I figure it, that ought to count for something, right?"

Will Chambers stopped in his tracks. "No. It doesn't count for anything. Ethically, a lawyer can't split fees with non-lawyers for case referrals. And that's what it would be if I give up a fee from you because you send me a case. Give me a break, Tiny."

"Okay, well, hey, I'm trying here. You know. Just give me some time. You'll get your money."

"Look, Tiny, my partners are putting pressure on me about my receivables. I know you and I go back a long way. I wouldn't be hammering you unless it was important. We have to get your fee collected, okay?"

"Sure, Will, okay," Tiny reassured him, wiping some of the sweat off his brow. As they turned the corner in the hallway they heard the echoes of voices ahead of them from the area outside the courtroom. There they saw several protestors with signs denouncing abortion. They were being lectured by two federal marshals. With news of the New York City truck incident spreading, security at federal buildings in the District was on full alert.

"Protest signs inside the courthouse. That would be a big no-no. Judge Ramington is going to have their heads on a platter," Chambers said as they approached the group outside the courtroom doors.

Heftland grabbed Will's arm and stopped him short.

"Look, Will. I really need you to do some magic here. I know you can do it. If I get convicted, my license is going bye-bye. I'm done. You've really got to get me off on this one."

"Tiny, I don't do magic. I do law. I'm not Houdini." And then Will looked at Tiny's panicked expression and patted his big shoulder. "I'm going to do my best. I promise."

They skirted the group of protestors, and as they entered the courtroom Tiny grabbed Will's arm one more time. Looking down at Will's feet, he began muttering something.

"Look, Tiny, it's going to be alright," Will said, brushing him off and pointing for him to sit with the large group in the audience section. Will turned and made his way to the front row.

A thin, plain-looking young woman with long brown hair grabbed Will's coat sleeve as he walked by the rows of benches. He noticed a little brass pin on her blouse in the shape of tiny baby feet.

"I am praying for you," she said quietly.

"My client is not part of your antiabortion group," Will said, trying to pull away from her grasp.

"That's okay, I am praying for you anyway."

"Sure," Will said. "That's good." He quickly sat down with his briefcase and tried to catch his breath.

A few seconds after Will had sat down, the side door swung open violently, with a bang. Judge Roger Ramington strode out, his black robe flowing. The bailiff barked out with a loud voice, "All rise, this court is now in session, the Honorable Roger K. Ramington is presiding, silence is commanded, God save the United States and this Honorable Court."

"Be seated," Judge Ramington called out, and he perched himself behind the bench. He was completely bald, with a head that had a shiny, even polished, appearance. His eyebrows were dark and bushy, and he carried a square-jawed look that let you know he was rarely amused, always in control, and relished presenting himself as the veteran Marine that he was.

"I have been informed by the clerk that all of the defendants on the docket today are here on Complaints alleging violations of federal law, namely 18 United States Code section 248, the Federal Access to Clinics Act, otherwise known as F.A.C.E.

"These Complaints all apparently have to do with alleged antiabortion protest activities three weeks ago at the Tri-County Women's Health Center," the Judge continued.

"Now listen carefully, each and every one of you. I am about to explain why you're here. I want absolute silence. This is *not* your day of trial. This is only a preliminary hearing to determine whether there is probable cause to continue your case forward toward trial. That means that merely enough evidence need be presented by the prosecution to show that a crime was probably committed and that you probably committed it. That's all. Nothing more is needed.

"I am informed that all of you, except one, are defending yourselves and do not wish to have lawyers representing you. That is your right. On the other hand I've always believed that, as they say, anyone who is his or her own lawyer has a fool for a client.

"Now, the prosecution will present its witnesses and evidence. You may then cross-examine those witnesses, but your right to ask questions will be extremely limited. It will be limited by the rules of evidence, of which you may know very little. It will also be limited to the issue of probable cause—not guilt or innocence. And in all likelihood you won't know the difference there either, because you're not lawyers.

"You need not testify on your own behalf—in fact you have a Fifth-Amendment right not to. If you decide to testify today you are running a great risk because, A) You may say just enough to hang yourself, and B) I'm not your lawyer. Don't ask me what you should do. And C) if you start telling me about your pro-life views and beliefs, I don't want to hear them because they have nothing to do with these charges against you as far as the law is concerned. If you violate this rule and start telling me why you are against abortion I will cite you for contempt.

"Now, with that, let's all have a nice day here in the United States District Court." Judge Ramington capped off his speech with a smile. Though it was not exactly a smile. It was more like the grin that a Doberman pinscher gives you when it pulls its lips back to bare its teeth.

The clerk called Will Chambers' case first, as it was the only one with a defendant who was represented by an attorney.

"Case number 01 CR 657, *United States of America vs. William Tinney Heftland.*"

Will Chambers and Heftland approached the bench.

"Are you William Tinney Heftland?" the judge asked.

"Yes, Your Honor—but my friends call me 'Tiny.'"

"Don't mistake me for one of your friends, Mr. Heftland. That would be a serious error. Are counsel ready?"

Will and the prosecuting attorney both nodded.

"Before you call your first witness," the judge said to the prosecutor, "does anyone want to make a *short* opening statement?"

But then something caught the eye of the judge. He lunged forward and leaned over the bench to get a better look.

The judge was staring at Will's feet. Will looked down and his heart sank.

"Counsel, approach this bench, and I mean now," Judge Ramington snapped.

Chambers and the smiling prosecutor approached the bench. Ramington gave a discreet nod to the court reporter and she stopped typing on her steno machine.

"Counsel," and with that the judge looked down at the file on the desk to remind himself of the name of the defense counsel. "Mr. Chambers. Yes. I've had you in my courtroom before. Would you care to explain your footwear to me?"

Will glanced down at his woven leather sandals. He had forgotten to replace them with the dress shoes that he kept by his desk specifically for court appearances.

"These are imported, hand-tooled leather sandals from Italy, Your Honor." And then he quickly added, "And I do apologize that in the rush to arrive at court on time—and I know that Your Honor is a keen observer of time—I apparently forgot to put on my dress shoes."

"You ever come in here again with sandals, looking like a hippie, you're in contempt, sir."

"It won't happen again."

"And get a decent haircut, mister," the judge added.

"Yes, Your Honor," Chambers replied. And then he added, once he noted that the court reporter was getting everything down on the record again, "And I do appreciate the Court giving me a critique on my hairstyle."

Judge Ramington shot a steely-eyed look at the court reporter, who then took her fingers off the keys again.

"Don't go there, Mr. Chambers. Don't play games with me. I was doing you a big favor. You want me to put my opinions of you on the record, I will be glad to do that. You want everything on the record, be my guest. You've got some kind of chip on your shoulder, counselor. I really don't care where it came from. You get it off. Now go back to the counsel table and take care of your client's case."

Will nodded silently. The prosecutor, who had been standing as a mute witness at side-bar during the entire colloquy, was grinning.

Will sat down at the counsel table next to Tiny. His exasperated client only had two words for him.

"Nice opening."

The prosecutor called, as his only witness, a police officer who had been on duty on the day that several dozen pro-life demonstrators showed up at the abortion clinic and sat down in front of the doors. Will knew that Tiny had been there that day. But he also knew that he didn't block the doors.

In fact, Tiny was there that day to serve a Summons and Complaint on one of the doctors for a medical malpractice lawsuit. In order to get closer to the front door and then to make his way inside to serve the papers, he had pretended to be one of the pro-lifers. That was when he was arrested.

The officer methodically described the scene that day. The blocking of the doors. The fact that women could not get in to get abortions. The arrests.

Then the officer described how one William Tinney Heftland had been there, in the midst of the protestors, and how he had been arrested as he was seated with them in front of the doors.

"Your witness," the prosecutor announced to Will after concluding direct examination.

Chambers paused for a minute. The courtroom became silent. The officer shifted in his chair. Judge Ramington began tapping his pen on the bench.

Then Will began.

"Are you sure my client was there that day?"

"Sure."

"How do you know?"

"He's hard to miss."

The judge chuckled.

"What was he wearing?"

"Red suspenders, I think."

"How do you know?"

"I remember."

"You don't remember it just because he's wearing red suspenders now?"

"No, of course not."

"You are sure my client, Tiny Heftland, was *sitting down in front of the doors*—rather than simply *standing up?*"

"I'm fairly sure."

"Is there some question in your mind about the suspenders, though?"

"Perhaps."

"Do you have pictures in your file there that could refresh your recollection?"

The prosecutor jumped to his feet.

"Your Honor, I think we know where this is going. Mr. Chambers is trying to go on a fishing expedition here. He is using the preliminary hearing simply to get discovery about the prosecution's case. He just wants a look at the police photos."

"Oh, so you do have photos," Will snapped at the prosecutor sarcastically.

"Where are you going, Mr. Chambers? You're wasting our time," the judge barked out.

"Your Honor," Will replied, "the federal rules of evidence permit me to have a witness refresh his recollection with anything that can revive his memory on a material point."

"How is this 'red suspenders' thing material? I'm not going to let you endlessly test the credibility of the witness—that's not what you do at a preliminary hearing."

"It is material," Will continued, "if we can show that a large man—and I think that we can all agree that Mr. Heftland is large—that a large man wearing red suspenders who was a private investigator and a process server—and who matches my client's description—was not seated on the ground obstructing the clinic doors, but was in fact trying to *get into the doors* to serve lawsuit papers on one of the doctors when he was arrested."

Judge Ramington stared at Chambers. Then he pulled out the charging document from the court file and started reading out loud.

"Alright. The violation here is that the act was done with obstruction... or that he intimidated or interfered with someone trying to get reproductive health services...*because that person*...who is obstructed is trying to get those services. In other words, a process server...may or may not be part of an obstruction—and I suppose he would not be there *because* people are trying to get in to get abortions done. He would be there for some other reason. Objection overruled. Officer, answer the question."

"Yes, the police photos would probably refresh my memory."

The officer glanced through the pack of photos in his file.

"I can't tell."

"Why not?"

"Because your client—Mr. Heftland—is not in any of these photos."

"Your Honor, I would like to see those photos."

The judge glanced over at the prosecutor.

"At this point I guess I don't have an objection," the prosecutor deadpanned, "if Mr. Chambers wants to help prove the government's case by identifying his own client in the photographs and placing him at the scene of the offense."

Will took the pack of photos and quickly spread them out over the counsel's table. He began staring at several of them, but none showed his client.

"Okay, counsel, proceed," the judge said.

But one of the photos had caught Will's eye, and he lifted it up to look at it more closely.

"*Now,* Mr. Chambers," the judge said.

Will did not flinch, but stared at the photo—transfixed by something he thought he saw.

"I will be terminating your cross-examination, Mr. Chambers," the judge said, his voice rising.

Now Will was holding only one photograph in his hand as he turned to face the witness.

He looked the officer directly in the eye. The officer shifted a little in the witness chair.

"Is it a fact, officer, that my client—rather than sitting down in front of the doors of the clinic and obstructing patients from getting in—was actually standing up, in his bright-red suspenders, and waving the lawsuit papers that he was trying to serve on one of the doctors inside the clinic—in fact, waving those papers over his head?"

"No, I don't believe so. I would have remembered."

"Would it refresh your memory to look at a picture that shows *that very thing?*"

"No. Because I just looked at those pictures. They don't show that."

The photo in Will's hand was taken to the clerk and marked as an exhibit and handed to the officer on the stand.

"Look at the picture. Look very closely. Look through what is on the surface and look deep into the picture...deep into the photograph," Will said.

"I'm sorry, but this is absurd, Your Honor," the prosecutor blurted out. "This is starting to sound like some kind of cheap parlor trick—maybe defense counsel would like to hypnotize the officer into seeing something that isn't in that picture."

But the judge was not looking at the lawyers, he was looking at the witness. And the officer had changed his expression as he was looking at the photo.

"Does that photo portray something different than your recollection, officer?" the judge asked.

"Not exactly, but..." the officer responded.

The prosecutor was on his feet again, but before he could say anything the judge reached over and grabbed the photograph from the witness and looked at it himself.

"There's nothing here, Mr. Chambers," the judge said, "that shows your client at all. All I see is a group of the other protestors sitting in front of the doors of the clinic."

"Your Honor," Will said, and now his voice was calm and deliberate, "look at the glass—the reflection in the plate-glass window of the clinic—not at the people sitting in the foreground of the photo, but into the glass..."

The judge stared at the photo, and then silently passed it back to the witness. The officer's shoulders slightly slumped. There was a little turning-up at one corner of his mouth, as if he were trying not to smile nervously.

"Officer," Will continued, "an overcast day that day?"

"Yes."

"A lot of reflection on the glass—almost like a mirror?"

"Yes, counselor, that would be one way to describe it."

"And that reflection in the glass of the window shows—faintly perhaps, but clearly enough—it shows my client, red suspenders and all, standing off in the distance with his hands held over his head, and papers in them?"

"Yes."

"And there is someone else in the reflection of that glass, approaching him?"

"Yes, counselor, there is."

"Who is that?"

"That's me, I think, in that reflection, coming up behind him...I guess to arrest him. While he was standing up."

"And certainly not *obstructing* the doorway?"

"No. To be honest, I guess not."

The prosecutor wisely decided not to attempt the hopeless task of trying to rehabilitate his witness. He waived any redirect examination.

That is when Judge Ramington gave a short and dispassionate explanation for his decision to dismiss all of the criminal charges in the case of *United States of America vs. William Tinney Heftland.*

Will and Tiny walked out of the courtroom together. Tiny gave him a huge bear hug while Will fought back a little embarrassment in front of the court personnel walking by in the halls.

"Oh, man, I owe you big-time," Tiny said. "I don't just mean paying my bill. I will do that. But if there is some way I can repay you. Some favor—anything." He was beaming.

"Sure," Will said. He was smiling too. Then Will hooked one of Tiny's suspenders with his finger and pulled on it. "Lucky suspenders."

"You got that right!" Tiny said and strode off with a big wave.

Will turned around to leave. He noticed the fragile-looking woman with the little baby's feet pin, standing in the hallway, smiling at him and waving. He thought he heard her say something like "praying for you" again. Will gave her a half-wave as he walked out of the courthouse toward his car.

4

Washington, D.C.

WHILE WILL CHAMBERS WAS CONCLUDING HIS CASE that morning, a meeting was being held at the law firm of Kennelworth, Sherman, Abrams & Cantwell on K Street in downtown Washington, D.C. K Street was affectionately known as "central power" in legal circles. Its glass buildings housed the most powerful lobbyists, lawyers, and political insiders in the most powerful city on the planet.

In the law firm's cavernous suite of offices, attorney Jay Foxley Sherman, senior partner and long-reigning chief of the firm's litigation section, was seated at the twenty-foot-long mahogany table in the large conference room. Next to him was a law clerk with a legal pad and an associate attorney.

Sherman had distinguished looks, with silver-white hair and wire-rim glasses. As one of Washington's elite trial lawyers, he was at the top of his game. *Beltway* magazine had just voted him the best litigator in D.C. for the rich, the powerful, and the politically connected. He had represented Senators caught in scandal, and a foreign ambassador accused of spying. Sherman had won a successful defamation lawsuit on behalf of a former president whose name was maliciously tarnished in a television news program. Fortune 500 companies came to him when their executives were indicted for white-collar crimes. These were the caliber of clients that paid Jay Foxley Sherman his six-hundred-dollar-per-hour fee.

But today, "J-Fox" Sherman (as he was called by those who knew him) was not happy. He was struggling to look friendly and diplomatic. But underneath his calm demeanor and his twelve-hundred-dollar Italian suit, a volcano raged. Sherman was the kind of lawyer who insisted on absolute control over his clients. He demanded that they never talk to the press, never give interviews—and *never* appear on national television—without his prior approval. Control was his ultimate addiction. His trial experience had taught him that when you lose control of the client, you lose control of the case. And when that happens—more often than not, you end up losing the case itself. J-Fox Sherman didn't try cases to lose them. Sherman's expression was neutral, but his face was flushed.

The beltway lawyer had good reason to be irate. Just a few weeks before, he had filed a libel and defamation lawsuit on his client's behalf in the United States District Court of the District of Columbia. Shortly afterwards, and without consulting Sherman, the client had appeared on national television to discuss matters that went to the very core of his case.

Sherman's client, Dr. Albert Reichstad, sat across the conference table with a strained look, but his raised eyebrows and subtle smile revealed a measure of arrogance. Reichstad's hair, professionally dyed a dark brown to cover the gray, was short, and his beard was well-trimmed. His retiring good looks went well with his expensive Harris-tweed jacket and imported tie. Though Dr. Reichstad was a scholar and an academic, he was not at all the rumpled, absent-minded-professor type. His clothes, and his manner, disclosed the kind of financial power that few professors ever experience within the cloistered life of the university.

"Start the video," Sherman barked to the law clerk.

The clerk jumped to his feet and scurried over to the big-screen television that was smartly situated inside the floor-to-ceiling mahogany wall cabinet. He slid the video into the VCR and clicked it on with the remote control.

"When did this program air?" Sherman asked, with the tone of a man who was about to see his client jeopardize his lawsuit on national television before his case was even a month old.

Before Reichstad could answer, the associate attorney snapped out the answer.

"Four nights ago."

"Good," Sherman rapped out. "With all the news coverage that just broke this morning on the truck incident in New York, there's a good chance no one will even remember it."

The video started in the middle of a commercial. A sleek automobile was gliding through the wet streets of a big city at night. Mellow jazz music filled the air. A deep voice in the background said, "This kind of power and prestige isn't for everybody. But then, you aren't just anybody."

Sherman was impatiently tapping his black onyx pen with pure gold detailing on the table. He glanced momentarily at his reflection in its dark, rich wood.

Then the commercial ended. The program began with the pounding rock music of a studio band. The camera zoomed in to the host, who was seated at the desk with the distant lights of Los Angeles in the background—Billy Hampton, former college English professor, former comedy writer, former Las Vegas stand-up comedian, and now the driving force behind *America PM*, the hottest late-night show on television.

Hampton was leaning back in his chair, his head bouncing to the band's accompaniment. The music ended and the studio audience applause died down.

"Tonight we have a real treat. Harking back to my days as a college professor, I've asked Dr. Albert Reichstad, professor of anthropology at Harvard University, to join us. Dr. Reichstad has recently shocked the world with his revelations about an ancient document that he discovered. And get this—he believes that this piece of papyrus is a missing part of the world's oldest writing about Christianity."

With that Hampton held up a picture from a *Time* magazine article. It showed Reichstad studying a large lighted display on his desk, which contained a magnified replica of a fragment of papyrus writing. In the photo, a pretty young female student was standing next to Reichstad, looking on. The title on the magazine page read, "The Resurrection Disproved? Dr. Albert Reichstad Finds the Missing Key to the Gospels."

Hampton continued, "He's here to impart his impressive knowledge about one of the world's most profound subjects, the *real* Jesus of history—and while he's at it—he's also going to reveal an even more important mystery—how an old guy like him gets dates with the really good-looking young women in his class"—Hampton held up the magazine photo and said, "I didn't know you had a PhD in that subject—" (the audience laughed loudly) "won't you welcome Dr. Albert Reichstad, or as I like to call him, *Big Al!*"

Dr. Reichstad entered the studio stage smiling brightly, confidently. He shook Hampton's hand vigorously and sat down next to the desk, waving to the studio audience.

Before Billy Hampton could launch into his initial questions Reichstad interrupted him.

"You know, the woman in the magazine picture was one of my best students," Reichstad explained. "But I'm surprised at you, Billy—we are in the twenty-first century now. Women really shouldn't be viewed as mere sex objects or just dating partners. In my class, I'm happy to say that every young woman is encouraged to reach her full intellectual and professional potential." The audience ignited in raucous approval.

"Okay, so I deserved that one," Hampton came back lightly. "I guess that just shows how desperate I am—trying to pick up chicks with the help of a guy who is old enough to be my grandfather." The audience laughed and applauded loudly.

"No, but really, Doctor, all kidding aside, it's great to have you here," Hampton continued. "Now this subject is really heavy. And you, of course, you're kind of a heavyweight yourself in the scientific community. Professor of anthropology at Harvard—author of numerous books—two PhDs—and this one really gets me"—(Hampton was studying the "bio" sheet in front of him) "'voted by the students at Harvard as the most beloved professor for the third year in a row'—you know, when I was a teacher, I bribed my students with A's but it never got me anywhere."

When the laughter died down Dr. Reichstad bowed his head slightly and then said, "You know, that honor is the one I prize the most. You see, I believe that impacting students—touching them and showing them something about the truth of where the human race has been, and where we might be going, that is the greatest thing an educator can do. Now, in my field—Middle-Eastern anthropology and archaeology—I try to give my students a glimpse into the cradle of civilization. Teach them what motivated people thousands of years ago to believe the way they did."

"Well," the host jumped in, "that brings us to this discovery of yours—and this is really, I guess, a little like Columbus discovering America or Edmund Hillary being the first guy to make it to the top of Mount Everest. I mean, this is gigantic. Truly amazing, Doctor. You come across this little scrap of ancient paper that is part of the first—I guess you would say part of the actual original 'gospel,' if we can use that term, about the life—or actually more like the death—the burial of Jesus. Suddenly, this could be the most important discovery in the history of religion. From this little scrap of paper we realize that what the Christian religion has been teaching about Jesus, the folklore and the myths about his being raised up on the third day, and the whole Easter thing—we really have to give that up now. And you are the man—Dr. Albert Reichstad—you are the guy who did it all. You are the one who has really caused—if I can say it this way—you have caused a religious revolution."

Reichstad paused and smiled. Then he reached out and touched the coatsleeve of the television host.

"You know, Billy, I must tell you and your wonderful viewing audience something. I believe that what is really amazing is the human spirit. It is the ability of the human race to continue to seek out truth—and then when it is found, to embrace it even when it's uncomfortable. Even when it is very scary for us because it makes us face new horizons of our evolutionary adventure as humans. But I really think the Christian church—and not just Christians, but all people of good will everywhere, and all religions—I really think we are all coming to the realization that the story of Jesus being raised from the dead and being God, the mythic story that some of us learned in Sunday school as little children—it was a wonderful story, and it made us all feel good, but now, as twenty-first-century humans, we must honor the real truth about Jesus.

"We now know with certainty, because of the discovery I was privileged to make, that he was not God, and he didn't walk out of a tomb after he died. I believe the evidence from this remarkable papyrus fragment—we scientists call it the 7QA fragment—that was written just after his death and burial really does prove that beyond any doubt. But, you know, Billy, something of Jesus did live on. And that's what is really important. Jesus stood for love and tolerance among all people. Now that is the enduring truth he left for us. And of course, the truth—as the words of Jesus tell us—the truth will make us free."

The audience applauded wildly, and a few people were whistling. Billy Hampton was beaming from ear to ear. And then he applauded the moment himself, nodding his head up and down. "Dr. Albert Reichstad, ladies and gentlemen," Hampton said, inviting the audience to convey their love to this distinguished man of science. "We will be right back after this."

The video screen went to fuzzy white as the tape ended.

Sherman was silent. His face was no longer red. His brow was relaxed. He tossed a thick, stapled packet of papers across the table to Dr. Reichstad.

"That is the libel and defamation lawsuit that I filed in federal court here in D.C.," Sherman intoned, "to vindicate your professional reputation as a scholar and a scientist against the lies and accusations of murder published against you and your discovery of the Jesus papyrus—by that Christian fundamentalist preacher, MacCameron. I suggest you read it again. Take it with you."

Then the master trial lawyer eased back in his chair slightly.

"I will say this—I think you handled yourself fairly well on television. Not everyone can sell themselves on the tube," Sherman said. "But I am telling you right now, if you go to the media any more—or if you start showing up on Geraldo Rivera, or Jerry Springer or whatever—any more media whatsoever—and I mean *anywhere*—I don't care if it's on the morning farm report in North Platte, Nebraska—if you do any more media on this subject without talking to me first, I am off this case. And you will be looking for a new lawyer."

"I understand," Reichstad replied quietly but smugly. Sherman started to rise from his chair, but his client raised an index finger in the air.

"Just one final question, Mr. Sherman, before you go."

"Yes?"

"Has our defendant been served with these lawsuit papers yet?"

Sherman looked to his associate, who glanced at his file and said, "Reverend Angus MacCameron was served by our process server last week."

"Have we heard from MacCameron's attorney yet—do we know who he hired as his lawyer?" Reichstad asked as a follow-up question.

"That's *two* questions," Sherman shot back sarcastically. Then he smiled at his law clerk and nodded for him to answer.

"Not yet," the law clerk answered.

"We will get notice from his defense counsel in a week or so," Sherman said blandly. "Some local schlepp, some country-bumpkin attorney, will probably give me a call, asking if I will agree to an extension of time to file their response to our Complaint for damages. And of course, I will be ever so courteous—and I will courteously tell him that I have no intention of granting any extensions in this lawsuit." At that the law clerk and the associate snickered.

"No, I really don't think we should worry about who opposing counsel is going to be," Sherman continued. "I doubt that this guy—this Reverend MacCameron and his little magazine, *Digging for Truth*—have libel/slander insurance. It's just too expensive for some little shoebox publication like this. So you're not going to see him defended by one of the big insurance defense firms. Here you've got this right-wing, fundamentalist pastor and his little magazine—which, by our estimate, has a circulation of a couple of thousand readers if they are lucky—so, who is a guy like that going to be able to get as his lawyer?"

"What about religious institutions, foundations—conservative religious groups?" Reichstad questioned. "Won't they offer to fund the defense of his case? Make this case a cause célèbre?"

Sherman chuckled a little. "We've investigated this MacCameron. He's such an oddball—even as fundamentalists go, he is on the fringe. He's on the outs even with the conservative Christian groups. He seems to have offended everyone in the evangelical camp. And the Catholics won't touch him with a hundred-foot pole because he's insulted them too. No, I don't see him getting any help from other groups. He's out on a gangplank, all by himself. Besides, whoever the guy gets to represent him, I don't think we're too worried, are we, fellows?" With that, Sherman looked to the associate and the law clerk who were both smiling confidently.

The associate knew that this was his cue. He was now about to spread the final layer of gold-tinted public relations.

"There is a saying around town, Doctor, about Mr. Sherman as a trial attorney," the associate explained proudly. "When Mr. Sherman goes to court, they call it 'Sherman's March to the Sea.' You know, like setting fire to the crops, burning the homes, and laying waste to the enemy."

Sherman smiled broadly at that, and then added, "Now Dr. Reichstad, when we've won this case and decimated the other side, you will have to answer one little question of my own."

"Oh?" Reichstad responded. "What is that?"

"Well, it's your money—and believe me, you and your institute will be spending lots of it on this case..."—at that, Sherman's associates smirked—"but," he continued, "I'm still not clear why you are suing an obscure, penniless eccentric like MacCameron. Really, why bother?"

"I'll answer that right now," Reichstad snapped back, his eyes widening. "If I don't finally take a stand against the quacks like MacCameron, then pretty soon the scientific community starts to take shots at me as well. This lawsuit is designed to send a message, Mr. Sherman."

J-Fox Sherman smiled agreeably, though he still doubted his client's explanation. He stood up from the table, shook hands with Dr. Reichstad, and paused a second to stare him in the eye—the last reminder of who would be controlling this case—who was the client, and who was the lawyer. And then Sherman walked out of the room. He glanced at his Rolex. He didn't want to be late for his lunch meeting on Capitol Hill.

5

WITH WILL CHAMBERS OUT THE DOOR and on his way to court, Betty Sorenson could finally catch her breath. She straightened her silver-and-black hair and lit a cigarette as Will's Corvette taillights disappeared from view. But she had barely taken her first puff before she noticed a small entourage coming directly toward her on the sidewalk.

In the lead was a slightly disheveled man who looked to be in his sixties, carrying an old, very tattered briefcase. He had thick glasses but a square-jawed, handsome face with a fair complexion. Behind him was a strikingly beautiful woman in her mid-thirties, with dark hair and a flashy designer outfit. Following behind was a man in a dark suit with a small briefcase.

"Excuse me," the older man in the lead asked, "is this attorney Will Chambers' office?"

Betty quickly tossed her cigarette down and smiled politely. "Yes, his office is on the second floor. I am his secretary, is he expecting you?"

"My name is Angus MacCameron," the man said with an accent tinged by a subtle burr. "This is my daughter, Fiona. You may know her from her music and records. She's a famous Christian singer, you know."

Fiona cut in, smiling. "Just like a father, he's always bragging on me! My father has an appointment with Mr. Chambers. My manager and I would like to sit in, if that's alright."

Betty tried to smile and look detached and professional, but inside she realized that several more spinning plates in her boss's circus act were smashing to the floor.

"Won't you follow me?" she said, and motioned for them to follow her up the stairs, secretly hoping that Jacki Johnson, the assistant lawyer in the office, was free to meet with them—and somehow explain why Will Chambers wasn't.

The threesome was seated in the lobby. Betty then disappeared quickly down the hallway toward the rear. She poked her head inside a neat, well-furnished office. Jacki Johnson was dictating into the video desk recorder, but when she saw the look on Betty's face, she stopped in mid-sentence.

Jacki was a woman in her mid-thirties, with short, sculptured hair, large, pretty eyes, and smooth, coffee-colored skin. She was petite, but carried herself with the confidence of someone who could be tough and forceful.

She straightened her tailored suit as she swung around in her executive chair.

"Judging by the look on your face, I'd say you need my help," Jacki said.

"We've got a couple of new clients in the lobby expecting to see Will."

"Oh. And of course Will isn't here, I suppose?"

"Naturally."

"You want me to handle it?" Jacki asked calmly.

"Look I'm sorry to do this…again," Betty said with exasperation.

"I'll be glad to meet with them. Do you have any idea what this conference is about?"

"Haven't the foggiest," Betty replied as she walked with Jacki down the hallway. Then Betty stopped and turned to Jacki, and in a hushed and serious tone said, "I think you should also know that Hadley Bates was on the phone this morning, just before Will ran out the door."

"And?"

"And, he didn't want to talk to Will. Not exactly."

"What did he want?"

"Well," Betty continued in a whisper, "he wanted to know Will's schedule. And he wanted to know whether he was going to be *out* of the office all morning. So I told him that Will was scheduled to be in court all morning."

"And what did our esteemed managing partner have to say?"

"He just said, 'Very good.'"

"Is that all?"

"Yeah. He just said, 'Very good.' You know how he does, in that 'I'm HAL the IBM computer' voice of his."

"So what was that all about?"

"I really don't know. I got the feeling that Hadley was glad that Will was going to be out of the office this morning. I've got to tell you, I have a bad feeling about today. Okay, so we all know that Will and Hadley have never gotten along. But I think Will has finally pushed him too far. Will doesn't return his calls. He never attends the partnership meetings anymore. I think that the other shoe is really about to drop. I've got really bad vibes about this."

Jacki smiled and walked past Betty, straight to the lobby, where she shook hands warmly with the threesome. They introduced themselves and she invited them into the conference room.

Jacki explained that Will Chambers had been "detained" in court and that she was going to handle the interview. She offered them coffee but they declined. Jacki quickly sized them up as folks who were friendly and courteous—but who definitely wanted to cut to the chase.

The older man started first.

"Miss Johnson, I have to ask you a question before I get into my case. It may strike you as a bit odd. But, considering the unique aspects of my case, I absolutely have to ask. You see, my case—the reason that I am here—really deals with the most important question that has ever been asked in the last two thousand years. And even a bit more than that, this case is about a full-scale attack, a massive conspiracy, by the prince of darkness—against the church of Jesus Christ. So here is the question—are you a believer in God, Miss Johnson?"

Jacki paused. She was used to strange cases and strange clients, particularly after practicing law with Will Chambers for a while. Will had often remarked to her about that great paradox of the law: how the most profound civil-liberty issues often seemed to be wrapped around the lives of difficult, bizarre, and obtuse people. And working with Will, she had met a lot of them. Yet even in that, she had never heard a more audacious description of a lawsuit than the one just delivered by this man with the soft, friendly Scottish accent.

"Well, I was raised by my aunt to be a good Mississippi Methodist," she answered. "Church on Sunday mornings, and Sunday evenings, and Wednesday nights. I won a couple awards for church attendance and Bible readings back then. Yes, Mr. MacCameron. I am a believer in God."

"You see," MacCameron continued, "I ask you this for a reason. The Bible says that 'the fool says in his heart there is no God,' so I want to make sure that my lawyers are not fools." MacCameron's face lit up with an impish smile, and for a moment Jacki couldn't tell whether this old man was pulling her leg. She studied him closely and concluded that beneath his warm and infectious smile he was deadly serious.

"Which brings us to Will Chambers," Fiona MacCameron said. "Because he is the senior lawyer in this office, we are interested in some of his background. I assume that Mr. Chambers would be the one primarily handling this case. My father is very interested in hiring Mr. Chambers. But to be honest, I have some—well—some questions."

"What kind of questions?" Jacki asked.

Fiona sat poised and attentive, and waited for a moment before responding. Jacki recognized the line of clothes—strictly New York fashion. Fiona's makeup and hair had the touches of an expensive salon. As she folded her left hand over her right hand and rested them on the conference table, Jacki noticed the French-manicured nails. She also observed that there was no wedding ring on Fiona's hand.

"I've read some background research that Bob, my manager, provided to me about Mr. Chambers," Fiona continued. "I was impressed and certainly intrigued. Will Chambers is a fascinating and obviously a very talented man. But our questions have to do more with his personal life."

"The truth is, we have heard some unsettling things about Mr. Chambers," the man in the dark suit stated. "Since I am Ms. MacCameron's business manager, when she found out that her father seemed intent on hiring Mr. Chambers, she contacted me. I, in turn, contacted some people in the legal community to check up on him. I know that in the past Will Chambers handled some high-profile cases. But the word I've received is that the man now has some serious personal issues. In point of fact—that he is an alcoholic and his days as a trial lawyer may be over."

Jacki's eyes flashed with irritation. Controlling herself, she began to explain.

"Folks, let me tell you something. I came to this law firm because of Will Chambers. I was a law student at NYU. And I probably would have stayed up in New York to practice after law school. But I read an article in a magazine about this attorney down in Virginia. How he took on a case on behalf of a young Hasidic Jewish boy and his family up in the Bronx. The Jewish boy had been beaten up, set on fire, and left for dead by some neo-Nazi group in New York. Somehow he survived, miraculously, but he was terribly burned.

"Now, two of the thugs who did this horrendous thing were caught, tried for attempted murder, and convicted. But the ringleader was never caught. Will Chambers filed a lawsuit for the Jewish family against the owner of a trucking company in the Bronx who was suspected of being the driving force behind this racist Nazi group. One of the two convicted guys had tipped Will off to the fact that the trucking company owner was the guy who gave the order to 'be sure and burn a Jew tonight.'

"So I read in this article how the Virginia lawyer—Will—was poring over the records of the trucking company one night in his law office at three in the morning—searching for something that could tie this trucking company owner to the Nazi group and to the torture of this little Jewish boy. He went through the papers, page after page. Document after document. The rest of his staff had already gone home and were asleep. But he wouldn't give up. Then, in the middle of these thousands of pieces of paper that had been produced to him in the lawsuit, he found a little crumpled note in the handwriting of this trucking guy, talking about 'Kristallnacht tonight.' Kristallnacht—the 'night of broken glass'—was the name given to the evening when the Nazis went out on a rampage through German cities, smashing the windows of Jewish stores and killing Jews. Well, the note had been written on a little calendar pad and ripped out—and the date on the calendar was the *same day* the little Jewish boy was attacked.

"Well, that broke the case wide open. Will tried the case in front of a jury and collected ten million dollars in damages against the trucking guy, and he ended up getting the trucking company as part of the damages. The company was turned over to the Jewish family. They are still running it to this day. And the former owner, based on the evidence that Will discovered, was later charged with criminal conspiracy and is now serving thirty years in prison.

"After reading the magazine article about that case I decided to come down and interview with Will's law firm when I graduated from law school. And I asked him about that lawsuit, and about why he was so certain that he could find that *one piece of evidence* to prove his case."

The room was silent as Jacki finished the story.

"Will looked at me, and he said this: He said it's like being buried alive in a tunnel, or a cave, and you're in total darkness—but you know that as long as you keep digging, and if you are going in the right direction, you're going to break out. He said his cases were the same way. He told me that if you keep digging for truth, and you're heading in the right direction, you're bound to break through to justice on the other side.

"So that's why I came down here to Virginia to practice law with this firm. I wanted to practice with a lawyer like Will Chambers. As for these 'personal problems'—his wife died tragically about two years ago. He had a bit of a setback. But despite that, Will Chambers is still probably the best trial advocate I've ever met."

Angus MacCameron threw his hands up in the air as if he were a referee at a football game and someone had just scored a touchdown.

"Praise Jesus!" he exclaimed. "Did you hear that, dear Fiona? 'Digging for truth!' He said *'digging for truth!'*"

Then he looked at Jacki, who was staring at him with a puzzled look.

"Don't you see, Miss Johnson? *Digging for truth*. That's the very same as the name of my magazine. I wrote the truth about this fraud—Dr. Reichstad—and his phony 'discovery' in my magazine, in *Digging for Truth* magazine. And that's why I've been sued. And your boss, Mr. Chambers, is going to vindicate me and help me to tell the truth to the whole world! God has his mighty hand upon us today, can't you see it?"

The business manager tried to break in, but MacCameron interrupted him.

"Oh, Bob, I know you want to protect me, and I know that my precious daughter wants me to be careful. But God has been in this from the first. When I hired that private detective to do some investigative work for me on this lawsuit, I asked him if he knew any good lawyers. And in the very next breath he mentioned your boss, Miss Johnson. He said that Will Chambers is the best in the business. So here I am. As far as I'm concerned, it's settled. I want to hire Mr. Chambers and your firm to defend me. I want to hire Will Chambers to save the Christian church from the deception of the evil one."

And then, patting the conference table with his hands, MacCameron added, "So, we start today, aye?"

6

FOR WILL CHAMBERS, WINNING IN COURT had always been the first thing and the last thing. But now—and in fact for a long time—it was not enough. Now it merely provided him with a handy excuse for celebration, usually alone, usually drinking himself into the regions of full-blown self-pity, of which he was already hovering at the borders on a daily basis.

Driving back on Interstate 95 after winning Tiny Heftland's case, Will entertained the idea of going straight back to the office. Working through lunch. Getting things under control at the office. As he cruised along in his Corvette convertible with the music blasting he decided to turn his cell phone off. He started to sour on the idea of skipping lunch. He needed to celebrate.

Will pulled off the freeway and into Monroeville. He decided he would go over to the Red Rooster tavern and grab a sandwich and a few drinks.

At the tavern, he ordered a steak sandwich but only took a few bites. He downed several vodkas while he pretended to watch the Orioles game on the overhead television.

Will lost track of time. But he got to thinking that maybe he had had too much to drink. He figured that he would go to the office, put in an hour or so, and then go home early and sleep it off.

When he pulled up in front of the law firm building he noticed a truck parked in front with men loading it. On his way up the stairs he noticed the moving men were carrying furniture that looked familiar. Then he realized they were walking down with the lobby chairs from his office. He began to run up the stairs but missed a step and almost fell facedown.

Jacki Johnson was waiting for him in the empty lobby area of the office.

"What is going on?" Will yelled out.

"We've been trying to call you on your cell phone."

"I turned it off."

"Well, what can I say?" Jacki said, visibly upset. "Things are real bad. The partners voted you out, Will. They're taking you out of the firm. They pulled the plug on you. The partnership property—the furniture and everything—is being taken down to the Richmond office. They're closing the office here in Monroeville."

Jacki could see that Will was thunderstruck.

"I'm really sorry to hit you with this," she continued. "They're sending you a check for your share of your partnership interest—less the amounts they say are due to the firm from you. We got the message by email and then by fax just a few minutes before the moving men arrived. They've taken all the files, and they say they have contacted all the clients. You're closed out for good, Will—I'm so sorry."

"This is not the partners, I'm telling you that right now. This is all because of that twisted 'managing partner' Hadley Bates—he's behind this, that little scumbucket." Will ran toward the telephone in his office.

Jacki grabbed him and looked him in the eye.

"You've been drinking," she said in an irritated voice.

"I'm going to kill that…"

"No. You're not going to pick up the phone, not right now. If you do, you'll end up saying something to Hadley that you'll regret."

"He can't do this."

"He can. And he did. You have to move on. I think I'd better drive you home in your car. Betty can follow us in mine."

Will was shaking with rage, but he was too humiliated to look at Jacki, so he kept his back to her.

"Come on," Jacki said sympathetically, putting her hand on his back. "I'm going to drive you home to that big old mansion of yours. I just wish you had someone to be with you tonight."

"I'll be fine," Will muttered, but his voice was barely audible.

Jacki drove Will's Corvette away from the office with Will sitting in the passenger seat.

"This is ridiculous," Will snapped, "I had two drinks."

"Oh? Just two?"

"Maybe three."

"That's all you'd need now. To get arrested for DUI. You know, you don't need an assistant lawyer. What you need is a full-time nanny, a drill sergeant, and a priest, all rolled into one. And frankly, Will, that person is not me."

"Give me a break."

"No. You give *me* a break. I tell people you're one of my heroes. Which is really a remarkable thing considering the fact you're white, and you're a guy. But I'm tired of handling your screwups, like that client conference this morning."

"What client conference?"

Jacki sighed heavily and shook her head.

"There is other stuff going on out there in the world, Will, besides your pain. You are going to have to get around to doing whatever you have to do—forgiving yourself for Audra—getting on with your life. Check yourself into rehab. I don't know."

"I'm no alcoholic."

"Maybe not. But I'm seeing you heading for a cliff. And I'd rather not go along for the ride."

Then Jacki took her left hand off the steering wheel and, reaching over across to Will, waved her hand in front of his face.

"Look at this, Will, what do you see?" Jacki asked.

"Nice manicure."

"The ring, Will, the ring. Howard proposed to me two weeks ago. I've been wearing this diamond on my finger for two weeks. I wanted to see how long it took you to climb out of that cave you live in and notice it."

"I noticed it."

"Then why didn't you say anything? 'Congratulations.' 'Jacki, I'm happy for you.' Anything."

Will looked at her, then he laid his head back against the headrest, and looked out the window.

"Congratulations."

They drove in silence for a few minutes. Then Jacki said, "We need to talk business, Will. You and me. My life is taking a different turn now. Howard and I are going to be married. I have to have my career settled. I can't afford to work in an office where I don't know what my future is."

"Come on, you know what your future is with me."

"Do I? Hadley said in his e-mail that the firm has secured written consents from every one of your clients in the last forty-eight hours—to dump you, now that you are out of the firm, and to continue with the firm instead."

"Every client? He's a liar."

"Let me amend that," Jacki said. "Every client except two. One is that big loser Tiny Heftland. Bates said that you can have him, and any money due to the firm from him—as if you will ever recover it—you can keep. And then there's just one other client."

"Yeah. Well, I just finished Tiny's latest case today, so I guess that means I've got only one client."

"What happened in court?"

"We won. Great, huh? A victory for a nonpaying client, and on the same day that I get booted out of my law firm."

"Will, stop feeling sorry for yourself."

"Listen, Jacki, Hadley has got to know that I will be taking him to court over the way he is dissolving my partnership share."

"You want a friend's advice?" Jacki's voice was rising. "And frankly, I may be one of your only friends right now. Let it go. If you need to negotiate the figures with Hadley, let me work on him for you. But don't make this a bloodbath."

"Okay, so where do you fit in this mess?" Will asked.

"Hadley wants me to stay on with the firm—relocate up to the D.C. office," Jacki said, a little bit more softly. "Which actually works out well, I guess, because I'm barred in D.C. And Howard works up in northern Virginia, so I would be closer to him and have a shorter commute. And what I guess I am saying is this—Will, I can't afford to stay on with you if you're going to go it solo now. I mean really, besides Tiny, you've got only one client."

"Jacki, listen to me. I can build up the practice in a very short period of time. I want you to hang in there with me."

"Will, I don't want this to be any harder than it already is. Maybe I can help you out a little here or there, on the side. You know, if you need someone to cover for a deposition once in a while or do some legal research. But I have to stick with the firm. I know that sounds like I'm copping out on you. But my mind is made up. I'm sorry."

Will gazed ahead blankly and said nothing for a few minutes. Jacki had made her point. He had been her mentor and friend. As of late she had covered for him, and even nurse-maided him since his wife had died. But that was all changing now. As Will sat slumped down in the seat of his prized Corvette, his long hair whipping in the wind, he was simply tired of fighting—tired of caring.

Finally Jacki broke the silence.

"So, you want to know something about your sole survivor? The single client that you've got left?"

"Yeah. Who's the lucky winner?" Will asked sardonically.

"Angus MacCameron. *Reverend* MacCameron to be exact. He's the new client I took for you this morning. A little weird—he actually made me take a 'loyalty oath'—he wanted to make sure I believed in God. I'm going to be real interested to see whether he asks you the same question."

Will gave Jacki a strange, puzzled look. It was the kind of look you would expect from someone at a Chinese restaurant who had just opened a fortune cookie and then read his own name inside.

Jacki continued talking, not noticing Will's expression. She was looking for the cross street to start leaving the city—to leave the historic district with the two-hundred-and-fifty-year-old churches and the little shops and houses that were cloistered together, shoulder to shoulder—with their wood-planked front doors and black-iron door knockers—tucked up close to the cobblestone sidewalks of Monroeville.

"So this MacCameron definitely has a one-of-a-kind case. He wants to be defended in a defamation and libel case. You've really got to read the Complaint to believe it. Angus MacCameron and his magazine, *Digging for Truth*, are both defendants. He's alleged to have written an article that libeled this big-wig professor about an archaeology discovery," Jacki explained. "Some kind of ancient writing found over in Israel. The plaintiff—Dr. Reichstad—has published some scholarly journal stuff about the writing—it's apparently a two-thousand-year-old piece of papyrus. Reichstad has been saying that the fragment proves that Jesus was never resurrected. MacCameron really flipped out over that and then wrote some nasty stuff about Reichstad in his little magazine."

"Angus MacCameron. Why is this sounding familiar?" Will was musing.

"I don't know," Jacki replied. "You sounded like you didn't know about the appointment."

"I don't remember this meeting being scheduled," Will commented. "But Tiny was telling me about referring some new case to me. Oh man, this must be the case." Will gave out a low groan. "You know, I don't think Tiny has sent a decent case over to me in all the years I've known him."

"No, that's not true. Remember that case involving the police chief—I think that one was a referral from Tiny. Remember? The city wanted to terminate him for drinking on the job."

"Yeah. I guess you're right," Will said, sounding distracted and distant.

"What was the deal on that case?"

"They said he showed up drunk at a bank robbery in progress."

"Yeah, that's it. He was the chief of police of some small town in southern Virginia, wasn't he?" Jacki asked.

"Yep."

"Yeah," Jacki said, "I remember that. They had the bank surrounded. A single gunman was holding some hostages. And somebody died, right?"

"An officer died in a shoot-out," Will responded quietly. "The board of inquiry blamed him for giving the order to go in shooting rather than waiting for the hostage negotiators. They said his drinking was a contributing factor."

"So how did the case end?" Jacki continued.

"I got him his job back. There was a technical mistake in the way they fired him. We won on a procedural argument."

"Whatever happened to him—the police chief?"

Will was silent.

"What ever happened to that guy?" Jacki asked again.

"He died."

"Oh, yeah?"

"Yeah."

"How?"

Will was silent again, but Jacki probed a little more. "So what was the deal with that guy? Did he stay on with the police department awhile, before he died?"

Will didn't respond at first. But when he did, his voice was almost inaudible.

"After we won the case I tried to contact him. I called him at his house. He hadn't showed up at the police station for a couple of days. He didn't answer the phone. So I took a drive over to his house. His car was parked outside. The shades were drawn, so I couldn't see in. I knocked on the door. No answer. I called the police." Will paused for a few seconds. Then he concluded. "They broke down the door. They found him sitting in a chair with a glass of booze in his hand. Eyes wide open. His liver disintegrated—or he had a heart attack—something like that."

They were in the Virginia countryside now, and Jacki pulled the Corvette into the long driveway that led, through the arch of trees, up to Generals' Hill.

Jacki pulled the car to a stop near the front pillars of the old mansion, and then turned it off. She eased back in the seat for a moment. There was only the sound of the breeze rustling in the leaves, and a few birds up in the trees.

"Can he pay? This MacCameron guy?" Will asked.

"He's got funding from the magazine, so he may be able to pay a fairly substantial retainer. I really didn't talk money with him. I figured you ought to do that. His daughter, Fiona, was with him. She's some kind of Christian singer. A very classy-looking woman. I did notice she didn't have a wedding ring, which is interesting. Especially with a face that looks like it belongs on a fashion magazine. I got the feeling she's sort of looking after dear old Dad. But Dad says he won't take a penny of his daughter's money—he insists on funding his defense himself. This guy MacCameron, he's really a hoot. You know, a real 'praise the Lord' type, except I think he's Scottish or something. And I read the article he wrote against this Dr. Reichstad; it's something else. He brought the article with him. He really goes after Reichstad."

"Oh. Like how?" Will asked, trying to act uninterested.

"Like accusing him of fraudulent scholarship in interpreting this piece of ancient writing he found. And MacCameron even implicated Reichstad in the murder of an archaeologist friend of his in Jerusalem."

"Boy, that's a bad start to the case. Accusations of professional incompetence, coupled with the imputation of the commission of a crime. Classic examples of defamation per se," Will noted. "Tiny told me J-Fox is representing the plaintiff. Arguing a case against Sherman is like getting your teeth drilled."

"Yeah. This Professor Reichstad must be really well-connected to snag the Sherman firm," Jacki said, her voice trailing off. And then she added, with some genuine empathy, "Will, even if the money for your fees is there, maybe you need to let this case go. Sherman is going to try to bury you," Jacki continued. "Once he finds out that you are on your own, and that you're out of the firm, he's going to smell blood—it's going to be like a great white shark in a feeding frenzy. Not that you couldn't handle it. But is it worth the hassle? Maybe you ought to cash in your 401(k) and just take some time off."

But Jacki could already see that Will was thinking about the case.

"Anyway," Jacki continued, "the way MacCameron describes it, this Reichstad is a media hound, and he's clearly a public figure. So that means that your only real defense is to prove a lack of actual malice on MacCameron's part. I mean, that's basically what your defense would be, right?"

Jacki's question hung in the air as the leaves rustled around them in the treetops.

"Maybe not."

"Oh?" Jacki gave Will a strange little smile. "So what's the defense? I mean, assuming you even want to get involved in this dogfight. What would the defense be?"

"Truth," Will said as he reached over for the car keys and pulled them out of the ignition.

And then added as he climbed out of the car, "Truth is always a defense to a lawsuit for libel and defamation."

Down at the bottom of the long, winding driveway Betty pulled up with Jacki's car.

"You going to be okay?" Jacki asked.

"Sure. Me and Clarence. A man and his dog."

Jacki then told him, with strained optimism, "I checked on our office space. The rent is paid up through the month. The firm gave notice they were vacating. I called the landlord. I hope that was okay. I told him that you would be personally renting the space from then on. He said you can keep working out of the same office, as long as you can come up with the rent."

"Fine. Say hello to Howard for me," Will said. "Tell him he is a very lucky man."

"Look, it will take me a couple days to clear out. So you'll be seeing some more of me. I do think you will have to talk to Betty. She wants to know if you can afford to keep her on," Jacki added.

"Tell her I'll talk to her tomorrow."

"I'll do that," Jacki called out as she made her way down the driveway. "Oh, don't forget, you've got this Reverend MacCameron coming back in again tomorrow. He wants to meet you personally."

Will Chambers waved goodbye and trudged in the front door. Clarence, his golden retriever, came loping across the living room, his big pink tongue flapping. Will gave his dog's head a quick pat as he headed for the liquor cabinet.

7

After pouring himself a glassful of Jack Daniels, Will settled into the oversized chair in front of his big-screen television. He flipped through the channels and began downing the glass of whiskey in generous gulps. After losing interest in a made-for-TV movie, Will switched back to the news.

But he found himself thinking back to the police chief in Hadleysburg. He couldn't forget the day that he entered the house with some of the officers from the police department. He remembered the stench, and he recalled the bizarre and terrible sight of his client sitting, in full uniform, in his chair in front of the television set. There was a full glass still in his hand. His eyes were empty, fixed straight ahead. The chief's skin was yellowish and artificial looking, with black discoloration around his lips and eyes and in the folds of his skin.

Will got up and poured the glass out in the kitchen sink. He went to the refrigerator, found some orange juice, and poured it into another glass. And then he sat down at the table that overlooked the rolling green hills and the white-flowered mountain laurels that spotted the acres of what he used to think of as "*our* property."

No, he thought to himself, *it is not "our property."* There was no "ours" anymore. It was only *his.* The whole world had been divided into that which was *his* and everything else that belonged to everyone else in the world. But *us,* and *we,* and *ours,* no longer existed. Audra was gone. She was no longer part of this huge house. Her perfume didn't precede her into a room anymore. Her laugh didn't make him smile anymore despite himself. She was not there to keep him from taking himself, or his work, too seriously. He thought about the feel of her hair when it brushed against his face. He felt the aching loss of her touches and caresses.

He had met Audra at Georgetown during his law-school years. She was in the art department. She was an earthy blonde with a quirky sense of humor and an easy, winning smile. When he moved from his first job at the ACLU in New York to rural Tennessee for the Law Project of the South, she supported him. Audra sold her paintings at galleries in the tourist towns and taught art in the community colleges.

But when Will was fired from that office and then finally got the job with what was then Bates, Burke, Meadows & Bates, Audra had hoped it would last. And it did, for a while. But after five years, the rest of the partners suggested that Will move up to central Virginia to open a branch office. They said it was to get him closer to D.C., where they wanted to open their third branch, but Will felt the real reason was to get him out of the Richmond office, where he had become a constant irritation to the others.

Yet after the move to Monroeville, both Will and Audra felt an immediate sense of belonging. It was a city with a lot of charm and history. Monroeville was connected with several of the Founding Fathers. General Robert E. Lee had once marched down the street, right past the very building where Will's office was now located. The buildings and shops had carried their age quietly and well among the pear trees that lined the streets, trees whose blossoms would draw tourists in the spring through the fall.

But it was Generals' Hill, situated prominently in the rolling Virginia countryside just outside of Monroeville, that most symbolized the couple's sense of belonging.

They had bought the dilapidated pre–Civil War mansion with the idea of restoring it. Audra poured herself into the loving reconstruction of the great house. It was small as Southern mansions go, but to them it was a thing of beauty. It had tall white columns in the front, and a huge fan-shaped window just below the peak of the roof. Inside there was a curving staircase that led to the second floor.

Audra taught a few art classes at the local college. She split the rest of her time between the restoration of the house and painting in watercolors and acrylics in the studio that they had created in one of the extra rooms. She loved the house, but with her pacifist's heart had tried to get Will to agree to change the name of the mansion from "Generals' Hill" to something less warlike. But Will was too wedded to historical truth for that. The mansion had switched hands between the South and the North several times during the course of the Civil War. The name of the place was enshrined in local history. Besides, Will liked the idea of living in a house that had been near the focal point of great battles. After all, he thought, he made his living as a legal combatant in the new civil wars of justice. "Generals' Hill" just seemed to fit. There was something poetic about living in a place with a name like that.

But their idyllic life did not last. Audra longed for a baby but could not get pregnant. She threw herself into her painting and created a successful career as an artist. Her showings increased around the country. Tensions grew in the marriage. Audra moved out of Generals' Hill—just a temporary separation, she told Will—but he was too proud to ask her back. He had stared at the phone a hundred times, thinking about calling her at her apartment in Georgetown, but each time he had decided against it. She would call Will from time to time. He had lived for those calls, carefully disguising how much his heart and soul were dying without her.

And then one day the calls had stopped. When he learned of his wife's terrible death during the robbery of her apartment, the walls of Will Chambers' life had started crumbling down around him. More than anyone else in the world, Betty and Jacki had had ringside seats to Will's slow-motion collapse into cynicism and booze.

Will lost track of time as he sat at the kitchen table. But he suddenly became aware of the news report on the television. The announcer had said the words "nuclear weapon just outside New York City."

Will bolted up and stepped into the living room.

The news anchor was dialoguing, in a steady but tense voice, with an on-location reporter outside the FBI office in New York. The reporter was talking.

"Unconfirmed reports have come in that the rental truck was bearing Vermont license plates. Also unconfirmed, at least as of right now, is what kind of weapon the truck was actually carrying. There is no word yet on what seems to be the foremost question on all our minds: Is this rental truck, with its cargo, tied to last year's bombing on Wall Street? Some are wondering whether today's activities signal an all-out terrorist attack on the United States."

The anchor solemnly took over. "The FBI has refused up to now to specify exactly what was in the truck. However, sources in the State Department have reported that—and I am quoting here from one source—it was 'apparently a device designed for mass destruction.' And when we pressed the issue with one high-ranking source in that department, asking whether it was in fact a 'thermonuclear weapon,' that source refused to comment. Jim, are you hearing anything on that down there at the FBI headquarters in New York City?"

"No, but there is plenty of speculation that the truck may have been carrying some type of thermonuclear device. But, of course, no one will admit or deny that," the reporter responded.

"Jim, what about the fact that the State Department is tied into this incident?" the anchor continued. "We usually think of the State Department as having oversight only in matters of foreign policy. But here we have it involved in domestic national security. What's your take on that?"

"That is one of the strange twists in an already very strange story," the reporter said, and then glancing down at some papers in his hands, he noted, "yet we do know this. On April 1, 1999, in a move that really did not make many ripples in Washington, there was a bureaucratic reorganization of sorts. That in itself is certainly nothing new. What happened was that the Arms Control and Disarmament Agency was merged with the Department of State. So ever since that time, there has been within the State Department an Undersecretary for Arms Control and International Security Affairs. The present undersecretary is Kenneth Sharptin. He is also doubling in his prior capacity as Assistant Secretary of State for Near Eastern Affairs. Or as most folks would know it, 'Middle Eastern' affairs."

"So," the anchor announced, "filling in the gaps, the State Department has an interest in this case from an arms-control or international-security standpoint?"

"That's certainly the speculation down here on the street. Which only fuels the idea that the weapon on that truck may have been—well, the kind of weapon we reserve only for our worst nightmares."

"Thank you, Jim." Then the news anchor turned full face to the camera.

"In case you have just tuned in, we have a breaking story. This morning, a rental truck entering New York City was apprehended as it exited the New Jersey Turnpike for what appears to be a major weapons violation, at the very least. And potentially a very grave risk to our national security.

"Action was taken by the U.S. Joint Forces Command, a joint military and law enforcement network created back in 1999—in this case, the Defense Department, the National Security Agency, the State Department, and branches of the military, together with the FBI, and working in conjunction with the New Jersey State Police and the New York City Police. As a result of investigation by this massive task force it was learned that a truck, carrying what officials are now calling only 'a very menacing and very dangerous weapon,' might be heading toward New York City. Such a truck was in fact stopped. Its driver, a middle-aged man of Syrian descent, but a citizen of Jordan—Rahji Ajadi—was arrested. There were no passengers in the truck. The contents within the truck are—at this time—still a mystery. But unconfirmed reports within the State Department have suggested that it may have been carrying some type of device of mass destruction—possibly a thermonuclear weapon.

"The driver, Mr. Ajadi, is in custody in New York City at an undisclosed location. We have been told at this time only that he does not possess a valid passport. We know of no criminal charges as of yet. But we will certainly keep you apprised of any further details as we receive them.

"But one final interesting note. Jim Williams, our reporter in New York City, has already commented that this is a story of 'strange twists.' Well, here is yet another one.

"In a twist of remarkable irony, the truck was stopped by a New Jersey State Patrolman, Ezer Nabib, an Arab and apparently a devout follower of Islam. He had been put on the alert for the make and model of the truck. Apparently the United States government had also received an anonymous tip that the truck might be carrying a very dangerous weapon, and federal authorities and the military all converged on the scene.

"By the time the FBI and the Pentagon and all the other high-powered agencies had arrived, Officer Nabib already had the driver under arrest and the truck secured. Clearly, if there is one hero that is emerging in this story, it is State Patrolman Ezer Nabib, who just may have single-handedly averted one of the worst terrorist attacks in the history of our nation.

"Lastly, there is of course much speculation that this incident may also be tied to Abdul el Alibahd, one of the world's most-hunted international terrorists and a suspect in the Wall Street bombing of last year. Folks up in Manhattan who have had to recover from the horrendous World Trade Towers tragedy, then had to deal with the truck bombing may nearly have had to face yet another terrorist attack—but this one much worse. It is too early to tell—yet—how close we may have come to the brink of nuclear destruction within our own borders if it had not been for the courageous work of New Jersey State Trooper Ezer Nabib."

Will kept the television on into the night, catching every detail of the news story. While there were a variety of opinions given by military and law-enforcement experts, authors on terrorism, and cultural and religious commentators—who noted the irony of an Arab Muslim foiling the apparent suicide mission of an Arab terrorist—no new information was forthcoming.

Will wanted to pick up the telephone and call someone—anyone—to talk about the news. But he realized he had no one to call. When his eyes were too heavy to stay open, he plodded up the curving staircase to go to bed. His faithful dog, Clarence, followed him close behind.

8

IN PREPARING FOR THE DAY'S MEETING, Kenneth Sharptin, undersecretary of the State Department, made sure that the committee members would not enter the State Department building through the main entrance at C and 22nd Street. The press, smelling a story connected to the frightening events of the day before, was already posted there.

Instead, he had his staff usher all the members of the committee in through two separate side entrances. All except one—Colonel Brad Buchingham, the special envoy from the Pentagon. By contrast, he made sure that the Colonel—in uniform, his chest heavy with medals—came in through the main doors in the front. That way he could be seen, with the full press corps there, coming to meet Kenneth Sharptin—coming to confer with Undersecretary Sharptin—coming to advise him.

Five minutes before the Pentagon sedan was to show up, Sharptin strode out of his spacious office and down the hallway with flags of all the nations of the planet arrayed along the top of the walls. He got on the elevator and headed down to the first floor. He glanced at himself, mirrored in the reflection of the smooth steel in the elevator. Perfectly razored Ivy League haircut. Blue pin-striped suit. Light blue shirt with a red tie, and a tiny American flag pin on his suit coat lapel. Just right.

Several dozen television cameras were already perched in the driveway in front of the State Department building. The entire gathering could be seen from a large stretch of C Street—in the heart of D.C.'s power lane of government real estate.

Two of Sharptin's deputy assistants were already waiting for him by the front doors with briefing folders in hand, at the security clearance gate. The guards stepped back and opened the doors for him.

The press was there waiting for him. And then Sharptin heard one of his favorite sounds—the click of handheld cameras and the whir of shoulder-mounted video units.

"This is not a press conference," announced Sharptin as he smiled and paused on the front steps. "The White House released a statement yesterday, and we all stand by the President's words on the apprehension of the suspected terrorist and the rental truck yesterday in New York City."

Then Undersecretary Sharptin, with a slightly furrowed brow, pleaded with the reporters: "Please—please, ladies and gentlemen, please let our special envoy from the Pentagon in."

Colonel Buchingham was getting out of the sedan with a small briefcase in his hand. He didn't wait for the reporters to part. He cut, weaved, and dodged past them and through them, like a halfback.

He strode up the stairs to Sharptin, who was waiting with hands outstretched as if he were a high priest granting a bureaucratic blessing to the Colonel.

Sharptin extended his hand. But Buchingham did not shake it. Instead, Buchingham stopped directly in front of the Undersecretary, looked him in the eye, and said, "Kenneth, what you've got here is a media dog-and-pony show. Do not—I repeat—do not ever do this to me again."

Buchingham did not wait for Sharptin, and walked past him and through security, directly to the elevator. Sharptin and his assistants scurried to catch up and caught the elevator just before the doors closed. On the floor above, the group exited and made their way to the large conference room.

As soon as the Ad Hoc Committee on Cultural Engagement convened and the roll call was recorded, Undersecretary Sharptin made a short introductory statement. He explained how fortuitous it was, in his opinion, that the regularly scheduled meeting of the committee just happened to land on the day after the terrorist truck incident of the day before. He assured them that there would, indeed, be some discussion on the truck incident. But he urged them to see that event within the larger picture of the agenda of the committee. Sharptin then reviewed the history of the Ad Hoc Committee and its ever-evolving mandate.

First, he reminded them of the announcement, a year before, of the disappearance of Saddam Hussein and his family members in Iraq. How they were presumed to have been assassinated in a coup in Baghdad. Sharptin reviewed how he acquired authorization from the Secretary of State to put this committee together as a means of dialoguing about the possibilities of democracy in Iraq and other Middle Eastern countries.

This was followed by a few democratic reforms in Iran, and even talk of modest attempts at equal rights for women in countries like Saudi Arabia. The United Nations Conference on Women was ecstatic. The leading feminists from around the world began to meet and draw up hasty plans for combating patriarchy in the Middle East. All of this had kindled a wave of enthusiasm in the Department of State. Now, it seemed, was the time to take daring new steps to bring the Middle East into the new century—to make them economic and even cultural partners in peace.

And then came the classified reports from within the White House of potential oil shortages and projected petroleum production shortfalls for the United States in the coming years. As a result, there was renewed urgency in trying to find areas of common ground with the Arab OPEC nations.

But now, a Middle Eastern terrorist had been caught in the midst of an apparent plot to smuggle, and perhaps even detonate, a thermonuclear weapon within the shores of America.

"This is the time," Sharptin said in concluding his introductory comments, "for us to embrace a whole new vision—a new way of thinking about international security and global peace.

"Let me suggest this as the question we have to face: Where can we find an ultimate common ground between the East, with its rich heritage of Islam and obedience to spiritual conscience—and the West, with its powerful belief in individual responsibility characterized primarily by the Christian tradition? Is there a way we can bring unity and peace between these two important traditions, and in doing that, really secure the safety of America more than we could have ever dreamed before?

"Let me suggest—a whole new construct for peace. Let me suggest that violent religious differences and cultural differences are not a necessary part of the international equation. People—let me dare to suggest that this pattern of religious and cultural conflict can be changed—it is not just a part of the inevitable. And we all know that religious and cultural conflict between East and West is a matter of grave national security."

Sharptin then called on the members of the committee who were from the Arab–American Cultural Alliance to comment.

"What can be accomplished through finding common ground between the Arab and OPEC nations on the one hand, and the West on the other, is this," one member noted. "First, a community of sharing in oil reserves. Second, a chance at expanding democracy in the Middle East. And third, we can achieve what could never be achieved before this. There is a good chance that the Arab nations will give absolute assurances of a willingness to police, and even punish, the terrorists within their borders as long as the West shows appreciation—and not suspicious denigration—for their religious traditions."

Colonel Buchingham was clearly irritated.

"So," the colonel shot out, "if the U.S., England, Canada, if these nations show some respect for Allah, then the OPEC nations are going to keep their oil prices down and their production up—and they will even start arresting the terrorists that are currently roaming at will within their borders? Is this what you are saying? Is that your idea of national security?

"When you geniuses come up with the newest, dumbest idea for national security, then the very first folks who pay the price for it are those kids from your hometown who wear the uniforms," Buchingham continued. "They're the ones who get turned into hamburger helper because one day you woke up with this really bright idea about national security."

Sharptin tried to redirect the conversation.

"Colonel, your life has been devoted to the use of military force to protect American interests. And we all are very grateful for that. But now is the time to wage peace, rather than wage war," Sharptin chided. "Now, the Pentagon may not appreciate the need for the West to respect the traditions of Islam, but here in the State Department, we take that very seriously. This is not a new idea. Both government leaders and nongovernmental groups have been working for years on the issue of reconciliation with the Islamic countries."

But Colonel Buchingham was not about to be diverted from his course, and he kept charging ahead.

"And what I was about to say was that last, but certainly not least," the Colonel concluded, "it strikes me that you are talking about getting the U.S. government into the Islam business. Isn't that what you're really talking about here?"

Sharptin jumped in. "Colonel, I'm afraid you have made several flawed assumptions. We are not talking about the United States government officially promoting Islam. We are merely talking about fostering an atmosphere of tolerance toward the cultural traditions of our Muslim partners in peace. After all—who but the Arab nations themselves has the best opportunity to stop the terrorists within their own borders? The only thing the Arab nations lack is the *motivation* to do so. That's what we are talking about here. Simply providing the *motivation* to the Arab nations to do the policing within their own nations that we—as a separate Western nation—could not possibly have the right or the ability to do ourselves."

Several members of the committee started talking among themselves excitedly.

A question was then raised regarding the nature of the weapon on the rented truck that was stopped the day before.

"Right there is another problem I've got," Buchingham protested. "Do you realize that this operation is being pulled out of the hands of the military—and has been entirely co-opted by the FBI and the State Department? We have absolutely no intelligence on the nature of the weapon or device in the truck. That vehicle was whisked away before our Pentagon representatives had an opportunity to inspect it. We've been boot-kicked right out of the loop. This whole operation stinks."

"Thank you for your enlightening comments, Colonel," Sharptin commented, evoking a few chuckles from the group. "But I think that what we have got to focus on is this: By what means can we create a new way of thinking about the common ground between the rich tapestry of Islamic tradition—and the relatively young, but democratically vibrant traditions of the West? Let's all think on that—let's focus on possible answers to that question for our next meeting."

The meeting was adjourned. Colonel Buchingham, as the others were leaving the room, leaned over to the center of the large conference table toward the starfish-shaped speakerphone in the middle of the table. He touched the ON button and the green light went on. He touched it again, and the light went off.

"I noticed," the Colonel growled, "that the green light was off during our meeting. I presume, therefore, that there was no one else listening at the other end."

"That sounds a little paranoid," remarked Sharptin curtly.

"Sure," Buchingham responded. "But a little paranoia builds a lot of national security. By the way, isn't this the same conference room that the Russians were bugging a couple of years ago?"

"You can rest assured that after that incident we had it swept for bugs. And we've doubled our security measures."

"That'll make me sleep like a baby tonight," Buchingham said. "It truly will." Then he donned his cap, grabbed his briefcase, and exited the room.

Sharptin went over to the door of the conference room and locked it and then sat down at the long table and looked through his notes. He glanced at his watch. At exactly fifteen minutes to the hour he pushed the ON button of the speaker phone.

"He will speak to you now," a female voice said.

"I'm ready," Sharptin replied.

After two more minutes of silence a man's voice came on.

"Fine meeting, Kenneth, I'm pleased."

"Thank you, sir. Did everything come through alright?"

"Reception was limited. A little too much echo. That Buchingham's a problem," the voice said.

"I can handle him," Sharptin responded, with a sense of bold reassurance.

"I hope so. I'll be in touch."

"What's the timetable?" Sharptin asked.

"I'll let you know."

"Things are moving quickly," Sharptin said, with a little urgency in his voice.

"I don't like repeating myself. I said that I will be in touch."

With that the voice was gone from the speakerphone. Sharptin sat for a minute at the conference table. He relished it all. And he particularly enjoyed the thought that he had confidential access to perhaps the most powerful man in the world.

Sharptin made his way back to his office. There was a letter lying on his desk that had been couriered to him from the White House Chief of Staff while he was in his committee meeting. Sharptin smiled. Perhaps things were moving faster than he had thought. The convention was twelve months away. The vice-president's colon cancer had come at an opportune time. He had been assured that he was on a short list of consideration by the President and the party leaders for the vice-presidential slot. The only downside had been his lack of name recognition. Yet he was confident that, too, was being remedied.

His years in Washington had taught him that two kinds of people could engender power in Washington—the feared and the revered.

Yes, Kenneth Sharptin thought to himself. *And very soon, I shall be both.*

9

WILL CHAMBERS ARRIVED AT THE OFFICE a few minutes ahead of his conference time with Angus MacCameron so he could talk with his secretary.

Betty was there waiting for him, sitting at the reception desk with her arms crossed in front of her.

He had barely closed the door when Betty started in.

"I don't want any loss of benefits. No salary cut. Same hours. I want my financial package to be exactly the same as it was when I was being paid by the firm."

"No argument from me," Will replied, trying to be cheery.

"No offense, but are you going to be able to afford me?"

"Oh yeah, of course," Will said, keeping up his usual confidence.

"One more thing."

"Yes?"

"As I'm sure you noticed, the firm took our law clerk and our paralegal. They were put back in the Richmond office. I trust you are going to be taking on extra help. Because I am *not* going to double as a paralegal as well as a secretary, and whatever else."

"Sure. No problem."

"And just one more thing," Betty said, her eyebrow slightly raised.

"What is it?"

"Well," she said, "you're a connected guy. Tell me something."

"Yeah?"

"Are we all going to be blown off the face of the earth?"

"Well, no, I don't think so. But this thing is scary, huh?"

"I was telling Teddy last night as we sat there watching the news, 'Teddy, honey, we've had a good life together. But I don't want it to end in some kind of nuclear explosion.'"

"No, I know what you mean," Will replied. "Nothing like being melted into the concrete to ruin your whole day."

Just then Angus MacCameron walked in through the door. His daughter Fiona was with him.

Will stood looking at Fiona as she smoothed her hair back slightly. He searched momentarily for something to say, but failed. He wondered whether he had met her before. Yet he knew that could not be true. Whatever the connection was that he felt, he couldn't put his finger on it. He struggled to say something witty, but failed again, and only managed a wide smile.

"I hope you don't mind that I brought my daughter, Fiona, with me. Bob, her business manager, couldn't make it," MacCameron said, looking for a response from Will.

Will was still studying Fiona when Betty chimed in.

"Please pardon the state of the office. They've taken the old lobby furniture away. We are...in the process of doing some reorganizing."

"Refurnishing," Will added.

"Well, shall we sit down and have a chat?" MacCameron said. "Somewhere where there is a chair?"

"Sure. Let's have a...chat." Will replied smiling, and led them into the conference room.

He shook hands formally there. Fiona had small hands, but a firm grip. When he introduced himself to "Ms. MacCameron," she smiled brightly. Will noticed that when Fiona smiled she had little dimples in both cheeks.

"MacCameron was my family name," Fiona remarked. "But when I started performing I decided to take my Scottish clan name—Cameron. I go by Fiona Cameron."

"That was my idea," Reverend MacCameron interjected, smiling broadly at his daughter.

When they were settled in, Will led his client through the initial questioning. He started with his personal and family background. Then Will moved on to interrogate him a little more thoroughly about his professional credentials.

Will learned that MacCameron had been born in Glasgow, Scotland, to working class parents. He gave a little background on why the family, some two-hundred-fifty years before, had changed the family name from Cameron to MacCameron—to avoid retaliation by the English, who were at war with Scottish patriots at the time.

He was educated at Aberdeen University. He received further schooling, in archaeology, at the University of Edinburgh, where he did some teaching while he was pursuing his graduate degree. He did not complete his studies—moving instead to the United States. Once in America he received both a master's in Biblical Archaeology and a Master of Divinity from the College of the Piedmont in West Virginia. Later he became an assistant pastor of a small church in Pennsylvania, but after only a few years he left there and did some teaching and a little freelance writing for a few religious periodicals.

Then he founded his own archaeological magazine, *Digging for Truth*. It had started on a shoestring budget, but slowly he built up a following. Later he was able to move to Israel, where he and his wife settled into a small apartment in Jerusalem. MacCameron would scurry around to various digs and report back to his readers on them. He openly admitted that he was not well-received by the other archaeologists in Israel. And he was even less well-received by the academics back in the United States.

The only notable exception was a close friendship with a noted expert in Semitic languages and Middle Eastern history by the name of Dr. Richard Hunter. Hunter had worked for the British Museum but spent a considerable amount of time in Israel and the surrounding countries. MacCameron and Hunter had become good friends while they were students at the University of Edinburgh. They had remained close right up to the time of Hunter's death, which had occurred within the last year. Hunter had been found, shot in the head, in his tiny field office in Jerusalem.

Last, MacCameron described to Will with enthusiasm how he led several biblical archaeology tours every year—mostly for his faithful subscribers.

"Why did you leave the University of Edinburgh?" Will asked.

"I was teaching some classes to the undergraduates. I had an American student—a very pretty and wonderful girl named Helen," MacCameron explained. "Very bright. She just dazzled me. After she finished my class that term—by the way, she was an excellent student—I asked her out for tea. And then for walks down by the sea. And picnics. Well, we fell in love. She had to return to the States because she was over in Scotland for only a two-term study project. I followed her to America. We were married here in the States less than a year after that."

When Will started homing in on the allegations in Dr. Reichstad's Complaint, and on the details of the lawsuit, he turned to Fiona.

"Ms. Cameron..."

"Call me Fiona," she said, smiling.

Will knew what had to come next. But he regretted saying it.

"Okay, Fiona." Will responded. "I'm going to have to ask you to leave the room at this point. The attorney-client privilege of confidentiality protects everything your father and I say—because he is the client. But it does not protect you. If you stay in this room you could later be called as a witness by the other side and forced to divulge everything that we talk about."

MacCameron's face became animated, and he blurted out, "Well, let me assure you, Mr. Chambers, that I have nothing to hide from Reichstad's storm troopers—absolutely nothing. Anything we talk about here, he is welcome to find out about."

"That may be your gut reaction, but that's terrible litigation strategy," Chambers explained. "The way this game is played is this: We make them sweat for every piece of information. If they don't ask the right question, they don't get the right answer. And believe me—knowing this law firm that is on the other side—they will probably end up asking most of the right questions. So the point is, I'm afraid, Ms. Cameron—Fiona—I'm afraid that you will have to step outside."

At that Fiona stood up and put out her hand to Will. He shook it warmly.

"I think that's my cue," she said. "I noticed that little café across the street. I've got my cell phone with me. I'll see if I can get a cup of tea there. I can make some phone calls while I wait. I'll be there waiting for you, Da." She kissed her father on the cheek.

Then Fiona turned to Will, smiled sincerely, and said, "Mr. Chambers, it has been a pleasure. I will ask that the Lord give you special wisdom in dealing with my father's case."

"Sure, thanks," Will said, not knowing exactly how to respond. "It was a pleasure." Will studied her carefully as she left.

As soon as the door closed Will dove into the background facts of the lawsuit.

MacCameron had brought with him several back issues of his magazine to show to the lawyer. As Will probed his client and glanced through the magazine, he groaned inwardly at the titles on the covers. One of them—in bold print that seemed to scream—was "Christ's Second Coming and the Discovery of the Sacred Red Heifer!" Another pronounced, "Are We on the Verge of Discovering the Old Testament Ark of the Covenant?"

But Will was dumbfounded at the cover of the December issue that had caused the lawsuit. As he stared at it, he wondered why this relatively intelligent—and not entirely eccentric—fellow had not consulted a lawyer before printing such a journalistic monstrosity.

On the cover, in the upper-right-hand corner, was the picture of his friend, Dr. Richard Hunter.

In the left-hand corner was a picture of someone MacCameron described as a good-natured and well-liked antiquities dealer in Bethlehem, by the name of Harim Azid.

The face of each man was framed within a circle with red crosshairs. The point seemed painfully clear. Both men, who had died within a short time of each other—Azid by apparent suicide and Hunter in an unsolved murder—were being touted, by Will's client, as victims of some kind of murder conspiracy.

The black headline beneath their pictures proclaimed: "THEY DID NOT DIE IN VAIN!"

And then the subtitle underneath read: "Dr. Albert Reichstad's Phony, Anti-Christ 'Discovery'—and How It Is Connected to These Tragic and Suspicious Deaths."

Chambers, a champion of freedom of speech, suddenly found himself wondering why MacCameron's sophomoric and incendiary magazine should really be worthy of First Amendment protection. He thought back to another client of his—Billy Joe Highlighter, an evangelist whose case Will had handled—and it had cost him his job. Now, Reverend MacCameron. Did he really want to make a career of defending religious fanatics?

"Was it really necessary for you to refer to this Dr. Reichstad as the Antichrist?" Will asked.

"First of all, Mr. Chambers, I did not call him the Antichrist. I described his so-called discovery as an 'anti-Christ discovery.' Which it was."

"Okay, explain that one to me."

"Most certainly. The Bible teaches that the spirit of this world—the whole world system of the world, the flesh, and the devil himself—is the spirit of Antichrist. So therefore, Dr. Reichstad's 'discovery' is being used by the spirit of this age—in fact by the devil himself—as the most cunning form of deception yet to be unveiled in our day."

Will hardly knew where to start as he heard MacCameron's preposterous minisermon. *The spirit of this world,* he thought to himself, *includes me. And Audra. Was our marriage part of the spirit of anti-Christ? And what about Jacki? And a whole lot of other wonderful, decent people?* As Will thought about it, this MacCameron had apparently consigned them all to condemnation and everlasting hell because they hadn't stashed their brains in their dresser drawers with their socks—as MacCameron obviously had.

MacCameron must have noticed that Will was thinking deeply about something and not paying attention.

"Well, do you want me to continue?" MacCameron asked.

"Sure. Go to it."

"As I was saying. First, this so-called 'discovery' is being used by the spirit of anti-Christ. Second, you, Mr. Chambers, have no idea who this Dr. Reichstad is."

Will then asked his client what he knew about Dr. Reichstad's background. MacCameron described Reichstad's scholarly background in detail. He then produced a thirty-five-page curriculum vitae of Reichstad's that had been dug up by Tiny Heftland, whom he had hired to investigate Reichstad immediately after being sued.

Flipping through the massive professional bio of the plaintiff—Reichstad's degrees, and honors and awards, and twenty pages of published scholarly articles, books he had written, teaching assignments around the world, and the conferences he had hosted—that was when Will thought he heard the voice.

It was the voice somewhere in the unconscious that trial lawyers learn to heed. Will knew that all-important voice; it was the one that tells a lawyer later on "I told you so." He had always felt that it must be similar to the whisper in the back of the brain that tells some very lucky folks not to get on that airplane—the one with the ice on the wings, the one that everybody is going to read about in the morning newspaper.

That was the voice Will had learned not to ignore. It would warn him about those cases that started out looking good and ended up going real bad. And now that voice was telling Will Chambers that this case would not only turn out to be a dog—but it would be a dog with really big teeth.

"And third," MacCameron continued. His voice was getting quieter and even more intense. Now he was bending over toward Chambers.

"Third, and you have to get this one if you're going to be any good to me at all—third, while Reichstad pretends that this so-called discovery is the ultimate proof of who Jesus really was, I say—and much more importantly, God says in his holy, and immutable, and living Word—that this papyrus fragment is not about Christ at all. It is about that which is *not Christ*. Therefore, it is *anti-Christ*. Jesus said anyone who is not with him is against him. This papyrus discovery by Reichstad is a fraud against the truth of Christ."

Will found himself reeling from MacCameron's theological rantings. He strained to pick out the one, cogent string of information from his client's tangled ball of medieval religious thinking.

"You've got to tell me something," Will asked. "Why do you insist on calling this archaeological find by Reichstad a 'so-called discovery'?"

"You will begin to understand after I tell you about my last meeting with Richard Hunter. Then what is hidden from you now, will start being revealed." There was a labored sadness to his voice as he said that. And then, as if beginning the narration of some obscure epic, MacCameron intoned the beginning of his story.

"It all began in Jerusalem."

10

WILL LEANED BACK IN HIS OFFICE CHAIR as he listened intently to Angus MacCameron. As MacCameron began telling the story of his last, fateful meeting with Dr. Hunter, Will knew he was getting close to pay dirt, whatever it might be. If there was to be any hope for a valid defense to the lawsuit, this would be it.

As MacCameron recounted it, he and Dr. Hunter happened to be in Jerusalem at the same time last year. But MacCameron hadn't seen him for some time. His calls to Hunter's field office went unanswered. Then Hunter called MacCameron out of the blue. He said he had to meet him immediately. All Hunter would say was that it was incredibly important. He was breathless and excited, and he even sounded a bit frightened. But he wouldn't give any details over the phone.

MacCameron remembered that phone call from Hunter very clearly. "We've got to meet, and it's got to be quite soon," Hunter had insisted in a hoarse whisper.

MacCameron suggested a few restaurants, but Hunter rejected them immediately.

"Angus, it has to be somewhere in the old section, close to my office. I can't afford to leave this part of town, it's just too dangerous. I can't tell you why. You just have to trust me, my friend. It's got to be somewhere close to the western wall, and somewhere nicely hidden from view."

MacCameron thought for a minute and then made a suggestion. "How about the old Between the Arches Café? The streets there are always crowded with tourists heading to the wall and you can make your way to the restaurant without being noticed. Besides," MacCameron added, "the space used to be an old Roman cistern, remember? So the tables are at least two stories down."

Hunter agreed. The next day they met in the early afternoon in the café. MacCameron was already seated when Hunter showed up a few minutes late, wearing his usual wide-brimmed straw hat, the one with the dirty red bandanna for a hatband. His threadbare golf shirt was soaked through with sweat and his ruddy English complexion was almost purple with the heat. He was perspiring profusely.

"You look like a mess," Angus exclaimed in astonishment.

But his friend was busy turning around and looking behind him as he sat down at the little glass-topped café table.

"I had to double back several times on my way here." Hunter spoke in a hushed tone. "I am sure I was being followed, but I think I lost them."

"What in the world are you talking about, Richard?" Angus asked. "Followed by whom?"

As the waiter approached the table with their menus, Hunter fell silent, swabbing the sweat off his forehead.

MacCameron tried to make some small talk. "I read about the archaeology conference that Albert Reichstad is sponsoring. I assume that you were invited to speak there. What's the name of it?"

"'The Final Quest for the Historical Jesus—a New Way of Looking at the Archaeo-Biblical Data,'" Hunter responded distractedly. "I *was* invited to speak, but I have come across something much more important than anything they could address at that conference. So I told them I would be unable to attend. Angus, I am sure that the British Museum will be outraged when they find out that I canceled. But when you see with your own eyes what I've got, you'll understand. You'll see why it is much bigger than anything Reichstad and his traveling band of scholars could ever come up with."

"What is it?" MacCameron asked expectantly.

"I can't go into specifics," Hunter responded, bending his head down and leaning forward over the tabletop. "Let me just say this—I have come across a discovery that is about to erase two thousand years of religious history right off the map."

MacCameron was flabbergasted and searched for a response. But before he could speak, Hunter added, "That's why I want a second opinion. You and I have never been on the same page theologically, Angus. Which is exactly why I want you to see what I have discovered. One thing I know about you—you are a man of integrity."

"Can't you give me some idea—"

"It's a papyrus fragment," Hunter blurted out. "Almost certainly first century in origin, and absolutely from the Jerusalem area. I came across it through Harim Azid. You remember him?"

MacCameron nodded. "Yes. Everyone calls him 'Tony.' But—"

"Exactly," Hunter affirmed. "He was the antiquities dealer in Bethlehem. Before his death, Tony handled a lot of ancient artifacts, a number of them quite valuable. One day, he called me to come in and take a look at something. When he unwrapped it and showed it to me, I immediately knew this was going to be an earth-shaking find. Tony told me that this papyrus fragment he was showing me had been brought in by a Bedouin. Apparently, the man had found it in a cave at Qumran when he lived by the Dead Sea as a boy and had kept it under wraps for some fifty years. Then he finally decided to take it to Tony, who was some kind of shirttail relative, to find out what he could get for it. And then, well, poor Tony..." With that, Hunter's voice began to tremble.

"Yes, I heard he had committed suicide," MacCameron said quietly. "I was very sorry to hear that."

"That was certainly the story that was given out. Both the Israeli and the Palestinian police came to the scene, but the Palestinians had jurisdiction. They ruled it a suicide—apparently they found a revolver near the body, and they said that he had put the revolver in his mouth and pulled the trigger. Their report indicated that he had been despondent over his marriage. The strange thing is that he had been separated from his wife for a long time, and the last contact I had with him, he was in a very chipper mood. Certainly he kept a revolver. But then, most antiquities dealers do. I am telling you, Angus—this was no suicide."

"What *are* you telling me?" MacCameron asked.

"I am telling you that the same people who killed him are trying to get to me. They are trying to get the fragments I've got.

"I want you to meet me, Angus, in four days at my apartment here in Jerusalem. I've got to fly out of Tel Aviv tomorrow morning back to England. I am hoping to meet with the staff at the British Museum—if everything goes well, I know I can get their support on this project. I am telling you, Angus, this fragment is so powerful that men will kill over it."

As the waiter came to take their orders, Hunter whispered, "Come to my apartment in four days and I will show you." Then he shakily rose to his feet and walked rapidly up the stone stairwell that led out of the restaurant.

Will was trying to digest the story he had just heard. After a moment he asked, "Did the meeting ever take place?"

"No," MacCameron said with a sigh, then he shook his head and explained how three days later he had received a phone call from the Jerusalem police. They had found Hunter's body in his office. He had been shot to death, and the office had been ransacked. Considering Hunter's occupation, the police concluded that the motive was probably robbery. Antiquities, after all, were always a lucrative business for thieves.

"Why did the police call you?" Will asked.

"Richard had scribbled my name and telephone number in his calendar—apparently to remind himself of our meeting," MacCameron added. "Poor Richard must have been under incredible stress, knowing that his life was in danger."

By this time Will was feeling confused and uncertain about MacCameron's case. He stood up to stretch his legs and walked over to the window that faced St. Andrew's Episcopal Church.

The church across the street dated back to the time of the Revolutionary War. In its graveyard, officers who had fought in that war were buried under stone grave markers rubbed smooth and illegible with the years. Its tall steeple housed a bell that had rung two-and-a-half centuries ago to celebrate the news of General Washington's victory at Trenton, New Jersey, after he had led his troops across the frigid Delaware River. The bell had continued to toll every day since then, its ropes pulled by hand.

The great bell started slowly gonging to mark the hour as Will looked out the window, his back to his client.

"Look," Will said to break the silence. "We are going to have to schedule several more meetings so I can get a good feel for all the facts of this case."

Will found himself going on automatic pilot—giving his "I am your lawyer and you are my client" speech, against all of his better judgment.

"But let me give you the two ground rules for this game," Will continued, still ignoring the little voice in the back of his head.

The voice was saying, *Why not just blow this strange guy off—let it go—cash out what's left of your investments and go on a long holiday? Decide what you want to do with your life. Maybe travel. Or take up mountain-climbing. Or wildlife photography.*

"So here are the rules," Will heard himself explaining. "They are very simple. First rule—I will try very, very hard to win your case.

"The second rule is also very simple. You pay my legal fees in order for me to try very, very hard to win your case. I focus on the first rule—and you have to focus on the second rule. Those are the rules of the game. And now I need to talk some specifics about my fee structure."

"I must tell you something," MacCameron said, sounding a little agitated. "I know you are the lawyer. And I am the client. And I do get the point of your little recitation about the two rules of the game. But I must tell you this is not a game. No, not at all. This is deadly serious business. I consider this to be a struggle of titanic proportions. I believe that the very angels in heaven are bending down with listening ears, waiting to find out what happens in this case."

Chambers took a second to respond.

"Look," the lawyer said, "when I use the word 'game,' let me explain what I mean. There are always two sides to every game. When the gladiators went into the ring with animals during the time of the Roman Empire—to the gladiator it was the ultimate game of life and death. But to the animal, well, it was just another opportunity for dinner. With me it's a game. That's how I win—I keep myself focused on the fact that even though I am fighting for justice, I have to win it like any other game. Preparation, perspiration, perseverance—as my high school football coach used to say. So for you it's not a game—but for me, well, it's the game I've been playing most of my adult life."

"Tell me, Mr. Chambers," MacCameron asked. "When they put the Christians in the Coliseum with the lions—do you think that was a game, too?"

Will studied his client. He really had no desire to debate with the Reverend. Now he simply wanted to finish the arrangements for the retainer fee and get home.

"No, that was not a game," Will replied.

"Wrong!" MacCameron exclaimed. "It *was* a game."

Will looked at him with a blank stare.

"You see, it *was* a game—for someone. It was a game for the pagans up in the stands. To see the Christians thrown to the lions. They came to watch because they thought it was wonderful sport."

Will raised an eyebrow.

"And do you want to know something else, Mr. Chambers?" MacCameron went on.

Will Chambers had the feeling that this persistent Scot was going to make his point whether he wanted to hear it or not.

"Tell me," Will responded with a little resignation in his voice.

"That game is still going on today—the Christians and the lions. Metaphorically, of course. I would be the Christian," MacCameron noted with some measure of self-satisfaction.

"And I suppose," Will noted, "that Reichstad and his lawyers, they are the lions."

"You're catching on, my boy!" MacCameron shouted out. "And the courtroom—that is our coliseum."

"And what would that make me?" Will asked, not sure if he wanted to hear the answer.

"Oh—well, I will tell you," MacCameron said. "Yes, I will tell you. You are the gladiator. You're paid to defend me against the lions. Only, eventually you will have to ask yourself that all-important question."

"And what would that be?"

"When the time comes to choose—and believe me, Mr. Chambers, that time always comes and you'll have to answer this question—will you be standing with the Christians, down in the blood and sand, when the lions come charging—or will you be up in the stands, cheering with the pagans?"

Will was still doubting whether he ever wanted to climb into the arena to find out.

11

THE HUGE STADIUM WAS FILLED TO CAPACITY. Tens of thousands of teens, college kids, and "twenty-somethings" had flooded into the rock concert from the greater Los Angeles area that evening. The crowd, illuminated under the stadium lights, was on its feet, screaming in one massive wall of sound. Curt Razzor, lead singer of the rock band Zylon-B, was on the stage trying to quiet them down. But he was enjoying it, and was grinning and nodding his head violently up and down, absorbing the tidal wave of adulation.

Hundreds of musclemen with headsets, dressed in black T-shirts with white lettering that read "BEHOLD THE NEW CENTURY," paced up and down through the aisles.

Razzor stepped back from the microphone. His head was shaved in a bald circle on top, like a monk's, but he had long tangled dreadlocks cascading down from the sides and back of his head, and as he walked away from the microphone, bouncing his head to some unheard beat, the long ropes of hair swung wildly over the shoulders of his black spandex jumpsuit covered with yellow lightning bolts.

The crowd screamed louder. Razzor said something to the members of his group, who were all hanging back by the drum set that was poised on the raised platform at the rear of the stage. And then he laughed and walked back to the microphone. After a few more minutes he quieted down the ocean of people.

"I know why you are here. I know you have come so you can really trip on the music."

Screams began to rise up from the illuminated heads and arms and waving hands of the army of forty thousand.

"Now you have to shut up and listen. Okay? There is something really powerful coming down here. I'm like this historian of music. Okay? And I read about how the Beatles went over to India because they wanted to trip out on some spirituality from the Maharishi Yogi. That was the '60s."

The screams were getting louder again.

"Shut up, shut up," Razzor yelled mechanically, his voice reverbing over several acres of humanity.

The screams started dying down.

"That was the '60s. Now, we're not there anymore, are we? I mean, this is called evolution. We are out of the '60s, so listen up. Because there is someone who's going to talk to you. This dude's name is Warren Mullburn. He is like one of the most wired guys in the universe. And don't trash him with a lot of noise—cuz if you do I'm not coming back to end this show. Got it? So, you got to listen to him. But I'm telling you—I think he's got a shock-trip for you—he can blow your minds in ways that you can't believe. I personally have been consuming the power trip from this guy's ideas myself. So listen up."

Razzor walked to the rear of the stage, where he quickly disappeared down the back catwalk with his group.

The rock promoter, a man in a Hawaiian shirt and jeans, ran up to the mike.

"For just a few seconds I want to tell you something about Warren Mullburn, who is going to talk to you for just a few minutes, that's all it will take, I promise. Now, how many of you went to see the movie *The Planet Eaters* last year?"

There was a mild yell from the crowd.

"Great sci-fi horror flick. It's up for two special-effects Oscars this year. Well, the guy who wrote the book and then it was turned into the screenplay—the guy who wrote the story was none other than Warren Mullburn.

"Now, Mr. Mullburn is a true genius. He has been rated as the third-richest man in the world. He holds degrees from MIT and Stanford University. He has written a dozen different books. He speaks four different languages. The *International Financial Times* calls him 'the closest thing to an economic spirit master we've got.' The *Greenwich Village Echo* says 'despite his incredible wealth—one might even say *obscene* wealth—he may actually be a kind of contemporary prophet of what he calls the "new-century generation."'

"He is going to talk for only ten minutes. That's all. And in ten minutes, I guarantee you that, if you listen carefully, you will be able to see the way to change your life as you now know it.

"So now. I present to you Mr. Warren Mullburn."

Suddenly the lights went out, plunging the entire coliseum into darkness. A few shrieks were heard. Then a few seconds later, blazing lights flooded the stadium from the back of the stage—blinding, dazzling lights shining out into the crowd. There was a symphonic crescendo of timpani drums. Music was rising and getting louder as a figure approached the front of the stage, framed within the molten lights that backlit him like a sun.

Then suddenly, the stadium lights went back on. The man was alone on the stage.

Warren Mullburn did not go to the microphone but began strolling slowly across the front of the stage, taking in the audience, smiling and waving. Mullburn was slightly balding. His hair was blondish-grey on the sides and was trimmed neatly. He was wearing blue jeans and had a trim waist. His forest-green shirt was stretched over a muscular body that looked like it belonged to a twenty-five-year-old rather than a man of sixty years. His face and arms were tan. He walked with the energetic gait of an athlete.

Mullburn discreetly touched his shirt collar, where he had his wireless microphone, and heard the muffled tap reverberate from countless speakers in the stadium. Now that he knew his mike was hot, he was ready to roll.

Just then, four mammoth jumbo-trons that had been sitting darkened and dead in the stadium blinked on. Their huge screens lit up with the image of Warren Mullburn walking to the center of the stage.

"BEHOLD THE NEW CENTURY," he said, his voice ringing like a shot.

"I am here to bring a gift to you, and it is worth more than any amount of money you could ever win in the world's biggest lotto. It is an idea that will change your life.

"You came to hear some music. And it's great music. And this is a great night. But after the music is over you'll all get in your cars and drive home and nothing will have changed. Nothing will be different for you.

"I know that down deep you are better and smarter than your teachers think you are. You guys are stronger and much more hip, much more unique than your girlfriends give you credit for. You young women are smart and tough, and talented, and beautiful—and you wonder why the guys don't realize it.

"You've got jobs, some of you, and college degrees and you're making good money—but let's be honest—you're not being paid what you're really worth, are you? You're working for bosses who don't know half of what you know—who can't do half of what you can do.

"So you are stuck. You feel like something is keeping you down. As if some invisible force is preventing you from being the superstar you know is down there—deep inside. You guy musicians know you could be a Curt Razzor. And you young women know you could be a Missy J.J. So why aren't you?

"Here is why. There *is* an invisible force keeping you down. But it's not fate. And it's not God. And it's not the laws of nature. You can forget all of that.

"In the medieval ages sailors were being kept back from sailing across the ocean. You know why? It wasn't fate, or God, or the laws of nature. It was the fact that they hadn't learned a secret. What was the secret? The secret was that the earth was not flat—and big sea serpents were not going to eat up their ships. When they had the courage to learn the secret, then they had the power to become gods of the sea and sail around the world.

"For thousands of years men and women believed in this idea of a big God up in the sky, and as a result they were kept from learning the secrets of science, kept from flying in the air, kept from learning how the human body worked. They were kept in darkness."

Just then a picture of medieval monks flashed onto the screens, followed by an ancient painting of someone being burned at the stake.

"But then about a hundred years ago, suddenly the secret was out. We learned that we are all part of an evolution, an evolving power. Through science we learned that all human life started with little molecules, and turned into one-celled animals, and then into reptiles and fish and birds and mammals. And eventually into humans."

A picture of Charles Darwin came on the huge screens.

"But did you ever wonder why that evolution took so long? Why it took billions of years? It took so long because those little molecules, and the single-celled things swimming around in the sea, even those higher forms of animals—they hadn't learned the secret. They hadn't learned the secret that they were evolving. They were caught up *in the middle of* their own evolution—but they hadn't learned to *master* their own evolution.

"Almost all of the important discoveries of science, medicine, computer technology, astronomy—almost all of the great discoveries have happened since the discovery of evolution. And that is because we started to learn the secret—the secret that we are evolving upward into something better. We have started—whether we realize it or not—to speed up our own evolution."

The jumbo-trons showed a picture of the first moon landing.

"And now we come to this moment. Right here. Just you and me. Some time ago I learned the secret. I learned that every one of us can be the master of our own evolution. That's right. You can do it. I did it, and so can you. It's not that I am smarter or better. It's just that I happened to stumble across the secret. And you can learn that secret too.

"But to do it you only have to do three things. First you have to look in the mirror and admit that you are evolving into something better.

"Second, you need to throw the crutches away that are holding you back. Drugs are a crutch. Sure, it's fun to trip out and feel good for a little while."

Some cheers rose up from the crowd.

"But where does that get you when it's over? It slows you down. It keeps you from evolving.

"Now other things can hold you down too. You know, I went to Sunday school like some of you did. I know all of the Bible stories, and they were nice little stories. But while we were listening to those stories we were missing the real secret.

"Here's the secret, and here is the third step. Jesus was not some super-God who died and then got resurrected so he can send you all to hell when you don't behave. There is a really powerful discovery that was just made by a great scientist by the name of Albert Reichstad that proves, beyond any question at all, that the old Sunday school, Bible make-believe story about Jesus just isn't true. And the whole scientific world is now agreeing with him."

Up in the cheap seats a man with a T-shirt that simply said "Jesus" on the front yelled out, "You're a false prophet! Tell the truth. Tell them that Jesus is the Messiah!"

Then two of the musclemen in the black T-shirts quickly approached and whisked him out of his seat and down one of the corridors that led out of the stadium.

Smiling, Mullburn continued in his powerful and emphatic voice.

"But here is what is true. Jesus was just like you and me. He was just like one of us. So that means that he had learned the secret of his own evolution. He was able to do miracles and wonders and rock the world with love because he had mastered his own evolution.

"BEHOLD, THIS IS THE NEW CENTURY. It is time to put the old ideas away. I want you to join me in being the master of your own powerful evolution. Being smarter—being better—being richer—being more successful—being on top and not on the bottom. And all it takes is for you to reach out and have the guts to grab it. Grab it now. It's there for the taking.

"Face it. Realize it. You always wanted to be part of a real revolution. Now it is here. When they sang about the Age of Aquarius back in the '60s they knew something was coming. The real revolution now is spiritual. Be prepared for a real mind-melding experience—a real coming-together of the old religions of the world. Can you imagine it? The mystical secrets of Eastern Islam magically melding together with the Christian ideas of justice and love—coming together and creating something entirely new, and awesome, and powerful, in this new century.

"You have got to be open. Be open in order to catch the wave of this evolution that's going on.

"I love you people, every one of you. I love you all! Rock on!"

The lights dimmed except for a single spotlight on Warren Mullburn. He then wheeled around and strode off the stage, his back to the audience, as a symphony of percussion filled the cavernous arena.

Then for the next two hours, under the bluish white iridescence of the stadium lights, forty thousand young people screamed and cheered and leaped and danced to the rock music that had brought them together, that had made them one under the warm California night sky.

A chauffeur drove Mullburn and his bodyguards to the private jet that was waiting for them. The billionaire was quickly airborne, making phone calls around the world—to his contacts in the Asian markets, to the geologists in his several oil companies, to the executives in his multinational computer networking company. Soon he would be circling his modern-day castle in the Nevada desert preparing for landing.

Mullburn clicked off the telephone and eased back in his chair. He turned to the men in the seat across from him and said, "I think those kids loved me tonight. I felt really good out there. I do think that we are just about at critical mass. And I don't think there's anything—or anyone—who is going to be able to stop this now. Not now." And then he smiled confidently and looked at the biggest of the men. "Don't you agree, Bruda?"

Bruda Weilder, his big, blond bodyguard, smiled a big smile in return, nodded his head, and then said, "You are so right, Mr. Mullburn."

12

WILL CHAMBERS HAD A LOT ON HIS MIND while driving back from the main office of his former law firm in Richmond. His meeting with Hadley Bates and the other partners had gone about as badly as he had expected. There were accusations, name-calling, and threats. But worst of all was the white envelope that Hadley had pushed across the conference table to Will at the end of the meeting.

"By our calculations, using the formula we just described to you, this is what we have determined that you are entitled to," Hadley Bates said calmly in his monotone.

When Will opened the envelope and looked at the check, he thought at first this was some kind of sick joke. But then, after reminding himself that Bates was incapable of humor, he decided that this was for real.

The check was for $9,756.22. Will had expected at least twenty times that as his portion upon the partition of his partnership share. But Hadley had talked the other partners into debiting Will for all of his uncollected billings. Even further, Bates and the partners were charging Will for office expenses the firm had paid to him over several years without protest but which now, in retrospect, they were vaguely claiming to have been "exorbitant, unreasonable, or otherwise unjustified."

They tried to calm Will's angry response by telling him that they would pay him a portion of his client receivables as they collected them in the future, but only after, of course, the firm had deducted a "fair" sum for their costs of recovery.

But Will was not sure whether it was the paltry check that offended him the most, or whether it was the envelope that contained it. In the upper-left-hand corner of the envelope was the new name of the firm. It read, "Bates, Burke & Meadows." Hadley had not wasted any time. He had already taken his deceased father's name off the letterhead, and now he had removed Will Chambers' name and put his own name first.

When Will rose from the table at the end of the meeting, the other partners extended their hands and tried, a little awkwardly, to wish him well. But Will Chambers did not shake their hands. He just looked at them, and then looked at Hadley Bates, who was still sitting, his head cocked just slightly to the side, smiling a razor-thin smile.

"Is there anything further, Will?" Hadley asked.

"Yes there is," Will said through clenched teeth. "May I express my fond hope, Hadley, that you die—after a prolonged and painful illness—and then rot in hell."

Going eighty miles an hour on the interstate about thirty minutes out of Richmond, Will started feeling some regret about his comment to Hadley Bates. He felt certain that his rage had not come from hate, or any emotion even similar to that. Instead, it had exploded out of the depths of some other very dark and very lonely place. And now he was feeling as if that abyss—whatever its origin, and whatever it was—was beginning to swallow him up whole.

Prior to his meeting with the firm Will had made some financial calculations, and the results had been dismal. His investments and retirement account were substantially less than he had recalled. When Audra and he were together they had poured huge amounts of money into restoring Generals' Hill. It was going to be their dream house. But now, the remodeling was still unfinished, and it had tapped much of Will's financial reserves.

Further, during his separation from Audra, Will had let the premiums on their life insurance slide. When she died there was no insurance on her life. He had always tried to push that thought out of his mind. The guilt over her death was so enormous that he had tried to just dismiss the whole insurance issue.

As his financial worries swirled around his head Will kept thinking back to his meeting with Angus MacCameron. It had been three days since their first conference, and his only potential client had not been in touch with him about whether he could pay Will's fees.

Will had quoted him a substantial figure that he would need as his retainer fee. Estimating the huge numbers of hours the case would take, and taking into consideration the extra gymnastics that J-Fox Sherman would put him through, Will had thought the figure was reasonable. But MacCameron had looked at him with a troubled expression and simply told him that such a figure would tap out the remaining budget for the magazine for the year.

MacCameron had also made it clear in their meeting, after Fiona had stepped outside, that he would not permit his daughter to contribute a single penny to his legal defense.

Through his experience with the ACLU and the Law Project for the South, Will knew the realities and opportunities of public fund-raising. But when he asked whether there might be other religious groups—those that shared his beliefs—that would contribute toward his defense, MacCameron just shook his head and laughed.

As Will spotted the exit sign for Monroeville he was beginning to think that the case had left his office for good. He tried to reassure himself that this would have been a crazy case, a strange client, and Sherman, of course, a vicious legal opponent. He had every reason to be happy that the case had not worked out.

But Will's mind also kept drifting to Fiona. After the meeting Will had gotten on the Internet and done some research on her. Last year she had won a recording industry award called the "Dove Award." She had cut several successful albums, all of them in the gospel, contemporary Christian music vein. She was thirty-five years old, single, and had never been married. This was intriguing to Will. Here was this beautiful woman, talented and charming. Why wouldn't she be married? He speculated that perhaps her music career had preoccupied her. Or maybe there was a secret she was keeping, some great hurt that kept romantic relationships off-limits for her. Yet somehow, none of that seemed to fit.

Will had to remind himself that he had only met her once, and then only very briefly. He really knew almost nothing about her. *You can know someone for years,* he thought, *and really not know them at all.* Why should he think he knew anything about Fiona based only on a short meeting in a law office and a quick Web-site search on his computer?

Besides, why was he still thinking about Fiona at all? She could not be further from his world—and he from hers. By all appearances she was one of these "I'm in love with Jesus" types. *Perhaps there was an explanation there,* Will thought. Maybe she was the Protestant equivalent of a nun. As Will saw it, perhaps her heart was already pledged to the cold, airy regions of spiritual fulfillment, where romance, love, and earthly intimacy would have no place.

In fact, the more he thought about it, the only thing that he and Fiona had in common was her father's lawsuit. Now it looked as if Will was not going to represent MacCameron in the case.

As Will pulled his car up in front of his office he felt angry at himself. His life seemed to be quickly unraveling. It was ridiculous for him to burn so much energy thinking about a woman that he would never see again, and who lived in such a different world.

Will turned off the ignition but didn't get out of the car. As he sat there he felt the flood tide of betrayal wash over him. Betrayal, certainly, but of who? Audra? After two years of grief he was still not ready to let go. Yet he wasn't sure what he was really trying to hang onto. It wasn't her memory that he was clinging to anymore, not exactly. One of the infuriating things was the fact that with every passing day it was becoming more difficult for him to recall the details of her pretty face, and her expressive, welcoming smile. So he would keep glancing at pictures of her to try to sweep away the cobwebs and dust and breathe life into his indistinct recollections of her—memories that were becoming like the vanished lines of some poem about love by a forgotten author, something that you had read once in school but could no longer remember.

The memories were blurred and faded. Now, only the pain and the absence remained. Somehow those things had survived intact, and were clear and distinct. "Just remember," he would tell himself. "Try to remember her."

As he sat in his parked car he fiercely told himself to get a grip. He had to try to rescue himself. Not just economically, but professionally. And emotionally. He really had to change the direction of his life. Will felt as if he had to climb out of a hearse that had been carrying him away—driving him silently out of the light and toward the great gaping and shadowy nothingness, to a place where there are no memories, no laughter, no embracing, no connection.

Will was not sure how long he had been sitting just staring ahead. He slowly got out of his car and went up to his office.

When he walked in, Betty was on the telephone. She motioned to the top of her desk. There were two envelopes, a small white one and a large brown one. The white envelope was thin, and the brown one was stuffed to bursting.

Will took them both into his office. He opened the white one first, wondering momentarily whether it was Betty's resignation. He had no reason to think she would quit so quickly. Yet he also knew that she had stayed on with a lot of reservations.

But he was surprised when he sliced the envelope open and a check fell out. The check was drawn on the checking account of *Digging for Truth* magazine and was signed by Angus MacCameron. It was made out for the sum that Will had demanded as his retainer fee.

In the big brown envelope Will found a collection of materials that MacCameron had sent for his review.

Betty poked her head in.

"Did you see what your client dropped off?"

Will nodded.

"Tomorrow's payday."

"Thanks, Betty. I won't forget." Then Will added, "By the way, you and I need to talk about a raise sometime."

Betty's eyes brightened. "Do you want to talk now? I've got some time."

"How about in a couple of weeks?"

"How about in two weeks—by my next paycheck?"

Will nodded in agreement. But Betty could see that she had lost him to the case. He was half-turned, already looking through MacCameron's papers.

As he reviewed the materials he saw that his client had rubber-banded them into three groups.

The first group was a stack of magazines—issues from a publication called the *Journal of the Center for Biblical Archaeo-Anthropology*. Albert Reichstad was the editor-in-chief of the journal and had authored a number of the cover articles. There were half-a-dozen other scholars, each with PhDs, who had written the other pieces. Several of the lead articles written by Reichstad dealt with what he referred to as the "7QA papyrus fragment." This apparently was the ancient fragment containing writing purportedly about the burial of Jesus, the document that lay at the core of Reichstad's lawsuit against Angus MacCameron.

Then there was a pile of articles from other recent archaeology journals and scholarly magazines. As Will glanced at their titles it became clear that these were articles by other experts, who were critical of the manner in which Reichstad and his team had been handling the 7QA fragment discovery. These critics felt that Reichstad and his small band of associates had been too secretive. In fact, the Reichstad group had refused to release any copies or photographs of the fragment to other scholars, and had declined to permit other experts to examine it firsthand.

Yet Will was disappointed to see that the only criticisms in these articles were of the *secretive nature of Reichstad's methodology*. The articles critical of Reichstad were also careful to recognize his impeccable credentials. Furthermore, these critics appeared to admit that, based on all of the evidence thus far, Reichstad's findings, which interpreted the fragment as first-century Jerusalem in origin and as a contemporaneous description of the burial of Jesus of Nazareth, were *probably accurate*.

What these other scholars wanted, they argued, was simply the chance to verify and corroborate Reichstad's findings for themselves. This was essential, they pointed out, due to the electrifying and catastrophic implications that this small fragment of ancient paper would hold for the entire Christian world.

There were seven archaeologists who had authored articles critical of the secretive nature of Reichstad's work. Will wrote down all of their names and the identity of their academic institutions on his legal pad. He thought these critics might be a good starting point in locating expert witnesses who would testify in favor of MacCameron and against Reichstad.

The third and last bundle of papers was a mix of newspaper articles and Internet research. It also included a narrative report from the East Coast Investigative Services, which was the official name of Tiny Heftland's private detective business. Will guessed that this bundle was all from Tiny's investigation.

One newspaper article described the groundbreaking for a fifteen-million-dollar building in Maryland to house Reichstad's Center for Biblical Archaeo-Anthropology. Another article from the business section, six months later, showed the completed building for the Center.

The Internet research contained a listing of several small scientific conferences that had been hosted by Reichstad's research center. The names of Reichstad's six full-time scholars and researchers were listed in the various programs and their names were circled. There were also snapshots of each of the scientists, along with one of Dr. Reichstad, and pictures of the license plates of their cars, and printouts of their driver's license information from the Department of Motor Vehicles.

What Will found most intriguing of all was Tiny's narrative report. The first few pages recounted his surveillance of Dr. Reichstad and each of his six experts.

There was a record of Reichstad's comings and goings during a one-week period of time, including a description of his rambling two-hundred-acre Maryland horse farm and mansion.

A surveillance summary about his associates was also included. Each of them had expensive dwellings, several with exclusive brownstones in Old Town Alexandria, Virginia, and some on the other side of the Potomac in the high-rent district. A few of them had yachts that they sailed on the weekends in Chesapeake Bay. All of them had very nice vacation homes, and they drove new cars—BMWs, Mercedes-Benzes, Lincoln Navigators, and Ferraris. All of their children attended expensive private schools.

There was also a curriculum vitae and professional backgrounder for each of the six scientists. They all had teaching experience at Ivy League colleges. Collectively, before being employed as researchers at the Center, they had done substantial work on-site in Israel—on the Dead Sea scrolls, and in important archaeological digs at Megiddo, Jericho, Capernaum, and Beersheba—and at Petra in Jordan, and in Egypt, Iraq, and Iran as well.

Tiny's report ended with some notes about the Center itself. There was no public record of its having filed as a charitable foundation, as most scientific centers do, or as a nonprofit scientific enterprise. It was Tiny's conclusion that this was a private, for-profit research facility.

Will placed the papers in a large expandable folder and stared at his yellow pad for a few minutes. Then he began to make a few notes.

First he wrote down,

"Nonprofit foundation vs. for-profit private research center."

Then after a few seconds Will jotted down,

"Question—why didn't they incorporate the research center as a non-profit, tax-exempt foundation?"

Lastly he listed some further thoughts:

"Answers—reasons for the research center not to go non-profit, tax-exempt:

> 1) No requirement of public listing (i.e., salaries—expenses—donors—sources of income);
>
> 2) Must not need tax-deductible contributions (how is that possible? huge private funding?)
>
> 3) Are they hiding something?"

After a few more moments of reflection Will took his pen and underlined point number three several times.

Then he grabbed the telephone and called Tiny. He caught Heftland on his cell phone.

"Hey hey, my man, how are you doing?" Tiny bellowed.

"Listen," Will said, "I've got a proposition for you."

"I'm all ears."

"You know the money you owe me?"

"Oh yeah—and listen, Will, I haven't forgotten. I'm working on a real big stakeout right now—important surveillance—I'll be sending you some dough right away."

Just then the Burger Hut order box next to Tiny's car squawked out, "Would you like to try our special new Double-Delight Cheeseburger Combo for only $3.99?"

"I guess you're not kidding," Will noted. "That would be a big *stakeout*—spelled S-T-E-A-K-O-U-T—right?"

"Hey, no kidding. I really am on a job. I'm just stopping here for some drive-through cuisine," Tiny shot back, and then he leaned over to the box and shouted out, "Give me the special, and make it a diet Coke with that. And use the low-cal dressing on the burger, will you?"

"Look Tiny, here's my proposal. I'm offering you a chance to work off the money you owe me."

"Doing what?"

"Do you remember that libel and defamation lawsuit you sent over to me?"

"You mean that nutty Scotsman with the magazine?"

"Well, yeah, that would be the case."

"Did he come across with some money?"

"Yes. He retained me," Will replied.

"Wow. I'll be. Yeah, he paid my bill, so I figured he might be a decent client. But you never know about a guy like that."

"I read your report. Nice work."

Tiny was all smiles as he pulled up to the window at the Burger Hut. "Thanks. I really don't know what he was after. He was a little vague. He just wanted me to dig up whatever I could on this scientist, whatever his name was..."

"Reichstad."

"Yeah. Reichstad. And the rest of his scientists. The Frankenstein doctors over there at that research center."

"What makes you say that?" Will asked.

"Remember the original Frankenstein movie? You know, with Boris Karloff. The scientist, this high-society English dude, starts out being straight as an arrow—not Karloff, because he was the monster—but that other guy, English actor, refined type. But he gets sucked into the chance to become the master over life and death—and creating life out of the corpses of dead people, and so he starts going a little wacky..."

"I know the movie, Tiny," Will broke in. "What's your point?"

"Well, it's just this. Remember in the movies, whenever your local law-enforcement gentry show up at the Frankenstein castle asking questions—and the Herr Doktor, the mad scientist who figured he was still smart enough to con the local yokels, would show them around, as if to say, 'See—there is nothing strange going on here...' but you, the audience, you knew that he wasn't showing them everything. And he would always be in a real hurry to shuffle them out of there so he could get back to his ghoulish deeds in the basement."

"So?"

"Well, as part of my investigation I went over to that research center of Reichstad's. I posed as an amateur archaeology buff, a tourist, and asked if they gave guided tours."

"And?"

"The receptionist was real cold to me. Real ice-maiden. She said at first that they don't *ever* give tours. But then she gets up from her desk and asks if I would like to see some things. I said, sure. So she walks me around to a couple of the awards and pictures on the walls of the little lobby there, and tells me a few things about them, and thanks me for my interest in the Center, and then asks me to leave."

"Well?"

"It was the Frankenstein thing all over again. Why give me a pretend tour of the lobby? This gal was pretty nervous. She was acting like she didn't want to admit that they wouldn't give me a tour of that place. She couldn't wait to shuffle me out of there fast enough. So that just got me to thinking—what kind of stuff are they doing in the basement of the castle, you know? Are they covering something up? Just food for thought, I guess."

"Interesting," Will commented. "So, will you work off the money you owe me by working on this *Reichstad vs. MacCameron* case?"

"Sure, why not? But you got to cover my out-of-pocket expenses. I'll keep track of my time, at my standard rates. I'll send you a monthly statement. When do you want me to start?"

Will ended the call by telling Tiny he would give him a call in a few days.

After hanging up with his private investigator, Will dictated a Notice of Retainer that would alert the court and opposing counsel that he would be representing MacCameron. He would fax it, and then overnight the hard copy, that afternoon. He looked at his watch and figured he had enough time to start roughing out a formal Answer to the lawsuit Complaint, and then it would be time to go catch some dinner.

Then the lawyer took his pen and added another note to his yellow pad. It simply said:

"Frankenstein?"

13

THE RED ROOSTER TAVERN WAS QUICKLY filling up. There was a bizarre excitement in the air. Pitchers of beer were already circulating. There were the usual after-work frequenters—mostly office staff, some younger professional types, secretaries, teachers, and salesmen. But tonight the crowd was bigger and louder than usual. Friendly arguments and lively speculations were already breaking out—the kind you would normally see only before the start of an important ball game.

But tonight there was no ball game scheduled—or at least no game that this crowd had come to see. The overhead television sets were normally set to the sports channels. Tonight they were all tuned in to the World Cable Network.

On the television screen there were some newsmen talking, and the word "live" appeared in the corner of the screen.

Four blocks away from the Red Rooster, Will Chambers looked out his window and noticed the sun going down. He set the MacCameron file aside, along with the Bible that he had in front of him and decided to stroll down to the Red Rooster for a meal.

It was still warm outside, early evening, as Will left the building. He walked down the cobblestone sidewalks that had grown uneven with age, and along the narrow, tree-lined streets. He kept thinking back to something he had been reading back at the office.

He had read the article that MacCameron had written in *Digging for Truth* magazine as a rebuttal to Reichstad's claims about the 7QA fragment. MacCameron's article kept referring to passages in the New Testament. So Will had sent Betty scurrying down to the bookstore to get a Bible.

When Betty returned she knocked on the door of his office. He called her in, and she handed him the plastic bag from the bookstore without saying a word. But she gave Will a quizzical look, like she had wanted to make a sarcastic remark but had then thought better of it.

The MacCameron article made a reference to the Gospel of John, chapter eleven, so Will fumbled unsuccessfully through the Bible to look it up. He finally checked the table of contents and located it.

It was the story of Jesus going to the funeral of a guy named Lazarus, who had already been dead and buried for several days. Jesus told the people to remove the stone. They were all concerned because the body was already beginning to rot and stink. But they removed the stone, and then Lazarus walked out of the tomb, with his grave wrappings still wound around his entire body.

Lazarus, so dead that his corpse had already begun to decay, had been brought back to life in front of a number of witnesses.

Will read about the conversation Jesus had had, just before the "resur rection" of Lazarus, with one of the sisters of the dead man.

In verse twenty-five Will read this:

> Jesus said to her, "I am the resurrection and the life; he who believes in Me will live even if he dies, and everyone who lives and believes in Me will never die. Do you believe this?"

When Will read this, it was as if he had been hit full in the face, like a swimmer in the ocean slammed by a huge unexpected wave.

For just an instant, Will felt as if that question—"do you believe this?"—had been directed to him. As if there were someone in the room—sitting across from him—who had just asked him, "Will Chambers, do you believe what you are reading?" For some reason that question, in the silence of his office, had taken on the roaring power of a tidal wave.

Will rarely trusted his emotions. So he had chalked up his strange reaction to either stress or fatigue or both. As he neared the Red Rooster, Will realized he hadn't had a drink for a while. Maybe it was time to start catching up.

When Will walked in he couldn't see a spare table available, so he grabbed the last open stool at the bar.

"It's crowded," Will noted to the bartender. And then he ordered his usual—a steak sandwich and onion rings.

"What're you drinking tonight?"

For a split second Will struggled with his decision on how he was going to respond. So he ignored the bartender and glanced over at the television set. On the screen two news anchors were talking at a desk. Behind them there was a country outlined on a map, with the words "Saudi Arabia" in large letters.

"What'll you have, Will?" the bartender asked again.

Just then a foreign reporter came on the screen. The crowd in the Red Rooster suddenly quieted down.

"Hey, what's the deal here?" Will asked.

The bartender looked at him a little incredulously.

"Are you kidding? Where you been lately, on the space shuttle?"

"No, seriously. What is this?" Will questioned, nodding his head toward the television.

"The Wall Street bombers—or at least some of the guys who planned it—they are going to be executed today. It's been all over the news the last twenty-four hours."

"They finally caught them? Was there a trial I missed?"

The bartender laughed. "This is Saudi Arabia, Will. I don't think it works the same over there. They probably beat a confession out of these guys. Hey, who cares. The point is they're getting what they deserve. The death penalty. No appeals. No drawn-out legal case. Just quick justice. That's fine by me."

Somebody yelled out to turn up the television. The bartender bent over to a knob and turned the volume up.

The reporter was warning the audience that what they were about to see would be both shocking and graphic. He calmly explained how, after the New York truck incident, the U.S. State Department had put additional pressure on the Saudis for cooperation. As a result, new information had come to light about last year's Wall Street bombing, and the Saudis, based on that information, had immediately arrested two suspected terrorists. They obtained quick confessions, conducted a cursory magistrate inquiry, and imposed a sentence of death on both of them.

The method of execution would be by public beheading.

Then two men with black hoods over their heads were led by armed guards onto a platform. Their arms were tied behind them. Their legs were shackled, so they had to make little shuffling steps forward until they were in front of two large wooden blocks that came up to their waists. They were pushed down to a kneeling position.

Each guard held a long pole with a wire neck loop at the end. With the poles, the heads of the two men were forced and held facedown onto the wooden blocks from behind.

Two executioners in long robes and with huge silver-bladed axes appeared beside the prisoners.

Before Will could process what he was seeing, the two executioners swung their axes over their heads with blinding speed and brought them down onto the necks of the criminals. Two kneeling bodies fell over to the side, blood flowing from the headless necks.

The crowd in the Red Rooster jumped to their feet, cheering and yelling.

The noise continued as people raised their fists and continued to cheer at the television sets, giving each other high-fives.

One couple left immediately, the woman shaking her head. The man with her was grimacing slightly.

Will stared at the television set but did not speak. After a while the bartender came back and asked him again what he was going to drink.

"You know, I just remembered that I've got to be somewhere," Will said, and threw some money on the bar.

"Aren't you going to stick around for your steak?"

"Lost my appetite," Will replied.

"Oh, I forgot, Will, you're one of those bleeding-heart liberals," the bartender shot back with a little laugh.

"Exactly when did the world start getting so strange?" Will asked, but directed his question to no one in particular and did not wait for an answer. He was quickly out on the street, walking back toward his office.

Now all he wanted to do was get to his car and go home. Suddenly, the company of his loyal golden retriever seemed preferable to that of the human race.

14

IN WASHINGTON THE NEXT DAY, NEWS REPORTERS were crowding into the room at the Press Club. In the front of the room, the moderator of the press conference glanced at his watch, and then looked out over the room filled with television cameras and reporters.

Behind the moderator there was a row of six men and three women, standing and smiling stiffly. One of the women had a clerical collar, as did three of the men. Another was arrayed in bishop's robes. Then the moderator stepped up to the tangle of microphones at the podium. He smiled and thanked everyone for coming.

"Let me say first," the moderator explained, "that we are *not* going to be commenting today about the fact that two men were executed on live international television last night."

There were a few snickers from the reporters.

"That is the subject for another press conference, perhaps, at another time. We are here today to comment on the 7QA fragment and its implications for twenty-first century Christianity."

Then the moderator looked down at his prepared notes and began.

"This coalition represents a broad cross-section of the Christian denominations in America. As such, we have representatives from the National Council of Churches, from the American Conference of Bishops, and from most major segments of the mainline Christian community.

"Each of our representatives will be giving a short statement. But by way of introduction, I want you to know that a Joint Statement has been prepared by our coalition. And there should be enough copies of the Statement for all of you on the table in the back of the room, so you can pick one up as you leave."

The moderator introduced the representatives, who each, in turn, made three-minute statements.

Then the floor was opened for questions. The first question came from a newswoman in the front.

"Doesn't this 7QA fragment mean that Christians everywhere will have to start questioning everything they used to believe in the Gospel stories—questioning who Jesus really was?"

In response, several speakers from the panel emphasized that faith and science were partners in truth, not combatants. Yes, there would perhaps be a new understanding of Jesus, but that is the essence of faith—that it is a living and evolving concept, not a static, rigid, absolutist experience.

What if this archaeological discovery disproves the resurrection? one reporter asked. Wouldn't that be the end of Christianity?

Not at all, the panelists replied. One speaker emphasized that "the jury was still out" on 7QA, while on the other hand, the verdict on the traditional idea of Christ had been settled for two thousand years. Another panelist pointed out that the resurrection was a spiritual idea, with spiritual aspects to it. If Jesus was not physically resurrected, that did not mean that there was not, in some sense, a *spiritual* resurrection. In order to successfully survive in the twenty-first century, the panelist pointed out, Christianity needed to, in effect, reinvent itself. That included being willing to rediscover who Jesus really was.

Then a question came from a reporter in the back of the room. Jack Hornby, a veteran from the *Washington Herald* stood up and said he was addressing his question to anyone on the panel who would like to respond.

"This 'spiritual resurrection' that you are talking about sounds pretty safe—pretty bland. And if you will pardon my observation, pretty meaningless. In light of this 7QA fragment discovery, why not fight for the idea that either Jesus really walked out of the grave, or else he didn't? If he didn't, then maybe it's time for Christianity to take him down from the throne, in a manner of speaking."

After a few of the panelists tried, somewhat unsuccessfully, to respond, the moderator stepped up to the microphone. This was a difficult and complicated issue, and couldn't be answered, he said, in a simple way. Indeed, the moderator pointed out, it could not be answered in the kind of abbreviated and simplified format that many reporters would prefer.

"Then why did you bother to call a press conference and invite the press?" Hornby shot back. But before the irritated moderator could close, Hornby launched a final question:

"I would be interested in your reaction to the lawsuit that was recently filed by Dr. Reichstad, the scientist who discovered this fragment. He has sued a Reverend Angus MacCameron, who criticized his interpretations of the fragment. Are you aware of that lawsuit, and if so, what is your response?"

The moderator responded firmly. "We are aware of that lawsuit. As we understand it, this lawsuit is some kind of blood feud, if I can call it that, between Dr. Reichstad and this fundamentalist preacher MacCameron. Further, we do not believe that a right-wing religious extremist like MacCameron has anything intelligent to add to the debate over the 7QA Jesus fragment."

As the reporters quickly pushed their way out of the room, one of them came over to Hornby.

"Did you make it over to the press conference of the Union of Conservative Baptists and the American Evangelical Alliance this morning?"

"Yeah," Hornby said, "I caught most of it."

"I missed it," the other reporter noted. "I didn't think I could make that one and still get here for this one and then make my deadline by noon. So, anything interesting?"

Hornby smiled. He knew he was being pumped for news by a competitor. Some reporters really took a hard line on that sort of thing, and many of them would ignore that kind of ploy and walk away; others, even more direct, would tell another reporter to "buzz off."

But Jack Hornby had worked out his own approach over the years. Being a veteran reporter and having won a Pulitzer Prize had given him a certain leeway that others didn't have. He didn't mind tossing a few bones to the competition. He believed in freedom of the press—and maybe that meant letting the other guys know what was going on. In the end, though, Hornby had his own line in the sand, where his cooperation with other reporters ended and his own personal drive for the story took over.

"Those guys are the right-wing conservatives," Hornby explained. "These guys at the Press Club, on the other hand, are the moderate-to-liberal mainliners," Hornby noted. "Same lineup as usual this morning. The conservatives were suggesting a couple of possible explanations for the 7QA fragment. How it really doesn't conflict with a bodily resurrection of Christ. Some of them still had doubts about its validity. I also heard that a couple of TV preachers are planning a big rally down in Atlanta over this."

Then the other reporter opened the door for Hornby, and as they stepped out onto the sidewalk, he followed up this thought, squinting a little in the noonday sun.

"Jack, I think a lot more people are going to end up trusting this 7QA thing than the Bible. I think as time goes on, even a lot of churchgoing people are going to start thinking that, hey, you don't bow down and worship Jesus if you know that he's really still dead and his body is out there in a grave somewhere. The more I'm thinking about this, the more I believe we may have a real religious revolution in the making."

Hornby was silent, but he was eyeing the other reporter intently.

"Right?" the reporter asked.

But Hornby just kept looking at him, tight-lipped. The other reporter smiled. He knew he was getting close to Hornby's line in the sand.

"Maybe," Hornby finally replied. "Maybe not. One thing I've learned in this business—things are not always as they seem."

"So what's your take on this lawsuit by Reichstad?" the reporter asked as he flagged down a cab.

"You take this cab, I'll catch the next one," Hornby shouted out as he walked in the opposite direction. The other reporter had just crossed the line.

As Hornby walked away he paged through his small notebook, looking for the telephone number of attorney Will Chambers. Earlier that day he had checked the court file in *Reichstad vs. MacCameron and* Digging for Truth *Magazine*. Chamber's Notice of Retainer had just been filed.

The reporter hadn't talked to Will Chambers for a couple of years. The last contact was over a story that Hornby had written about one of Will's cases. Will had sued a federal agency for retaliating against his client, a low-level federal employee who had become a whistleblower over some illegal practices in the agency. Since that story had broken, the attorney had fallen off the reporter's radar screen.

Hornby pulled his cell phone out of his pocket and started dialing Will's office. He was getting close to his deadline for getting the Reichstad lawsuit story in the next morning's paper, but so far he had been running into a brick wall. J-Fox Sherman, who was usually more than happy to talk to the press, had not returned any of his phone calls.

The veteran reporter figured he could coax some lively quotes out of Will. With that, and with his background investigation on the lawsuit, his editor would certainly run the story. It had all of the elements of a great feature: a controversial religious issue, defamation of the professional reputation of a renowned scientist, and an interesting match-up of lawyers.

But earlier, when he had stopped at the U.S. District Courthouse just off Constitution Avenue and reviewed the file in the clerk's office, he had found the defining reason why the lawsuit ought to make great copy. The case had been assigned to be tried before the brilliant and controversial jurist Judge Jeremiah Kaye.

Kaye was the judge who had banned prayer at the meetings of the D.C. school board. Yet he was also the judge who had ruled in favor of the right of a Christian rescue mission to violate zoning laws by running a soup kitchen and "salvation chapel." Unpredictable and always interesting, Judge Kaye never backed down from tough decisions. In one case he had ordered the President of the United States to obey a subpoena from Congress. In his order, Judge Kaye had given the President forty-eight hours to comply, and had indicated that he was prepared to send U.S. Marshals to the White House to enforce the order if necessary.

Hornby walked down the sidewalk with his cell phone to his ear. As he waited for someone to pick up the phone at Chambers' office, he felt certain that this case was as newsworthy as any story he had ever covered.

Betty answered the phone and transferred the call to Will. In his typical blunt style Hornby zeroed in on the issues of the case. He said he wanted to do a feature—possibly the first part of an ongoing series on the lawsuit as it progressed. So, what did Will think of the allegations against Reverend MacCameron?

Will gave him a few well-scripted comments. As Hornby walked past the statue of Blackstone, the famed English jurist, that stood guard over the front of the federal courthouse, he furiously scribbled down Will's comments on his notepad.

"Thanks, Will," Jack said at the end of the conversation. "Look for it in tomorrow's *Herald.*" Then Hornby circled the quote from Will that he planned on using at the conclusion of the piece:

> Our Constitution protects the right of free speech because that is how we can ensure that our nation will remain free. But in this case the stakes are even higher. If my client was correct in what he wrote, and it is our contention that he was—then truth itself is on trial.

Hornby hailed a cab and started back to the paper. He decided to call his editor, and told him that he would be able to put the final touches on this story within the hour.

Hornby kept his word, turning the piece in with five minutes to spare. But by late afternoon the reporter had heard nothing. He sauntered over to the city editor's office. The door was closed, so he grabbed a cup of coffee and waited outside in the hallway. After a few minutes the door swung open.

The managing editor stepped out of the office, giving Hornby a less than polite nod as he walked past him and disappeared up the stairs.

When Hornby walked into the room the city editor did not look surprised.

"Jack, sorry, we've decided not to run your piece," he said matter-of-factly.

"Why?" the reporter asked, bewildered.

"Space. Several late-breaking things came in and bumped your story out."

"Like what? You mean like someone gets bit by the presidential poodle? I noticed that the story about the White House dog is going to be on page one. Is that the kind of really important late-breaking news you're talking about? What's going on here?"

"Settle down, Jack. You always take this stuff so personally. Look, all you've got is a lawsuit—sure, some interesting stuff *may* eventually come out. But lawsuits get filed every day in this city. Let's give it time. See if it grows some legs."

"Lawsuits get filed," Jack bulleted back, "but not like this one. You know that. Come on, tell me what the bottom line is here."

"Bottom line? Here it is," the city editor shot back, "Your story got dumped by the managing editor. Go talk to him."

"I will," Hornby snapped as he strode out of the office. And as he walked away he shouted, "I'll be back."

"I'm always open to a good story," the city editor yelled.

"Sure," Hornby muttered to himself as he charged up the stairs to the managing editor's office, "as long as it's got the President's poodle in it."

The city editor immediately punched the extension number for the managing editor, and in a few seconds was warning him that Jack Hornby was on his way up.

"He's coming to pressure you about that Reichstad libel lawsuit story."

"What did you tell him?" the managing editor asked.

"That we got crunched for space—late-breaking news—he didn't buy it. But then, what else could I tell him?"

"Keep Hornby out of this," the managing editor said. "I'm getting some real clear signals from the publisher himself on this one. This story is considered *not newsworthy*."

"And since when does the publisher tell the journalists what is, or is not, *newsworthy?*" the city editor asked, slightly irritated.

"You sound like a rookie when you talk like that," the managing editor growled. "Get with the program. There will be no story on this lawsuit until

I say so—and only *if* I say so. Meanwhile, if Hornby gives you any more problems, try this—tell him this is a religion story—and we've got religion reporters that will cover the story, if it needs covering. His beat is not religion."

"Sure," the city editor sighed, "I'm sure a Pulitzer-winning reporter like Jack Hornby is going to swallow that."

"Then let me make it crystal-clear," the voice on the other end of the telephone said. "This story on the Reichstad lawsuit is dead. And buried. Now, you just make sure it doesn't miraculously rise up and walk out of the tomb on the third day, all right?" Before the city editor could respond, his superior had hung up on him.

The city editor cleaned up a few things on his desk. As he grabbed his coat to leave early for the day he heard footsteps coming down the hallway. He knew it was Hornby—the footsteps were heavy and they were coming fast.

As he braced for Hornby to blow into his office again, he said to himself out loud, "This is not going to be pretty."

15

IT HAD ONLY BEEN TWO WEEKS since Will had filed his response to the Reichstad lawsuit and served it on the opposing side—the offices of J-Fox Sherman. The case was still in its infancy.

So the item in Will's morning mail took him by surprise. As he sat in the lobby of his office, Will opened up the envelope from Kennelworth, Sherman, Abrams & Cantwell.

In it Will found a Notice of Deposition from Sherman. Will's opponent had announced his intention to take the testimony of his client, Reverend Angus MacCameron, by deposition. It was scheduled to take place at Sherman's offices in D.C. the following week.

It was not the *fact* of a deposition that startled Will. Such procedures were the lifeblood of any lawsuit. Depositions—the giving of pretrial testimony—were usually taken in the offices of one of the attorneys and were more informal than a court proceeding, with only the opposing attorneys, a court reporter, and the witness present. With no presiding judge in attendance, they often created a free-wheeling kind of psychological drama as one attorney questioned, probed, and cajoled the opposing party under oath. At the same time the other attorney would object, obfuscate, distract, and defend, all the while hoping that his client would not make that one thoughtless, careless, case-destroying admission that the court reporter would dutifully transcribe for the court, for the jury later to read.

The thing that intrigued Will Chambers most was the fact that it was coming so *early* in the lawsuit. Conventional litigation wisdom was that you go to written discovery first—questions that would have to be answered under oath, or written demands for the other side to produce notes or documents that might relate to the issues of the case.

After getting the responses to written discovery a lawyer would then have a factual road map and could set up a deposition of the other party in order to gain live testimony on the precise issues—aiming for the center of the target with questions like heat-seeking missiles. The lawyer could hammer at the weak points as well as ask questions designed to fill in the blind spots of the case.

So why, Will asked himself, was Sherman racing to take the testimony of MacCameron so quickly out of the gate? Was it merely bravado from one of Washington's finest trial lawyers? Perhaps, although Sherman was too arrogant to feel he needed to impress anyone else. He was the kind of lawyer that just assumed you were already in awe of him.

Will was mulling over that question when he walked into the coffee room. Betty was pouring herself a cup.

"You know something, Will," she commented, "I've read the *Washington Herald* every day since you had the telephone interview with that reporter. I don't think they ever ran that story."

Will merely grunted in response, discovering a little sourly that Betty had taken the last full cup of coffee, leaving only a sinister black film at the bottom of the pot.

"Betty, how about making some more coffee?"

"How about you and I talking about my raise? Then we can talk about my making some more coffee."

"End of the day, today. We'll talk."

"I'll be there," Betty said, half-smiling and walking back to her desk.

The promise to give Betty a raise had slipped his mind. He had been preoccupied over the last two weeks. He had received inquiries from about a half-dozen prospective clients—however, only two had panned out. This was not good news. He was starting to shift into some heavy-duty anxiety about his professional future.

Will had met with his mortgage lender in an effort to borrow some cash against his house. But he was told, flatly, that he was already mortgaged to the hilt. In fact, the state of the house—with its uncompleted renovation—made it bad collateral for another loan.

Will had also been busy trying to negotiate a higher buy-out figure from his former partners. Despite his confrontational final meeting, he somehow believed that they would cut him some slack. But now that they were no longer returning his calls, Will was feeling desperate.

The only complex litigation he had was the MacCameron lawsuit, and he wondered how long it would be before the money from the fundamentalist preacher's tiny magazine would start drying up.

Will buzzed Betty on the intercom and asked her to get J-Fox Sherman on the line. He knew that he had to buy some extra time before exposing his client to deposition questioning from someone as cunning as Sherman.

Besides, Will was still unsure about the facts of such an unusual, complicated case. He was not expecting a report back from Tiny for at least another two weeks. Will had asked the big private eye to contact each of the archaeological experts who had written articles critical of Reichstad's handling of the 7QA fragment. In Tiny's interviews, hopefully some damaging information about Reichstad or his discovery of the fragment would surface. He was looking for any information they had in their back pockets—the kind of stuff that would be too controversial or scandalous, perhaps, to have made it into their polite scholarly writings.

Betty's voice came over the intercom, telling Will that Sherman's office was on the line.

Will picked up the phone. It was the receptionist from Sherman's law firm. Chambers asked for Sherman, and he was transferred to the receptionist in the litigation department, and after that, to the personal secretary for J-Fox Sherman. Then Will was put on hold for several minutes.

Finally, Will was able to explain to Sherman's secretary that he needed to speak to Sherman personally about a case they had pending together.

In a few minutes Will was transferred again.

Then he heard a man's voice at the other end.

"Mr. Sherman, Will Chambers here. I am calling on the *Reichstad vs. MacCameron* suit."

"I am not Mr. Sherman," the voice at the other end responded. "I am Mr. Sherman's chief law clerk. Mr. Sherman cannot talk to you right now, he is unavailable. Can I help you?"

"I need to talk to Mr. Sherman personally about a deposition he just scheduled on one week's notice, in a new lawsuit that isn't even out of the cradle yet. I would like to get that deposition moved down the track a week or two."

"Oh yes, I'm familiar with that case. You would like to get the deposition adjourned for a few weeks?"

"That's what Mr. Sherman and I need to talk about."

"Just a moment," the law clerk said. And then Will waited on the line for another ten minutes.

When the voice came back on the other end it was the law clerk again.

"I'm sorry, but Mr. Sherman regrets that he will be unable to reschedule the deposition. He looks forward to taking the testimony of your client next week at the exact time and date indicated in our Notice of Deposition."

"Mr. Sherman was capable of speaking to you."

"Why, yes," the clerk replied.

"Then he is fully capable of speaking to me about this."

"No, I'm afraid Mr. Sherman is too busy to talk to you."

"Mr. Sherman's not attempting to intimidate me, is he?" Will bulleted back. "Because if he is, then Mr. Sherman is going to end up taking my self-improvement class—I call it 'phone etiquette for the self-impressed, self-aggrandizing D.C. lawyer who likes to hide behind his support staff so he can try to look lofty and powerful.'"

After a moment of silence, the law clerk said, "I will inform Mr. Sherman of your comments, Mr.…" and then the law clerk stifled a little laugh and said primly, "I am sorry. We've never heard of you before. What is your name again?"

"Let me make it easy for you," Will responded abruptly. "Just remember me as the lawyer who ended up winning this case," and with that, he slammed down the phone.

After spending twenty years in courtrooms around the nation, Will Chambers had learned at least this much: Every lawsuit is like a war. So he had developed the habit of naming his bigger lawsuits after famous military conflicts. Some were like the War of 1812. Others were like the Civil War. Still others he labeled the War of the Roses, or the Hundred Years' War.

After his short conversation with Sherman's office Will was already visualizing the contours of this particular legal battle.

D-Day—Omaha Beach, he thought to himself. The only problem was that, unlike General Eisenhower, he was not commanding a massive invasion force. Yet the analogy still seemed to fit. After all, it seemed certain that there were going to be heavy casualties.

He called for Betty to contact MacCameron and tell him that he had to be in Will's office at one o'clock the next afternoon. Will would finish his initial planning and review in the morning, and then he and MacCameron would immediately start planning for the deposition.

For a fleeting moment, Will's concentration was interrupted with a vision of the casualties of war—of old newsreel footage of soldiers' bodies, floating in the waters off Normandy. Then he realized how absurd that thought had been.

No matter what the casualties of this case might be, Will mused to himself, at least no one would be trying to kill him.

16

WORKING AT HIS DESK AT THE Center for Biblical Archaeo-Anthropology, Dr. Reichstad was told by his secretary that he had a call on line one. Reichstad picked up the telephone.

A digital voice at the other end gave him a number to call.

Reichstad sighed, irritated at receiving a command to make another call when he was busy editing the next issue of his scientific journal. Those calls always came at the wrong time, and he didn't like the feeling of being someone else's caged bird.

He unlocked the bottom drawer of his desk and pulled out the telephone in it. He punched in the numbers on the phone. It was a familiar routine. He was dialing into a telephone number that had been disconnected by the phone company, and which was being electronically pirated by the caller for his temporary use. Thus, if the call was ever traced, it would simply lead to an obsolete number. The caller was keen on high-tech methods to ensure both his secrecy, and his complete control.

A man's voice answered on the other end of the telephone line.

"Are you alone?"

"Why bother asking me that?" Reichstad said, bristling slightly. "You can see for yourself."

He looked up at the corner of the ceiling, where there was a small circular dot, the size of the end of a pen, with a little red light inside, and then said, "How do I look?"

"Smug," the voice at the other end replied, "and smug men make mistakes."

"I'm very busy, what do you want?"

"An update on your lawsuit."

"I have sent you a memo already," Reichstad responded impatiently.

"I wanted to ask you directly," the voice said.

"What is it?"

"Please look up, and speak clearly and distinctly when you answer," the voice commanded.

"Sure," Reichstad said, getting visibly irritated. "I will look right at you, and I'll speak clearly so your voice-stress analyzer and your physio-psychologist who are undoubtedly watching and listening can get a good read on whether I'm lying—okay?"

"Please answer this question: Have you told your attorney, Mr. Sherman, any facts of this case that you should not have told him?"

"I have only told him as much as he needs to know," Reichstad answered.

"Please answer the question. Yes or no. Did you tell him things about the case that you should not have told him? Specifically, details about Azid and Hunter; and exactly how you came into possession of 7QA?" the voice asked.

"No," Reichstad answered.

"I've had some reservations about your lawsuit. Like you, I did see some potential benefits, and I felt that the benefits outweighed the risks. But, if I change my mind, you are going to pull the plug on this case immediately."

"Anything else?" Reichstad asked.

"Yes," the voice said. "MacCameron's lawyer, Will Chambers. We've looked into Mr. Chambers."

"And?" Reichstad questioned.

"I'm not sure yet. Mr. Chambers may be a problem for us."

"How much of a problem?"

"I don't know yet. But we may have to take him out of the equation. I think he fancies himself a kind of champion of lost causes. That's very unfortunate. I'll be in touch." And then Reichstad heard the familiar recorded message that always followed those phone calls: "The number you have dialed is no longer in service. Please check the number, and dial again."

Reichstad hung up the telephone, closed up the drawer, and locked it. After his clandestine telephone contacts it always took him a few minutes to get his mind back on track. He despised these cloak-and-dagger exercises. And he despised interruptions to his work: the work for which he was so brilliantly qualified, and for which he had already become a world-class celebrity.

He pulled himself up to the desk and began sorting through the papers he was editing for the cover story of the journal. Then he found the rough draft of the article he was authoring. It bore the title—"Why the Old Mythic Jesus Must Go: Further Implications of the 7QA Fragment."

17

THE BRIEFING ROOM IN THE SMALL MILITARY INSTALLATION twenty miles outside of New York City was jammed with investigators, law enforcement agents, and government lawyers. The U.S. Army command post had been converted into a makeshift jail in order to house one single prisoner. Gathered there was a larger consortium of federal agencies than had been involved in either the Oklahoma City bombing or the World Trade Center attack. The group had assembled to participate in the interrogation of Rahji Ajadi, the truck driver who had been arrested entering New York City a few weeks before.

An army major general stepped up to the front of the sparsely furnished room, and everyone quieted down.

"Gentlemen and ladies," he began, "I think we are all here, so I will begin.

"We have present with us today representatives from the U.S. Attorney's Office, the Justice Department, the Pentagon, the FBI, the Bureau of Alcohol, Tobacco and Firearms, the National Security Agency, the Central Intelligence Agency, the Defense Department, Immigration and Naturalization, the National Emergency Response Team, the Federal Emergency Management Agency, and the Department of State.

"As you all know," the major general continued, "it took us some time to work out the kinks in the overlapping and sometimes conflicting jurisdiction between the agencies here. And of course you know all about the dogfights going on over who was to head up the national terrorist response team in the event that something like this ever happened. We can thank the media for spreading that all over your morning papers. But let's be clear about one thing. The Pentagon is now running this show. That was the final decision of the White House.

"You will all be given a crack at interviewing Mr. Ajadi. You should have already received the backgrounder on his case. The government lawyers will talk to you tomorrow about some of the specific problems they see in prosecuting Mr. Ajadi under existing federal laws. But let me just summarize them.

"First, there's the fact that a New Jersey state trooper arrested Ajadi just after he had crossed over into the state of New York. At page twenty-three of the backgrounder you'll see where the lawyers explain the problem of 'territorial jurisdiction' for the arrest. Bottom line, a state law enforcement officer from New Jersey can't make an arrest across the state line unless he's in 'hot pursuit.' But the rotten fact is that there was no chase going on here, so the arrest was probably illegal. Therefore, the search of the truck was probably illegal too. That means we've been gut-shot in this case. Guys, this is not rocket science here. Most of you probably learned about how not to make an illegal arrest in the first class at the police academy. Our MPs learn that in their first training session. But that's what happened here, like it or not.

"Second, at pages thirty to forty you have a rundown about the weapon that was found in the back of Mr. Ajadi's rental truck. Again, just to summarize, what we've got here is an American-made W87 MIRV thermonuclear warhead. The identifying serial numbers had been removed—but we know it was one of ours.

"Now here is the real kicker." The major general walked over to a large engineering diagram of a warhead that was on a display stand at the front of the room.

"Now this little puppy is standard nuclear technology." With that he started indicating areas of the diagram with a little laser pointer.

"The trigger mechanism is a chemical explosion that combines beryllium and plutonium-239. That starts the fission explosion. That's boosted by DT gas. Then X-rays compress the second component right here. That, in turn, causes the massive fission/fusion reaction. And when that happens, well, that's when you and everyone else within about two-and-a-half miles of you buys the farm.

"People, the MIRV they found on that truck had no plutonium-239. It had no beryllium. It had no DT gas. Nor did it have uranium-238, or 235, or any lithium deuteride."

Then the major general clicked off his laser pointer and looked over the audience.

"In other words," he said, "the MIRV in that truck was a blank."

He waited a few minutes for the unruly conversation to die down in the room.

"The agenda in your report tells you when each agency is given the chance to interview this guy. Your time allotments are listed. None of you will be allowed to be present during the interviews of the other agencies, primarily because you have different security clearances, as well as for jurisdictional and secrecy reasons that should be pretty clear. Only the lawyers from the Justice Department will be present during all of the interviews, and of course, Mr. Ajadi's lawyer.

"Now because the Department of State has the fewest questions and they need the least amount of time talking to this guy we've put them at the end of the interrogation list. They are batting cleanup."

Someone shot his hand up.

"Are we supposed to assume that this case is being plea-bargained with Ajadi? That seems to be the only logical explanation as to why his lawyer is allowing us to talk to him, rather than having him take the Fifth."

"I'll let the Justice lawyers elaborate on that in tomorrow's session. But the bottom line is this—it's pretty clear we don't have any shot at a nuke-related criminal prosecution against Ajadi. He will enter a plea to a minor immigration violation and will be deported, of course. But hopefully we can all get some useful information and be able to trace this incident back to the source—who put that empty nuke in that truck, and why. And in the process we can improve our national security status. I am sure you are just as disappointed as we are that there will be no major criminal prosecution against Ajadi. Now each of you can stand down until your interview time comes up."

The major general dismissed the assembly. The federal agents began filing out of the room, talking angrily and shaking their heads in disbelief.

Meanwhile, in another part of the building, Rahji Ajadi was sitting in a small room, across a plastic table from the public defender who had been appointed to represent him. Ajadi was outfitted in a prison-issue sweatsuit that was too big for him. He pulled the sleeves up over his elbows as he waited for his lawyer to speak.

"First of all," the lawyer began, "let me start with the good news. It looks like the government is going to charge you only with the immigration offense we talked about. No other criminal charges. That assumes that you will fully cooperate over the next few days with each of these federal agents who will be interviewing you. You will have to be truthful. You can't hold anything back. If they discover you are lying, the deal is off."

"And how soon can I see my family?" Ajadi asked.

"I don't know yet. There will be a court hearing called a 'presentment.' The charges will be filed. We will be pleading 'no contest,' which is the same as guilty—we talked about that at the last meeting. The government is going to be asking the judge to sentence you to the exact time you have spent in jail. And then you will be deported. We have agreed, as you will recall, not to fight the deportation. The government will return you to Jordan."

Ajadi shook his head. "This has been such a nightmare. I am no terrorist. I know that I was wrong in staying here in this country after my visa expired. But I had no idea what was in that truck. They told me not to look, so I didn't."

"Look, Rahji, just answer all of their questions. I will be there with you the whole time. It will be fine. And remember the big question everybody wants to know."

Ajadi nodded his head in affirmation.

"It's the question we've been over and over. Why you?" the lawyer asked. "Why would some complete stranger have started up a conversation with you at a bus station and then end up offering to pay you fifty thousand dollars to drive a truck from Vermont down to New York City, but insist that you do it via a swing through New Jersey? To the feds that doesn't make any sense. They are going to be interrogating you with that question in mind. In the back of their minds they are thinking that you are a terrorist. They think you work for Abdul el Alibahd."

"This is crazy," Ajadi exclaimed, "I have never met that man. I don't even know any person who knows him. He is a terrorist—a murderer. As I am driving the truck, I start thinking about the bombing last year on Wall Street. I tell you for that reason I was very afraid, as an Arab, of driving a truck into New York City. But the idea of getting fifty thousand dollars, it made me blind. I had those gambling debts I had to pay off. I was very frightened. I thought that the men who ran the casino would come and hurt me. And I was concerned that my family would find out and I would shame them. I thought I could just drive the truck and collect the money. I got the twenty thousand in advance to drive the truck, like I was promised, so I thought everything would be so easy."

The lawyer nodded. He had heard all of it before during his earlier sessions with his client. But his eyes narrowed now and he looked at him intensely.

"So the question remains," the lawyer stated. "Why you?"

Ajadi shrugged his shoulders, and then as he pulled his baggy sweatshirt sleeves over his elbows he said, "Maybe because I am an Arab."

The lawyer leaned back in his chair. He had heard that before too. Then the public defender asked the follow-up question that he had asked himself, and his client, several times earlier—the question he'd never received a good answer to.

"And why would someone want to randomly set up an Arab by putting him behind the wheel of a rented truck with an unarmed, nonoperable nuclear weapon in it, and then head him toward the heart of New York City? And then, why would a mysterious dispatch from the New Jersey State Police order a rookie Arab state trooper to illegally stop that truck after it was already across the border into New York?"

Ajadi just stared back at his lawyer blankly. Outside the door they could hear the sounds of the guards approaching, bringing a meal to the prisoner on a cardboard tray.

"I'd really love to get the answer to that," the lawyer said, rising from his chair to stretch as the jailers opened the heavy metal door and entered the room with the food.

18

ANGUS MACCAMERON WALKED INTO WILL'S OFFICE at one o'clock sharp. He was carrying a worn brown-leather Bible under his arm.

Before Will could focus the discussion on the upcoming deposition, MacCameron smiled and raised his index finger dramatically in the air, and with the other hand began fishing in the pocket of his suit coat. After a few seconds he found what he was looking for, broadened his smile, and placed the contents on the table in front of Will.

Will looked down on the conference table and saw two concert stage passes.

"Do you have any plans this weekend, Mr. Chambers?"

There was an awkward silence as Will wondered what his client had up his sleeve.

"Perhaps we can discuss my plans later," Will replied. The lawyer folded back the first sheet of his yellow legal pad to reveal a clean sheet of paper. This was a subtle reminder that he was ready to start to take notes about the case.

"Come now, Mr. Chambers. Surely you can take some time off from your strenuous pursuit of justice to enjoy some spectacular musical entertainment," MacCameron urged.

Chambers tried to resist. But as he looked at his client, who was peering through his thick glasses with that twinkle in his eye, the lawyer found the corners of his mouth slowly breaking into a smile.

MacCameron was pressing in. "You need to get away from the office and have some real fun and fellowship. Now here are two tickets to my daughter Fiona's gospel concert this coming Friday night. One for each of us. It's at the Concert Pavilion in Baltimore, down by the harbor. The concert starts at 8:00 P.M. Just meet me a little ahead of time outside the stage door, and Fiona will greet us backstage."

MacCameron took one of the tickets off the table and put it in his pocket. Then he pushed the remaining one toward Will.

"What do you say?"

"I will try to make it," Will answered with a tinge of hesitation in his voice.

"Truly?"

"Sure. Why not?" Will was secretly intrigued by the idea of watching Fiona perform in concert. He had, he admitted to himself, nursed an interest in the beautiful singer. Yet at the same time, the thought of sitting through a "Jesus" event made him uneasy. As Will reached for a copy of MacCameron's *Digging for Truth* magazine from his file, he figured that he would put the concert on the back burner, and decide later.

Will quickly began to walk his client into the core of the lawsuit's allegations against him.

"I want to focus on the essential facts: In other words, I want to go into the article you wrote, why you wrote it, and what investigation you had undertaken before you wrote what you did about Reichstad's discovery. Then I will go over the deposition itself, what it will be like, what questions will be asked."

Will pointed to a copy of the lawsuit papers on the table in front of MacCameron.

"Now here is Reichstad's lawsuit in a nutshell. He has the burden of proving four things. First, that in your article you communicated '*defamatory*' statements about him. Something is 'defamatory' if it injures someone's reputation, particularly their professional reputation. Frankly, they will be able to nail that one. Implying that Reichstad was connected with the wrongful death of Azid the antiquities dealer and the murder of Dr. Hunter, your archaeologist friend—that is defamatory. And going after Reichstad's lack of professionalism—in fact suggesting scientific incompetence in his interpretation of the 7QA fragment—is also defamatory.

"Second," Will continued, "Reichstad has to show how this article damaged his *reputation*. That means actual damage to his professional reputation among his peers and friends. He is also claiming the right to huge punitive damages against you.

"Third, he has to prove that what you wrote was *false*. And fourth, they have to show that you wrote it in '*actual malice*.' Reichstad has the burden of proving 'malice' because he is a 'public figure'—that means that he is someone who is well-known and has been in the public eye. When it comes to 'public figures', the First Amendment protects what you write about them unless they can show that you did it with 'malice.'"

"By 'malice' do you mean something like hatred or animosity?" MacCameron asked.

"No, not really. What it really means is that you had a reckless disregard for whether what you wrote was true or false. That you exhibited a lack of care for the truth about Reichstad and his discovery, and his possible connection to the deaths of Azid and Hunter."

"So what is our response?" MacCameron asked, thrusting an index finger in Will's direction.

"Our defense is twofold. First of all, we are arguing that you did not act in 'actual malice.' That you did an adequate investigation of the facts before you wrote the article. You weren't reckless about the information you wrote."

"I'm not a reckless man, Mr. Chambers. I am passionate about what I believe, but that doesn't make me reckless."

"That's true. But what is important is what the judge and the jury hear and see in the evidence. They aren't going to care about your good intentions if the evidence shows that you were careless and disregarded the facts."

"And what is the other defense?"

"The truth," Chambers replied. "While they have the burden of proving the falsity of your article, that only requires Reichstad to testify that what you wrote about him was not true. That's it. Then the burden of proof shifts to us. We have to then persuade the jury and the judge that what you said in that article is the truth."

"But it is the truth," MacCameron said with his voice rising. "As I stand here in the sight of God, I tell you that what I wrote is the truth."

Will lifted up the magazine article. "Okay. Then let's get into it. You make two statements that Reichstad and his lawyers say are false and defamatory. Here is the first. This is the one about Reichstad and the two deaths." With that, Will began reading from the article from MacCameron's magazine:

> Remember, my dear reader, that Harim Azid and Dr. Richard Hunter were both in possession of the 7QA fragment before they died. The facts show that Dr. Reichstad, who now possesses the 7QA fragment, must be connected to the suspicious death of Mr. Azid and the tragic murder of Dr. Hunter.

"We will go over that one separately tomorrow," Will explained. "Today I want to focus on the second quote that they are suing you for. In the same article you also write this, which they are claiming is also false:

> Dr. Reichstad has brazenly concluded that the 7QA fragment is written about Jesus of Nazareth, and that it shows us that he was

> buried but did not rise again. By concluding that, Dr. Reichstad is either deliberately lying, or else he has committed scientific malpractice.

"Now," Will said, "what proof do you have that what you wrote there is the truth?"

MacCameron flipped open the pages of his Bible, and a second later he said, "Paul's first epistle to the Corinthians, Mr. Chambers, chapter fifteen, verse fourteen:

> And if Christ has not been raised, then our preaching is vain, your faith also is vain.

"And also in verses seventeen through nineteen, the apostle Paul says this:

> And if Christ has not been raised, your faith is worthless; you are still in your sins. Then those also who have fallen asleep in Christ have perished. If we have hoped in Christ in this life only, we are of all men most to be pitied."

Will Chambers shook his head in bewilderment. What he was looking for was not pious pronouncements from the Bible, but cold, hard, credible, and convincing facts. Will's disappointment was clear in his face.

"Is there something wrong?" MacCameron asked.

"Those are *not facts*."

"But what I just read you is the truth."

"Religious truth. Your own private, subjective, religious viewpoint. That is different than factual truth," Will countered.

"The Bible is God's Word. That makes it true. Therefore the facts in the Bible are true. And therefore what I just read to you is a factually true statement," MacCameron shot back, his voice passionate.

"Look, I don't want a theological argument. And I don't want a debate over semantics. Your deposition is being taken next week by a lawyer who could have taught the Spanish Inquisition some new tricks. He does not want to just question you. He wants to humiliate and destroy you. Do you realize that?" By now Will's voice was just below a shout.

"I know better than even you what is at stake here," MacCameron replied loudly and firmly. "But you have to give me a chance to explain before you jump to conclusions."

Will's face was slightly flushed, and his jaw was clenched. He looked over the table at this strange religious zealot who had pulled him into a libel and defamation case that was beginning to look impossible to win.

"Go ahead," Will responded in an exercise of control. "Try to explain. But do it concisely. And make it clear—and factual."

"What you have to realize is that this case is not just about the law," MacCameron explained. "Or even about the 7QA fragment. This case is about the resurrection of Jesus Christ from a tomb in Jerusalem. What people end up believing about—that historical fact—changes the course of world history. And it changes the eternal future of every human being who confronts that question. That's why I began with the Bible, Mr. Chambers. I gave you the wide-angle lens. Now, I believe that what you want me to do is start with the small picture. The microscopic view. That's fine. So let's start with the 7QA fragment itself.

"Now," MacCameron said with a somber look, "what I am about to tell to you is exactly what the 7QA fragment says."

19

Before Angus MacCameron could begin his detailed explanation about the 7QA fragment, Will wanted to clear something up. It was clear that he would have to get up to speed on the basics of biblical archaeology.

"One question," Will interjected, feeling a bit more at ease now with MacCameron. "Explain the reference to 'Q' and the identifying number and letter."

"Well, the Q stands for the source of the fragment—here, Qumran. It's by the Dead Sea."

"The Dead Sea scrolls?" Will added.

"Yes. I see you have been doing your homework. Qumran was a Jewish religious community in the desert area near the Dead Sea in Israel. Most scholars believe that as of A.D. 68 the community either fled, or was decimated by the advancing Tenth Legion of the Roman army. Now near the Qumran community there was a series of caves in the jagged, arid hills of the desert. In the late 1940s some members of a Bedouin tribe of sheepherders—part of the Taamireh tribe—discovered a collection of ancient scrolls and other writings in those caves. Those are the 'Dead Sea scrolls.' The significance was that they contained the oldest manuscript versions of the Old Testament ever found."

"So, are the Dead Sea scrolls just parts of the Old Testament?"

"That's an interesting question. A few experts believe that some fragments from cave number 7 at Qumran may actually be versions of the New Testament Gospels, but the majority of scholars reject that view," MacCameron explained, his voice beginning to race. "The widely accepted view is that the Dead Sea scrolls only contain Old Testament writings. Versions of the books of Isaiah and so forth."

"So why is Reichstad's fragment called '7QA' if it isn't part of the Old Testament Dead Sea scrolls?" Will asked.

"When archaeologists, and papyrologists, and others refer to a fragment of the Dead Sea scrolls, they start with the number of the cave where the fragment was found. That is followed by the 'Q' reference, and then it is followed by an indexing number that refers to how that particular fragment is indexed and inventoried with all other fragments from that cave. Now Reichstad chooses to call it 7Q because he claims that when he bought it from Azid he was told it was from cave 7 in the Qumran area, and that was according to what some unidentified Bedouin who found the fragment said when Azid purchased it from him originally."

"What do you think?" Will asked.

"From my one conversation with Richard Hunter in that café in Jerusalem, I have no reason to doubt that."

"And what about the 'A' reference in 7QA?"

"Reichstad simply chose that to identify it as the first fragment of its kind from cave 7 that he obtained, and to distinguish it from the other fragments from that cave that were discovered back in the 1940s."

"So," Will probed, "what is there in Reichstad's interpretation of 7QA that supports what you say in that article?"

"Let's start with what we know about 7QA," MacCameron said. "Let's review what Reichstad *claims* that the Greek letters say in that fragment." He opened the magazine to a different page.

AND THE BODY OF JESUS OF NAZARETH WAS LAID IN THE TOMB. THEY DESIRED TO ANOINT IT BUT COULD NOT RETURN TO PREPARE THE BODY. THE BODY REMAINS IN THAT TOMB TO THIS DAY.

"What is the significance of 7QA being written in Greek?" Will questioned.

"That makes it consistent with the rest of the New Testament," MacCameron said matter-of-factly. "The whole New Testament was written in a version of the Greek language called Koine Greek. That was the common, street-language form of Greek. 7QA appears to be Koine Greek. So to that extent it is consistent with the Gospels in the New Testament."

"But isn't that the argument that Reichstad is making? That this 7QA is actually the original and authentic ending to the Gospels?" Will asked. "That later on the Christian church doctored up the ending to say that Jesus actually rose from the grave?"

"Exactly," MacCameron responded.

"But aren't you supporting Reichstad's own argument?"

"Look, Mr. Chambers, there are a lot of things I do not dispute about 7QA. I agree that the papyrus is likely from Jerusalem from the middle of the first century. I agree that it's written in the same New Testament Greek language as the Gospels. And frankly, I don't have too much dispute with how Reichstad and his people have interpreted the Greek text."

"Well, then what is left for us to hang our hat on?" Will asked, his voice tinged with exasperation.

"Three major points." MacCameron replied. "First, there is what you lawyers call the burden of proof. Just a few minutes ago you told me that Reichstad has the opening burden of proof on the four elements of his case."

"Right," Will replied, happy to see that his client had been paying attention.

"But he also has the burden of proof *historically*." MacCameron explained. "There are four Gospels in the New Testament. All were either written by eyewitnesses or based on firsthand information from eyewitnesses. And they all contain resurrection stories. We have manuscript evidence that dates those New Testament writings back to a time period within the generation of the eyewitnesses of the actual events. We have better evidence of the authenticity of the Gospels as accurate historical accounts than we have for any other ancient documents from any other ancient period.

"The apostle Paul wrote his first letter to the Corinthians around A.D. 50, when the witnesses to the life, death, and resurrection of Christ would still have been around. In that letter Paul cites the fact that Jesus Christ appeared in bodily form to more than 500 witnesses after his resurrection. Now for the last two thousand years, not one document claiming to be from an eyewitness source has ever surfaced to contradict any of that evidence. Until now. So 7QA is the first and only attempt to seriously question the resurrection based on claimed eyewitness testimony.

"When I read to you from Paul's letter about the importance of the resurrection, I did so because that single historical fact is the core of what Jesus Christ is about. Jesus predicted that he would be crucified, and would die, and would rise again three days later. The resurrection proves that he was not a liar, but in fact foreknew, and fore-willed, his own miraculous victory over death."

Will was listening intently. For some reason his memory began to conjure up, seemingly out of nowhere, the recollection of a card table down at the ocean cabin of his Uncle "Bull" Chambers. His parents would take him there to visit when he was a boy. The table was on the porch, overlooking the crashing waves off the Cape Hatteras coast. There was always a huge, complicated picture puzzle spread out on that table, in varying degrees of completeness every time he visited.

His Aunt Georgia was crazy about doing picture puzzles. As a young boy, Will would stare at the partially assembled picture and the mess of little oddly shaped pieces spread around it. But before he could understand what it was, he would have to grab the cover of the box and see what the completed picture was supposed to look like.

"Are you following me?" MacCameron asked.

"Sorry. I was just thinking about something," Will responded.

"May I continue?"

"Sure," the lawyer replied.

"Now secondly, Reichstad has refused to produce the actual 7QA fragment for anyone else to actually view firsthand. All we have are the indistinct photos in his magazine. Experts need to examine the *texture* of the fragment. And the *edges*—that is critical. No one can arrive at any conclusions about the edges without either much better photos, or better yet, by examining it."

"How about Reichstad's associates?"

"Do you mean those in-house experts he bankrolls at his supersecret private research facility? Those scientists?"

"They have excellent credentials," Will noted.

"Sure they do. But they are all on a well-padded payroll. You read Mr. Heftland's investigative report."

"Where does Reichstad get his funding?"

"I don't know. The man attracts money like a magnet," MacCameron said, shaking his head. "He is a person of great public-relations talent, most certainly."

"He gets no tax-deductible donations," Will noted, "no major foundation grants. His research center deliberately declines to file as a charitable, tax-exempt organization. That means that they don't have to file any public reports."

"To get back to your point, Mr. Chambers, we really do not know how much access the other experts in his research center have been given to the actual fragment, as opposed to photocopies, or X-ray copies, or scanned telemetries. But even if they did have actual access, the point is that they are not free to contradict their director, Dr. Reichstad. To hold 7QA hostage from the scientific world is an outrage."

"But isn't this déjà vu?" Will asked.

"How so?"

"I've been reading the archaeology journals you sent to me," Will explained. "There was a tremendous hue and cry about the Dead Sea scrolls at one time too. Small groups of scholars were accused of hoarding them and not allowing other scientists to evaluate them. As a result some wild conspiracy stories started circulating. Theories about what the scrolls might contain. But when the scrolls were finally released to other experts, the whole thing appeared to be a tempest in a teapot."

"The difference here is that we have something that is being touted as a contradiction of the whole two thousand years of Christian faith," MacCameron countered. "The world needs a chance to refute Reichstad's claim by hands-on evaluation of that fragment."

Will couldn't disagree with that point. In his litigation experience, forensic testing usually required experts to evaluate the material itself—not just reproductions. "Let's assume that you—or some other expert on your behalf—gets a chance to evaluate 7QA," he suggested to his client. "What would you expect to find?"

"That brings me to point number three. There may be other fragments, or other parts of this fragment."

Will was thunderstruck. This was the first time he had heard MacCameron suggest the possibility that there might be missing parts to 7QA.

"And exactly why do you say that?" Will asked slowly and deliberately.

"Because of the message."

"Message!" Will exclaimed. "What message?"

"Why, the message that Dr. Hunter left me the night before he died. The one he left on my answering machine."

"Where is that answering-machine tape?" Will had bolted up and was leaning over the table toward MacCameron.

"I have it at home."

"Is it safe?"

"Why yes, I am sure it is."

"What does it say?"

"I think you had better hear it for yourself, Mr. Chambers."

Will Chambers looked at his client. The bells from St. Andrew's Church were tolling five o'clock.

"I need to stretch my legs, if I could," MacCameron said pushing himself away from the conference table. "Walk around and get a bite to eat before I head home. Tonight's my night off. I have someone watching my wife—Helen—for me. So I thought that perhaps I could take in a bit of history about your charming little town."

"Sure," Will said. "But why don't you just tell me the gist of what was on that tape-recording first."

"You know, I'd rather not. I really want you to hear it for yourself. That's essential before I tell you what *I* think is on it. Now if you will excuse me," MacCameron said as he rose from his chair a little stiffly, "I will get some fresh air." With that he loosened his necktie slightly. "I understand that St. Andrew's Church across the street has some fascinating history behind it. I may take a gander over there. Is it open to tourists?"

"Almost everything is open season for tourists in this town," Will replied, still trying to figure out why his client had become so evasive about the message that Hunter had left. And then he added, "I'm sure you can look around in the church. The bell in the steeple is the same one they rang to announce George Washington's first great victory during the Revolutionary War."

MacCameron grabbed his Bible, gave a wave, and then was out the door.

After his client had left, Will remembered something MacCameron had just said about his wife, Helen. Will realized that he hadn't asked him much about her. He wondered why he needed to have someone watch her.

It was early evening, and Will knew that Betty had gone for the day. So when he heard a noise in the lobby he poked his head around the corner, expecting to see MacCameron there, perhaps returning for something he had left behind.

Instead, Will saw it was Hattie, the elderly black cleaning lady for the building. Hattie was a tiny woman with glasses and white hair. She walked slightly bent over, and had one leg that looked like it had a hard time catching up to the other. Will usually knew that Hattie was coming because the soft sounds of her humming or singing would waft down the hallway ahead of her. She was dressed in her usual attire: a gray work uniform with the words "Hattie's Clean-Up Company" across the back.

"Evening, Mr. Chambers," she said with her usual glowing smile, tilting her head down so she could peer through the top half of her bifocals.

"Hattie, I thought you were someone else. How are you?"

"As good as good can get, Mr. Chambers. Say, where is that good-looking young woman lawyer that used to work here—Miss Johnson? I haven't seen her around for a while," she asked, picking up the wastepaper baskets.

"She doesn't work here anymore," Will explained, hoping that Hattie would not ask for details, which she usually did in her unabashed style.

"Well, now that's a shame. You lost yourself a good lawyer. I always liked her. Seemed like a real sharp one."

"Yes, she was sharp all right."

"What happened—didn't pay her enough money?" And with that Hattie chuckled and gave a little stomp on the ground.

"No. That wasn't it, Hattie."

"Oh, I know. She must have gotten married to that boyfriend of hers—Howard. That must be it."

Will felt embarrassed that the cleaning lady seemed to have known more about the details of Jacki's life than he had. He couldn't help but think back to his last conversation with Jacki, while she was driving him home in his Corvette the day the law firm had given him the boot.

"Not exactly," Will replied. "Jacki did get engaged to Howard. But the fact is that I am no longer in the same law firm. Jacki stayed with them, and they moved her up to their D.C. office. I'm in this office by myself now."

"Well, you say hey to her for me if you see her, won't you? The Lord bless you now, Mr. Chambers."

Hattie shuffled slowly out of the office. A few seconds later Will could hear her gently humming a hymn, and it was echoing down the stairwell.

Will walked back to his office and looked out the window. He gazed out at the old, cream-colored brick of the church across the street, at its tall, green-tiled spire that rose to the tallest point in Monroeville.

He saw MacCameron down below, opening the front door of the church and stepping in.

As Will glanced over to the church's graveyard and its black wrought-iron fence, his thoughts returned to the lawsuit. He reflected on the wording of the 7QA fragment that seemed to so clearly contradict the resurrection story in the Gospels.

Dead men don't walk out of graves, Will thought to himself.

And then he asked himself the logical and inevitable question: *So how do I prove that once, two thousand years ago, one man did?*

20

AS REPORTER JACK HORNBY SLIPPED INTO THE BACK of the pressroom in the federal building he figured that this was going to be just one more government press conference. He struggled to be optimistic, speculating that it might be mildly interesting because it had to do with oil—and the possibility of oil shortages always made great press. There had been no official statement about oil shortages. But the Department of Energy had released a report that questioned the "availability of oil at the current range of prices at the wellheads" and the "ability of oil production to keep apace with the growing demand." Hornby saw this as bureaucratic mumbo-jumbo for the fact that there might be some real concerns about oil supply/demand ratios.

Hornby knew that oil, like money, was one of the great motivators of human events. It moved nations to war, built empires, and fueled the transportation that reduced the size of the planet down to a cozy global village. But at least at first blush, the veteran reporter could see nothing eventful or even mildly exciting in this particular press conference. Ever since the meltdown he had had with the city editor and then the managing editor over his story on the Reichstad lawsuit, Hornby had been given increasingly insignificant assignments.

He wondered if they would soon have him covering the increase in cab fares, or the traffic problems created by the unpatched potholes in the Washington, D.C., streets.

The Energy Department official at the podium was droning on. He was explaining how the world thus far had burned about 850 billion barrels of oil. Daily consumption of oil was running about 80 million barrels a day.

He went on to describe how the rate of oil use around the world had been increasing by a few percentage points every year. However, oil discovery and production had not kept up with the same rising curve.

Every nation of course maintained oil reserves, he noted. But the oil reserves of almost all of the major oil-consuming nations had been dropping by several percentage points every year. This was also true of the United States. For reasons of oil pricing and availability, America had been dipping into its strategic oil reserves.

All of this would be of little concern, the official pointed out, if the results of oil exploration had reflected the optimistic predictions from the last decades of the twentieth century. Unfortunately, the last major oil field to be discovered—Safaniya in Saudi Arabia—dated all the way back to 1954. There had been great expectations about a deep-water site off the Gulf of Mexico, however that field ended up containing only about one billion barrels—barely enough to supply the needs of America for a mere fifty days.

Hornby was hoping against hope that this fellow at the podium would get to the point.

Meanwhile, the speaker pointed out, OPEC's oil policies and its production reserves were not audited, so the West could only guess about how well OPEC was supplying the oil needs of the rest of the world.

But now, the official was happy to announce, the United States was exploring a new oil initiative with Saudi Arabia.

Because of the recent trend of cultural and international cooperation between the Arab nations—specifically Saudi Arabia—and the United States, talks were underway, he explained, that could be tremendously beneficial to the future industrial needs of our country.

The United States—through the Department of State—and the OPEC nations were now engaged in high-level talks that could open up the OPEC oil monopoly to some Western influence and monitoring.

When the speaker was finished, the hands shot up instantly. The reporters wanted to know the specifics. How would the U.S. benefit? What new arrangement with the OPEC consortium could we expect? What was the motivating factor behind the Arabs' opening up their oil monopoly to the United States?

The official avoided answering any specifics, indicating that he did not have the answers to those questions. Hornby decided not to raise his hand. Instead, he studied the speaker with that combination of intuition and exacting observation that a seasoned reporter develops. Hornby was trying to determine if this fellow, a relatively low-level Energy Department representative, *really* didn't know anything more than he was letting on.

Finally, when the questions slowed down, Hornby raised his hand.

"Yes, one last question," the speaker said, recognizing Hornby in the back of the room.

Hornby's voice boomed through the room.

"I have reason to believe that you may be hiding information from us. The only question is, *why*? Are the American people on the verge of being denied gasoline at the pump for their cars? Are we heading for a catastrophic oil crisis? Is that what's going on here?"

The speaker's eyes widened. A flustered look spread over his face. "I really don't know how to answer such a question. Really—that of course—is an outrageous question. There is nothing being hidden here at all. There is enough oil to go around. I—really don't understand what you're coming from—or I should say, where you are coming from."

Hornby didn't try for a follow-up question. He wheeled around and left the room. The awkward nonanswer he had received from the government official had answered it all. If this man had known anything of substance, his department would have prepared him with several slick avoidance-and-deflection responses. He would have been able to cover the weakest and most vulnerable parts of his position with a fifty-dollar smile and some well-crafted, but empty, hundred-dollar ambiguities.

Instead, this fellow had tripped over himself. No one with real inside information would have reacted with such public-relations clumsiness. Clearly, the Energy Department had chosen as its spokesman someone who *really didn't know anything*.

That told Hornby that the government had dangled a pawn in front of the press on an issue that was apparently very sensitive—so sensitive that they had to build a firewall between it and the poor department underling who had the job of facing the press.

Hornby didn't care whether this story was going to get published or not. He had another reason. He wanted to get to the secrets of this oil story just to prove that it could be done.

21

TWO POLICE CARS WITH LIGHTS FLASHING were parked directly in front of Will's law office building when he arrived at work the next morning. When Will entered the front door he heard the crackling sound of police walkie-talkies reverberating in the halls. Employees from the first-floor accounting and investment firms were mingling and talking with each other. In the background he saw one blue-uniformed officer. Broken glass was scattered over the carpeted floor of the hallway.

Will scurried up the curving stairway to his office. Before he had reached the last step he saw two more patrolmen. They stopped him and asked whether this was his office, pointing to the open door at the end of the hall.

As he responded that yes, this was his law office, Will looked down to the open door and noticed that the frosted glass bearing his name was smashed out of the door frame. Glass shards lay in the hallway.

"What's going on?" Will asked urgently, looking around for signs of Betty.

"Break-in," the older of the two officers replied. "We have secured the crime scene, but because it's a law office and you've got confidential files and things we had to wait for you."

With broken glass crunching under foot Will stepped gingerly into the office with the officers following behind him.

There in the lobby, Betty was surveying the office with bewilderment.

"This is crazy," she blurted out.

"If you could size up the office for us, tell us if you see anything missing, we'll make a note of it," the officer said.

Will and Betty walked around the office. The equipment and computers were intact. The lamps and furnishings all seemed to be there.

That was when he noticed that the storage doors and file cabinets had been pulled open and not closed up. The plastic box for their backup tapes was open. The yellow light on the computer screen was still on, and the computer was humming.

"The computer was on when I got here," Betty noted, "when I walked in the door with the police."

"Check all the backups," Will told Betty as he sat down in front of the computer.

The screen blinked on and he checked the computer directory for the last computer file that had been accessed. It was the file on the *Reichstad vs. MacCameron* lawsuit.

"Computer backups are all still here," Betty replied.

"What was the last file you worked on yesterday?" Will asked.

"That one," she said, pointing to the computer screen. "I was working on the MacCameron case."

"Is it possible that you just forgot to shut off the computer yesterday?"

"Absolutely not," Betty shot back, "that is something I don't do. I don't leave for the day without turning the computer off."

"I don't mean to interrupt this Sherlock Holmes mystery," the older police officer quipped, "but we need to know if anything was stolen."

Will and Betty both shook their heads.

"Appears to be petty vandalism," the officer remarked, closing up his notepad. "It looks like they entered down at the end of the hall on the first floor, smashed some windows in those offices—but they didn't gain access to any of them. They ran up here, smashed the glass in the door of your office, got inside, looked around, and left. Might be kids. Sometimes it's somebody looking for quick cash that might be lying around the office—you know—cash for drugs or whatever."

Will reached over to the side drawer of Betty's desk and pulled it open. There in the top tray was their petty-cash fund, still perfectly intact—two twenty-dollar bills and some singles.

"They must have been in a hurry, or just sloppy," the officer said as he prepared to leave.

"Aren't you going to dust for fingerprints?" Will asked.

"How many people do you think have touched the doorknob to your office in the last two weeks?" the officer asked. "I'm not putting you down, counselor, but the glass in the window of your office puts this at about one hundred bucks worth of property damage. Do you want to know how many minor-crime reports we get in a week?"

The telephone rang, and as Will was nodding to the departing officer, he answered it. It was Tiny Heftland. Tiny was calling from Maryland and wanted to meet Will on Friday night, just outside of Baltimore, to go over the results of his investigation in the MacCameron case.

"Why don't you come down here to my office?" Will suggested. "Or better yet, let's just talk by phone."

"Well, I really think you need to see Reichstad's research center for yourself. Besides, on Friday I'm on my way north to Pennsylvania for a new case I've got. Your office is in the wrong direction, good buddy. I'm going to be tailing the husband of some really rich society lady in Philadelphia. If you get up here by seven, we can spend some time together and then I can head straight up to Philly."

Tiny gave Will directions to a small grocery store a few miles from the research institute. They would meet there on Friday evening.

As Will hung up the phone, he noticed that Angus MacCameron was in the doorway, looking down at Betty as she was kneeling to clean up the broken glass.

"Good heavens, what happened?" MacCameron asked.

"Vandals, I guess," Will responded, motioning MacCameron into the conference room in the back.

"Vandals?"

"That's what the police think."

"Was anything stolen?"

"No."

"Were there signs of a search—of somebody going through your office?"

"Reverend MacCameron, we've got it under control. So let's pick up where we left off on your case."

But MacCameron wouldn't let the matter rest.

"Reichstad and his cronies are ruthless," he declared. "This is exactly the kind of thing we should have expected."

"Are you saying that they are behind this—my office being broken into?"

"I'm saying," MacCameron noted with a slightly raised eyebrow, "that you can expect a leopard to act like a ruthless man-hunter, even if he has changed the spots on his coat."

Once again, Will was enduring another of his client's wandering witticisms that always seemed to be off the mark—and forever irrelevant to the lawsuit. Will shrugged it off and got to the issue that he had been pondering since their last meeting.

"Did you bring the tape?" Will asked.

MacCameron pulled out a small brown-paper bag and emptied it onto the table, revealing a single microcassette and a small handheld tape recorder.

The two looked at the little cassette.

"You have listened to it recently?" Will asked.

MacCameron nodded his head and said, "Now it's your turn." But then he quickly added, "Before you turn it on, tell me—are you coming with me this Friday to Fiona's concert?"

"I'm afraid not," Will responded. "I just found out I have to be somewhere this Friday night."

MacCameron shook his head and gave Will a strange smile.

Will snapped the cassette into the player and turned it on. There was a moment of fuzzy background noise. Then he heard the obnoxious, warbling beep at the end of MacCameron's answering-machine greeting.

"The next voice you hear will be Richard Hunter's," MacCameron said solemnly.

And then they listened, mesmerized, as they heard Richard Hunter leave this message:

> Sorry to change plans on you chap, but strange things...dangerous things...I was followed again from our lunch meeting. I had to take two different cabs. I think I've lost them. Can't meet you as we planned. I'm taking an earlier flight to London, back to the British Museum.

Hunter's voice was hushed and out of breath. He continued:

> I'm sending the fragmentseparately...in case something happens to me...

Will grabbed the tape player and hit the pause button. Then he said, "I need to hear that again."

"Yes!" MacCameron shouted, his arms outstretched. "By God's everlasting grace you caught it. You did hear that, didn't you?"

"I don't know what I heard."

"Yes, you do. You heard it. Tell me, what did you hear?"

Will's finger was on the pause button. He looked the Scot in the eye and said, "I don't know what I heard."

"Well then, play it again by all means. Play it twice. Play it three times," MacCameron said, as he bounced in his chair with glee.

The lawyer rewound the tape and played it again. But this time he moved the little side switch to slow play. This is what he heard, as he listened to Hunter's voice in slow motion, basso profundo:

> I-m...s-e-n-d-i-n-g...t-h-e...f-r-a-g-m-e-n-t-s...s-e-p-a-r-a-t-e-l-y...
> i-n...c-a-s-e...s-o-m-e-t-h-i-n-g...h-a-p-p-e-n-s...t-o...m-e...

"There it is," MacCameron cried out. "Now look at me and tell me, Mr. Chambers, what did you just hear?"

Chambers had a little smile in the corner of his mouth. "What I *heard.* What I *think* I heard was Hunter saying that he would be sending the fragments separately."

"Fragment*s!*" MacCameron exclaimed.

"Yes. *Fragments.* As in *plural.*"

"More than one!" MacCameron cried out.

"Yes. Which is what plural means, I guess," Will noted with a touch of sarcasm.

"More than one fragment. So obviously," MacCameron said, his enthusiasm growing, "7QA is only *one* part of a whole. Thus there are other missing pieces to the puzzle. Which is exactly what I had in mind when I wrote that article in my magazine accusing Reichstad of fraudulent scholarship. He had to have known that 7QA is just one piece, and that there are adjacent pieces to that papyrus writing that could completely change the meaning of 7QA once we see them all put together."

"On the other hand," Will continued, trying to bring his client back to reality, "we don't even know for sure whether Hunter's fragment—whatever it was—was the same fragment as Reichstad's 7QA."

"Here is what we know," MacCameron said, taking a handkerchief out of his pocket to wipe the heavy perspiration from his brow. "We know that Hunter said he got his fragment from Azid. Reichstad claims that he bought 7QA from Azid for fifty thousand dollars. That's point number one. Point number two. Hunter said that his fragment came from cave 7 in the Qumran area. Reichstad has admitted 7QA came from cave 7. Point number three. Hunter said his fragment would erase two thousand years of Christian history. Reichstad's interpretation of 7QA, if it's true, would do exactly that."

With that MacCameron leaned back in his chair, as if he were an English barrister who had just presented a smashing closing argument for the Queen's Bench.

"All of that is circumstantial evidence," Will responded. "It may make your case. It may not. But I don't trust my ears—or yours for that matter. I know a guy who is a freelance voice analyzer. He used to work for the FBI. I want to send this tape over to him to see if he can substantiate what the two of us think we are hearing."

"Be my guest," MacCameron replied.

"This also concerns you, because you are going to be paying for this analysis. And this guy doesn't come cheap."

MacCameron nodded knowingly.

Will continued. "I also plan on making a demand for access to the original 7QA fragment. I am preparing a Demand for Documents right now.

That fragment is on the top of the list of the physical objects Reichstad is going to have to produce to us."

"Did he know he would have to give us access to the original 7QA fragment?"

"I'm sure his lawyer warned him about that."

"Strange," MacCameron commented, shaking his head in disbelief. "He has fought off the rest of the world from getting their hands on that piece of papyrus. And now he is going to hand it over to us."

"Not that strange," Will responded. "They will probably get a protective order from the judge requiring us not to divulge anything, to anyone else in the world, what we learn about that fragment in our evaluation of it."

"Can't we divulge what we learn about 7QA during the trial?" MacCameron asked.

"Yes. Assuming this case goes to trial," Will said. The lawyer gazed off in the distance for a second or two. Then he added, "And when I get access to 7QA I know what I'm going to do."

"You mean, when *we* get access to it," MacCameron clarified.

"Yes. *We* are going to hire a materials engineer to examine the edges of 7QA under a microscope."

"Exactly!" MacCameron shot back. "To see if it has been cut. You know, Azid would do this monkey business with written antiquities. If he thought that an ancient writing was really valuable, he was known to slice it into a few pieces and then sell off the pieces one at a time—just to bump up the price."

"Do you have proof of that?"

"It was common knowledge. So who would you get to do this examination?"

"I've got somebody in mind," Will said. "I used him in another case involving a piece of paper that had been torn out of a calendar. We had to match that piece of paper with the calendar it came from—the calendar belonged to a guy who ran a trucking company we were suing. A guy who had a real problem with Jewish folks."

"You do have a heart for justice, Mr. Chambers," MacCameron said to his lawyer. "I know that. The same God who saved me from my sins blesses those who seek justice for the downtrodden. It's my prayer that you will come to know him—the Lord who is the source of all justice."

MacCameron was smiling at Will as he said that. Will felt a little embarrassed and glanced back at the tape player on the conference room table.

"Is there more on the tape?" Will asked.

"Oh, yes," MacCameron assured him.

Will took the tape off pause and moved the switch to normal speed. Hunter's message finished:

> If they get to me, I just want you to know that I have always felt you were a true friend. Give my love to your dear Helen.

There was a sadness to Hunter's voice. And then he concluded,

> So if you ever have to put the picture together, just remember this the next time you come to the halls of the British Museum. Remember your Bible. That won't be hard for you, old friend. And most important of all, remember the resurrection order.

And then there was the sound of the telephone hanging up.

"What is the 'resurrection order'?" Will quickly asked.

"I'm not sure what he meant. I can only guess that he meant the order that Jesus gave for Lazarus to 'come forth.'"

"Was Hunter giving some kind of clue to you?"

"No doubt it was a clue. But what he meant by it, I simply do not know," MacCameron admitted reluctantly.

Will rubbed his eyes. He felt a migraine starting to squeeze his head in a vise. They had been coming on ever since he had gotten off the booze. Now the MacCameron case was another reason for a headache. He was tired of the mysteries in a case that seemed to lead nowhere. He wanted answers. Time was running out. His client's deposition was just a few days away. Will knew that as they were speaking, J-Fox Sherman and his cadre of lawyers and paralegals up in the sleek glass-and-mahogany world of K Street in Washington were plotting his ultimate legal humiliation. Chambers the trial lawyer felt helpless, like a boxer who was going to enter the ring—but with all the lights out—where he would be punched by an opponent who could see in the dark.

An opponent who would be wearing brass knuckles instead of gloves.

22

INSIDE THE STATELY VILLA THAT WAS TUCKED within the thick woods outside of Vienna, Austria, a messenger was walking quickly through the great hall. His footsteps made echoing click-clack sounds on the marble floor. Two armed guards in flowing robes and turbans followed behind him. The messenger and the guards walked up to Warren Mullburn, who had been sitting impatiently on the velvet couch situated under the mammoth oil portrait of Empress Elizabeth for nearly an hour. Sitting near him were his two interpreters and his three personal bodyguards. Mullburn was dressed in a black suit with a white, tieless, buttoned-up shirt that gave him the look of a modern Islamic cleric.

"The Council of Islam extends its apologies, Mr. Mullburn, for the delay. Please follow me."

Mullburn and his entourage were led down the great hall and through an arched entrance that led into a smaller room with a receptionist in a gray suit and horn-rimmed glasses. She was sitting at an antique desk in the middle of the room. She picked up the phone, whispered something, and hung it up. She nodded to the messenger, who led Warren Mullburn and his group into an inner room while the two armed guards posted themselves on either side of the door.

The adjacent room was a spacious library of dark oak paneling with floor-to-ceiling leatherbound books. In the middle there was a huge, dark walnut table that filled the room. A ring of robed, bearded Muslim leaders were seated around the table. Across the table from Mullburn, one official in a gray-and-white robe and white turban, with a long salt-and-pepper beard, lifted his hand in greeting.

"In the name of Allah, the Merciful, the Compassionate, we greet you, Mr. Mullburn."

Mullburn smiled broadly, and clasped his hands together and bowed his head slightly to the assembly.

The leader continued. "Let me say first of all that we all speak very fluent English. So there is no need for your interpreters. Secondly, we have very good security here, so there is no need for your personal security forces."

With a little wave of his index finger Mullburn directed Bruda Weilder, his chief bodyguard, to lead the rest of his group out into the waiting room. When the door was closed behind them, the moderator proceeded to the heart of the matter.

"Time is precious, so allow me to address some concerns we have, Mr. Mullburn. First of all, you have confessed a belief in Allah. Is that correct?"

"Most certainly. I believe that Allah is God, he is the one God, and Muhammad, blessed be his name, is his prophet," Mullburn affirmed with a smile.

"And yet," one of the clerics blurted out, "we have read your writings. You have been influenced by the ideas of the German philosopher Hegel. Such ideas are the ramblings of an infidel. Do you renounce them?"

Several of the other clerics were nodding athletically.

"It is true that I find some of the ideas of Hegel to be intriguing," Mullburn calmly responded. "And I know that you are learned men. You too are probably familiar with Hegel's dialectic. He concluded that all of history, and all of man's ideas, shows how one great idea, the 'thesis,' is soon opposed by another, contrary idea, the 'antithesis.' And that this leads to conflict between the two. But in the end, regardless of which idea prevails, there is ultimately a 'synthesis' between the two. So the two formerly opposing ideas are eventually synthesized, melded, and coalesced into a new combination. And that process continues over and over, throughout history."

Another cleric jumped in. "But Allah is forever. And he is unchanging! This Hegel of yours speculates on an endless process of changing and ever-evolving ideas about truth and God. This is totally opposed to the Qur'an."

"Does not the Qur'an itself say," Mullburn countered, "in Sura 30:30 that God has created man with a religious nature? This means that man searches from a religious soul. In the process of seeking, and rethinking, and searching for Allah, man sometimes synthesizes different philosophies—differing ideas—and I would propose to you that the end product of that synthesis could be the vindication of Islam itself."

Mullburn surveyed the skeptical and unsmiling faces around the table. "Let us speak plainly," he said. "I have concluded that the ultimate synthesis—the great melding together of religious ideas—is now at hand. After this last great synthesis there is no further process—no further need for evolution to take place in man's religious ideas."

"Yes," the moderator noted. "We understand that you believe that Islam and Christianity can be—in your words—synthesized?"

There was laughter around the table. Then the moderator continued. "We all know that for many years there have been dozens of meetings between many organizations that seek to reconcile Islam and Christianity. But so far, they have only produced cordial handshaking and meaningless platitudes. And still, the West continues in the ways of the infidel."

"Let me be very clear on this," Mullburn stated. He raised his hands confidently, beginning to paint a picture with his words and gestures.

"Imagine, for a moment, that a man is riding on a camel across the burning sands of the desert. The two of them, man and camel, have been synthesized into one thing—combined into one image as they travel along under the deadly heat of the sun. Yet in truth, which of the two is more important? Is it the camel that needs the rider on its back to survive? No! It is the *man* who needs to ride on the camel's back to survive in his trek across the hot desert. The camel is the important thing. The rider is simply something that is carried along."

Then Mullburn smiled and folded his hands in respectful summation. "As a follower of Allah, it is my belief that in the grand synthesis, Islam is the camel—Christianity shall merely be the baggage that goes along for the ride."

The chuckling around the table had stopped. Now several of the Muslim teachers were looking intently at Mullburn, with thoughtful, wrinkled brows.

The moderator spoke. "Is it the wisdom of Allah that we are hearing? Or simply an American billionaire's clever use of Arab symbolism? We don't ride camels anymore, Mr. Mullburn. Personally, I prefer a Mercedes-Benz."

Another Muslim cleric followed up. "How is this synthesis going to happen in a way that does not compromise Islam?"

"What is the greatest dividing point between Islam and Christianity?" Mullburn asked. "Certainly it is the misguided belief that Christians have in the 'Trinity.' We Muslims believe that God is one. Christians apparently believe he is three persons, and have persisted in that mistaken notion for two thousand years. Now, let us ask ourselves this: What is it that lies at the heart of this false idea of the Trinity?"

"As we all know, it is the Christian idea that Jesus was truly God incarnate," one of the teachers responded.

"Exactly," Mullburn agreed. "If you take Jesus out of the Trinity, it collapses like a house of cards at a Las Vegas table."

"Interesting concept, Mr. Mullburn," the moderator noted, "but true Muslims do not play games of chance. And they do not gamble. By the way—you own several casinos in Las Vegas, do you not?"

"In light of my conversion to Islam, I am in the process of transferring all of my interests in those casinos."

"Of course you are," the moderator replied quietly.

"We know how you have spoken out about your ideas to large, public audiences," another of the Islamic teachers commented. "At a rock-and-roll concert in a coliseum near Los Angeles you said, and I quote: 'You have got to be open. Be open in order to catch the wave of this evolution that's going on.' End of quote. Now Mr. Mullburn, is it evolution or is it Islam that you are promoting?"

"Evolution is the train. Islam is the freight. Allah is the destination," Mullburn replied. "With the discovery of the 7QA fragment, we are witnessing the inevitable disintegration of the theological concept of the resurrection. Jesus is quickly becoming an admired prophet rather than a Christian savior. And, of course, a Christianity that considers Jesus to be a prophet—rather than a savior—comes very close to the teachings of Islam."

"Your idea that more people are now abandoning the belief that Jesus was God—what do you base that on?" the moderator asked.

"I own my own public opinion survey center," Mullburn replied. "Since the first public announcements of the 7QA discovery, attendance in mainline Protestant churches has dropped by almost 30 percent. Even more significant, 52 percent of Americans now believe that there is no substantial difference between the God of Islam and the God of Christianity.

"And you have probably read about the revolution that is taking place within the Vatican. As a result of the Pope's refusal to allow Catholic scholars to take a public position, either way, on the 7QA fragment, dozens of prominent Jesuit scholars have left the Church in protest. There has been a drastic dropoff in the number of Catholic seminarians. When you couple this with the continued rise of Islam around the world, there is no question that this is a historic opportunity for the triumph of Islam."

The moderator nodded and thanked Warren Mullburn for coming. Then he added, "There is also a lingering question—how can I put this delicately—about your motives, Mr. Mullburn. What is it that causes you to expend such energy—and such investment—to pursue this idea of leading Christians into the arms of Allah?"

"My concern for humanity—and my reverence for Islam," Mullburn said warmly.

"Yes, of course. Those would be fine ideals. Admirable motives," the moderator responded.

Mullburn stood up and shook the hands of each of the leaders. The moderator escorted him to the door.

"There are, of course, some of our more fervent leaders who would not agree with your approach," the moderator added as the two stopped outside the door of the library, and he gazed at Mullburn with an ironic look. "For instance, Abdul el Alibahd probably would not accept your position of trying to compromise with the Christian culture of the West."

"He is a terrorist. Surely you do not share his penchant for blowing up American cities?" Mullburn asked.

"Most assuredly not," the moderator responded. "But Allah has many who profess to serve him. Allah moves through his followers like a whirlwind. That wind, like a sandstorm, cannot be controlled. And sometimes people are destroyed by it."

With that, the moderator gestured in parting, and as he returned to the conference, the thick library door closed with a heavy thud.

Mullburn collected his several assistants who were waiting in the lobby of the villa, and quickly motored out to the landing strip where his private jet was waiting. On the way he was briefed on how he was doing on the NASDAQ, on his holdings in the foreign markets, and on a new oil field that was being surveyed by his geologists.

"Did the monthly income reports arrive from our casinos yet?" Mullburn asked.

"Yes, Mr. Mullburn, and I think you will be pleased," his aide said, passing him an e-mail report.

"Just make sure that I've got a few straw men listed as the new owners of those casinos," Mullburn ordered. "We don't want to offend our new friends on the Council of Islam—at least not yet."

23

WILL CHAMBERS WAS SITTING IN HIS CORVETTE with the top down, wondering where Tiny Heftland was. There was no sound that evening except for the chorus of crickets out in the dark. An occasional passing car would momentarily flood the parking area outside the little country grocery store with light from its headlamps that would then sweep by quickly like a searchlight.

The general store, a small, square clapboard building with a turn-of-the-century false front and an ancient-looking gas pump out front, was closed. Will had been careful to follow Tiny's directions to their rendezvous point. He had even arrived fifteen minutes ahead of schedule. Then his cell phone rang. It was the detective.

"Hey Will, did you find the spot?"

"Yeah, where are you?"

"Okay, so listen, good buddy, I'm really sorry to do this to you. Something came up on this other case I'm working on. I've got to get up to Philly earlier than I expected. So I'm really sorry I can't meet you. I feel bad about this."

Will bristled, and snapped back, "Tiny, I can't believe this. You're the one who insisted on me driving all the way up here to Maryland to meet you. This was your idea."

"Hey, I know your time is money, counselor," Tiny said, trying to smooth things over. "But look at it this way. The point was for you to get a firsthand look-see at Reichstad's research center. So you can still do that. I faxed you directions to the place. It's only about a mile-and-a-half away from where you are right now."

Will quickly finished up the phone call with Tiny. Still annoyed, he started up his car and wheeled it onto the country highway. He took two more turns onto smaller and smaller roads until, out of the darkness, he saw the small, unassuming sign announcing the Center for Biblical Archaeo-Anthropology. The building off in the distance looked unremarkable. It was a two-story, beige-brick office building in the middle of a clearing. There was a large satellite dish on the roof and several imposing antennas, but no other buildings or houses within sight. The only unusual thing, however, was that, with the exception of a plate-glass window at the entrance, there were no other windows in the structure. Yet in all, Will could not understand Tiny's insistence that he drive several hours just to look at it.

As Will started to drive away, he looked back at the building in his rear-view mirror. One more thing caught his attention. There was no fence around the property. If this building was as secret as Tiny had suspected, and as forbidding as MacCameron had painted it, why was there no visible security around it?

Within an hour Will was cruising on the interstate just outside of Baltimore. He started noticing signs for the city's inner harbor. He glanced at his watch. It was 9:05. He remembered that Fiona's concert had started at 8:00. If he took the exit for the harbor he could be down there in ten minutes.

Well, it really didn't matter, he mused, because he had forgotten where he had put the stage pass that MacCameron had given him. Of course, he could always go in through the front gate and try to buy a ticket like everybody else. But why bother? Then something jogged his memory, and he punched the button on the glove compartment of the car. The door flopped open, and the stage pass for the concert was lying there on top of his collection of maps. Off in the distance, as the signs on the freeway indicated, the exit ramp for the harbor area was approaching.

Without any reason that he could articulate, Will took the exit and made his way downtown. He knew where the Pavilion was. In a matter of minutes he was parking half-a-block away, and walking quickly toward the concert hall. He banged on the stage-door entrance, still wondering why he was there. A man with a headset and a T-shirt that read "Fiona In Concert!" opened the door. Will showed him the pass, and the man gave him a wide smile and welcomed him in.

"You must be a friend of Fiona's," he said in a semi-whisper. "Her dad was supposed to meet you here but he was not feeling well, so he couldn't make it."

The stagehand showed Will to a seat off stage left, next to a black curtain that draped down from the catwalk above. He could see Fiona inviting a group of children onto the stage. In one corner there were musicians at a grand piano, an electric keyboard, and a synthesizer, and in the other corner there was a drummer, a guitarist, and a woman with a violin.

In the center of the stage Fiona was laughing, and kissing and hugging each of the little children as they squirmed and scampered up to join her.

"Oh my, I love children," she said radiantly. "Aren't these little ones the most precious blessings from the Lord?"

And with that her voice cracked a little, and she covered her mouth with her hand. She apologized for getting teary and laughed at herself, and soon the audience was laughing with her. Off-stage, mesmerized by Fiona, Will began to grin in spite of himself. Even amid the staged unreality of a huge concert hall and in the glare of the spotlights, Fiona seemed uncommonly authentic.

Fiona arranged the children into a small semicircle on the floor around her. As she did, her musicians moved quietly into a simple, soothing lullaby.

Fiona sat in the midst of the children and began to explain her next song.

"One day Jesus was approached by a group of boys and girls. I bet they looked just like you!" And with that she touched the noses of a few of the children, who giggled with delight.

"Well," she continued, "the disciples of Jesus didn't want these boys and girls to bother Jesus. I suppose they thought that he had very important business to take care of—and they thought that being with little children was not important. But Jesus corrected them. He told them to let the children come to Him. Jesus is the kind of Savior who loves to hug children, and surround them with love, and bless them with his big strong carpenter's hands."

The music swelled and Fiona started to sing in a voice that was sweet and light—

> Let the children
> come to Me—
> My kingdom shall
> forever be
> Reflected in their
> joyful faith
> With beauty and
> simplicity.

Fiona finished the little ballad and helped the children to the waiting arms of their parents as the concert hall thundered with applause. Then the house lights dimmed and a single spot shone on Fiona. Though quiet at first, the music started slowly to build.

> When the two Marys
> came to the tomb,
> To anoint their dear Savior
> who lay there,
> They met, quite instead,
> an angel who said
> That a thing most amazing
> had happened.

The small orchestra then cranked up to a charging beat, led by the synthesizer, as she sang,

> HE HAS RISEN!
> HE HAS RISEN!
> He is not in the tomb
> He is meeting you soon,
> He has risen in power,
> Conquered death in that hour,
> HE HAS RISEN!
> HE HAS RISEN!
> HE HAS RISEN!

Some laser lights flashed across the stage at the finale and the crowd roared. But to Will, there was no sound, no audience—only Fiona. This dark-haired beauty who exuded joy and grace—she sang like an angel, yet had a down-to-earth sense of humor that seemed to spring not just from wit, but from generosity of soul.

Fiona ran off stage and gave a hug to the stage manager. He whispered something in her ear, and she stepped over to Will.

"Mr. Chambers, how wonderful of you to come." She took both of his hands in her hands. "I heard that my dad is not feeling well. I think my friends have him on the phone. Will you excuse me just for a moment?"

Fiona stepped away and picked up the telephone on the soundboard desk and talked for a few minutes. She ended by saying, "Love you, Da. Get better. Tell Mum I love her."

Then she turned to Will. "I had planned on going out with you and my father. Do you still want to go out? Have you eaten? I want to have you meet some friends of mine."

Before Will could really respond, she was whisking him out the side door and into a waiting limo. They chatted politely while the car cruised down toward the Little Italy section of Baltimore and stopped in front of a place called "Luigi's." The sign said "Closed."

The door of the restaurant swung open. A stocky man with dark hair combed in a high flattop, wearing a white apron, spread out his arms to greet them. He set them at a table by the window decked with a checkered tablecloth. The rest of the restaurant was empty. Will and Fiona were waited on personally by Luigi and his wife, Maria, a quiet, good-natured woman with gentle eyes and a gracious manner. They lit a candle on the table, and after they brought the food out Luigi and Maria joined them for dinner. Luigi folded his hands and said a short prayer, and then they all began a frenzy of dish-passing, eating, and conversation.

The four of them talked nonstop amidst the pasta, the meatballs, the thick aromatic sauces, the garlic bread, and the Neapolitan lasagna. Luigi and Maria talked about coming over from Sicily to Brooklyn as children, within a year of each other—about how their families had known each other back in Italy. They talked about their courtship—and their marriage—and their two little children. The little boy and girl were supposed to be asleep in the apartment above the restaurant, but they kept sneaking down the stairs and peeking around the corner at the foursome, and giggling until Luigi would chase them back up the stairs.

Will had the strangest sensation that he had known these people forever. Fiona would roar at Luigi's stories with a belly laugh that was a peculiar and potent contrast to her classic beauty. But when she was not laughing, and her face was bathed in the golden glow of the candlelight, Will found himself struggling not to simply stare unabashedly at her. In the warm laughter of these wonderful people, and in the presence of this woman, Will was starting to feel—resurrected within—the powerful joy of being alive. It was a feeling he hadn't experienced any time in recent memory. And it was a feeling he did not want to lose.

When the conversation slowed down it was late, and Luigi and Maria started collecting the dishes from the table. Luigi said he would call the limo driver to come pick them up. The two restaurateurs insisted on doing the dishes, and as they disappeared through the swinging doors that led to the kitchen Fiona and Will remained back at the table.

"So tell me frankly, how do you feel about my father's case?" Fiona asked.

"It's too early to tell," Will responded.

Fiona laughed and said, "That's a lawyer's response."

"I'm being as honest as I can. I'll be in a much better position to say after the opposing attorney takes his deposition next week."

"You know, my father speaks very highly of you."

"Well, I'm flattered. But frankly, he hasn't seen me in action on this case yet. Maybe he ought to reserve judgment," Will noted.

"He is a very good judge of people. I believe that the Lord has given him a real gift of discernment. I have to confess that I originally had some doubts about you."

Will was taken aback. He struggled a bit, and after a few seconds he said, "What kind of doubts?"

"My business manager had investigated you and recommended to Dad that he not hire you."

"Oh?"

"He had some concerns about your personal life. Personal problems that might affect your ability to represent my father."

"Like what?"

"Well, Mr. Chambers..."

"Please. Call me Will."

"All right—Will. I was told that your wife had died and that you took it very hard. That you were a heavy drinker, but you were getting the problem under control. You know, my heart breaks for you. To lose your wife has got to be so hard."

"Yeah, it's been hard."

"If I may ask, how did she die?"

Fiona had just moved into an area that Will was rarely willing to discuss. But tonight he was feeling different about life. So he answered her. He took a breath before he spoke quietly.

"She was murdered."

Fiona didn't speak at first. She brought her hand up to her face and closed her eyes. When she opened them Will could see tears.

"Dear Father," she said, fighting back the tears. "How awful for her—and for you."

Suddenly Will was conscious of a wall of emotion rising up, like a freak tidal wave that had appeared out of nowhere. It was threatening to engulf him. He struggled for control and said nothing for a while, but stared at the candle that was burning low. Finally he managed a question.

"You said that you had your own doubts about me. What were they?"

"Oh, I don't think that's important anymore. If my father's happy with you then I'm happy with you."

"No, that's not fair. I disclosed something personal to you," Will said. "Now it's your turn. What doubts?"

"Well," Fiona said, "in addition to the problems with alcohol, I just could not understand how an attorney who used to work for the ACLU could possibly represent someone like my father."

"You mean, how could a liberal like me represent a Christian fundamentalist?"

"I'm suspicious of that word when non-Christians use it," Fiona said firmly. "The media loves to use that term 'fundamentalist' to paint people—particularly Bible-believing Christians—as lunatics or fanatics."

"I don't think your father is a lunatic. He's unique, that's for sure. But he's no lunatic," Will said with a reassuring smile. "Besides, what makes you assume that I am a 'non-Christian'?"

"Well," Fiona replied gingerly, "you have a point there, Mr. Attorney. So, are you a Christian?"

"I have nothing against Jesus. I think he had a lot of great ideas. But when it comes to the big question about God, I'm probably more of an agnostic."

Fiona wrinkled her brow slightly and leaned toward him with her arms folded in front of her. "Everything I've heard about you is that you are a man who is not afraid of taking an unpopular stand—even against all of the odds—as long as it is something you can believe in. But here is the most important issue of all—the question of whether God exists and whether he loves you and wants to save you—and on that issue, here you are, sitting on the fence."

"Some questions just don't have easy answers," Will retorted.

"And sometimes the answers are right there in front of you. All you have to do is open your heart."

"I don't know what that means—'open your heart,'" Will countered. "Religious lingo like that really turns me off." For an instant Will regretted coming back at Fiona so aggressively.

"It turns you off?" Fiona shot back. "I thought you were in the business of pursuing the truth."

"I never said I wasn't."

"So if it's truth you want—then who cares whether it turns you on, turns you off, or turns you upside down," Fiona said, pursuing the issue. "Truth is truth."

"Okay," Will replied, but before he could make his point, Fiona pushed on.

"And just for the record, Mr. Trial Lawyer, if you dare to confront the *real truth* about God, he *will* turn you upside down. Which is a good thing, not a bad thing. So, the question is—are you willing to face the truth? Are you willing to have God turn your life around?"

Will smiled as he saw Fiona pressing in. She seemed to have a unique power of combining tenderness with a will as tough as an oak board. He paused for a minute and stared thoughtfully at the candle.

"Now that I've endured your cross-examination, it's my turn," Will started again. "Tell me, do you spend a lot of time on the road?"

"Yes, I do," Fiona said, "at least lately."

"For the record, I think you are a beautiful performer," Will said, and then realized that it had not come out the way he wanted it to. "I mean, you sing beautifully."

Fiona laughed and blushed a little, and then nodded in thanks.

"So, you must have a lot of dates with lots of men around the country," Will said somewhat indelicately.

Fiona hesitated for a moment. "No, I find my life very busy doing what the Lord has called me to do. I have a lot of friends who I love very much. And to answer your real question, I am single—as in not married. I am single by choice. I believe that God may have called me to singleness. And if that is the way I can best serve him, then I am happy with that."

The front door to the restaurant swung open and the limo driver appeared. Fiona and Will gave their goodbyes to their hosts. As they walked outside they could feel the wind picking up. While the limo took them back to the Pavilion the two of them made small talk. They could now hear the sounds of distant thunder. When the car arrived at the spot where Will had parked his Corvette, he climbed out.

Fiona lowered her window and stretched her arm out to shake Will's hand.

"Will, I will continue to pray for you as you handle my father's lawsuit. I believe that this is an incredibly important case," she said. "God bless you."

Will searched Fiona's smile for some glimpse, however fleeting, of something more than just cordial appreciation. But as he stepped back from the car he decided that there was none.

He watched the limo as it drove away down the boulevard. Then he climbed in his car and headed home. Rain was starting to fall, and the wet pools on the street were reflecting the red and green streetlights.

He turned his windshield wipers on high speed. As he listened to their mechanical thumping while driving through the shimmering sheets of rain, Will was beginning to feel that familiar sense of stark and utter loneliness.

24

ON THE TOP FLOOR OF THE OFFICES of Kennelworth, Sherman, Abrams & Cantwell, Angus MacCameron and Will Chambers were ushered into the spacious conference room. The court reporter was already set up with her steno machine off to the side of the massive conference table. Another court reporter, a videographer, stood next to his tripod, adjusting the camera lens as he readied his equipment for the deposition that was about to begin.

They were offered coffee, but both declined. As they waited, they were able to look out over Washington, D.C., through the wall of solid glass. They could see the Capitol dome and a corner of the White House in the distance. Several more minutes went by, and then the door swung open. Two associate lawyers with legal pads and thick files under their arms walked in and introduced themselves, quickly taking their seats. A moment later a law clerk scurried into the room with a file under one arm and a laptop computer under the other arm. He quickly plugged in the laptop and booted it up. Then he dutifully folded his hands on the table and waited.

"I wasn't aware that this was going to be recorded on video camera," MacCameron whispered somewhat nervously to Will, who was seated next to him.

"Don't let it throw you," Will whispered back. "Pretend the camera isn't there. Just focus on what we talked about. Listen to each question before answering. Make him rephrase any question you don't understand. Don't answer a question that isn't being asked. And just tell your story *your way* and not *his way*. That's it."

Another minute of silence passed. Then the door opened and J-Fox Sherman walked in. He was dressed down to his shirtsleeves, in an imported blue silk shirt, red suspenders, and a tie with a Picasso design.

Sherman strode over to MacCameron and extended his hand. MacCameron shook it, but Sherman said nothing. Then Sherman reached over to Will and shook his hand. But Sherman held it in a vise grip, and for a second the two men locked eyes.

Then Sherman moved away from Will, and as he went round the table to seat himself directly across the table he said off-handedly, "Sorry, counselor, I've forgotten your name." Sherman's law clerk announced, "Will Chambers. Attorney from Monroeville, Virginia, sir."

"Ah, yes. Monroeville. Cute little town. The life of a country lawyer. What brings you all the way up here to big, bad Washington, D.C., Mr. Chambers?"

"Justice, Mr. Sharman," Will responded.

"That's *Sherman,*" one of the associate attorneys snapped.

"Oh, I imagine that Mr. Chambers is just having some fun with us, isn't that right, attorney Chambers?"

Will did not respond.

Sherman stretched out his hands over the conference table and brushed it lightly. Will noticed that. It was no idle gesture—Sherman was making a point. He had no notes at his disposal. No legal pad. No file. Not even a pen. Just a naked tabletop in front of him. J-Fox Sherman was letting his opponent know that he was about to conduct a four-hour deposition completely by memory. As if to say, "I am already in complete and total command of this case. All of the facts, and the principles of law, and the points of persuasion are already ordered and neatly organized in my mind. Now stand back and behold how I destroy you."

MacCameron raised his hand and was sworn in. Then Sherman began, his hands folded confidently on the table and his face expressionless.

Sherman had the court reporter mark, with exhibit stickers, the December issue of *Digging for Truth* magazine that lay at the core of the case. He also marked as exhibits several other issues of the publication.

After MacCameron had identified all of the magazine articles on the record, Sherman began questioning him on his educational background. He did so, not by the use of the kind of harmless, non-leading questions most lawyers use in depositions, like, "please describe when and where you received each of your educational degrees," and then letting the witness give a rambling answer.

Rather, Sherman recited, by memory, each stage of MacCameron's educational history, putting forth each fact as a separate question to which MacCameron could only agree by answering "yes." It was a psychological tactic to begin exerting control over the deposition process. Even more importantly, it was intended to intimidate the witness and his lawyer, illustrating how J-Fox Sherman had already mastered all of the central facts of this case by heart.

Sherman finished MacCameron's educational background by asking a series of questions that Will found troubling.

"When you left the University of Edinburgh, a world-renowned institution, you went to America to attend the College of the Piedmont in West Virginia ?"

"Yes."

"Was the College of the Piedmont a world-renowned institution?"

"No, not really."

"In fact that college did not even offer a PhD program or its equivalent?"

"I think that is true."

"When you left this world-renowned institution, the University of Edinburgh, to attend a much lesser known and less-qualified school, did you leave on good terms?"

"Yes, I believe I did."

"You had been a good student at Edinburgh—good grades?"

"Yes, quite."

"You had no problems, such as misconduct of any kind, as a reason for your leaving?"

MacCameron took a while to answer.

When he finally replied he simply said, "No, sir."

Then Sherman moved on to MacCameron's employment history. When MacCameron affirmed that, yes, he did leave the Family of Christ Community Church in central Pennsylvania after only two years as the assistant pastor, Sherman paused.

"And you left that church under a cloud of suspicion, did you not?"

"I'm not sure what you mean," MacCameron answered.

"Were you asked to resign as assistant pastor?"

"It was a mutual decision."

"Did the board of elders and the head pastor tell you that they wanted you to leave, effective immediately?"

MacCameron took a few seconds to answer. Then he replied.

"Yes. They did tell me that. But may I explain?"

Sherman ignored his request to expand on his answer and launched into a volley of blows to MacCameron's credibility.

"Is it correct that the church wanted to kick you out because you had exhibited, and I quote, 'a lack of Christlike love and a total absence of tolerance toward our Christian brothers and sisters in other religious denominations'?"

"Well," MacCameron stammered slightly, "I really don't remember if that was the exact wording."

Will jumped in.

"Mr. Sherman, your question implies that a statement or document of some kind exists from which you are quoting. If that's true, then in fairness I want you to show it to my client so he can look at it and possibly have his memory refreshed."

Sherman smiled, and waved his hand to his law clerk. The clerk retrieved a document and set it on the table in front of his boss.

"Reverend MacCameron, do I need to show you these minutes from the board of elders meeting of that church to jog your memory about that unfortunate series of events?"

"I have a standing objection to any further questions about Reverend MacCameron's employment history that occurred prior to his becoming the editor-in-chief of *Digging for Truth,*" Will responded, "unless you can show me how it has any relevance to this case."

"Oh, that will be my pleasure," Sherman intoned. "We have alleged—and you have denied—that your client exhibited actual malice against Dr. Reichstad. I would contend, Mr. Chambers, that your client had not only actual malice under the law when he wrote his shameless and defaming article—he had, in fact, actual hatred of everything Dr. Reichstad stood for. *Reverend* MacCameron, in fact, held in contempt every religious, cultural, and intellectual group on the planet that did not agree with him."

At that point Sherman swung in his chair back toward MacCameron and bulleted out a series of questions designed to bring the point home.

"Is it correct that the church wanted to fire you because of your public statements condemning the Catholic Church and the Pope in particular—your statements that they were the 'most logical candidates to fulfill the role of "religious Babylon" in the end times predicted in the New Testament book of Revelation'? Is that correct?"

"Yes, I made those statements, and yes, the church did not agree with my preaching on that but—"

"And is it correct that you likewise condemned, in your preaching, many different denominations and religious groups?"

"Well, I did speak the truth about how certain denominations were not in line with biblical teachings..." MacCameron replied.

Sherman continued to batter the witness.

"You condemned certain sects of the Methodist church?"

"Yes, I suppose I did preach against some of their official positions on certain issues—"

"You condemned much of the Episcopal denomination?"

"I only attacked some of their official positions on matters which were clearly against Holy Scripture—"

"You criticized Presbyterians..."

"Yes, on occasion..."

"And certain of the so-called liberal branches of the Baptist denominations..."

"I imagine I did—"

"You criticized some of the so-called liberal factions of the Lutheran churches—is that correct?"

"In my preaching I tried to be biblical—but, yes, you are correct..."

"Can you think of a single Christian denomination, now as you sit there, that at one time or another you did *not* condemn in your preaching during your rather short-lived experience as an assistant pastor at that church in Pennsylvania?"

Will looked at his client. MacCameron looked pale and tired, and the deposition had several more hours left to go. Of course Will knew the tricks of the trade. He could have peppered the air with a number of objections. He could have demanded a time-out for his client, and then whisked him out into the hallway to regroup.

But Will had decided that it was sink or swim for MacCameron. If he could not hold up to a deposition with Sherman, surely he would not be able to handle himself in the emotional crucible of a full-blown jury trial.

"Do you want the question re-read?" Sherman asked.

"No, I don't need it re-read. The fact is that I cannot now remember which Christian groups I did, or did not, criticize."

Sherman's next area of interrogation went right to the heart of the case. He tossed some copied papers in front of MacCameron and asked him to read out loud what Sherman had highlighted with a yellow marker. It was a portion of the article that MacCameron had written in the December issue. In it MacCameron had contended that Reichstad "must be connected to the suspicious death of Mr. Azid and the tragic murder of Dr. Hunter." In the same article he also had written that Reichstad's conclusions about the 7QA fragment were the result of his "either deliberately lying, or he has committed scientific malpractice."

As MacCameron read out loud his seemingly outrageous condemnation of Reichstad from his own magazine article, Sherman studied his opposing counsel. But Will was stone-faced and unperturbed.

When MacCameron was finished reading, Sherman launched the next assault.

Prior to writing the article, had MacCameron ever conducted an investigation into whether Reichstad's conclusions about 7QA were correct?

"I read every scholarly and professional article about 7QA I could get my hands on," MacCameron replied. But when he was pressed on that point, he had to admit that not one of those articles suggested that Reichstad's conclusions were wrong—they only criticized the fact that he would not share the original 7QA fragment with other researchers so they could verify his findings. And he also admitted that not one scholar in the known world had ever written that Reichstad was deliberately *lying* about what the 7QA fragment was, and what it said.

Had MacCameron conducted any investigation, himself, into the suicide of Azid and the murder of Hunter, *prior* to writing that article? No, MacCameron agreed that he had not. Did he have anyone read the article before he published it, to ensure the factual accuracy of his statements? No, he had not. Was MacCameron in possession of any written document or any data from any law-enforcement agency that even slightly suggested that Reichstad might in some way be connected to the deaths of Azid and Hunter? MacCameron had to admit he had no such information.

As Sherman wound up that line of questioning, he had convincingly painted a picture of MaCameron as a fundamentalist preacher with a tattered employment history and a penchant for intolerance—certainly no professional match for the world-class Reichstad in either credentials or educational qualification. The portrait of MacCameron was of a man who published an outlandish libel against a beloved scholar, having made little or no prior verification of the accuracy of his conclusions.

Will's defense of "lack of actual malice" hung now by only one slender thread. The one area that Sherman had not yet entered was the only area left that could form a reasonable basis for MacCameron's published attacks on Reichstad: that MacCameron had had *personal knowledge* of the matters that he had written about. Sherman quickly breached that last stronghold.

"Did you have any personal knowledge or information that supported your attacks on Dr. Reichstad?"

"Yes," MacCameron replied, with a smile.

Sherman then commenced to unravel, in an interrogation that went on for another hour-and-a-half, every detail of Dr. Hunter's single conversation with MacCameron at the Between the Arches Café in the old section of Jerusalem. And he probed the message left by Hunter on MacCameron's answering machine.

Will studied Sherman for some glimmer of response to this thunderbolt of information: a twitch or a blink, or something in his posture that let on that Sherman was having some reaction to MacCameron's testimony—to his describing Hunter's fear of being pursued and Hunter's belief that Azid's death was not a suicide—or to Hunter's mysterious fragment that seemed to so closely resemble the 7QA fragment.

But Sherman revealed no emotion at the tale that MacCameron was telling. He calmly pursued his questions until the last bit of information was extracted.

Then Sherman turned to Will and said, "We are hereby demanding that you produce to our office, forthwith, that tape recording from your client's answering machine—the one with Dr. Hunter's message on it."

Will agreed, having no objection to lodge, but said that it would be a matter of a few days before the original tape could be produced. Will did not—nor was he required to—disclose that his own audio expert was analyzing the tape recording at that very moment in hopes of proving that Hunter's fragment was actually a comment about several "fragments."

Near the end of the deposition, Sherman leaned back and asked MacCameron the million-dollar question.

"Tell me, sir—was there anything in what Hunter told you in person—or on that taped message—that *directly proved* the truth of anything that you would later write against Dr. Reichstad in your little magazine?"

MacCameron, who was now slouched over and looking tired, glanced over at his lawyer. Will noticed that his client had a burdened expression, and there was perspiration collecting on his forehead and on his upper lip.

There were a few seconds of silence. The court reporter took her fingers off the keys of her steno machine and stretched them, but her eyes were glued on MacCameron, waiting for him to respond. MacCameron gave a little sigh, and then answered.

"No, sir. Nothing that Richard Hunter said *directly* proved the things I later decided to write against Dr. Reichstad."

Sherman leaned back in his chair. Will could smell death in the air. There was a carcass on the floor of the conference room of Kennelworth, Sherman, Abrams & Cantwell. What Will Chambers knew through his years of trying cases, but MacCameron naively did not know, was that the carcass on the floor was what was left of Angus MacCameron's legal defense.

But even Will Chambers did not expect what would come next. Sherman was about to personally bring in the vultures to pick at the carrion.

"You testified under oath today, Reverend MacCameron—right here in this very room—that you did not leave the University of Edinburgh because of any misconduct. Do you stand by that?"

"Yes. It is the truth."

"Oh, is it? Is it the truth? Mr. MacCameron, I would suggest that in fact you have committed perjury in this very deposition."

"No, sir, I have not," MacCameron retorted loudly. "My answer was truthful to the question, the way you put it."

"Is it a fact, sir," Sherman said, raising his voice, "that just before you left Edinburgh University, formal disciplinary charges against you were about to be prepared by the University—charging you with plagiarism in one of your research papers?"

Will couldn't believe it. In all that MacCameron had disclosed to him, this allegation had never surfaced. Sherman's question about why MacCameron had left the University of Edinburgh was one of the first questions Will had asked his client.

"Is that a fact?" Sherman pressed with a booming voice.

"Not like that," MacCameron answered, his face flushed.

"Is it a fact that you were told the University was going to prepare such formal charges?"

"That is not why I left," MacCameron tried to explain.

"Is that a fact—yes or no—you must answer, sir. Yes or no. Were such charges going to be brought against you?"

MacCameron took a deep breath. Then he replied very simply.

"Yes, they were."

Sherman stood up commandingly. He pointed his finger at Will Chambers.

"On the record, Mr. Will Chambers, as legal counsel for Reverend Angus MacCameron, defendant in this lawsuit, I am now giving you notice. Take heed, sir, that no later than tomorrow by the close of business, my office will deliver to your office a petition for attorney's fees to be assessed against you under Rule 11 of the Federal Rules of Civil Procedure. You will have fourteen days to formally withdraw your frivolous defense of 'lack of actual malice' in this case. If you do not, we will proceed to move the trial court to dismiss that defense for total lack of evidence of your part. It should be painfully clear to all of us that your client made no effort to verify the slanderous lies he printed against Dr. Reichstad. He therefore exhibited reckless disregard for the factual accuracy of the allegations printed in his article, and is guilty of actual malice.

"After getting the trial court to dismiss your defense of lack of actual malice, we will then proceed to ask the court to issue sanctions against you for asserting that totally unfounded and unsupported defense. The sanction we will demand is one-half of the attorney's fees generated by our firm on this case thus far. I have calculated that sum as of yesterday—not including my legal performance for nearly five hours today. And we will be asking that the court assess our legal fees—not against your rather sad client. No, sir. Instead, we will be asking the court to assess these fees against you personally, as his lawyer."

With that Sherman pulled a piece of paper out of the pocket of his silk shirt and tossed it over to Chambers. Will opened it. It simply said,

Total fees of law firm for work on Reichstad case: $490,000.00

One-half of fees, to be assessed against Chambers: $245,000.00

Now there were two carcasses on the floor. And Will Chambers felt as if the vultures were already picking at his eyes.

Sherman's legal team gathered around him and shook his hand, murmering their hushed adulation at his tour-de-force handling of the deposition.

MacCameron was mopping the sweat off his face and managed a struggling smile toward his lawyer, who was standing at his side. As Will glanced at J-Fox Sherman's gloating smile, he knew one thing for sure. He knew that he couldn't give up the last word to this pack of wolves that had encircled his aged and isolated client.

Will looked at the piece of paper he still held in his hand, and he waved it toward Sherman.

"Gee, I really am surprised that your legal fees aren't higher than this," Will said mockingly. Then he tossed the paper onto the conference table. "Now what's really going to be interesting, Mr. Sherman, is when Reverend MacCameron and I win this case," and with that Will put his hand on MacCameron's shoulder, "and I send your law firm a demand for *my* attorney's fees."

J-Fox Sherman mumbled something, turned, and left the room, sweeping with him his two legal associates and the law clerk, who followed dutifully behind. The court reporters quickly packed up their equipment and slipped out. In the silence of the conference room, there was only Angus MacCameron, attorney Will Chambers, and the small piece of paper that still lay where Will had thrown it on the middle of the conference table.

25

SO FAR, EVERY LEAD THAT JACK HORNBY had followed had turned into a dead end. He had still failed to uncover the nitty-gritty reality of what was going on between the United States government and the OPEC cartel. He had struck out with his contacts within the Energy Department.

As Hornby stood in front of the reporter's assignment board at the *Washington Herald,* he noticed that one of the religion reporters had been assigned to cover a seminar at the Smithsonian Institution entitled "The History of Islam and Prospects for Cultural Reconciliation with the West." Hornby also noted that, at the event, State Department undersecretary Kenneth Sharptin was scheduled to receive an award for "Cultural Achievements in Peacemaking." Hornby knew the reporter assigned to cover that story.

Clearly, he concluded, the newspaper wanted this to be a "puff piece" on the seminar and the fêting of Undersecretary Sharptin.

Across from Hornby's name on the chart was an assignment for him to cover a budget meeting of the D.C. control board. Here was yet another lackluster assignment that would end up being buried on page eight of the Metro section.

But the thought of financial issues triggered something. Not exactly something about the OPEC–United States oil story. But it triggered a thought of Hornby's longstanding "pickpocket rule." Greed and financial gain were the common denominators of many a great news story. The question became, who is picking whose pocket?

So he started thinking back to the Reichstad lawsuit story being killed. Then he remembered how he had first talked to his city editor and then had marched up to the managing editor. And finally Hornby had gone back and nailed the city editor again as he was trying to leave for the day. He had said something very significant, and Hornby was surprised he hadn't clicked on it before now. It was not the kind of thing an editor would usually admit to a reporter.

As the city editor had tried to dash past him he had blurted out, "Give it up, Hornby—when the owner and publisher want to kill a story, it stays dead."

Why would the ownership of the *Washington Herald* care about a story on a lawsuit over an archaeological discovery of a Harvard professor? For the owners and publishers of the newspaper the top and bottom line was always financial. So, who was picking whose pocket? And what did it have to do with the Reichstad lawsuit? And why did Hornby suddenly have the hunch that it had something to do with the OPEC oil story?

According to the Energy Department's statement at the press conference, the State Department was the catalyst in breaking new ground with the OPEC nations of the Middle East. And Hornby was cognizant of how State Department Undersecretary Sharptin had been actively marketing himself as a kind of cultural peace-broker between the Islamic East and the Christian West. In fact, Sharptin had been portraying himself as a kind of diplomatic chief for religious reconciliation.

The veteran newsman took out his notepad. First, at the top of the page he wrote: REICHSTAD LAWSUIT.

At the bottom of the page, in the lower right-hand corner, he wrote: STATE DEPT./SHARPTIN.

Then Hornby wrote a third entry in the lower left-hand corner of the pad: OIL/WHOSE POCKET?

Hornby glanced at his notepad. Then he drew a line connecting the three points and forming a triangle:

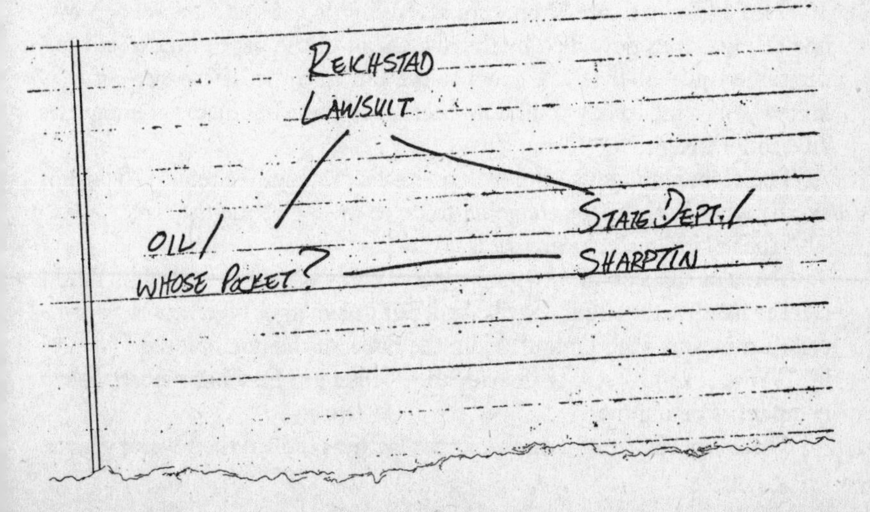

Hornby picked up the phone on a nearby desk in the newsroom and called up one of his college buddies, who worked as an accountant down in mergers and acquisitions. He glanced at his watch. It was perfect timing for lunch. His friend answered. Hornby invited him to catch up on old times over lunch at the Federal Grill.

"Who's buying?" the accountant asked wryly.

"I owe you one from the last time we went out," Hornby said.

"What decade was that?" the accountant asked. "You know, we work for the same newspaper. But you're too busy getting Pulitzer Prizes and ticking off the editors to take me out to lunch. It's about time."

They grabbed a cab together and arrived at the Grill just before the rush. The two slid into a quiet booth and ordered their meals, then started catching up on personal things. His accountant friend sounded disgruntled about his position in mergers and acquisitions. For Hornby, the trail was getting warm.

Halfway through the luncheon special of crabcake sandwiches and soup the accountant started getting the drift. There was more to this meeting than just old college comradeship.

Hornby was asking about any big mergers that the *Washington Herald* had been recently involved in.

"It's constant," the accountant said, hedging a little. "You know, mergers, acquisitions. Diversification. That's what my department is all about."

Hornby could sense something lurking just under the surface.

"Tell it to me straight. If you become a source I won't divulge it to anyone."

"What is this? Are you doing a story on me or what?"

"No," Hornby assured him, "I'm just trying to get some answers on why one of my stories got killed by the ownership of the paper. You would feel the same way—after all the years you've put into the newspaper—if they knifed you in the back—you know, because of some big financial merger, as an example. Right?"

The accountant got a grim look on his face. "Yeah," he replied, "which is exactly what I think they are going to do to me—give me the axe."

"You're kidding," Hornby said. "Why?"

"A major shakeup in ownership. We're into a big merger all right. And I can see handwriting on the wall. We'll put this merger together. New ownership comes in. And I'm out. I join the ranks of the unemployed."

"Wow," Hornby said with sympathy, "this must be a big merger. What company is taking over?"

There was silence at the table as the waitress refilled their water glasses.

"Look—I'm real concerned about telling you anything," the accountant whispered.

"Hey, you know my reputation," Hornby assured him. "I have never disclosed a confidential source. Remember when I spent thirty days in jail for contempt because I refused to divulge the source to the court?"

The accountant looked uneasy as he eyed his water glass. Then he said, "After all the years I put in with this newspaper. Boy, what a raw deal."

"Yeah. Really raw deal," Hornby added. "So come on, what's the name of the company buying out the *Herald?*"

There was a moment of silence while the accountant looked around at the surrounding tables. Then he lowered his head, and in a low voice he replied, "Global."

"Global what?"

"Global Geo-Technology, Inc."

Hornby thought about it for a few seconds, and then he responded, "Never heard of them."

"Sure. Not exactly a household word," the accountant added. "You'd probably know the parent company that controls them."

"Oh," Hornby asked, "who is the parent company?"

"Global Petroleum."

"So the *Washington Herald* is about to be purchased by a wholly owned subsidiary of Global Petroleum?"

"That's the deal," the accountant said, looking over the check that the waitress had left.

"Hey, don't worry about that. I'm picking up the tab for lunch," Hornby said. And then he asked his follow-up question.

"Isn't Global Petroleum owned by Warren Mullburn, the world's third-richest man? The reigning guru of religious synthesis? The master of evolutionary self-help?"

"Yeah, that's the guy. I've read some of his books. His science-fiction stuff is great. But his other stuff is kind of wacko. But you're right. If you can believe the business trade papers, he's number three in the whole world in accumulated wealth per net assets."

Jack Hornby tossed the money for the lunch and a healthy tip on the table. But before the accountant could ask him about sharing a cab back to the newspaper building, the reporter, with his notepad in his hand, had already left the restaurant and was running down the street.

26

As PROMISED, THE DAY FOLLOWING THE DEPOSITION of Reverend Angus MacCameron, the courier from J-Fox Sherman's law firm hand-delivered to Will Chambers a written motion under Federal Rule 11, seeking a court-ordered award of attorney's fees against Will Chambers in the amount of $245,000. The motion was conditional, however. In it, Sherman indicated that the request for attorney's-fee sanction would be withdrawn if, in return, within fourteen days Chambers formally withdrew, in writing, the defense in the lawsuit that MacCameron lacked "actual malice" at the time he wrote the article against Reichstad. In other words, Sherman was demanding, in return for dropping a demand for attorney's fees against Will Chambers, that Chambers admit that his client had been reckless in his writing of the defamatory magazine piece.

Sherman knew that the attorney's-fee motion would place Chambers and his client on the horns of an intractable dilemma. If Will Chambers agreed to withdraw his defense of "lack of actual malice," he would be conceding one of the major issues of the case.

On the other hand, if Chambers refused to withdraw that defense in two weeks, he faced a great risk. He might be ordered to pay a quarter of a million dollars in legal fees to Sherman's firm, provided that trial judge Jeremiah Kaye agreed with Sherman that the issue of MacCameron's recklessness was clear beyond any question.

Sherman had also coyly attached to the motion, for Chamber's reading enjoyment, a copy of a recent decision by Judge Kaye under Rule 11 in another case. Just three months before, Judge Kaye had hit a losing attorney with an attorney's-fee sanction in the amount of $150,000 for making unsupported allegations in a lawsuit. J-Fox Sherman had been the winning attorney in that lawsuit.

When Sherman met with Reichstad a few days later to report on how the deposition of MacCameron had gone, he was aglow with cautious optimism. He detailed each of the blows that he had inflicted on the fundamentalist preacher and magazine publisher in his questioning.

But Dr. Reichstad seemed unusually distracted in the conference. He had only one matter that he wanted to discuss with Sherman. Reichstad repeatedly demanded that Sherman discover everything he could about whether MacCameron might be in possession of certain "papers" dealing with the 7QA fragment.

"What do you mean by 'papers'?" Sherman asked his client.

"I'm sure you know what 'papers' are," Reichstad countered. "I simply want you to demand that MacCameron produce to me any piece of paper that he might have in connection with the 7QA fragment."

"Other than the actual article that MacCameron wrote—and copies of the research articles he accumulated on the 7QA fragment, what kind of 'papers' would you expect him to have?" Sherman asked, with a growing impatience at his client's ambiguity.

"I don't know. Perhaps some kind of paper that might be—well—connected directly with the actual 7QA fragment itself," Reichstad answered somewhat evasively.

"And what type of 'paper' would that be? What type of 'paper' would be, as you say, 'connected directly with the actual 7QA fragment'?" Sherman asked, now clearly irritated.

"That is for you to find out, isn't it, Mr. Sherman? That is, after all, what you are being paid huge amounts of money to do as my lawyer, is it not?"

"I'm being paid to be your lawyer," Sherman barked back, "not your mind reader. Lay it out for me, Doctor. What kind of 'paper' are you talking about? Spell it out."

Reichstad straightened up slightly in the leather chair in Sherman's inner office. Then he asked, "Of course, everything that is said here is confidential, right? Everything you and I discuss is protected by attorney-client privilege?"

Sherman nodded, but he narrowed his eyes as he surveyed his client. He suspected that with a modicum of encouragement Reichstad could be led to disgorge some information that was at least disagreeable, and perhaps even nasty. J-Fox Sherman had the stomach, of course, for things disagreeable and nasty. But he had no stomach for losing—no desire to hear something that might undermine the stellar case that he had painstakingly prepared.

"Of course," Sherman responded. "Everything here is secret. Although, there are some ethical conditions placed on me by the bar association. If, for instance, a client were to describe an ongoing conspiracy to commit a crime, plans to perpetrate a crime in the future, or cover up a crime committed in the past—or if the client fabricates a case that is built on lies and commits a fraud on the court—then sometimes," Sherman continued, speaking very slowly for the benefit of his client, "sometimes an attorney has to turn a client into the authorities. That is why a client should be *very careful* what he tells even his own attorney."

There was a moment of silence as Reichstad managed a smile. Then he said, "Yes. I think I understand."

"Do you?" Sherman asked.

"Yes."

"Now," Sherman continued, "about that 'paper' that you want me to demand from MacCameron. Exactly what are you looking for?"

"Hmm. Yes. Well, let's just say that if you were to demand from MacCameron that he produce any piece of paper that he believes was at one time *connected to* 7QA..."

Reichstad's voice trailed off.

"Let's just say," Sherman added, picking up the cue from his client, "that MacCameron believes that there are other fragment pieces that were once part of 7QA. Let's just assume that. Then perhaps I should make a demand for such fragments to be produced to us."

"That sounds like an excellent idea," Reichstad responded, smiling. "And if he does not have possession of such fragments himself, perhaps he could be forced to describe who *does* have possession of them."

"Yes. I can make that kind of discovery demand in this lawsuit," Sherman noted. "But of course, I don't recall your ever telling me that 7QA was originally part of a bigger fragment. And I have an excellent memory. Now such a revelation, if it were true, could be very damaging to your case."

"Perhaps. Perhaps not," Reichstad said as he rose from his chair. "But then what is more important, ensuring that my 7QA discovery remains in the history books—or winning one little lawsuit?"

After a career as one of America's most celebrated trial lawyers, J-Fox Sherman already knew the answer to that question—even if his client didn't.

27

THE SUN WAS OUT AND THE AIR WAS WARM as Will Chambers motored along the North Carolina coastline. The top was down on his Corvette convertible, and the sunlight felt good on his face after some days of cloudy weather. His golden retriever, Clarence, was in the passenger seat, his head in the wind, his ears flapping, and his eyes closed in dog delight.

Off to his left Will saw the white band of beaches and the azure blue of the ocean. No whitecaps today. The Atlantic was calm. As he drove up and over the bridge that led out to Cape Hatteras he wondered how long it had been. Ten, fifteen years perhaps since he had last visited the ocean home of his Uncle Bull and Aunt Georgia. He had talked with them a few times by telephone. Some letters and Christmas cards had passed back and forth. The last time he had met with them face-to-face was at Audra's funeral.

When Will had started on his four-hour drive from Virginia down to the sand dunes and fishing boats of the Outer Banks he had told himself that he was really going there to meet his uncle for professional reasons. Bull Chambers had been a well-respected North Carolina county judge. Now that he was retired and lived year-round on the coast, from what Will gathered he spent most of his time ocean fishing and beach walking with his wife of fifty years. Bull was one of the wisest men Will had known in the law—full of the common-sense side of legal issues—studied, calm, and deliberate. And while Bull was smart, he always knew that the underside of the cold, objective standards of justice included a healthy dose of mercy. Beyond even that, Will had a bond with Uncle Bull. When Will and his father had become estranged many years back he always felt he could turn to Bull, his father's brother, to talk things out.

Will had told his client Angus MacCameron only that he needed to consult a trusted "legal advisor" regarding the thorny dilemma with which they were presented at the end of the deposition. MacCameron consented and told Will that whatever he decided to do about the Rule 11 motion—or anything else in the case for that matter—had his complete support.

Yet as Will drove down the sandy dirt road to Bull and Georgia's weathered ocean house he felt that perhaps there had been other reasons for this trip. Personal reasons. Subjects that had been put away like you put away a closed file on the shelf or hang clothes in the back closet because they're out of season. Put away, but not forgotten.

He came into view of the little home with wooden siding worn and bleached gray by the sun and wind and salt air. The two-story beach house with the screened-in front porch was perched up on a bluff overlooking the white dunes, which were spotted with occasional clumps of tall saw grass blowing in the breeze.

As Will pulled his car down into the driveway, Georgia Chambers, a woman of sixty-nine with salt-and-pepper hair, scooted out of the back door and into full view. Will had always remembered her as a creature of eternal optimism and energy. Georgia was wearing blue jeans and a sweatshirt, and her head was cocked slightly to the side, with an enormous grin, and both hands were on her hips in her characteristic pose of spunk and love.

"Willie Chambers, you come over here right now and plant a big kiss on your Auntie Georgia's wrinkled face!"

Georgia held her arms out wide, and Will hugged her slight frame, smelling the lilac water she always wore.

She put her arm through his and led him into the kitchen, where she had a glass of lemonade waiting for him. Clarence bounded in after them. She scolded him gently for not coming down to visit over the years. She ran her fingers through the tangle of his long hair and said, "You are getting to look so like your daddy."

Georgia explained that Bull was waiting for Will at the harbor, where he was working on his big fishing boat. She walked Will out onto the screened-in porch.

There on the porch, just as Will could have expected, was a table with the pieces of a picture puzzle, some connected, some in disarray. Will looked at the semi-completed jigsaw puzzle and reached for the box cover that lay on the floor.

Georgia quickly grabbed his hand away. "No fair. You have to guess first, Willie. Now what does it look like? Guess."

Will studied the collection of pieces that were already fitted together in the middle of the table.

"Looks like a cave," Will remarked.

"Close," Georgia chimed brightly. "It's called the Garden Tomb. That's the tomb that a British general by the name of Gordon discovered in the 1880s. A lot of folks think that was the place where the Lord Jesus was buried and rose again."

"How long have you been working on this?" Will asked.

"Oh, a couple weeks. Only when I get the urge. Bull and I have been so busy doing absolutely nothing that I don't get to it very often!" She laughed loudly and then added, "You know I'm trying to talk your Uncle Bull into taking me over to the Holy Land next year. You know, I've never been. What a thrill that's going to be!"

As they left and walked over to Will's car, he looked back toward the porch.

"I remember you reading to me on that porch when I was a kid."

"Oh yes," Georgia replied. "Remember the little Bible lessons and stories I used to teach you and the other children on the porch? Your daddy would throw a fit! Oh my, he didn't care for that. Well, you know your daddy!" And then she laughed some more.

Will kissed her and hopped in his car with his dog. He promised he wouldn't be such a stranger anymore, and would visit again. Then he started driving along the beach road toward the marina where he expected to find Bull Chambers.

28

DOWN AT THE DOCKS BULL CHAMBERS was working on the deck of his big fishing rig, named *Sweet Georgia Mine.*

A tall, lanky man, Bull had a face that was weathered and deeply lined and showed all of his seventy years. But his arms were tan and muscular. Bull was a man who was lean and sinewy and tough but always met folks with a smile and a gentle voice. From his physical appearance, his gait, and his folksy manner, one might think that Bull had spent his life as a woodsman or a fisherman, rather than presiding over a court of law.

The retired judge gave a big wave from the boat's bow when he saw Will, and the two shook hands warmly as Will climbed on board. Clarence scampered behind him and then quickly plopped on top of one of the boat cushions.

"Thought we'd do some fishing while we talked," Bull said. "Push us off from the pier, will you, while I back her up."

Bull navigated the big fishing boat out of the channel, moving slowly until they started heading toward the open ocean.

On the telephone Will had only told Bull that he had a case to discuss with him. Now, while Will stood next to Bull in the little wheelhouse of the boat as they ventured out into deeper waters, Will launched into the details of *Reichstad vs. MacCameron and* Digging for Truth *Magazine.*

By the time Bull had arrived at his favorite spot for the big ocean tuna and marlin and was gearing the engine down, Will was just finishing his overview of the case, including J-Fox Sherman's ruthless Rule 11 attorney's-fees motion against Will.

Along with his review of that case, however, Will had also talked about a great deal more—his being forced out of his law firm, his money problems, his frustration with his legal career, his irritation at his former managing partner Hadley Bates, his night with Fiona at the little Italian restaurant, and his general impressions of Angus MacCameron's religious views.

Bull addressed Will's legal concerns first.

"I know a little about how J-Fox Sherman operates," Bull said in his slow tarheel drawl, as he baited the thick rod that was locked in next to the fishing chair at the stern. "I had him in my courtroom a number of years ago. It was a complicated product-liability case. He marched down from Washington with his army of legal assistants, you know. Sherman's a lawyer who does to his opponents what I do to those sea bass I like to catch—first he guts them, then he pulls out the spine."

Bull slowed the boat to trolling speed and set Will up in the chair with the wide leather belt around his waist. Will slowly started reeling the line in.

"Hey," Will said, "it's been a lot of years. I hope I remember how to do this."

Bull yelled out, "How do you like the name of my boat?"

"Yeah, I noticed it," Will replied. "Aunt Georgia must have been honored."

"Well," Bull said, "it was kind of a bribe. She hates fishing—and I love it. So when I retired I figured that I had to give the woman her due, somehow, for all the time I spent out on this thing."

After Bull killed the engine he reached into the Styrofoam cooler and pulled out a can of diet soda.

"Georgia thinks I'm a backslider. She's really been working on me. So far she's gotten me to give up my cigar-smoking, give up my drinking, and she has me back at Wednesday-night, midweek services at the Baptist church. I told her I draw the line at my Thursday poker-playing, though."

Bull passed a can of soda over to Will.

The boat was creaking rhythmically as it was buoyed gently on the rolling waves.

"You're not helping me with my legal problem," Will said after a few moments of silence.

"What are you after?"

"I need to know what you think, Bull."

"About what?"

"What have I been talking about here? My case. I've got a decision to make. If I cave in to Sherman and we admit the issue of recklessness in my client's publication of that article, we only have one single thin defense left at trial to try to win this case on—we would have to prove that MacCameron's allegations about Reichstad were substantially true. That's a pretty tall order. On the other hand—if I gamble on the fact that they can't prove recklessness and we take our chances, and Judge Kaye rules against us on that, I may be facing a quarter of a million dollars in legal fees assessed against me."

"Maybe," Bull replied. "But I've seen you pull more legal rabbits out of more legal hats, I swear, boy. You've been in tough spots before."

"This time it's different."

"How?"

"I'm not sure. Maybe I'm just tired. Maybe I'm getting tired of trying cases. Maybe I want to chuck it all and come down here and open up a fishing guide business with you—make a lot of money off the tourists. And maybe it's something else. It just seems like nothing makes any sense. And frankly, I don't think I care anymore," Will said in a distant kind of voice.

"Well, I've been listening to you talk about your case," Bull said. "I've been listening. But I don't really think this is about your case. Not really."

Will glanced at his uncle, then stared out over the slowly rolling blue ocean.

"The last time I saw you was at Audra's funeral. I'll never forget the look on your face. You know, when I was in Korea I remember whenever a soldier would get hit in a serious way—you know, like if he just got gut-shot and his insides were all tore up. And the man would look up at you with that look. The look that said he knew that the life was pouring out of him, and he knew that all hope was gone.

"Well," Bull said, tossing his empty soda can in a bucket, "that was you. My heart just about busted for you when I walked into the funeral parlor and saw you. You looked just like you'd been gut-shot. You honestly did."

Will wanted to say something, but he couldn't. He stretched out his legs so his feet rested on the stern rail, and folded his hands on his fishing rod.

"I'm no great expert on the human heart—no psychologist—" Bull continued, "but I will say this. I think you've probably been carrying the weight of the world around since Audra's death. What happened to that poor, beautiful wife of yours was terrible. She must just have been at the wrong place at the wrong time.

"And you probably figured that if you had done things differently—if you'd have wooed her back to you during the separation—if you'd have put down your pride and gotten her back to you there in Monroeville, things would have been different. Then she wouldn't have been alone in that apartment in Georgetown that night when the break-in happened. And then she wouldn't have been murdered. Now I'll tell you something about regrets,

Will-boy. Regrets are a big load to carry on your back for the rest of your life."

Will choked as he tried to fight back his tears. Bull came up from behind him and placed his hands on Will's shoulders but said nothing. There was quiet for a while, except for the lapping waves and the sound of the boat rolling gently.

"I still miss her," Will said. "Down to my bones." The two men were still again for a few minutes.

Then Bull broke the silence. "I come out here on the big water, especially when everything is calm and blue—the sky and the ocean, like it is today—and I bring up a lot of memories about folks we lost. I think about you losing Audra. And I think about my brother—your dad—and how I wished I could have said goodbye to him. And I think about the two of us, as boys, fishing together. Hiking along the edge of the swampy flats that were a few miles from where we grew up."

"Did Dad ever tell you why he divorced Mom?"

"Never did," Bull replied. "I tried to talk to him about it. I could see that it was driving the two of you apart. But you know your Dad. Proud. A little pompous. Stubborn as the day is long. No, he wouldn't talk much to me about that. He and I were different. I stayed a good ol' boy down here in North Carolina. He moved up to Boston to go to school; he liked playing the part of a Northeastern intellectual.

"I loved your dad. He was a brilliant man. But he could be arrogant. Always wanted to figure things out his way. Never wanted to rely on other folks. That can be a lonely way to live. When he died all of a sudden, that must have been a real shock to you."

"I always figured Dad and I would patch things up. But it never happened," Will mused. "Then one day I got that call from Mom in California. She said she'd been contacted by some of the folks at the newspaper. They'd found him on the floor of his office."

Bull was going to say something—but he was interrupted by a noise. Will's rod bent down violently, banging on the rail. Will straightened up and pulled back on the rod. He muscled the line as he fought the pull at the end of his pole so he could begin reeling in; suddenly a large blue and yellow and green tinted marlin broke the water and leaped in the air, its head jerking frantically side to side as it fought the hook in its mouth.

Bull jumped over to the wheel and straightened out the boat so the line wouldn't get tangled in the motor, and sang out to Will not to lose him.

The marlin dove deep and Will pulled the rod again. He could feel the big fish struggling, pulling, and swimming first in one direction and then another.

Will's arms started tiring as he tenaciously reeled in the fish closer and closer. After twenty minutes of struggle, as Will brought the huge catch up to the side of the boat, they could finally see the glimmering ocean colors of the marlin through the water, just below the surface.

Bull reached over with his long gaff hook and hooked it in the gills. Will unstrapped himself from the chair, and the two pulled the fish up and over, into the bay of the boat. As the heavy weight of the fish slammed down on the deck, Clarence woke up and began barking wildly.

Bull and Will both laughed and congratulated each other, and took a minute to admire this elegant brute of a fish with its huge spiny fan spread out, its gills opening and closing as it lay in the boat.

"How about a catch and release on this one?" Will asked.

"No matter to me. I don't eat 'em," Bull said. "And I'm too cheap to mount 'em."

Then Bull fished around in his bag for a moment and pulled out a little camera. "Here," he said, "let's at least prove to my wife that we were fishing, rather than loafing and drinking down at the Harbor Lights Tavern."

Will needed both hands to pull the marlin up and hold it by the stringer line in front of him as Bull clicked off a couple pictures on his camera. Then they took the pliers, worked the hook out, and slowly lifted and then pushed the big fish back over the side of the boat. The marlin slipped into the water, then made one last, quick break at the surface before it disappeared into the deep.

The two men motored back to shore on the calmly rolling deck of the *Sweet Georgia Mine*. When Clarence started scenting land, and the harbor was coming up close, he began running around excitedly in circles, barking and wagging his shaggy tail.

"You never did give me your advice on my case," Will commented as he leaned into the ocean breeze that was hitting his face and blowing his long hair straight behind him.

"Hmm. Okay. Here it is," Bull said. "This is what I've got to say to you, Will-boy. I think that this case you've got here is more than some fine legal points. And I think that the Good Lord has got the right lawyer on his side in this case. And I think that he is going to make sure that you do the right thing, whatever that is.

"Besides," Bull said as he turned the wheel and powered the boat down, "I'll get your Aunt Georgia to start praying about your case. And after that happens, I wouldn't want to be in J-Fox Sherman's shoes for all the tea in China."

Up ahead where the ocean met the harbor, it was peaceful and clear except for one lone sailboat that was skimming along, parallel to them. Bull Chambers waved to the sailors and began guiding his boat slowly toward his designated slip. He cut the motors, and with his weathered hand on the wheel, he guided it perfectly and effortlessly dockside.

29

WILL WAS CRUISING BACK TO VIRGINIA on the interstate. He knew he had to make some decisions while he drove. Clarence lay, exhausted and sleeping, on the car seat while the lawyer began to rev up his mental engines.

He thought back over each of the details of MacCameron's deposition. And about the issues in the case, and the evidence they had to support their defenses.

But mostly, Will was riveted on Sherman's motion to sanction him with attorney's fees. In order to prevail, Sherman would have to show that MacCameron was reckless in his publishing of the article; but even further he would have to show that Will was contesting that issue with absolutely no evidence to support his conclusion—the conclusion that MacCameron had at least some facts to back up his article when he wrote it.

So, hadn't MacCameron had *some* facts when he wrote the article to indicate that Reichstad might have erred in his conclusions about 7QA? First, there was the possibility that 7QA might have been part of a larger fragment—this was implied by what Richard Hunter had said. And if that were so, then how could Reichstad be so sure that his interpretation of 7QA was correct without also looking at and interpreting the other fragments that might originally have been part of the same piece of writing?

But Will was aware that unless—and until—they could prove the existence of those other fragments, and then actually produce them, this argument was based entirely on inference rather than direct proof.

As to the other accusation that MacCameron made against Reichstad—that he might have been implicated in the deaths of Azid, the antiquities dealer, and Hunter, Will could only see three facts in his favor: 1) Reichstad was in Jerusalem at a conference during the times of their deaths in Bethlehem and Jerusalem, respectively; 2) Hunter believed he was being followed and possibly stalked by someone who wanted his "discovery" (whatever that was); and 3) Reichstad had admitted in his own journal articles that he had obtained the 7QA fragment from Azid—though he said he had purchased it shortly before Azid's "suicide" and of course vehemently denied that Richard Hunter had anything to do with 7QA.

Will thought through the variations in how Judge Kaye might rule on the recklessness issue, and then on whether Will ought to be punished with a huge attorney's-fee sanction for contesting an issue that could not be defended. And, of course, Judge Kaye was always unpredictable.

But there was something else here in the picture that did not make sense. Why did J-Fox Sherman need to slam Will with a motion for attorney's fees so early in the case?

Was there something that Sherman was afraid of? Beyond that, was there some piece of information that they were trying to get from MacCameron and his attorney? Is that why they were using the blackmailing power of an attorney's-fee motion to start squeezing them to settle the case—at almost any cost?

So what did Reichstad really want? wondered Will. He had to know that MacCameron would not have the money to pay any substantial damage judgment, even if one were awarded against him. Will asked himself again: *What is it that Reichstad really wants?*

Of course, Sherman had made a routine demand for the tape from MacCameron's answering machine, the one with Hunter's message, during the deposition. Was that it? Bringing a lawsuit just to get that message tape hardly seemed worth the bother.

Then Will remembered that he had received a large envelope from Sherman just before he took off for North Carolina. In a hurry, he had tossed it unopened into the trunk of his car with the other parts of the MacCameron file.

Will pulled the car off the interstate at a rest stop where there were some picnic tables. He got out of the car, opened the trunk, and retrieved the envelope from Sherman.

In the envelope was a document headed "Plaintiff Dr. Albert Riechstad's First Demand for Documents to Defendants MacCameron and *Digging for Truth* Magazine."

Will scanned the Demand that Sherman had sent him. He was asking for MacCameron to produce to them

> Any and all documents, or papers, in any way connected with, or which are purported to have ever been, at any time, part of, or

> adjacent to, or appurtenant with, that document of antiquity known as the 7QA fragment.

Will read it again. It was the typical language-tortured, overcomplex information request that trial lawyers love to make during discovery. But the meaning behind it was crystal-clear. Sherman and Reichstad were obviously concerned that MacCameron might have, or know something about, other fragments that were originally part of 7QA.

Will grabbed his cell phone and punched in a number. When the voice on the other end answered, Will said, "This is Will Chambers calling on the *Reichstad vs. MacCameron* lawsuit. I want to talk to Mr. Sherman immediately."

After a few moments Sherman's secretary answered, and Will identified himself.

She asked Will to please hold. Then, in less than twenty seconds, Will heard Sherman's voice at the other end.

"Yes Mr. Chambers," Sherman said warmly and confidently. "What can I do for you?"

"We've got some unfinished business," Will added.

"That we do. In fact, I was just reminded that tomorrow is our little deadline on your response to my motion for attorney's fees."

"That was why I called," Will replied, but then said nothing else.

After a pregnant pause Sherman spoke up.

"You know, Will, you and I are both professionals. We do what we have to do to serve the interests of our clients. I can't say that I enjoyed bringing that motion against you. Nothing personal. Just had to be done. And here in this law firm we always do our homework. We've checked up on you and on your legal career. Some nice little cases you've won around the country over the years. So you are a lawyer who can read the law and appreciate the facts of this case just like I can."

"Hmm," Will replied.

"And so," Sherman continued, "I'm sure you know that we've got your client nailed down real tight on the issue of recklessness in publishing that crazy article about my client. You're dead in the water. You're going nowhere with that defense."

"Food for thought," Will responded.

"And that only leaves your defense of 'truth.' And as to that—" Sherman gave a little chuckle, "well, what are you going to do here, turn this lawsuit into some kind of trial of the century? Are you going to solve the mystery of two millennia of Middle Eastern religious history using a guy like Angus

MacCameron as your only expert witness? Of course not. We both know that. I know you are starting your own office now—you are no longer with that Richmond firm any more. Need to pay the bills. Keep the lights on. Build a practice. Of course, this case could destroy you. That would be a pity."

"Yes, wouldn't it," Will commented.

Sherman finally began to unveil the molten core—the golden center.

"Look," Sherman continued, "if you concede in writing that MacCameron was reckless in publishing that article, I will withdraw that motion for attorney's fees against you. And then, perhaps I bring you up here for a real nice lunch. We get special catering from Pierre's. His lobster thermador is out of this world. And you and I talk about the rest of this case—where it is going—perhaps there is something you and your client want that we can give you, and perhaps something you can give us. Negotiation rather than nuclear warfare. What do you say?"

It was now clear to Will. There was something that Reichstad wanted from MacCameron. And he wanted it desperately. He wanted it badly enough to wage a legal war to get it. And it had something to do with other fragments that may once have been part of 7QA. But whatever it was, Will was ready to do hand-to-hand combat before they would get it.

There was another long pause. Then Will said, "I have one question for you."

"What would you like to know?" Sherman asked.

"Tell me something," Will began, bending over his car and scratching the top of his big dog's head. And then Will Chambers smiled and put his last question to J-Fox Sherman:

"Are you ready to rumble?"

30

THE WHITE HOUSE ROSE GARDEN WAS SURROUNDED by a horseshoe of reporters and photographers. The President was smiling as he shook the hand of New Jersey State Trooper Ezer Nabib. The officer and the President were both smiling, frozen in a pose for the cameras, as they held between them a bronzed plaque that read,

Officer Ezer Nabib
For valor and bravery in the line of duty
and for protecting America

After the photo op ended the President waved and was hurried back into the White House.

The President's press secretary walked to the podium. He said, "I apologize for the short notice in announcing this press conference. I know that this was originally just scheduled to be the presentation of the commendation to Officer Nabib. However, we do have some information we would like to give you."

The reporters scurried closer to the podium, elbowing each other for position.

"First, the U.S. Joint Forces Command has finished its initial investigation of the incident involving the rental truck entering New York—the incident for which Officer Nabib was decorated today. It is their conclusion that the truck was in fact carrying a MIRV-type missile outer shell. However, it was *only a missile shell* and was carrying no nuclear load; it was incapable of detonating. Our national security was never imperiled. The U.S. Joint Forces Command had an opportunity for a real-life, real-time test, and it performed admirably.

"Second, the driver of that truck, Mr. Ajadi, was apparently an unwitting pawn in this incident. He has no known ties to any terrorist organization.

He was paid handsomely to drive that truck, but we have every indication that he never looked in the truck, and never knew its contents."

And with that the press secretary smiled, and turned the page of his notes.

"And that leads to our third point. The State Department and the Justice Department have informed us that the new Islamic Democratic Republic of Iran has taken into custody three individuals who they believe were involved in the MIRV missile incident. While this investigation is still in its tentative stages, this much we know: The MIRV missile was American-made.

"We can only surmise that it must have been stolen from an American base during the time of the prior administration and under the watch of the prior President. Apparently, a Russian crime syndicate was given this weapon, and it in turn arranged for its transportation into the United States for reasons that are not now clear. But there is every indication that the Russian operatives were smuggling the missile into the U.S. at the behest of someone with great power and influence—the international terrorist Abdul el Alibahd, we suspect.

"The President believes that we are witnessing a triumph of cooperation between America and its Arab partners in peace in stamping out the threat of terrorism. After all, it was Ezer Nabib, an Islamic Arab, who courageously apprehended and secured a truck carrying a device that may well lead us to the world's number-one terrorist.

"We have Saudi Arabia apprehending, and bringing to swift justice, the two perpetrators of the Wall Street bombing—both of those criminals, of course, were operatives of Abdul el Alibahd.

"And today we have the announcement of Iran's cooperation in the capture of three suspects in the MIRV missile incident. All of the bridge-building that our President has accomplished with the Islamic and Middle East appears to be bearing fruit. And of course, a special thanks goes to the State Department, and particularly Undersecretary Kenneth Sharptin for his visionary diplomacy in aiding that bridge-building process."

A flurry of hands shot up but the press secretary ignored them and indicated that no questions would be taken at this time. Someone shouted out,

"The Convention is still six months away, but already there is a lot of talk about Kenneth Sharptin as the President's choice for replacing the vice president in light of his advanced colon cancer. Can you comment on that?"

The press secretary smiled but did not answer, and waved as he walked toward the French doors of the White House.

Jack Hornby was in the back of the news pack. He had his notepad flipped open to the triangle he had previously drawn. He pulled out his pen and wrote down, off to the side of his triangle, the words "nuclear scare."

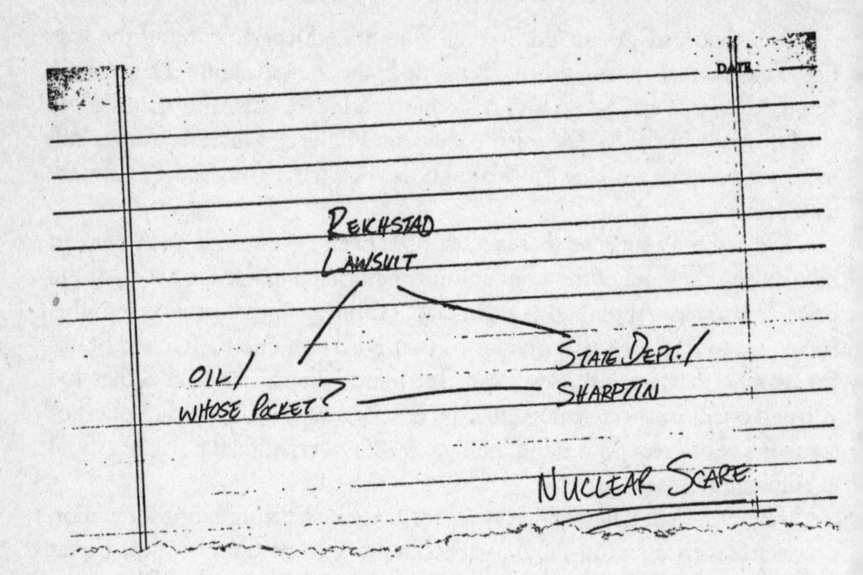

Hornby looked at "nuclear scare" and wondered how it might fit into the picture he was trying to put together. Perhaps it didn't fit in at all.

The reporter looked down at the list of people he was calling. Each name was a candidate who Hornby thought might be able to make some sense out of the three points of his triangle. Attorney Will Chambers was next. He hadn't spoken to Will since the ill-fated Reichstad story, but it looked like this was the time to reconnect.

31

When Will returned from North Carolina he drove straight to Generals' Hill. After dinner he wandered through a couple of the rooms in the first floor. They lay in various stages of incomplete renovation. Each room had its own fireplace, but the tuck-pointing in the brick and stonework was not finished. The walls were still demolished down to the studs. Bringing back the Virginia mansion to its original charm and elegance had been a dream of Will and Audra's.

That evening, for the first time in a long while, Will started thinking about completing this job. Maybe he could start spending his weekends doing some of the carpentry work himself. It would be a welcome relief from the pressures of his law practice, and a way of starting to get his life back together.

When Will went to sleep that night, Clarence was already curled up at the foot of the bed. Will's sleep, since Audra's death, had been fitful and restless. But that night he would sleep deeply and peacefully. And when he woke up, somehow things would feel better.

When he arrived at the office the next morning, Betty was not at her desk. On the desk there was a telephone message that Jack Hornby, reporter from the *Washington Herald*, had called.

There was also an envelope addressed to Will. He opened it up. It read,

> Dear Will:
>
> In light of your repeated failure to follow through with my raise I am hereby tendering my resignation, effective this very moment.
>
> Yours very truly,
> Betty

"Great," Will muttered to himself. With the Reichstad lawsuit starting to build up steam and the trial only a few months away, this was no time to train a new secretary.

The telephone rang and Will picked it up. It was a lawyer from the public defender's office in New York.

The man explained that he had met Will once, many years ago when Will was trying cases for the Law Project of the South. He had been a law student at the time and had sat in on one of Will's trials. Will had sued a rundown mental health institution that had covered up the deaths of handicapped children who were being abused while in its care. The public defender explained how, after the winning verdict was announced, he had come up and congratulated Will on his victory.

Will thanked him for remembering the case he had handled but no, he did not remember him.

"How can I help you?" Will asked.

"It's only because I remembered your name. That's why I'm calling."

Will wondered why this lawyer was not getting to the point.

"So, what's up?"

"Well," the public defender said, "I don't know how much I want to discuss over the telephone."

"Can you give me a hint what this is about?"

"I am the lawyer for Rahji Ajadi."

Will paused for a moment. The other lawyer spoke as if that name were supposed to mean something.

"You must have read about my client. He's the guy who was driving the rental truck in the MIRV missile incident."

Now Will clicked. "Yeah, I know exactly who you are talking about. So, what can I do for you?"

"I just wanted to know whether you were working for the government in any capacity."

"No," Will said, "I've been in private law practice."

"Did you have any connection at all with the case that the government was trying to build against my client?"

"None whatsoever," Will answered, a little mystified.

The other lawyer took a second and then he said, "Okay then. If you're sure about that, then I'm sorry I bothered you."

"Wait a minute," Will interjected. "Why do you want to know?"

"I am calling from my office phone. I don't feel comfortable going into details. Since the point that I was appointed to represent Ajadi, I have been under a microscope because of the national-security aspect of the case. For all I know my telephone is tapped."

"Can you tell me what this has to do with me?"

"Possibly. Your name came up."

"How?"

"My client, over the course of two days, was questioned by almost every agency in the federal government. But at one point, just one question was asked—it was a little bizarre actually. They obviously didn't realize that I might know who you were. Someone asked my client about you."

"Are you sure they got the name right?"

"Yep."

"Are you certain they were talking about me—maybe there is someone else out there with the same name."

"Not unless you've got a twin brother with your name who is also a lawyer in Virginia."

"So who…how did this come up?"

"I'm really not hot on saying a lot over the phone."

Will thought a minute. "If I come up and visit with you there in New York, would you be willing to explain this to me?"

"I've already got a waiver from my client to discuss his case. He wants to get to the bottom of this, like I do. Frankly, I got him an unbelievably sweet deal considering how things could have come down. But he still insists that someone set him up and he wants me to get him some answers if I can."

"Will you talk to me?"

"Yeah. I will. But you have to come up here. Give me your fax number and I will fax the location where I want to meet you. How about tomorrow?"

"Fine," Will replied, "I'll probably take the train up."

Will gave him his fax number and they hung up. Will racked his brain for some explanation as to why his name would have surfaced during the interrogation of Rahji Ajadi, but could come up with nothing.

But there had to be a reason why his name had been mentioned in that investigation up in New York. Facts have causes, he had always believed. Sometimes to find the causes it just took the right kind of digging.

The phone rang again and it was Tiny Heftland. Tiny explained that he had finished his investigation of every scholar and researcher who ever wrote an article critical of Albert Reichstad. None of them had any hard information disproving Reichstad's conclusions about 7QA. And none of them, except one, wanted anything to do with being an expert witness for Angus MacCameron and against Albert Reichstad.

"Who's the one who might be an expert witness for us?" Will asked.

"Her name is Mary Margaret Giovanni," Heftland said. "American-born, but raised abroad. Former nun. Was a consultant in ancient Semitic languages and biblical antiquities at the Vatican. Has written and lectured on the subject of..." With that, Tiny had to look at his notes to remind himself of the word.

"...written and lectured on the subject of first century *papyrology*."

"That's the study of papyrus writings," Will noted.

"Bingo."

"Is she going to help us?"

"Don't know. She said she wants to think about it. When I mentioned MacCameron's name she said she wanted to check out our guy first before she was willing to sign on as an expert witness on his side."

"When will she let us know?"

"Couple of weeks."

"That's too long," Will said. "Our trial date is only about four months away. Our deadline for naming experts is in three weeks."

"I'll have her call you," Tiny responded. "Hey, did you see Reichstad's research center up in Maryland?"

"Yeah. Nothing particular. No fences. No security. Just a plain office building."

"That's my point," Tiny explained. "That's why I wanted you to see it yourself. Remember, I did security work for the State Department in my bygone days when I worked with their security forces in the Middle East. So, I crawled around on that property with Walter Ugett—the electronics whiz kid I work with sometimes. What we discovered is that this research center has very sophisticated remote sensors set up on the grounds. I mean, like the kind you find on the White House lawn to prevent crazy guys and terrorists from getting onto the property. That kind of sophisticated security. It beats me why a bunch of ivory-tower experts in ancient history would need that kind of world-class security."

"Have Giovanni call me," Will said, trying to cut short his conversation, since he heard the fax machine ringing in the other room. But then he thought of one more question.

"By the way," Will asked, "do you have any kind of dope on the MIRV missile incident—anything turned up for you?"

"Only what I read in the papers or get from the TV," Tiny responded.

"Do you have any thoughts on it?"

"In my professional opinion," Tiny said with a measured sense of importance, "that whole deal stinks more than my garage when I forget to put out my garbage bags for pick-up. You know, when it's summer, and it's really hot, and things really get cooking up?"

"I think I get the picture," Will added.

"That operation was just not right. Something's really weird about that deal."

After hanging up with Tiny, Will walked to the copy room. On the fax machine was a note from the public defender in New York. It read simply,

> Meet me tomorrow at noon on the steps of the New York Public Library. Please come alone.

Will picked up the fax. He was starting to get the feeling that there just might be a healthy side to paranoia. As much as he did not want to admit it, he was starting to wonder whether there was more to *Reichstad vs. MacCameron* than just one more lawsuit—even an unusual lawsuit at that. Rather than leave the fax in his office he folded it and stuck it in his pocket.

After trying to return Jack Hornby's call and only getting his voice mail, Will left a message for him. Then he called Jacki Johnson at the D.C. office of Bates, Burke & Meadows. Jacki was on her way to court so she couldn't talk long, but she was warm and asked how Will was doing.

"Betty quit today," Will explained.

"Sorry to hear that," Jacki said. "What are you going to do about office help?"

"I thought you might know someone."

"Let me think about it," Jacki said. "Say, what did you ever do about that lawsuit that came in—you know, the one with the old professor or whatever he was. J-Fox Sherman was on the other side."

"I took the case," Will replied.

"So, it's Will Chambers versus the great and powerful OZ?" Jacki said with a laugh. "Well, you always liked those kinds of odds. Listen, I've got to run. I really have been thinking a lot about you. Howard says hello. We have to get together for lunch sometime. Please keep in touch."

Will hung up the phone. It felt good to touch base with Jacki. He could have used her help on the MacCameron case. But that was not going to happen now. Will was facing the fact that this case would have to be a solo flight.

32

WILL RESERVED A TICKET FOR THE FOLLOWING morning on the early train to New York City, and then sat down to review the transcript of the MacCameron deposition that the court reporter had dropped off. He knew that analyzing the precise wording of Sherman's questions and MacCameron's answers would be essential.

One of Will's first conclusions was that MacCameron had not committed "perjury" at the deposition, as Sherman had suggested—not even close. Sherman's question had been whether the "reason" for MacCameron's leaving the University of Edinburgh was that the University was entertaining charges of misconduct against him. MacCameron had denied that the "reason" he had left that University was that they had been thinking about bringing plagiarism charges against him.

After the deposition, Will had asked MacCameron about the incident at the University of Edinburgh.

MacCameron admitted that at first the University officials had thought he had plagiarized the rough draft of a paper of another graduate student. MacCameron had denied it when they interviewed him about the incident. While the matter was pending, he had decided to follow his heart and go to America to join his future wife, Helen. It was only after he had arrived in the United States and enrolled in the college in West Virginia that the University of Edinburgh officials learned the truth: It had actually been the other graduate student who had tried to use the ideas he found in one of MacCameron's papers as his own. MacCameron invited Will to contact the University administration in Edinburgh to verify that fact.

But Will had been genuinely concerned about MacCameron's physical demeanor during the deposition. When Will mentioned that, his client then confessed that he had a history of heart problems and was prone to fatigue. He apologized for not being "on the mark" during the deposition.

In further review of the transcript, Will saw very clearly that Sherman and Reichstad wanted to put MacCameron on trial. They would try to match the Scot's modest educational qualifications against the world-renowned Reichstad's credentials. But this case, Will concluded, could not be about Reverend Angus MacCameron. It was bigger than the personal problems, or professional accomplishments, of either of the parties.

Will thought back to one of the sound bites that he had given to Jack Hornby. Will had commented,

> If my client was correct in what he wrote, and it is our contention that he was—then truth itself is on trial.

What Will now realized was that his description of the case to Hornby was more accurate than he could have imagined.

Sherman and Reichstad would want to make it a trial of the smallest and most precise details. Sherman would try to force the case into a small and tortured box of carefully controlled facts.

Yet Will knew that, while he would have to answer all of the minute factual details raised by Sherman in order to prevail, he would have to go one step farther. Will Chambers would have to paint the big picture on the big canvas. "Truth itself is on trial." But the truth about what? Or who?

Will was beginning to understand. This case was really about the very question raised by Reichstad's sensational revelation of the 7QA fragment. It was the question that Will had not wanted to face, perhaps for reasons more personal and more profound than he had ever thought. But it was the question that he now had to answer for himself and ultimately prove to a jury and a federal judge: Did the remains of the body of Jesus of Nazareth still lie in a tomb somewhere in Jerusalem as the 7QA fragment seemed to indicate? Or did Jesus walk out of his own grave—thereby making Reichstad's interpretation of 7QA false, or at the very least, grossly inaccurate?

What if, Will now reasoned with himself, a world-class historian informed the whole world that he had discovered a single small fragment of a historical document from the late 1700s that proved that George Washington was not the leader of the Continental Army during the Revolutionary War? How would such a report be treated? Clearly, he concluded, it might cause experts to call such a person either a liar—or at least an incompetent historian.

But would that situation be any different from the 7QA dispute? The difference probably rested, Will thought to himself, in the degree of certainty we have about the facts surrounding George Washington's life. We are all pretty certain about George Washington. We are less certain about what happened in ancient Israel two thousand years ago.

But what if, after objectively viewing the evidence, there was only one reasonable conclusion about Jesus? What if the credible facts all pointed to his actual resurrection? Could that ever be proven in a court of law? Was this the ultimate defense of truth that Will would have to produce in trial? Will wondered how he could ever hope to be able to prove something of such monumental significance—something that had been debated by historians, theologians, and philosophers for two thousand years.

As Will was packing up for the day, the phone rang. When he picked it up there came over the line a voice that he had not heard in years—a deep, booming southern drawl.

"Will Chambers—how are you, my friend?"

"Is this brother Billy Joe Highlighter?"

"Yes, my friend, it certainly is. Will, how are you?"

"Fine, Billy Joe. How about yourself?"

"Oh, I will tell you, my friend, I am Spirit-filled and blessed by the Lord!"

Highlighter was an old client of Will's. After Will had left the ACLU in New York out of disgust over its new policy of using federal racketeering laws against pro-lifers, he had joined the Law Project of the South as one of its civil rights trial lawyers. He had won a number of brilliant victories, but after only two years had found himself on the street again. The cause was simple: He had publicly insulted his legal director in an argument over a case.

The case had involved Reverend Highlighter. Against the direct orders of his boss, Will had agreed to represent the controversial and flamboyant evangelist. Brother Billy Joe ran a large church called The Church of the Golden Road in Nashville, Tennessee. He had been preaching a series of sermons against immorality that were televised on a local cable channel. And in each of the sermons he railed against the local district attorney, who had refused to prosecute prostitution, gambling, homosexual bathhouses, and other "vice" crimes in the greater Nashville area. Highlighter finished his series of sermons against public immorality by marching his congregation down to city hall. There he preached, in his typical athletic style, on the sidewalk right outside the prosecutor's office.

The district attorney happened to be running for re-election at the time, and he didn't care for the "hair-shirt exhortations," as Billy Joe would call them. The prosecutor also didn't like being called the "Herod of Nashville."

Unfortunately for Brother Billy Joe, that was about the time that a fire broke out one night in the sanctuary of the church and the whole property burned to the ground. But the building had been recently insured for a million dollars. When it was learned that the church had been considerably in debt at the time of the fire, the local prosecutor, who had managed to win re-election by only a dozen votes, saw his chance for revenge.

He wasted no time convening a grand jury and charging Highlighter with criminal arson. Brother Billy Joe, feeling that he was being unjustly persecuted in retaliation for the exercise of his First Amendment–protected right to verbally tar and feather the prosecutor from his pulpit, contacted Will Chambers.

This was the kind of thing Will Chambers relished. By then, the affair had attracted national attention, and Will's boss ordered him to withdraw from the case and accused him of being a glory hound and a grandstander. Will stayed with the case anyway. And when one newspaper reporter asked him if the rumors were true that his boss had disagreed with his decision to represent Highlighter, Chambers gave one of his classic self-destructive comebacks. According to newspaper reports he said,

> Anyone who cannot see the clear First Amendment implications of this tragic and unjust case has one of two problems. Either he cannot read the clear language of the Constitution, or else he has suffered a serious head injury—the kind that makes you think you are a visitor to planet earth and your real home is somewhere outside our solar system.

Chambers' boss was not amused and Will was summarily fired. He continued representing Highlighter on his own, out of a local motel-room-turned-law-office. Will won an acquittal for Brother Billy Joe, and his victory made headlines around the country. But he paid a price. His liberal colleagues considered him a traitor of colossal proportions. Not only had he alienated himself from the ACLU, but now he was representing Bible-thumping fundamentalists like Highlighter.

Will hadn't spoken with Billy Joe in years. But the television evangelist wasted no time explaining why he called.

"Will, I was just at an evangelists' conference in Biloxi, Mississippi. And while I was there I heard via the grapevine about a case that I believe you have going on, involving a Harvard professor by the name of Albert Reichstad. And I was further informed that your case concerns that snake-oil piece of parlor-trick chicanery known as the 7QA fragment. Is this true?"

Will smiled. Brother Billy Joe had apparently not mellowed over the years.

"Yes. The case involves 7QA."

"Well," the preacher continued, "back when you vindicated me against the false charges of criminal arson I covenanted with the Lord. I told the Lord that if ever I could do something for you—consistent with the commands of Scripture—I would do it. Now the first and most important thing I could do for you is to introduce you to the person of the Lord Jesus Christ. In the years since we last talked, have you considered getting to know Jesus Christ in a personal way, Will, by accepting his finished work on the cross and inviting him into your heart?"

"Let's just say that I am looking into the person of Jesus as we speak."

"Good. Very good. I will pray to that end," Highlighter responded. "Now, secondly. I am, as you know, schooled in Bible exposition. If there is any way I can assist you in this highly important case, please let me know. I would be honored to be an expert witness for you. You know, I am also schooled in New Testament Greek. It is quite important, particularly if you are going to be disproving this preposterous 7QA hoax, to understand New Testament Greek—the language of the Gospels."

Will thanked Brother Billy Joe for calling and indicated that if he needed him to assist he would certainly give him a call. Will knew that there was no way that he could use Brother Billy Joe as an expert witness. The reasons exceeded the number of fingers on both hands. Yet one of Highlighter's comments did seem important.

Will closed up the office. In the hallway he greeted Hattie as she was humming some vaguely familiar tune and pulling her rolling cart, mop, and bucket.

After leaving the office Will decided to take a detour over to the big bookstore that stayed open late. He wandered over to the religion section. After a few moments he located a Greek New Testament. He flipped through it and discovered that it contained an English translation of the New Testament side-by-side with the Greek. He also picked up an introductory text on New Testament Greek.

From the bookstore Will headed home to Generals' Hill. As he got out of his car and locked it up for the night, he stopped for a moment outside and smelled the powerful fragrance of boxwoods, and listened to the rustling trees of the surrounding woods. He did love this place. As he walked up to the towering columns on the front porch, he could hear Clarence barking joyously in the front room, waiting for him on the other side of the big front door.

33

IT WAS EARLY IN THE MORNING, and there was a warm mist in the air from the rain that had fallen the night before. From the back window in his kitchen Will looked out over the orchards and the acreage beyond. In an hour or so the fog would begin dissipating, but now it lay like a carpet of white vapor in the green rolling terrain past the orchards and all the way to the little creek that served as the boundary of his property. By the time the mist would lift, Will would already be on the train bound for New York City.

Will hugged the neck of his big golden retriever, grabbed his briefcase and raincoat, and strolled the eighth of a mile or so down the long tree-lined driveway to the county road. He had decided to leave his Corvette locked up at the house and take a cab down to the train station. By the time he reached the end of the driveway the cab was still nowhere in sight. Will glanced at the overcast morning sky, and then pulled out his cell phone and called his answering service. Only one call had come in, one from Angus MacCameron. In the final part of his message, MacCameron explained,

> So, I have received your bill, Will. I do know the costs are going to mount in this case. Unfortunately, subscriptions to *Digging for Truth* have dropped drastically. We have serious budget problems. But I am sure the Lord will provide. I'm not quite sure how we are going to pay you from this point on...but don't worry. We'll figure something out. Thanks.

Will had learned early on in his legal career that, while justice may be equal, that doesn't mean it comes cheap. Tiny Heftland, through his work thus far in the case, had all but paid back the debt he owed to Will for past services. From this point on the meter would be running. They had hired the voice expert to analyze the tape-recorded message from Richard Hunter. Will had sent a written demand for Sherman to get his client to turn over the original 7QA fragment so that Will's experts could evaluate it. Those experts would have to be paid.

And then there was Dr. Giovanni. If she agreed to testify for them, she would have to be paid. And there were depositions to pay for. And Will's time commitment on this case, which had already been considerable, was about to become enormous. Now there was a doubt as to whether his client was able to continue paying him.

As if that were not enough, the question of Sherman's quarter-of-a-million-dollar motion against Will still hung in the balance. After Will had thrown down the gauntlet to him in their last conversation, J-Fox was going to come after Will like a buzz saw on wheels.

As the cab pulled up, Will felt the burden of the stakes against him. A one-man office versus one of the nation's largest and most prestigious law firms. MacCameron's dwindling financial resources versus a funding source for Dr. Reichstad that seemed to be limitless. Reichstad as a plaintiff, the man who had become the darling of America's cultural and religious intelligentsia, and who taught at Harvard, published books, and ran an internationally recognized research center. On the other side there was MacCameron as a defendant, a man who had graduated from a little Bible college in West Virginia that no one had heard of and ran a hysterical little magazine that fewer and fewer people were buying.

The ride to the train station was quiet. The cabbie tried to engage him in conversation, but Will's mind was somewhere else. He had been in tough spots before. But not quite like this. Yet he knew that, while there was nothing that could be done about *some* of the odds against him, there was something he could do about *his* preparation for the case. He had a five-hour train ride, each way, up to New York City and back. Will had planned on using that time to school himself on the rudiments of the New Testament Gospels. He would block out of mind the mounting pressures and focus all of his mental energy on the case. That was a knack he had developed in his career. He would have to draw on that ability now more than ever before.

As Will settled into his seat on the train, he pulled out a Bible, the Greek New Testament, and the introductory text to the New Testament Greek language. He planned on reading the Gospels on the way up to New York City, and then delving into some of the basics about Greek on the way back. MacCameron had suggested that Will start by reading all four of the Gospel accounts of the resurrection.

When, after a little fumbling, he found Matthew, Mark, Luke, and John, he then took out a little pad of colored sticky tabs. He marked the pages where, in each Gospel, the story of the burial and resurrection began. That way he could flip from one to the other and compare them.

The train was not crowded, and he had space to spread out his books and files on the seat next to him. As the train rocked and creaked Will read through the accounts in all four Gospels. Then he went back and read them again.

But he was having a problem focusing. After the second reading he discovered his problem. He had never spent any time reading the Bible before. These New Testament books had immediately confronted him with tales of angels and a dead Jesus who had arisen from the grave. He found the entire story too incredible to take seriously. He set the Bible down for a minute and thought. Then he had an idea—really, more of a new perspective. A change of focus.

What would happen, he thought to himself, *if I forget that this is religious literature?* Perhaps that was the key. *What if I treat this as if it were an ancient transcript from a long-since forgotten court proceeding? If I look at the accounts as the testimony of witnesses in court?*

Will started reading again. He then went back and reread the accounts for a fourth time, but this time he did so with a legal pad on his lap. At the top he wrote four headings: Matthew / Mark / Luke / John.

As he read each account of the resurrection he numbered and charted the essential facts, descriptions, and events. Will ignored the "religious" component of the stories, merely treating them as testimonies of eyewitnesses (or accounts that could be traced to eyewitnesses)—something he had done for years as a trial lawyer.

After he had charted the basic facts of each account in each column, he went back and started evaluating them.

The first thing he noticed in the Gospel stories was the factor of "consistency/individuality." Will knew from his trial experience that, when several witnesses to an event later describe that same event, in order to warrant belief, their stories had to possess both of these two convincing facets—much like the two sides of a same coin. The first facet was basic consistency. Though differences are always present in multiple-witness accounts of the same event, the basic facts must be able to mesh.

In Will's review of his notes, he saw that all four of the Gospel accounts contained the same basic factual pattern, with more than a dozen factual components in common.

All four of the Gospels reported that some women—all of whom who were familiar with Jesus and had personal knowledge of the site of the tomb where he was buried—had returned to the tomb several days after the corpse of Jesus had been buried. They were there to anoint the body. 7QA, by contrast, specifically indicated that some unspecified persons "could not return to prepare the body..." Thus, on that point alone, 7QA was irrefutably at odds with the four Gospel accounts, and in particular the Gospel of Mark.

Will saw that all four of the stories also said that the visit to the tomb occurred very early in the morning—just at the break of dawn, on the "first day of the week." All four accounts prominently mentioned a disciple by the name of Mary being among those visiting. All of the stories mentioned that the women had witnessed the fact that the large stone that had been rolled in front of the tomb to seal it had been moved before they got there, and that the tomb was open, and that the tomb no longer contained the corpse of Jesus. And all four accounts included a reference to a subsequent face-to-face meeting between a resurrected Jesus and his disciples.

There were some other significant consistencies that Will noted. Three out of the four Gospels mentioned an encounter at the tomb between Mary and at least one being described as an "angel," who announced that Jesus had risen. And those three were all consistent in describing the emotional response of Mary to that encounter.

The flip-side facet of "individuality" was also present in these accounts. Will knew that the hallmark of accurate multiple-witness testimony was not only that all must agree as to the central facts, but that each observation should differ slightly in the details—details that one witness may have observed but another may not have noticed. When four witnesses recite exactly the same facts in the same way, that immediately points to the possibility that the witnesses consorted together to fashion a unified story, or even worse, to manufacture a lie.

Will observed that each story bore the hallmark of setting forth individual and unique facts—but not in a way that would logically contradict the other Gospels. In particular, Matthew and Mark mentioned one angelic meeting with Mary and the other women. Luke mentioned two. Dr. Reichstad, in some of the writings Will had reviewed, had ridiculed the Gospel accounts for such "discrepancies."

But to Will it was much like the situation at an armed robbery. One witness on the street corner sees, and later testifies that he saw, "*one*" police officer draw his gun on a robber he was chasing. Another witness, closer and at a better angle, might see that same officer and also a *second* officer, obscured from the first witness's view by a parked car, also pursuing the bank robber with his gun drawn. Are the two witnesses to be disbelieved because they both accurately observed the same incident from two different positions? To Will, the point seemed so elementary, it surprised him that someone with Reichstad's qualifications would have missed it.

Will looked out of the window as the train reduced its speed and the cadence of click-clacks of the rails beneath him slowed down. The train eased into the station at Philadelphia for a short stop.

An influx of passengers was arriving, and Will moved his books and papers off the seat next to him so an elderly man with a cane and a gray fedora could sit down in the neighboring seat. Will had already moved onto the second characteristic he had noted in the Gospels—the "credibility" of the witnesses.

Will was impressed at the believable way in which the main characters were portrayed. Three out of the four accounts specifically described the kind of awe-struck emotion one would expect in a person who confronts a supernatural event. Matthew described the "fear" and "joy" of the women; Mark mentioned their "trembling" and "astonishment" as they ran, pell-mell, from the scene. Luke detailed how the women were "terrified" and fell with their faces to the ground during the angelic encounter at the tomb.

Will remembered hearing ghost stories as a child when he was at camp, and how the hair would rise on the back of his neck. There was something authentic about the way these stories recounted the very human reaction of these followers of Jesus.

Yet something struck Will even more strongly: the credible way that the disciples of Jesus were portrayed. Genuine doubt and initial disbelief was a constant theme in the Gospels. If these accounts were fabrications and lies, why hadn't these disciples portrayed themselves in a positive light? Why hadn't they written themselves into the stories as paragons of unswerving faith and fidelity to Jesus, their hero?

In one of his journal articles, Riechstad had written that the writers of the Gospels, and the disciples, and the believers in the early Christian church were infected by the naivete of nonscientific first-century ignorance and superstition—thus, they were able to talk themselves into believing the miracle stories that they themselves were actually inventing.

But Will found something quite different in his study of the accounts. When Mary first encountered the empty tomb—when it was "still dark," and presumably before she met any "angel"—she ran and told Peter and the other disciples. Her first reaction was *not* to believe that Jesus had miraculously risen. Rather, she had the kind of common sense, empirical skepticism that Will appreciated. According to the Gospel of John, she had initially concluded simply that "they have taken away the Lord out of the tomb, and we do not know where they have laid Him."

According to Luke's account, when Mary reported the empty tomb and her encounter with an angel to the disciples, their initial reaction was exactly what Will would have expected from the most skeptical twenty-first century witness: "These words appeared to them as nonsense, and they would not believe them."

And in Matthew, even when the risen Jesus bodily presented himself to the disciples, not all of them instantly believed: "But some were doubtful." Will found that, in John's Gospel, one follower by the name of Thomas had refused to believe until he had had the chance to personally inspect the nail holes in Jesus' hands, and the scar in his side where the Roman soldier had thrust in a spear.

To Will, these New Testament witnesses and followers were simply not gullible or naive in the way that Reichstad and his compatriots had assumed.

As the train slowed down and entered Newark, New Jersey, for a short stop, Will had begun examining his third conclusion. This one he had labeled "factual irrelevancies."

He knew that one of the marks of factual accuracy is the presence of the seemingly *irrelevant* detail that a witness initially gives. When Will would meet with a new client for the first time—someone who had experienced some great trauma or injustice, or had some important story to tell—often the client would just spill out needless and seemingly irrelevant factual information. The reason for this is that the client knows only that he or she has a story to tell. A person with a story wants to tell it all, and let the lawyer figure out what the facts mean in the eyes of the law.

As Will viewed the accounts of the resurrection, this was the one aspect of the story that impacted him more than any other. In the Gospel of John, there was an abundance of factual detail about the inspection of the empty tomb—much of it secondary and seemingly irrelevant to the main point that Jesus had been resurrected and was no longer there. Yet all of it bore the marks of eyewitness observation and therefore corroborated the story.

One of the disciples ran faster than Peter and got to the tomb first. Then in order to look into the empty tomb Peter ended up "stooping and looking in," implying a small opening with a low doorway.

And when they looked into the empty tomb they didn't just see that Jesus' body was absent. Peter also saw something else—something having powerful testimonial value to Will as a trial lawyer. He "saw the linen wrappings lying there, and the face-cloth which had been on His head, not lying with the linen wrappings, but rolled up in a place by itself."

If the body had been stolen, or simply moved from the tomb, there would have been no reason, Will concluded, to have taken the time to painstakingly remove the linen wrappings from the body—and certainly no reason to take the time to carefully "roll up" the face covering

But secondly, the reference to "the face-cloth which had been on His head, not lying with the linen wrappings, but rolled up in a place by itself" told Will that there had been deliberate and intentional action—by someone or something. That action had taken place within the tomb between the time Jesus had been buried and the time, Sunday morning, that the witnesses had arrived and found the tomb was empty. The linen wrappings had been intentionally removed and discarded. The face-cloth had been carefully rolled up and placed down in the tomb at a slightly different spot.

All this could not have been the result of grave-robbing followers who grabbed the body and dragged it out so as to bury it elsewhere—in the hopes of perpetrating a fraud on the world. And the enemies of Jesus would certainly not have had any reason to disturb the body. In fact, they had every reason to try to ensure that it remained exactly where it lay.

The more that Will thought on it, the more he felt that what he was reading in the Gospel accounts was an authentic description of a corpse that was simply not acting like a corpse. There were evidences of an event that was convincingly factual and observable—yet unexplainable by human reason or scientific theory. Dare he admit it to himself? Here were the powerful, tangible traces of what should happen when the mundane, physical world is intersected by the supernatural. When the ordinary facts of life encounter the divine.

Will had lost track of the time. Raising his head, suddenly he was aware that the train was pulling into Penn Station in New York City. The elderly man next to him glanced over at the Bible in Will's lap.

"You a preacher?"

"No," Will replied, "I'm a lawyer."

The old man gave him a strange look. As if the idea of a lawyer reading a Bible didn't make much sense to him. After a moment the train came to a slow, rocking stop.

After getting to his feet stiffly and with difficulty, the old man turned to Will and said, "Don't care much for *that* stuff," nodding his head toward the Bible that Will was holding. Then he added, "I've got more important things to worry about."

The old man cautiously inched his way to the steps, leaning heavily on his cane as he walked, with Will impatiently walking behind him.

34

WILL MADE HIS WAY OUT OF THE DINGY, cavernous confines of Penn Station and into sunlight, where he was greeted with the roar of New York City street noise. He hailed a cab over to the New York Public Library.

As he climbed out of the cab on the west side of Fifth Avenue, Will realized that he had not asked for a physical description of the lawyer he was supposed to meet. So as he walked across the wide plaza in front of the library he quickly scanned the crowds of pedestrians, some walking, others mingling in front of the huge stone columns and high arched entrances of the library.

Then he noticed a short man in his thirties with horn-rimmed glasses, wearing a corduroy jacket and a tie loosened at the neck, with a newspaper tucked under his arm. The man was walking toward him. When he was right in front of Will he extended his hand but kept it close to him and looked around as he did. His expression was worried-looking and his face was locked in a kind of a grimace.

"You haven't changed much," the man said. "I'm the guy from the public defender's office. Let's start walking." The public defender then gave a little nod of his head.

With that the two lawyers started strolling down toward Fortieth Street, wading through the tide of pedestrians that was cramming the sidewalks during the noon hour.

Will didn't waste any time.

"How did my name come up in this MIRV missile incident?" he asked as they walked along.

"There was this long line of federal agencies that were interrogating my client, one after another. The last agency in line brought it up," the public defender answered, still glancing around him.

"Which one?"

"The State Department—their lawyers."

"Why?"

"You got me," the man answered. "We had two days of interviews. I had worked out a really sweet deal for my client, but it required him to spill his guts about everything he knew about the truck, the guys who hired him to do this, and so on. Most of the people interrogating my client were either prosecutor types or experienced investigators. Except at the end. These two pencil-pusher types from the State Department came in at the end, basically with a shopping list of names, and wanted to know if my client ever talked to—or had any contact with—this long catalogue of people."

"What kind of people?" Will asked.

"I didn't recognize any of the names except for the last name they asked about—yours. They mentioned it and I couldn't believe what I had just heard. They wanted to know if Mr. Ajadi, the driver of that rented truck, had ever talked to you after his arrest. Now, I don't think they realized that I knew you."

"What did Ajadi say?"

"Of course he had no idea who you were."

The other lawyer stopped in front of a hot dog wagon. "You want one?" he asked Will.

"Are you kidding?" Will responded. "I don't eat anything that's served on the streets of New York City."

"I was the same way when I moved here," the other man said, squeezing mustard on his hot dog. "But I figure after living here for the last five years without getting dysentery I must have developed the NYC superimmunity to all of the bugs that swim around here."

"So what is your theory as to why they brought up my name?"

"It beats the heck out of me what they were after."

"Tell me about the State Department's involvement in all this."

"Well," the other lawyer continued, wiping mustard off his chin with his napkin, "these lawyers worked in the department headed up by Undersecretary Kenneth Sharptin."

"Isn't he the one that all the TV talking heads think has the inside track for the vice-presidential slot at the convention?"

"Same one."

"So why was Sharptin involved in your case?"

"Because Sharptin is head of something called the Arms Control and International Security Affairs branch within State. I think it was created back in 2000. It has input into nuclear threats against the U.S. from an arms-control standpoint. At first, just after the truck was stopped, the State Department took the position that they were going to have joint control of the investigation, with Sharptin at the head. But after a power struggle, the Pentagon won out."

Something triggered Will's thinking. "Maybe you can help me understand something," he said. "I heard on the news that the warhead on that truck was empty—a blank. It was never an actual threat. So why all the talk about national security?"

The other lawyer frowned, and stopped walking.

"Look. Forget what you hear and see out there in the news. There is something very weird—maybe even very scary—going on here."

Will could see that the other lawyer was weighing how much he wanted to say.

"Let me just spill it here," the other man said, stopping in his tracks and looking Will in the eye. "I learned in this case that the guys in the Pentagon think that there is no way that this MIRV missile is at all connected to Abdul el Alibahd. Now I know that someone was leaking stuff to the press that Alibahd was behind all of this—even the White House had suggested that. But it's not true."

"So who was behind the truck incident?"

"I'm going to give you my best guess," the lawyer explained, for emphasis jabbing into the air the rolled-up newspaper he was carrying.

"And it's partly based on what I got from some of the feds I met with," he continued. "That Russian crime syndicate didn't get the missile housing from someone in Iran who's connected with Alibahd. They got it from someone within the U.S. who has either a lot of inside pull—or a lot of money to pay people off at one of the nuclear test labs—or both. The MIRV was loaded on the rental truck. My guy was hired to drive the truck because—as an Arab—he looked the part of a terrorist. The whole thing looks like a bizarre setup. The arrest was deliberately ordered to be made on the wrong side of the river—on the New York side—by a New Jersey state trooper so the thing could not be prosecuted. This Arab Muslim state trooper—by the way, what are the odds there, right?—the Arab cop gets a call from dispatch to stop this truck. Only one problem—the dispatch tapes don't show that the call to him ever came from the State Patrol headquarters. Anyway, he gets this mystery call and 'saves the day.' The President of the United States ends up giving an Arab follower of Allah a medal for bravery for protecting us all from the 'radical Arab terrorists.' Only there was no Arab terrorist plot involving that truck. That was a fantasy. The whole thing looks like a Disney World put-on."

"Why?" Will asked. "What's the point?"

"That's what I can't figure out," the lawyer said. "There's a closed-door select Senate subcommittee investigating this whole thing. But because it involves national security—or so they claim—we couldn't get any leads there. Besides, you know as well as I do that the politicians in Washington are never going to figure this one out."

By that time they had made their way back to the plaza in front of the massive library. Will still was mystified.

"Why would the State Department care whether I was involved in your client's case?" Will asked. And then he answered his own question. "Unless Sharptin's department was concerned that I would somehow get insider information that the so-called nuclear threat by Arab terrorists was really a put-up job. But how could they think—"

The public defender's face suddenly lit up with something he had remembered, and he broke in. "Oh, and one more thing I found out. Don't know how important it is. But the two assistant U.S. attorneys who were assigned to my client's case were the same ones who were investigating the Wall Street bombing. They told me privately that—even though Alibahd was definitely the mastermind behind the bombing—the two guys who got executed in Saudi Arabia may not actually have been part of it. But suddenly the Saudis are the international buddies of America for getting the guys who blew up Wall Street. Only one problem—there is no actual proof that the guys who got their heads cut off were anything but small-time pickpockets who happened to get arrested at the wrong time."

Will was trying to process what he was hearing.

"Look," the other lawyer said slowly and painstakingly. "The executions were showpieces to make it look like the Arab nations are now policing their own borders for terrorists and offering full cooperation to the U.S. Saudi Arabia was merely looking for someone to execute."

The lawyer continued, "The point was to make the American public think we need the help of the Arab states to keep the terrorists from blowing up our country. Alibahd had already bombed Wall Street, so somebody figured that he would be a credible bad guy to take the blame for this 'nuclear threat.' I know I'm sounding like a conspiracy nut, but I'm giving it to you straight."

The public defender glanced at his watch and said, "Got to get back to the office. Just so you know, you and I didn't talk. This didn't happen." And he started to turn to leave, but then spun back. "Hey Chambers, what did the State Department want with you, anyway? What have you gotten yourself into?"

Will thought for a moment and replied, "The resurrection."

The man gave him a baffled look, and then turned and quickly disappeared into the crowds of New Yorkers rushing to get back to their desks by the end of lunch break.

As Will looked for a cab he did not notice the two Middle Eastern–looking men strolling about fifty feet behind him. They had been following him and the public defender during their walk down Fortieth Street and back to the Public Library. And as Will ducked inside a taxi, the two men quickly hailed their own cab—and started in the same direction, directly behind Will's cab.

35

JACK HORNBY WAS STILL TRYING TO CONTACT Will Chambers, but they were now playing phone-tag by voice mail. Hornby had gone home for the day and was standing at the front door of his condo unit in Bethesda, fishing for his keys.

A nondescript car with government plates pulled up to the curb behind him. Colonel Brad Buchingham was at the wheel. He lowered his window and yelled,

"You interested in a story?"

Hornby turned and eyed the car, walking closer until he recognized the driver.

"Buchingham, is that you?"

"Get in," the Colonel snapped back.

"Oh, I don't know. Is this safe? The last time I tried to talk to you I think you called me a Communist sympathizer."

"That's not what I said."

"Oh?" the bemused Hornby replied.

"What I really called you was a scum-sucking, gutless Communist sympathizer."

"Good memory."

"Are you getting in or not?"

Hornby laughed a little then stepped back and looked at the car and at Buchingham. Then he slowly worked his way to the front passenger side. He gingerly opened the door and, with a dramatic flourish, peeked over into the backseat as if to make sure he was not going to be jumped from behind.

"Hornby, you're a real clown," the Colonel said through a tight grin, and when the reporter was finally seated Buchingham started away from the curb.

"Got your little notepad?"

"Never leave home without it," Hornby said.

"Let's start with the DIA."

Hornby had covered the Pentagon long enough to know that the colonel was talking about the Defense Intelligence Agency. Its duties included—among other things—assessing the military and national-security risk to America from its dealings with other nations. Dealings such as sales of technology and military hardware.

Buchingham explained that he had never before gone to the press—*never.* And he reiterated his distaste for Hornby and what he perceived as his anti-American, antimilitary perspective. Yet this time, the Colonel continued, someone had to blow the whistle. He had seen an internal Pentagon memo that discussed upcoming sales of sophisticated arms and military technology to Saudi Arabia, Kuwait, and Egypt, with a timeline of similar sales six months later to the newly formed regime in Iraq and to Iran, and possible sales to Syria nine months after that. All of the sales were planned to take place *after* the upcoming presidential elections.

This was unprecedented, of course, and Hornby was quick to understand that. Buchingham had to confess that the sales were not final, and were subject to "contravention." Yet such military hardware transfers to Arab nations would be a major shift in the balance of power in the Middle East, and a major change in American foreign policy.

But there was another red flag he had noticed in that internal memo.

"The memo goes on to say," Buchingham said, "that the DIA is *not*—I repeat, *not*—to exercise its usual oversight in assessing the risk to American national security if these military sales go through."

"Who's the prime mover in this?" Hornby asked.

"Well, the memo says that the decision to take the DIA out of the loop on this came from 'upstairs.'"

"How far upstairs?"

"Way far upstairs," Buchingham explained.

"Names. I need names."

"Well," Buchingham said, pausing a little, "let's just say I was going to a horse race. And let's say that Undersecretary Kenneth Sharptin over at the State Department was a horse. I bet he would be named something like, oh, 'Crazy for Power.'"

Hornby smiled as he jotted it down in his notepad.

"So," Hornby continued, "what happens to this horse—'Crazy for Power'? Does he win, place, or show?"

"That all depends."

"Depends on what?"

"On whether somebody takes him out of the race first."

Buchingham pulled back in front of Hornby's condo. Hornby got out of the car and walked over to the driver's side.

"Say, what do you know about oil?"

Buchingham had to think for a second before he responded. It was clear to him that Hornby had been doing his homework.

"It's black."

"Yeah. And what else?"

"The largest single share of it is controlled by OPEC."

"Yeah?"

"They're headquartered in Vienna, Austria."

"Okay. So far what you've given me I could have gotten off the Internet."

Buchingham eyed Hornby, and then growled, "You tie this to me and you're finished."

"No problem. 'Reliable sources at the Pentagon.' That's as far as I will go in my story," Hornby assured him.

"So I did hear, through a friend down at the Defense Threat Reduction Agency, that the United States is about to get dealt a seat at the OPEC meetings," the Colonel said. "That would be the first time a major non-Islamic nation from the West would be sitting in on those meetings. A seat on OPEC would give us a major advantage in protecting our oil supplies."

"So what is the United States giving to OPEC in return?"

"I bet that's a question that has an interesting answer," Buchingham said, and then put his car into gear.

"You said 'non-Islamic nation...'" Hornby shouted out to the departing car, as he stepped back to the curb. And then he repeated himself, speaking into the air as Buchingham's car drove away.

"You said, the United States as a 'non-Islamic nation.'"

36

WILL CHAMBERS DECIDED TO SPEND the rest of the afternoon visiting some old haunts in New York, since he had not been there for several years. The last time was when he and Audra had attended a small art show featuring some of her work in acrylics. Later, they had caught a Broadway play, stayed at the Plaza, and then taken the train back to Monroeville. In those days they were up in New York City several times a year—either for Will's cases or because of Audra's connections with the art community there.

That weekend had begun with her success at the art show. At first, it had seemed as if the old feelings of romance and friendship had been rekindled between them. But then, for reasons he couldn't even remember now, it had all ended in bitter, explosive arguments as it had so many times before. Will never could understand how they could have been so deeply in love, yet have acted so cruelly toward each other. Shortly after that, Audra had moved out.

Now, when Will revisited the art gallery, it was still there, but the proprietor was out for the day. The college-age girl at the desk did not remember the work of Audra Chambers or the art show Will asked about. That was before her time, she said.

After going past the Plaza he decided to catch a cab down toward Greenwich Village. He had dinner at a café the two of them had often frequented. Yet, as he paid the waiter and walked out after his solitary meal at their favorite table, he was surprised how none of these places now held any emotional connection for him anymore. They had merely become recognizable places. Now he was simply a tourist, following memories as an out-of-towner might flip through a guidebook.

On a lark he headed down to the harbor area and nosed around the shops. He had an idea in the back of his mind that he wanted to pick up a gift. He would send it to Fiona Cameron as a way of thanking her for the dinner at Luigi's.

Will picked out a crystal replica of the Statue of Liberty. He asked the shop owner to ship it to the office of Fiona's business manager, which was the only address he had for her. Then he wrote a little note for them to include in the package. It read,

> Fiona—
>
> I don't know why this small gift made me think of you and our dinner together. But please accept it as my thanks for the meal, for the conversation, and for being the delightful person you are.
>
> Will

Will left the gift shop. As he was walking down the sidewalk, one of the two men following him quickly ducked into the same shop. Then Will decided he would make his way back to the train station, and he hailed another cab. As he did, the second man waved down a cab that was going in the same direction as Will's.

Once he was on the train, Will settled down for some more homework on the Reichstad lawsuit. He wanted to read some of the fundamentals of New Testament Greek. But as he tried to buckle down to his reading, a rush of thoughts bombarded him—static jamming his concentration. Thoughts of both Audra and Fiona kept interrupting his focus. This trip to New York had not been what he had expected. He wondered how Fiona would respond to his gift.

But a voice jolted him back to the case—the voice of the public defender asking, "What have you gotten yourself into?" Someone had an obvious concern about Will's activities. But why?

At the Newark train stop, Will got up and stretched. He was feeling tired, so he made his way down to the dining car to grab a cup of coffee—only to find it was closed. He returned to his seat and decided it was time to buckle down and learn something about Greek.

Will saw that MacCameron had started him off in the right direction. The New Testament was written in "Koine" Greek, the common, everyday form of the Greek language at the time of Christ. Koine Greek was the closest thing to the universal language of the known world then.

Will quickly discovered that the Greek alphabet resembled the English alphabet with some exceptions. He glanced at the spelling of the names of the four Gospels in his interlinear Greek-English New Testament that he had bought. The Gospel of "MARK," for instance, appeared as:

MAPKON

As he read further, he noted that words were arranged in sentence structure much like English, except that in Greek, word order was not critical—words could be moved around in a sentence without necessarily changing the meaning of the sentence, unlike in English.

Will began to realize how hard it was going to be to understand even the rudiments of New Testament Greek by the time of trial.

After an hour and a half of reading, Will's eyes started getting heavy. He didn't remember falling asleep, or his head sliding to the side against the train window. He would not wake up until the train shuddered to a halt at the little station in Monroeville.

37

IT WAS WELL AFTER MIDNIGHT WHEN WILL walked off the train. He trudged half-a-block down to the all-night cabstand. Still exhausted, he climbed into the back of a cab and gave the driver directions. Then he leaned his head back for a moment to collect his thoughts. In just a few minutes he was asleep again, his briefcase and coat still on his lap.

In a deep sleep, and dreaming, Will heard a voice. It was yelling. There was danger, but Will could not make out where the voice was coming from. It was saying, *Hey Mister. Hey Mister. Wake up.*

"Hey mister, wake up! Is that your house? It's burning! Man, that house is on fire!"

The cabbie was yelling to him in a panic and pointing out the front windshield of the car. "Your house is on fire! It's burning down!"

Will stumbled out of the cab with his things, still groggy, and looked up the driveway of Generals' Hill. The whole sky was red and orange and filled with black smoke. He saw his Corvette, still there where he had parked it. Then he saw his house.

There were flames shooting from every window in the huge Civil War mansion. Will started sprinting up the driveway. He could see that the roof was also on fire. He heard himself scream, "No, no, no, no!"

In the background he heard the cabbie shout that he would call 9-1-1. Then he yelled, "Is there anybody in there?"

Clarence! Clarence was still in the house. Will ran to the front door. It was black with soot, and smoke was billowing out from around the corners, from under the bottom.

He snatched up his raincoat from the ground where he'd let it fall, wrapped it around his hand, and grabbed the large iron doorknob. When he opened the door, a blast of smoke and fire blew through the opening, hitting Will and throwing him straight back as if he had been hit by a bomb.

As he was scrambling to his feet, the flames retreated back into the house, and he could see something lying on the floor just inside the door. It was Clarence.

Shielding his head with the raincoat he raced up to the entrance and reached around ahead of him into the black smoke and furnacelike heat. Then his hand felt the fur and body of his golden retriever. He moved his hand up to the collar and began dragging the dog out of the smoke and the fire.

He pulled Clarence down onto the front lawn. Will looked down—Clarence's eyes were open, but staring straight ahead. His large pink tongue was caught, hanging out slightly, between his clenched front teeth. He was not moving. Will stroked his head and felt something wet. In the flickering light of the fire he could see that it was blood.

Looking closer he saw the blood was centered around a black bullet hole in Clarence's skull. Will patted the head of his dead dog, and smoothed his ears down. After a minute, he rose to his feet.

Will stood before the house, which was now starting to collapse into the inferno. The walls, the wood shutters, the draperies and furniture, the floors and all else that had been there was being consumed. The great house, with its towering white pillars, and broad front porch, fan-shaped windows, and the charm of a century long past, was forever gone, incinerated in the raging ball of fire rising higher and higher into the night sky.

Out of nowhere Will began to feel it all fall away. The furniture he and Audra had picked out. Her artwork, which still decorated several of the walls. The photo album of their life together. The books. The clothes. The small things of a lifetime, each collected at a place, and carefully preserved for a reason. The photographs he had of his father when he had served in the Navy during World War II. His boyhood things: the old baseball glove, the trophies, the high school and college yearbooks. Love letters from Audra. It was all gone. And Clarence...

As Will stood in front of the wall of flames that roared upward he could hear the sirens of the fire engines in the distance, coming down the country road toward Generals' Hill.

Tears welled up in his eyes. He shook his head, engulfed with rage and sorrow.

Will's head hung down as if some invisible sinew had just snapped. Like a bull whose snorting and charging was now over. Worn and bloodied and receiving the final thrust of the sword from the matador. From the blade that pierces the tough hide and plunges down into the back of the neck, where it brings the bull, slumping and stumbling, down to his knees, and down to bloody defeat. Down into the dirt of the roaring arena.

38

UP IN HIS GLASS-AND-MAHOGANY OFFICE SUITE, J-Fox Sherman had assigned his multiple associates in the Reichstad case to two different tracks. His strategy would be like a combination of land invasion and air strike, exquisitely coordinated.

On one team, several of the lawyers in the firm, under his supervision had researched, drafted, and now completed a lengthy Motion for Summary Judgment. Such a motion can be brought when the facts are not in substantial dispute—and the law can be applied to the facts by the judge, thus bringing the case to an end without ever going to trial.

Sherman was asking the court to review the facts that had already been established—relying primarily on Angus MacCameron's own sworn deposition testimony. He would argue that the facts dealing with two issues were certain, clear, and undisputed. The first issue Sherman wanted the judge to decide was whether MacCameron had been reckless at the time of the printing of his article against Reichstad. Sherman felt that through MacCameron's own deposition testimony, recklessness had been established.

Sherman would also ask the judge to decide the second issue, the defense of *truth*—whether there was a substantial amount of truth in what MacCameron had said about Reichstad. Sherman would contend that there was no hard evidence that MacCameron could produce to support what he had written.

The Motion for Summary Judgment was the "air strike." If Sherman won both of these arguments, the case was over—except for his right to have a jury calculate the enormous damages that he also hoped to prove. In addition, he would argue his motion for attorney's fees against Will Chambers: that the defenses Will had presented at the beginning of the case were so lacking in evidence that he should be punished by having to pay the quarter-of-a-million dollars in attorney's fees to Sherman's firm. That would be the coup de grace—the final, decimating blow—Sherman's response to Will Chambers' obstinate and aggressive defense.

The second team of Sherman's lawyers were working on the "land invasion." They were preparing for a full-blown jury trial in the event that Judge Jeremiah Kaye did not rule in their favor on all of the issues. The attorneys had lined up several scholars in archaeology, papyrology, and cultural anthropology who would testify as expert witnesses in support of Reichstad's interpretation of 7QA. They had done a thorough review of MacCameron's background and were preparing a crippling cross-examination for him at trial.

As the commanding general, Sherman was ready for war. The Summary Judgment motion was five hundred pages long. Will Chambers would only have fourteen days to respond. Judge Kaye would hear arguments in open court the next week after that, and probably give his ruling from the bench.

A copy of the motion had been sent by Sherman to his client. At his research center, Reichstad scanned the thick packet of papers, but his mind was elsewhere.

Dr. Reichstad had only five days left before he had to produce the original 7QA fragment to MacCameron and Chambers' expert witness. Until now, Reichstad had been successful in jealously protecting the fragment from the outside world.

Reichstad had insisted that Sherman find a way to block the production of the fragment. The lawyer had told his client it was impossible—all he could do would be to delay it by filing motion after motion with Judge Kaye, asking him to issue orders that placed multiple layers of restrictions on MacCameron and Chambers—preventing them from doing any testing that affected the paper or the writing, or that had any effect on the humidity and barometric pressure inside the glass case which housed the 7QA fragment.

In addition, for reasons unknown even to J-Fox Sherman, Reichstad refused to have the opposing experts do their evaluation of 7QA on the grounds of his own research center. He insisted that it be transported by armored car to some neutral site in the D.C. area. He also demanded that his own staff be present during the defense's evaluation of the fragment.

Reichstad rose and examined himself in the full-length mirror in his office. He was preparing to drive to the studio to begin filming a TV documentary on his discovery of 7QA and its revolutionary effect on Christianity. The film would be titled, *The Dead Jesus.* Because the project would not air until *after* the trial date in his lawsuit, he had not bothered to tell his lawyer about it. After all, Sherman seemed forever preoccupied with holding Dr. Reichstad back in his meteoric climb to greatness.

Reichstad was certain that he could retrieve information from MacCameron that would destroy, and bury, two thousand years of religious history concerning Jesus. Only then could he move onward to the final project—one so daring and so dangerous that Reichstad could scarcely believe it was now within his reach. A project that would change not just two thousand years of Christianity, but more than five thousand years of Judaism—and which had the potential to shift the balance of world power to the Middle East.

Yes, Reichstad thought to himself, he was right not to tell his lawyer about the documentary film. No lawyer was going to rob him of his place in world history.

39

WILL CHAMBERS HAD NOT RETURNED HIS phone calls for the three days since the fire. He was now renting a room at a cheap motel, and putting in very little time at the office. He did check his voice mail—but there were no calls from MacCameron about paying Will's overdue legal fees.

From the beginning, *Reichstad vs. MacCameron and* Digging for Truth *Magazine* had been a bad omen in his life, Will concluded as he sat down on a bar stool at the Red Rooster. Now that MacCameron could not pay his bills, this was the time for Will to file a petition with the court to permit him to withdraw from the case altogether.

From the first day that the case had come into his life, he mused bitterly, it had been one catastrophe after another: kicked out of his law firm; all but one of his cases taken from him by his former firm; losing his staff as well as his friend and associate Jacki Johnson; his secretary quitting; his office broken into; and now his home burned to the ground and his dog cruelly killed.

After the fire the fire marshal and the fire inspector met with him and told him it was almost certainly arson. The fire appeared to have been set in several places on the first floor. The multiple sites of the fire's origin plus the gunshot to the dog's head made it clear this was no accident. Clarence's body had been analyzed for traces of evidence, and the bullet from his head was now at the crime lab.

But Will knew something about arson, and he knew that in this case they were not going to find the perpetrator. Whoever had done this was too clever and too determined. Will was convinced that because he'd left his Corvette outside it had given someone the impression that he was in for the night. After dark that person had gained entrance through the front door—it had been unlocked when he had tried to get in during the fire. Poor

Clarence was shot in the head to make sure he didn't give off a warning bark. Will had already heard from the crime lab that markings on the bullet indicated, at least preliminarily, that it might have come from a gun with a silencer.

Will believed that the fire had been set by someone who thought he—Will—was upstairs, asleep in bed. Someone wanted him dead.

Will was looking at the glass of whiskey and water in front of him. He hadn't touched liquor for weeks. Now it really didn't seem to matter. Will was still staring at the glass when Jack Hornby walked in the door and sat down next to him.

"Hey, how are you? Too busy to call a newspaperman back?"

"Yeah. Real busy," Will replied sarcastically.

"You have a minute?"

"I've got a whole lot of minutes. But I'm not sure I want to spend them with a reporter."

"Oh, I think you do."

"You think so?"

"Yes I do," Hornby said.

"How'd you find me here?"

"Well—a little birdie told me."

"Don't be cute. I'm really in no mood for cute," Will said, staring straight ahead.

"Look, reporters—good ones—gravitate to people who have two things: a story to tell, and a reason to tell it."

Will thought about it for a second. "You talked to one of my former partners?"

"Nope. But getting close."

"Betty Sorenson, my former secretary."

"Yes, sir. I located her. I said to her, 'Where can I contact this guy. He's not in the office and he's not at home.'"

The reporter continued. "She said, 'If you don't find him at either of those two places'—and this is a quote—'then check out the bar stools at the Red Rooster.'" And with that Hornby chuckled.

Will pushed the glass away from him and turned to Hornby.

"Why shouldn't I tell you to get lost? You know, you never ran the story on our lawsuit even after I gave you a beautiful quote."

"Look—Betty told me she'd read in the paper that your house had burned down to the ground. A pre–Civil War mansion. I feel for you, buddy. That's a rotten break. I'm sure you're in no mood to talk to a reporter. But I'm not just a reporter. I can be a help to you here, Will. Really, I can. I'm not supposed to say this—we all worship at this altar of 'objective journalism'—but I really am on your side. Whatever that means to you. I'm asking you to trust me a little bit. You give me some information, and I think I might be able to help you in return."

"Prove it."

With that, Hornby pulled out his notepad with the triangle diagram on it.

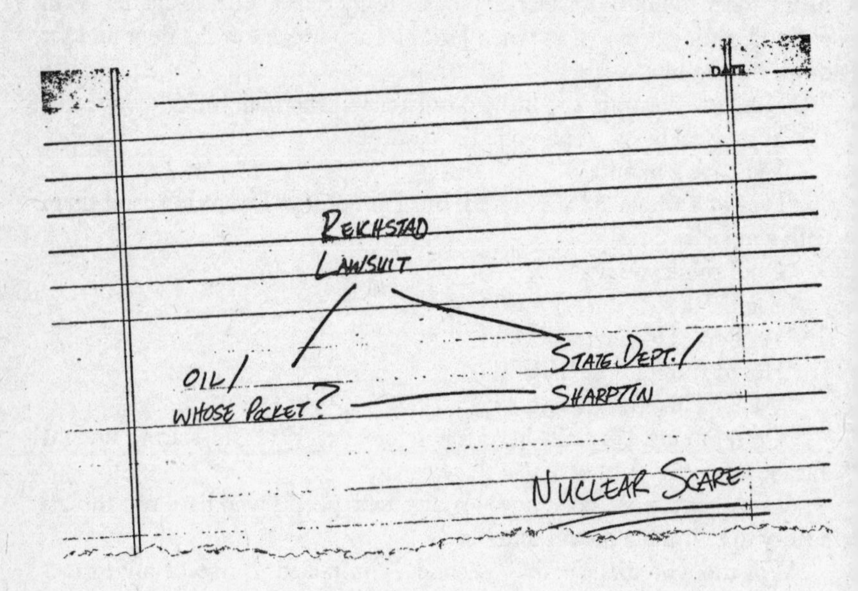

Then Hornby pushed the notepad over to Will and asked him, "Do you see the answer to this puzzle? Because I sure don't. But I will tell you this: You give me something that helps answer this puzzle, and I will tell you what I know. And after I do, I swear you are going to be able to make some big waves in your defense of the Reichstad case. I'm talking tidal-wave proportion. I'm talking about tsunami-type monster waves."

Will looked at the notepad and said nothing. Hornby was leaning from his bar stool, looking at Will expectantly.

Will realized that the pieces were now right there in front of him. He just did not want to see them. He wanted to grunt that he was tired, and disgusted, and then just walk away from all of it. But he couldn't. Not now. Down in the dark tunnel he was starting to see a small shaft of brightness. He had to start digging toward the light. Toward the truth.

Will took out his marker pen and drew a line connecting STATE DEPT./SHARPTIN to REICHSTAD LAWSUIT and pushed the notepad back to Hornby.

"What is the connection between Sharptin and your case?" Hornby asked.

"I recently found out from a real insider source that the State Department has been watching me. It's my conclusion that the State Department has some interest in my handling of the Reichstad case."

"Alright. Fair enough. Let me tell you," Hornby said in return, "that I found out from a very reliable source that the U.S. government is trying to establish unprecedented ties with the Arab nations. Militarily and economically."

Will took the notepad and drew a line connecting STATE DEPT./SHARPTIN to OIL/ WHOSE POCKET? and slid it back to Hornby.

"Well," Hornby responded, "that's no flash of brilliance. I figured that one myself. Sharptin has an interest in cutting Americans into the oil monopoly of the OPEC nations. That much I know already. Now, what I need to know is how NUCLEAR SCARE fits into this picture—or whether it's just a red herring."

Hornby pushed the notepad back over to Will. Will then took his pen and crossed out NUCLEAR SCARE and rewrote it—but right in the very center of the triangle. Then he drew lines connecting it to all three points of the triangle—to the Reichstad lawsuit, to Sharptin and the State Department, and to the issue of oil.

Hornby's eyes widened, and he said, "I'm listening."

Then Will explained everything he had been told on his trip to New York City about the missile incident—how it was a phony deal—how it was not really connected to Abdul el Alibahd—how the executions in Saudi Arabia had probably been showpieces to appease Americans over the Wall Street bombings. How the arrests in Iran connected with the 'nuclear threat' were also a put-on. And how all of this was done for the purpose, apparently, of convincing the American people that the Arab nations were America's best and last hope against terrorism and for global economic security in the oil markets.

After Will was finished, Hornby was silent for a moment. Then he slowly began to explain that he was going to trust Will with some highly sensitive information. Hornby told Will how the story he had written about the Reichstad lawsuit had been squelched because of an upcoming merger between the *Washington Herald* and a subsidiary of an oil company owned by billionaire Warren Mullburn. His investigation had shown that Mullburn, for some reason, did not want publicity about the lawsuit to surface—at least not now.

Hornby concluded by telling Will that he had traced millions of dollars of funding from one of Mullburn's many business enterprises to Dr. Reichstad's research center.

Will took the notepad once again and drew a line, this time connecting OIL/ WHOSE POCKET? to REICHSTAD LAWSUIT.

Then Hornby wrote down—underneath the word OIL—the name "WARREN MULLBURN."

Will looked at the finished diagram.

"There is only one problem in this little picture," Will commented. "The fact that we have a three-way benefit to the people in the three corners of this triangle doesn't mean we've got some kind of conspiracy.

"Mullburn supports Reichstad financially," Will continued thinking out loud. "The State Department—for whatever reason—wants Reichstad's lawsuit to be successful; Sharptin at State wants a new economic and political alliance with the Arab nations, as does Mullburn because of his oil interests. That's not enough."

"There is one more thing," Hornby said.

"What?"

"Mullburn has never directly intervened in any political campaign. Until now. I have found out that he has spent millions of dollars on a public-relations campaign to ensure that Sharptin wins the nod for the vice-presidential slot at the upcoming convention. Something is driving all of this," Hornby said, tapping his finger on the notepad.

Will glanced over at the bartender and said, pointing to his glassful of whiskey, "Dump this and give me a ginger ale, will you?"

Then Will looked at Hornby, managed a smile, and asked him, "It's interesting that you should have come here when you did. Do you believe in fate?"

"No. I believe that things happen for a lot of different reasons. People just call it fate."

"Do you believe in God?" Will asked.

Hornby paused. "Don't know. Never had the chance to get a story from him."

"You may end up doing exactly that," Will replied, "before the dust settles in all of this."

40

In a small, unassuming office in Newport News, Virginia, several Naval Intelligence officers were meeting with the Deputy Director of Operations for the CIA and two of his field agents.

Abdul el Alibahd had been tracked by the CIA as he departed Uzbekistan. American intelligence agents then later received reports that he was in Khost, a location in Afghanistan with a history involving old terrorist training camps. That is when he disappeared.

Alibahd had always been able to finance his worldwide travel, along with his terrorist cell groups, through complex channels of investments and disguised funds. To the American intelligence community, he had come to embody terrorism at its most effective and most dangerous: As one of the richest men in the world, he possessed unlimited but well-hidden sources of cash; he had access to terrorist camps around the world that provided him 'safe houses'; he had control of strike groups that could pick up and move locations on less than ten minutes notice; and he possessed a fanatical devotion to a violent purpose.

The supervising Naval agent was explaining information his unit had received on possible routes of travel for Alibahd.

"The thread in all of our intelligence is that Alibahd may be planning an unusual excursion by sea," he said.

The deputy director was intrigued by that. He put his finger on several points on the world globe that stood on the desk and commented, "This guy is almost always landlocked in his paths of escape; he scurries between the countries that give him refuge—from Northern Africa through most of the Middle East, to Afghanistan and Pakistan in the east and Uzbekistan to the north, and as far west as Turkey. Taking an ocean route doesn't make any sense."

"Gee," one of the agents commented ironically, "why don't we simply call up Iraq or Saudi Arabia and ask them to explain this to us? Aren't they part of our new 'partnership for peace'? I thought the Arabs were going to catch Alibahd for us, right?"

After the chuckles quieted down, the deputy director put his hand on the globe and spun it slightly.

"Gentlemen, there's a lot of blue on this globe. If we don't catch him boarding a specific vessel, or at least locate the right harbor, the ocean is going to hide him pretty well. We do know one thing for sure—our bad guy is on the move. But where is he going, and why?"

41

As a result of his conversation with Jack Hornby, Will was committed to continue his representation of Angus MacCameron up to the bitter end. Will called Tiny Heftland and told him about the arson and the shooting of his dog. Tiny offered to secure a full-time bodyguard but Will only scoffed at the idea.

He gave Tiny his temporary address at the Robert E. Lee Motel, where he was staying until the insurance company began paying off on his fire loss. The claims adjuster indicated that the fact that arson was involved would slow down the process, but that as soon as Will was cleared as a suspect (a "mere technicality," they said) they would get some money to him to cover his temporary lodgings. In the meantime, Will was going through his savings and his money-market account fast. Soon he was going to be seriously strapped for cash.

The motel where Will was staying was populated by truck drivers, transients, and traveling construction workers. The first night he was there the temperature dropped, and he tried to adjust the old-fashioned stand-up radiator. But the fitting for the pressure knob came off and steam and boiling water spewed over the room. He drifted off to sleep to the sounds of country music in the next room, an arguing couple upstairs, and a loud drunk out in the parking lot.

The second night a caravan of carnival workers checked in.

The man at the front desk was round and short, with a gravelly voice. Each night Will would ask if he had gotten any messages during the day. The man would give him a look that seemed to say, "You expect me to take messages too? That's gonna cost you extra."

After a few days, however, Will began to adjust to his downscale lodgings. He struck up a few interesting conversations with some of the truckers.

One fellow and his wife were long-haulers from Texas who traveled with a little white poodle. Another guy had a huge lighted cross on the grille of his truck and wore a black T-shirt that said "Truckin' for Jesus."

And there were some other lighter moments.

One night the telephone rang. Will picked it up. At the other end was the soothing voice of a woman.

"Hello. I don't know if you remember me," the prerecorded message began, "but I'm your psychic advisor. We talked not too long ago. Remember? You had a concern about money. Well, I've got some great news for you. All you have to do is call me back at the private number I'm going to give you, and I will give you a free three-minute psychic reading. I think that you are really going to be surprised with what I'm going to tell you! Remember—this is my private number, so don't give it out to anyone else! Here it is: 1-900..."

Will's belly laughs could be heard all the way out into the parking lot, where a few drunks and prostitutes were congregating.

When Will had made it into his office the day after his meeting with Hornby he had had a short telephone message from Dr. Mary Margaret Giovanni. She hadn't left a message but simply stated that she wanted Will to call her. She gave her telephone number where she was teaching at Catholic University. Will, hoping that she would be willing to testify for them, called her back immediately. Then he got the bad news.

"I am not interested in being an expert witness on your case," Dr. Giovanni said firmly. "I admit that the issues are fascinating—I've always disagreed with Albert Reichstad's conclusions about the 7QA fragment. But I will not, cannot, be an expert for your client—for this Reverend Angus MacCameron."

"Why not?"

"I've looked into his background. This man is a fundamentalist preacher type. He's said some very nasty things about the Catholic Church."

"Dr. Giovanni, I have personally reviewed everything my client has ever published. I know that he has levied some criticisms against the Vatican—but then again he has also attacked almost every other denomination and sect in the civilized world as well."

"Attorney Chambers, your client practically called the Vatican the whore of Babylon. I myself have had some disagreements with the Holy Father and the leadership in the Vatican. But I am still a loyal and devout Catholic."

Just then a delivery courier stepped into Will's office with a slender overnight envelope. Will signed for it and glanced at the sender's address as

Dr. Giovanni continued to express her concerns about MacCameron. The letter had been sent by J-Fox Sherman. Will ripped open the envelope and scanned the letter inside as he was listening on the phone.

Will interrupted Dr. Giovanni.

"Doctor, I can understand, I really can. But I've got two things to say. Just hear me out if you would. First, MacCameron's bark is worse than his bite. Actually he is a rather charming—though somewhat eccentric—fellow. I've read his writings. What he wrote is that, in his opinion, and taking literally the reference in the book of Revelation to the creation of a kind of religious Babylon in the 'end times,' he believes the Vatican may play an important role. He also believes that nearly all denominations within Christianity will be duped into this new religious Babylon as well. I don't know if that clarification helps."

"It doesn't," she replied.

"Well then, let me give you the second reason for you to rethink your position."

Will raised the letter from J-Fox Sherman closer to his eyes, making sure he was reading it correctly.

"Doctor, how would you like to be the first human being in the world, outside of Reichstad's own research team, to inspect and analyze the 7QA fragment?"

There was silence on the other end.

Then Dr. Giovanni asked, "You are talking about the actual fragment—not a replica or a copy?"

"I am talking about the very thing itself, yes."

There was another silence.

"Mr. Chambers, have you ever been to Israel?"

"No, I haven't."

"Well, I have spent much of my life there, and in various parts of the Middle East. Down near Jericho there is a place where, according to popular belief, the Mount of Temptation is located. Where Jesus was tempted by the devil. Are you familiar with that story?"

"I didn't used to be. But I've been brushing up on my New Testament lately. Forty days and nights in the wilderness. The devil appears and offers some tempting business options to Jesus."

"Yes," she continued, "the devil takes Jesus and shows him all the kingdoms of the world and promises to give them all to him; all Jesus has to do, in return, is bow down and worship the devil. Why do I feel like I am at the Mount of Temptation right now? You are offering me the most prized opportunity any antiquities scholar could have. But I simply will not deny my faith."

"Angus MacCameron is not the devil," Will shot back, "And I am not one of his demons, I'm just his lawyer. I know sometimes people get those two roles confused."

Giovanni laughed as Will continued.

"Doctor, you don't have to agree with his position on theological matters. You only have to be willing to tell the truth about 7QA after you study it—and tell the truth about Albert Reichstad. That's it. If you want to say from the witness stand that you detest what MacCameron has said about the Vatican—or anything else—be my guest. Just be willing to present your informed expert opinion about Reichstad's interpretation of 7QA."

Will could tell that Giovanni was softening.

"Let me think about it a little bit more. I have a lecture I'm giving this afternoon. I will call you back after that. It was good talking to you, Mr. Chambers."

Will looked back at Sherman's letter again. In it, Sherman had conceded that Reichstad would have to produce the original 7QA for inspection.

But the letter was attached to a motion that Sherman was filing, asking Judge Kaye to place numerous restrictions on the time, place, and manner of the inspection. If Will opposed the motion it would simply eat up the clock that was ticking rapidly toward the trial date. That was exactly what Sherman wanted. By the time the motion had been argued and decided by the judge, it would give precious little time to Will's expert—if he had one—to inspect the two-thousand-year-old fragment before trial.

On the other hand, would Dr. Giovanni be willing to tolerate the complicated restrictions that Sherman wanted to place on their scientific analysis of 7QA, even if she agreed to be Will's expert?

Will decided he would present the issue to Dr. Giovanni when he talked with her later that day.

As he pondered that, a Federal Express courier walked into the office with two large packages. They were both from Sherman's office. Will had a good idea what they were.

Inside was Sherman's massive, five-hundred-page Motion for Summary Judgment, which he had just filed with the court, asking Judge Kaye, in effect, to give Sherman and his client a slam-dunk victory in the case before even getting to trial. Will had less than two weeks to mount his written reply.

But Will was scheduled to take Reichstad's deposition in a few days. Perhaps he could blow the case wide open with Reichstad's own testimony;

if so, he could attach the deposition transcript to his written reply to the court.

Yet he also knew that Sherman and his troops would prepare Reichstad as if he were about to be examined by the French Academy of Science. Cracking Reichstad open in the deposition would be nearly impossible.

Will was deep into his review of Sherman's motion papers when he received a telephone call from his expert in voice and recording analysis. He had finished his study of the cassette tape containing the message from Dr. Richard Hunter, and had arrived at his conclusion regarding the part of the tape where Hunter mentioned either "the fragment," or "the fragment*s*."

"It's really very clear to me," he told Will. "I am very certain."

"Well, which is it? Fragment—or fragment*s*?"

"Whatever it means to you and your case—and I really have no idea what your case is about—but in my opinion..."

That was when Will heard someone call out his name in the lobby.

Will interrupted his caller, and poked his head around the corner. It was attorney Jacki Johnson, standing in the lobby. Will smiled and asked her to grab a seat.

"I've only got a few minutes..." Jacki said.

Will assured her that he would be off the phone in a second. Then Will returned to his caller.

"All right. Give it to me. Which is it? Fragment or fragments? Singular or plural?"

"Will, you've got more than one 'fragment.' When I slowed it down under my voice analyzer it showed a definite 's' at the end of the word. That guy on the phone said 'fragment*s*.'"

After the call Will stepped quickly into the lobby where Jacki was pacing. He hugged her, and she smiled and stepped back and took a long look at him.

"I didn't expect to see you in such good spirits! I heard about your house. That was terrible. I was so sorry for you. I thought of the parties with you and Audra. The good times we had out there. I just can't believe it."

"They killed Clarence. That was the icing on the cake."

"Oh no—who?"

"I don't know."

"What are you saying? Was this arson or something?"

"The fire marshal is convinced it was. And whoever did it put a bullet into my dog too. It seems pretty obvious to me."

"Who would have done this?"

"Jacki, I think they were after me. They wanted me out of the way."

"But who?"

"I'm not sure. I think it has something to do with the case I'm handling for MacCameron."

"Well, I want you to know," Jacki said, "that I was up in U.S. District Court in D.C. the other day when one of Sherman's legal associates filed a motion with the clerk that looked like it was the size of the New York City phone directory. I took a peek at it and recognized the caption. It's that MacCameron case, right?"

"Yeah, Sherman's motion just came into my office today."

"You have no secretary?"

"Nope."

"No paralegals—no clerks?"

"Not a one."

"Are you trying to work yourself up to a heart attack, or would you prefer a stroke? Or do you plan on maybe hanging yourself from the light fixtures when you finally realize you can't handle this case alone?"

Will chuckled. He missed having Jacki around.

"So, I was talking to Howard—by the way, he says hello and expects to see you at the wedding. Anyway, I told him about the motion. You know what my loving fiancé says to me? Can you believe it? He asks me if I still have any 'personal leave' coming my way from the Hadley Bates law firm. So I tell him, sure, I have almost two weeks. Then, get this—he says—well, then, why don't you take some of your personal leave time, and go down to Monroeville and help that poor guy Will Chambers? He needs you on this case. Can you believe the nerve?"

"Sounds like Howard. I can't imagine that you would let him boss you around like that," Will replied with a smile.

"Well, if we were married I wouldn't. But hey, the wedding is still more than a month away. So, I think I'm going to let him enjoy the illusion that he can call the shots. So, what do you say? When can I come down here and start helping you with this case? I mean, if you can guarantee my safety. I don't want somebody to start shooting at me because I'm helping you!"

"There is only one way to make sure," Will replied, in a serious and steady voice. "You need to stay entirely in the background on this. That's the only way I will accept your help. No one can know you are helping me. In fact, I want you to do everything on this case out of your home. Don't come to my office again. I don't want to take any chances." Will broke into a grin. "You know, you really are a peach, Jacki. And I think you're way too good for Howard. You tell him that, for me."

"Oh yeah, keep it coming, keep it coming! Flattery always works on a woman."

"No, I mean it," Will said. "You are a wonderful friend. I don't think I ever told you how much I appreciated working with you all those years. And I think you put up with a lot with me. I was a tough guy to work with."

Jacki looked at Will more closely.

"Something is going on with you, Will, I can see it," she declared. "Despite all of this stuff coming down on your head. I think I see some humanity peeking through again. The old Will is coming back."

"I'm not sure it's the old Will," he replied. "I feel like I'm on some kind of strange journey to somewhere. I'm not really sure where I'm going. But one thing I will do. I'll let you know when I get there."

42

After Jacki Johnson left, Will felt a renewed sense of optimism. Before she had volunteered her help, Will had been wondering how he could possibly defend against Sherman's Summary-Judgment motion, continue the rest of the work on the case, and still deal with the huge amount of work necessary to finish his property damage claim for the fire. And then there were the rather sinister undertones to the fire investigation.

Will had begun to see the focus of the arson investigation shift toward him. The investigators wanted to know why he had been in New York, and whether he had any proof that he had been there on the day of the fire. Will had indicated that he had had a "confidential meeting," and that he was not at liberty to divulge it. He had no intention of breaching his promise to the public defender.

The investigators had then explained that they knew he had been terminated from his law partnership. Perhaps, because of financial stress, he might have had a motive to set the fire himself. Will was outraged by their suggestion. Did that also mean, he argued to them, that he shot his own dog with a gun equipped with a silencer? Did any of that make sense?

The arson investigators had demanded that Will provide them with some proof of having been up in New York that day. That part of his story, according to the arson squad, was not checking out. Unfortunately, Will had paid cash at all the restaurants—and for his train ticket. All the receipts had been in his raincoat. And that had been incinerated on the front porch of his house, where he'd dropped it when trying to rescue Clarence.

Yet Will was determined not to let the lurking threats of an arson charge slow down his preparation in the case.

Will's immediate task was to sketch an outline of each point that Sherman had made in his Summary-Judgment motion. He was working on that when Angus MacCameron called him on the telephone.

MacCameron said that he had heard about the fire destroying Will's house, and how terrible it was, and how sorry he felt about it. He asked if Will had managed to find a place to stay. Will told him that he was staying at a motel.

He initially questioned whether to tell his client that he was a suspect in the arson of his own house. But he decided to divulge it. Will explained that the investigators were demanding proof that he had been in New York earlier that day.

"I know you must think I'm chasing hobgoblins when I talk like this, but Will, I have to tell you something straight," MacCameron responded somberly. "This is spiritual warfare. You are being opposed by evil forces from the province of hell. Forces you may not understand. The prince of darkness wants you out of my case because he knows that God himself, in his inscrutable wisdom, has hand-picked you to defend me. But don't give up. Finish the course! Run with zeal that race that is set before you, as the Bible says!"

Will didn't know whether it was just his increasing familiarity with MacCameron's bibliocentric style of conversation, or maybe something else—but regardless, Will was beginning to see the logic behind MacCameron's encouragement.

Then his client became very upbeat and said that he had some "great news" but wanted to tell Will in person. He invited Will up to Washington to have dinner in his apartment with him and his wife, Helen. He would tell Will the good news then. Will suggested they go out to eat at a restaurant to save the trouble, but MacCameron insisted he would prepare dinner for them in his apartment. That way, he said, Will could meet his wife.

Will recalled that Fiona had mentioned her mother briefly during their dinner at Luigi's—that she had health problems—but hadn't elaborated. Fiona had also said that she planned her tours so she could fly back to be with her parents almost every weekend. Will also remembered that Fiona was cutting her current tour short altogether to spend more time at home with her mother.

Touched by his client's offer, Will accepted. MacCameron suggested that they dine together that very night. Will said that would be fine.

Just as he was getting ready to leave for his dinner with the MacCamerons, Will received a call back from Dr. Giovanni. She said she had considered her involvement in the case. While she still had misgivings about Will's client, she would agree to evaluate the 7QA fragment and would testify about her findings.

Then Will hit her with the restrictions Sherman wanted to place on the analysis of the fragment. Giovanni did not like them. Will then explained how a long, drawn-out court battle over Sherman's conditions would delay their access to the ancient piece of papyrus, which would mean that they would be playing right into their opponents' hands.

Reluctantly, Giovanni agreed to the conditions listed in Sherman's motion. She had to admit that none of them would likely affect the validity or accuracy of her conclusions.

"When do I get a chance to look at it?" she asked.

"As soon as I tell the judge that I have no objection to the request, he should issue an order for them to produce it. Then we will be in business."

What Will did not explain was that Sherman might have other tricks up his sleeve to further frustrate and delay the production of the ancient fragment. With the trial date quickly approaching, Will knew that every day, and every hour, would be critical.

43

THE APARTMENT OF ANGUS MACCAMERON WAS a modest little place up in D.C. amid middle-income brownstones, and halfway between the lower-rent area and the upscale condos in Georgetown.

MacCameron greeted Will at the door with a hearty hello and a big smile. Will suddenly felt foolish that he hadn't brought a gift—or something to add to the dinner. That's the kind of thing Audra had always reminded him to do.

Inside, Will could see the evidence of a very simple existence. The furniture was old; much of it was worn. He noticed that in the living room a throw rug was placed over an area in the carpeting that was torn and frayed. In the corner was a small desk with a computer, with books piled on the floor around it. There were bookshelves in each room, all crammed with books, and with more books stacked in piles on top of each of them.

Will could smell dinner cooking. MacCameron urged Will to come in and meet his wife. As he approached the doorway of one room he turned to Will and lowered his voice.

"My dear Helen has a very rare form of cancer. The cancer cells take over the air sacs of the lungs. She never smoked a cigarette in her life, yet she still came down with it. They gave her a lung transplant a year ago. But the cancer turned up again in the new set of lungs. She has trouble breathing so she has to use an oxygen mask.

"I hope this doesn't bother you. But she is such a blessing to me, such a priceless woman. I wanted you to meet her before things get any worse for her. And, of course, she knows all about you and is eager to see you. Come in to her room, won't you?"

They stepped into a bedroom. Helen MacCameron was propped up in bed with a pink flowered bathrobe on. There was an oxygen mask over her mouth, connected to a tank next to her bed. Her right arm had an IV tube running to a metal stand from which were hanging a clear-looking solution and a darker solution, both in plastic bags.

Her brownish-gray hair had been neatly combed. Someone had put makeup on her face, rather inexpertly applied.

Her arms were laid on top of the covers. They were thin, and the skin seemed to hang a little from her bones.

Helen lifted one arm with great effort and vaguely directed it toward Will. He took her soft, fragile hand. It was cold to the touch. As Will studied her face he saw the features of a woman who would have been a striking beauty in her day. But he noticed something else. The skin around her eyes was crinkling ever so slightly, and the muscles of her face were tightening. Helen MacCameron was smiling at him from behind her oxygen mask.

"Mrs. MacCameron, meeting you is a great honor," Will said. "I know you've been a wonderful wife to Reverend MacCameron. And a great mother to Fiona."

Angus MacCameron bent over and kissed Helen's forehead gently, and then stroked it with his hand.

"Are you hungry, love? Would you like to eat now?"

With an effort Helen shook her head "no." Then she looked as if she wanted to say something. So MacCameron lifted her mask and she whispered something into his ear. Then he smiled and put his wife's mask back on, carefully adjusting it, and left the room with Will.

As soon as the two were in the kitchen together MacCameron told Will, "Helen told me you are very charming. That you are a good man."

"Your wife seems like a very courageous woman."

"I've been telling her all about you," MacCameron said as he opened the stove to check the pot roast. "I've learned to be a moderately decent chef since she's taken a turn for the worse."

"I am sorry she is not doing well."

"The prognosis for my dear wife—the soul of my soul—well, it's not good. I take comfort in knowing that things really do work together for good for those who love the Lord and are called by him, and who have embraced Christ by faith. My wife loves the Lord. She may be doing cartwheels on the golden streets of glory much sooner than I would want."

Then Angus MacCameron's chin trembled a bit, and his voice cracked as he said, "She is my very best friend as well as my soul mate. I fear that I may have a rough road trying to go on without her. I look to God alone for the strength to sustain me when that day comes." And with that he opened up his hands in front of him, as if to release his grip on some treasured but invisible possession.

"I lost my wife," Will said as he helped set the plates on the dining-room table, "and my life fell apart."

MacCameron was carrying in the pot roast on a large serving plate.

"The Bible says there is a kind of grieving everyone goes through, including those who belong to God. Even Jesus wept. There is the loss that God knows we must all experience. But then there is a kind of grieving for those who have no hope beyond the grave. That is the tragic, empty, lonely kind of grief. So, have you read that part yet, in the Gospels, where Jesus wept? You've been reading the Gospels like I suggested?"

"Straight through. All four of them. I even remembered their names. And your little rhyme helped."

"So, you do listen when I talk!" MacCameron exclaimed. "Yes, my Sunday school teacher in Glasgow taught me that as a boy: 'Matthew, Mark, Luke and John; saddle the horse and I'll get on,' he used to say. So, do you remember where it was that Jesus wept?"

"Yes. At the tomb of..." Will had to think for a moment. "Lazarus."

"Well done. Well done."

They both sat down to the meal, and Angus MacCameron prayed a blessing over the food.

"Oh, I nearly forgot!" MacCameron said. "The good news I had for you. I received a letter from a church I had never even heard of before. The letter was a note of encouragement for me to continue the fight against Reichstad's 7QA heresy. And with the letter was a check made out to my magazine. A very large check from the outreach ministry committee of that church. Enough to pay what I owe you and plenty more left over. I'm transferring that whole check to you. You can take it with you when you leave tonight."

The thought of leaving the Robert E. Lee Motel hit Will like an explosion of Independence Day fireworks. He couldn't help from beaming ear to ear.

"I told you my boy, the Lord provides; he really does," MacCameron said.

"Where's that church located?" Will asked.

"Tennessee."

"What was the name of the church?"

"Church of the Golden Road. I believe that was the name."

Now it was clear. And Will could only smile and shake his head. Brother Billy Joe Highlighter and his congregation were now supporting the work of Will Chambers.

"So, you have a church behind you now. That would make you a missionary of a rather strange sort, wouldn't it?" MacCameron noted with a gleam in his eye. "But if you are a missionary, then you had better know what your message is, right? So, barrister Will Chambers, what is your message? Exactly what do you believe?"

As Will thoughtfully chewed his pot roast at the humble table of his client, he knew that he did not have an answer to that question—not yet. But he also felt, just as certainly, that he was destined to discover it. Not just an answer to the mysteries of the legal case he was handling—but something even larger. He felt the powerful pull to some kind of unknown doorway. And he somehow knew that when he dared to open that door, it would lead him to something bigger than all of the battles he had ever fought. Bigger than his pursuit of justice. Bigger even than the dreams that were dashed, and the love he had lost, and the home that lay in ashes. Bigger even, perhaps, than life itself.

44

WILL WAS ON THE LINE WITH J-Fox Sherman's office when Fiona called and left a voice-mail message for Will to call her back.

He was in the process of telling Sherman's associate that he was agreeing to every single one of their conditions for the production of the 7QA fragment to his experts, and that he was overnighting to Judge Kaye his formal consent to the terms set out in Sherman's motion. He was faxing his consent as they were speaking.

Despite all that, Sherman's legal associate was hesitant to commit to an exact time when the fragment would actually be produced.

"The written order of Judge Kaye to produce 7QA to our experts should be signed by day after tomorrow," Will countered. "I do not want any delays. If there are, I will be filing a motion for contempt of court against your office."

The associate lawyer assured him that he would be in touch with J-Fox Sherman, who was presently in trial in a complicated antitrust case in New York, and that he would relay Will's concerns to his boss.

Will called Fiona back. "I'm looking at the area code on your voice mail; that's North Carolina, isn't it?" Will asked.

"Yes," Fiona replied, "I'm getting ready for a concert in the coliseum down here in Greensboro. Thanks for calling me back."

"Sure. How are you?"

"Well, I got your present. That was very kind. You didn't have to do that."

"I know. But I did want to thank you for the dinner. And it just seemed to have your name written all over it."

"I heard about your house burning down. When I heard I just cried. How awful. Da says that he finds the whole thing very—I think 'sinister' is the word he used."

That reminded Will of the problems he was having over the claim, and the cloud of suspicion hanging over his head.

"Fiona, this may come as a strange request. But I just wanted to ask you something. Was I thoughtless enough to include the sales receipt in the box I sent to you?"

"Gee, I don't remember. I don't think so," Fiona replied hesitantly.

"How about the box? Did it have the logo or name of the shop where I bought it?"

Fiona thought for a few seconds.

"I don't think it did. Just a plain white box with tissue paper and Styrofoam in it," she said. And then she asked, "Will, does this have something to do with your house fire? Da told me that they're trying to blame you. They are questioning your word on where you were that day."

"Well," Will replied, "I really don't want to burden you with anything else. Please just let me know if you recall anything about where I bought that statue. I'm sure this fire investigation will come out all right. No reason to worry."

"I sure will try to remember anything I can," Fiona responded. "By the way, I heard that you had dinner with my father and that you met my mother."

"Yes, I did."

"This is the last leg of my tour. I'm going home to be with her full-time. I really need to be with my mum now."

Will could tell that Fiona's voice was trembling slightly.

"It meant a lot, meeting her," Will said.

After a moment's silence, Fiona spoke again. "Will, I did have one other reason to call you." Her voice had changed a little.

"What is it?"

"Well—I guess when I received that package from you with that very thoughtful gift, I thought we ought to talk."

Somehow, Will knew what she was going to tell him.

"Remember our dinner together? You asked whether I was going out on dates. I told you I was single by choice. Like I said, I feel that it is probably God's choice for me. But even if I felt that God had prepared someone for me, it would have to be someone who knows Jesus personally and loves him with all his heart. I think that probably puts us light-years apart."

Will could hear her draw in a shaky breath. "You are a wonderful guy. So much love underneath that thick skin of yours. And a brilliant lawyer. My father was right—I think you are God's choice for his case. But I can't see how you could be God's choice for me. I hope you don't think I am being too harsh in saying this—this is not easy for me. You have such a precious place in my heart. But I just don't want you to have any expectations."

"No," Will said quietly. "I could see this coming some time ago. Just a feeling I had."

He could hear Fiona crying softly.

"Please forgive me," she said composing herself. "With my mum getting worse and everything else, this has been hard. But God has really been so good to us in the midst of all this."

"I wish I could make it easier," Will said. "I would do anything not to see you hurt. Listen, you've got to get ready to sing. I ought to let you go. I want you to sing like an angel tonight. How should I say this—how about, 'give 'em *heaven* tonight!'"

Fiona laughed, and promised she would.

After hanging up the phone Will knew he had heard a door close. He had no choice but to move on. The problem was, he had no idea what that meant, or how he was going to do it. Somehow he had to keep moving straight ahead, and not look back. He sat and stared out the window for several minutes, thinking about the hurt and the sadness he felt because of Fiona's call. He had to face the truth—he had allowed Fiona to become a major force in his heart, like the moon pulling the tide.

Will tried to pull himself together, while he trudged over to the conference room to where the papers for the MacCameron case had now expanded. He had to prepare for Dr. Reichstad's deposition. But he knew now that it would be impossible to get his experts in to evaluate the 7QA fragment *before* he would be asking Reichstad questions under oath. Thus, he would not have that arsenal of ammunition to use in his questioning. That fact would be a major hindrance.

As a result of questioning hundreds of witnesses over the years, he had learned the sad truth. When something *really important* was at stake, you had to corner the witness with the facts—*force* the truth out through well-placed and expertly timed questions. Truth-telling was not, with a biased and self-interested party like Reichstad, a matter that could simply be taken for granted. Rather, the truth was something that would have to be squeezed out like the last bit of toothpaste from a toothpaste tube.

And in just a few days, Will would have his opportunity to start squeezing.

45

JACK HORNBY WAS FOLLOWING UP A LEAD. He knew there had been a meeting recently, near the OPEC headquarters in Vienna. In attendance at the meeting had been the top Muslim clerics from each of the OPEC nations.

Hornby knew there was no *official* tie-in between Islam and the OPEC oil cartel. Yet there had always been a lurking suspicion that the original driving force behind OPEC was the desire to protect and preserve the most potent economic weapon that Islam had—the thick, black liquid that lay like a treasure trove, beneath the sands of the nations of the Middle East.

OPEC had been created in 1960 by a conference of Islamic nations that had met in Baghdad. Among the original five members, the only nation not overtly controlled by Islam was Venezuela. But even it had strong Islamic sympathies and had regularly appointed Muslim delegates to the OPEC conferences.

With the council of Islamic clerics meeting in Vienna at the same time as the annual meeting of OPEC, Hornby had begun to see a pattern emerging.

Then he had received a call from someone in the U.S. who had a relative in Vienna. According to Hornby's source, American billionaire Warren Mullburn had met with the Islamic clerics at a lavish villa just outside Vienna—at the same time the OPEC conference was going on.

Having already been alerted to Mullburn's suspicious connections, Hornby was now hot on the trail. He pulled every public speech, article, and book authored by Warren Mullburn.

After keyword-searching for "Islam, Christianity, Mullburn" on the Net, Hornby noticed the numerous times that Mullburn had made favorable mention of Islam and had advocated a merger of some type between the two religions. Was Mullburn's motivation just part of his eccentric philosophical meanderings? Or was his entrée into the Islam-OPEC connection a matter of brute economics? Or was it perhaps some combination of the two?

Hornby called Will Chambers to exchange information and get an update on the Reichstad lawsuit.

"Guess what I just finished doing," Will said after he had been greeted by the reporter.

"I'm bad at guessing games," Hornby replied.

"I thought you were the guy who was always running with 'hunches.'"

"I believe in hunches. That's different. What'd you come up with?"

"Well—but first I need to give you some background details. And these need to stay under wraps, unless and until the case goes to trial."

"You know my reputation. I only blow the lid at the right time—and on the right people."

"Okay," Will replied. He went on to recount MacCameron's meeting with Dr. Hunter in Jerusalem. And how and why MacCameron had become suspicious of the deaths of Hunter and Azid. Lastly, Will explained his client's theories about Reichstad's connection with the two dead men and the fragment that seemed so similar to 7QA.

"So what you're saying," concluded Hornby, "is that Reichstad must have come into possession of Hunter's fragment by some skullduggery—is that the case?"

"You're right on track."

"So—you're going to have your client testify at trial that Hunter gave him a description of the fragment that was identical to what's now known as the 7QA fragment—and if the jury believes your guy, you just might have ballpark triple on that issue. Okay, I see a story coming."

"Wait a minute—how are you going to get this in print?" Will questioned. "Your newspaper's in Mullburn's pocket now."

"Watch me," Hornby responded.

"Well, and Mr. Billionaire brings me to the punch-line. I did a computer check on the Israeli newspapers during the week of Reichstad's New Testament antiquities conference in Jerusalem," Will explained. "I pulled up a little blurb in the *Jerusalem Post.* Guess who was in town that week? *Our Mr. Mullburn*—on 'business.' The same week as Reichstad was there—the same week that Azid and Hunter show up dead. And shortly thereafter, Reichstad trumpets to the world that he has the 7QA—received from Azid shortly before his 'suicide.'"

"Then lo and behold—7QA spells doom to the story of the resurrection of Jesus Christ. And that is just swell to the Muslims—because calling Jesus the Son of God is blasphemy to them," Hornby added.

"So, what is it that you have for me?" Will asked.

"Well, speaking of Islam," Hornby went on, "I just learned that Mullburn was in on some supersecret meeting of the head Muslim clerics of the OPEC nations, in Vienna. That meeting was just before the formal OPEC meeting—also in Vienna. My hunch is that Mullburn is trying to convince the Muslims that the U.S. is Allah-friendly. In return for some 'cultural reconciliation,' to borrow one of Kenneth Sharptin's favorite phrases, Mullburn is trying to get himself appointed to this new American chair at the OPEC meetings."

"Well, in light of his campaign contributions for Sharptin, that certainly smells illegal."

"Of course," Hornby noted, "so Mullburn will get someone who is beholden to him—the guy owns everybody—to hold that seat at OPEC and to be his stoolie. Mullburn would have insider information on oil production and prices way before the rest of the world. It would be a goldmine for him."

"The Arabs will give all of that power to Mullburn for the price of a little religious compromise by the U.S.?" Will said skeptically.

"Well," Hornby laughed, "that, plus some advanced military secrets and real heavy duty weaponry—compliments of the United States government!"

"What does Undersecretary Sharptin get out of all this—assuming there is some kind of—I hesitate to use the word..."

"Use it. It won't hurt," Hornby broke in sarcastically.

"Okay. *Conspiracy*."

"What does Sharptin get out of all this? Why he gets a little card that says, 'Go straight to White House as vice president—don't stop at go.' Sharptin will have bought for the U.S. the perception of oil security and lower gas prices. He's already got the Arab nations looking like they are driving the terrorists into the sea. Helping America feel safe and secure in a new partnership for peace. No more Wall Street bombings. No more trucks with nuclear warheads. That makes Sharptin a valuable commodity to the President—because the current White House popularity ratings stink like a dead skunk."

"Does this all make sense?" Will asked, a little mind-boggled by the size of what he was hearing.

"I love baseball," Hornby said. "Yes, I do love baseball. And the real thing of beauty, in my book at least, is a gracefully executed triple play. Where those big two-hundred-twenty-pound athletes are gliding in the air, leaping, catching, bulleting that ball to the next guy all in one movement—like a ballet in the dust. How I do love to see a good triple play."

Will Chambers was waiting for the point.

"So here we have the chance to make a triple play. Reichstad is at first base: He gets money, fame, and fortune through the discovery of 7QA. Only he needs Mullburn, Mullburn is behind this somehow with his funding and his influence—and maybe even something more than that.

"Undersecretary Sharptin is at second base. He uses the 7QA discovery to plow the old-time Christian religion into the ground and create some 'feel-good' reconciliation with Islam; in return, the Arab nations appear to help the old U.S. of A. keep everybody safe from terrorism—and also keep everybody driving with cheaper gas. A huge arms deal to the Arabs through Sharptin's arm-twisting is the deal-sweetener. And Sharptin gets into the White House for his good sportsmanship and fancy footwork."

"And Mullburn is at third base?" Will asked.

"Right. He gets the inside OPEC track to more oil—and at the same time can lay claim to having fulfilled his own megalomania by creating a new religious merger—Islam and Christianity—mixed with some of Mullburn's own brand of evolutionary theology."

"Hornby, you are a conspiratorialist! I never would have guessed it."

"No, to the contrary," Hornby replied. "I just know a good story when I see it. But there is one little problem with all this."

"What's that?" Will inquired.

"We don't have a speck of clear proof that this science fiction story is really true. Without a smoking gun we've got no ball game. Now, aren't you going to be taking Reichstad's deposition soon?"

"In two days," Will said.

"Why not start testing our conspiracy theory by asking some pointed questions at the deposition?"

"No, I can't afford to let him know what we are thinking," Will responded. "If I can prove it—I will spring it on them at trial. If not, I can't let our theory see the light of day."

"Let me know how the deposition goes," Hornby said, and then hung up.

Will went back to his preparation for Reichstad's deposition. He knew that when he questioned Reichstad he would be walking the razor's edge—trying to gain the maximum amount of information, but trying not to tip off his opponents to the fact that he might have discovered a conspiracy so outrageous that it looked almost capable of consuming the truth itself—*almost*—but not quite.

46

Angus MacCameron had said he could meet with Will as soon as Fiona was off tour. She could relieve him in caring for his cancer-stricken wife.

When MacCameron arrived at Will's office a day before Dr. Riechstad's deposition, he was carrying a thin book in his hand.

"I thought I had given you everything that Reichstad ever wrote," MacCameron explained, "but I forgot to give you this one."

"What is it?" Will inquired as he grabbed his notepad and sat down at the table in his office, across from his client.

"A book that Reichstad authored about ten years ago. I think it's out of print now."

Will looked at the title: *A New Quest for Jesus.*

"Anything helpful in it?"

MacCameron shook his head and said, "I honestly don't know. I have been a little tired lately, and with Helen not doing well, I just have not had a chance to look at it."

MacCameron was pale and looked weary, so Will decided to cut the meeting short.

The two of them reviewed the areas of questioning Will had planned for Reichstad's deposition.

Next, they discussed the Summary Judgment motion that Sherman had filed. Will had prepared an affidavit for MacCameron to sign, explaining his version of the facts, and why his accusations against Reichstad in his magazine were well-founded.

Will gave a copy of the rough draft of the affidavit to MacCameron so he could take it with him and read it over.

"Check closely for any inaccuracies," Will advised him. "If you sign this thing, and then you say something different at trial, you are in real trouble. Also, see if I have left anything out that you think is important."

"When can we look at the 7QA fragment?" MacCameron asked.

"I called the court clerk yesterday, and Judge Kaye signed the order requiring them to produce it to us according to the terms that Sherman had demanded. I called Sherman's office, but he is still in trial in New York. But don't worry. I will put a formal demand on record at the deposition. Today is Thursday. I see no reason we can't have it by next Monday."

"Good," MacCameron said, his face lighting up. "Now that we know that Hunter said 'fragment*s*' in his message, I am even more convinced that when we get a look at 7QA we are going to see evidence that it was originally part of a bigger piece. Azid probably cut it into pieces. He was going to sell the fragments piecemeal and drive up the price."

"Have you got any further ideas on where the other pieces might be? Or how many there are?" Will asked.

"Hunter's message said he was sending the 'fragments' separately. I think at first, Azid gave only one piece to Hunter. Probably the 7QA fragment first, to see how much Hunter thought the British Museum might be willing to pay. I don't think Azid had any idea how valuable it was going to be. But I know Azid knew a little about Koine Greek—and I think he probably recognized the name 'Jesus' in the Greek. That's why he cut up the document and gave 7QA to Hunter first."

"What do you think Hunter's conclusions were?"

"I'm sure Hunter probably reached the same conclusion that Reichstad later did. Except for one thing."

"What's that?"

"When Hunter met with me at the Between the Arches Café in Jerusalem, at first he was talking as if there was *one* fragment that he had obtained from Azid. But later in the conversation, it started sounding like he was talking about *several* fragments. You have to remember, Hunter was very cryptic about all of this—he looked like he was under intense pressure."

"What do you think happened?"

"I believe that Azid cut the larger fragment into two, perhaps three pieces. He first showed the fragment that had the word 'Jesus' to Hunter because he knew that would create great excitement."

"So Hunter evaluates that piece—the one you think is 7QA, the piece that Reichstad later obtained?"

"Precisely," MacCameron replied.

"And Hunter looks at the 7QA piece," Will continued, "says to himself, this is first-century writing, and rushes back to Azid and demands to know the whole story behind it. And so Azid says, 'I've got these other fragments that belong to the same piece.'"

"Yes, that's what I think happened," MacCameron replied. "Azid shows Hunter that he has the other pieces. Hunter informs Azid that when he puts the whole puzzle together he will be able to secure a huge amount of money from the British Museum. I can only presume that Richard collected all of the pieces from Azid—because he mentioned 'the fragments' in his message."

"That means that the only people who knew of the existence of the other fragment pieces were Azid, of course, and Hunter."

"And someone else: Those responsible for killing them both," MacCameron added.

"Did Hunter mention other reasons why he felt that Azid's death was not a suicide? All we know is that there was no motive—no depression or despondency—and no suicide note."

"No, nothing else really. Hunter did say that the Israeli police had been at the scene also, but he said nothing about their observations."

"So if Hunter had all the pieces...Okay, the killers go to Azid first. He doesn't have anything. Then they kill him. But why?"

The two were silent. Then Will answered his own question.

"Whoever did the killing didn't do it just to sell the fragments on the black market. It wasn't just for profit—they wanted to be able to lay claim to them in front of the entire world. Therefore they couldn't afford to have any witnesses. Azid's death had to look like suicide—because Reichstad knew that he would have to eventually explain where he got the 7QA fragment—and that meant having to tie the fragment back to Azid. An allegation that he was murdered would cast suspicion on Reichstad."

"Why didn't Azid simply refuse to tell them anything?" MacCameron asked.

Will smiled at his client's naivete.

"He probably did—at first. But I have a feeling that someone used very strong persuasion to get him to talk before they killed him." Then Will had a thought—and wrote down "Israeli Police" to remind himself to call Tiny.

"You mean they tortured him before they killed him?" MacCameron asked.

"Yes, I would say that is likely."

"Why wouldn't the police be able to detect that when they looked over Azid's body?" MacCameron wondered.

"There are ways to torture someone, I think, where it's not so obvious."

"Poor Azid. And Richard. Such a waste of life. Such a terrible thing," MacCameron commented sadly.

Will got up and stretched. Then he said, "You have no idea where those other fragments are. And Reichstad either doesn't know—or he does, but he won't admit it. So how in the world are we going to find out where they are? That is the ultimate proof we need in this case."

"I called London and spoke to Richard's sister, with whom he had been living. She didn't know where the other fragments might be. I called the British Museum and asked about his papers and effects. They said they had gone through everything in his office—a matter of routine inventory of his projects—but they didn't find anything either."

"So," Will said, "that only leaves us with Hunter's riddle." With that, Will glanced at his notes. He recited the message:

> So if you ever have to put the picture together, just remember this the next time you come to the halls of the British Museum. Remember your Bible...Remember the resurrection order.

"I know those fragments are somewhere at the British Museum," MacCameron mused. "They have to be. I just don't know where to start."

"And if you were to find them—what if they substantiate Reichstad's claims that 7QA is proof that Jesus never rose from the grave. Then what?" Will asked his client.

"They won't."

"How do you know?"

"Because," MacCameron said with a smile, "I know that my Redeemer liveth!"

"How can you be so sure?" Will probed. "I've looked at the evidence while I've been preparing this case. While I can't understand it scientifically, I can see the evidence historically and logically. As a trial lawyer, I concede there's a persuasive case for the credibility of the Gospel accounts of the resurrection. But that doesn't push me over the line into faith."

"That's because," MacCameron noted with a smile, "reason can never 'push' you over the line into faith. It can bring you up to the bar, but it can't propel you over. That is the job of something else—something much different indeed."

"And what would that be?"

"The human will. Faith is like a muscle, exercised by an act—not just of reason, but of the will. God draws people to himself by his inscrutable and divine election—but at the same time you must be willing to exercise that muscle of faith yourself. You must take the first step of faith not because your sense of logic compels you, but because *you* have willed. God wants you to meet him, through his Son, Jesus Christ. He calls you. He woos you. He even chases and pursues you through a million steps and a million different paths. But he waits now for you to turn in his direction, and merely take that first step."

Will was quiet. After a moment MacCameron rose, getting ready to leave.

"Will, take the church bell tower across the street there as an example. Last time I was here I went over and looked around," MacCameron continued. "They say that its bells have been ringing, pulled by hand, every day since 1776."

"Yes, that's true. Everybody knows that."

"How do you know it?" MacCameron asked.

"Well, you just told me," Will replied.

"Do you trust me enough to bank your life on it?"

"Of course not," Will retorted.

"How else do you know the history of that church bell tower?"

"Oh, common knowledge of the folks here in Monroeville. And I'm sure that there are historical documents in the local museum that spell it out."

"The historical documents would be the best evidence?"

"Probably," Will answered.

"How do you know that you're not being lied to? That the chimes you hear from that tower are not chimes being sounded by some kind of recording? How do you know that the tourists aren't just being told a pack of lies?"

"I don't know that—not for sure."

"Is there a way to find out for sure that someone is still pulling those ropes by hand?"

"Obviously," Will said. "Just walk over and meet the bell-puller personally."

MacCameron smiled the kind of smile that told Will that his point had been made. Will was beginning to sense where MacCameron was headed, but he wasn't ready to acknowledge it.

"So what does that prove? What's your point?" Will asked as MacCameron started for the door.

Then MacCameron stopped and turned around. His eyes were soft and he had a big smile.

"The point," the old Scotsman said, "is this: It's time to take the step. It's time to walk up to the power that is pulling the ropes—to personally encounter the Great Master of the bell tower, the First and the Last, the Alpha and the Omega. The One who tolls the bells of heaven and earth. The One who spins the planets as if they were mere child's toys. Are you ready to take that step?"

There was only a shrug from Will Chambers.

"Ah, that's a pity. I will pray for you, Will. That you will take that step of faith. That you will invite his Son, Jesus Christ, into that place in your heart where the will resides, and where true love begins."

MacCameron said goodbye and left the office. Will sat at the table tapping his pen for a few minutes, feeling oppressed.

Outside, the bells of St. Andrew's Church began to toll.

47

IT WAS EARLY EVENING, AND THE SUN WAS LOW on the horizon, sending blazes of orange and red off the surface of the water, and casting long shadows along the decks of the U.S. Navy destroyers that were anchored in the harbor there.

Just off that harbor in Newport News, Virginia, things were crowded within the small office that was serving as an intelligence command center. The expanding team of federal agents who had been tracking the movements of Abdul el Alibahd now included the participation of the FBI and Army intelligence as well as the CIA and Naval intelligence.

As the team divided up their paper-wrapped dinners from a local hamburger joint, the Deputy Director of CIA Operations addressed the group.

"Our last information on the black gull had him heading into Khost near the Pakistan border. Then we had no further intelligence until late last night. That's when our sources told us that there was a report—unconfirmed as of yet—of a possible sighting of the black gull entering Libya. Then this morning we received a report of another possible sighting of several of his personal bodyguards in Lisbon. If he is with those bodyguards, and we believe he is, that means that he probably flew out of Libyan airspace and directly over to Lisbon by private jet. He's obviously moving fast. We contacted our CIA operations people in Lisbon, as well as the Portuguese authorities. And of course, we have red-tagged him through Interpol. We are trying to draw the net tight before he leaves Lisbon."

"What are the scenarios for his destination?" one of the agents asked.

"One bet is that he is heading down to some of the small islands along the western edge of Africa, possibly just off of the coast of the western Sahara. Maybe to establish some new training camps there."

"Any other scenarios?" another agent asked.

"Sure. It doesn't seem to make much sense that he would go north. So that leaves only one more direction."

"West. To the United States," a naval officer interjected.

"Yes," the CIA director affirmed. "But that could also mean Mexico. Or Canada—even the Newfoundland area, which is the closest. But how could that make any sense?"

One agent raised his hand and volunteered a thought.

"Maybe he's decided to take up commercial fishing," he quipped sarcastically. "In which case, I've got a boat with a big hole in the hull I could sell to him."

After the sardonic laughter died down, the director returned to the same question. This time there were no volunteers. There were only puzzled faces as they wondered why the black gull might choose to move across the Atlantic Ocean.

48

DRIVING ON HIS WAY TO DR. ALBERT REICHSTAD'S deposition, Will Chambers called Tiny Heftland on his cell phone.

He asked Tiny if he would get in touch with some of his old contacts in the Israeli police. He wanted to find out everything he could about the death of Tony Azid. Will told Tiny what he had discovered thus far.

Because Azid was an Arab, and was killed in his shop in Bethlehem, a city under the newly negotiated joint jurisdiction of the Palestinian police and the Israeli police, the Palestinian police had primary responsibility to investigate the antiquities dealer's death. As a result of their review, the Palestinian police had ruled it a suicide. The Israeli police had also showed up at the scene, but did not file an official report. That was apparently standard procedure in cases of overlapping police jurisdiction.

Tiny agreed to try to re-establish some of his Middle East contacts and see if he could interview the Israeli police who had been at the scene of Azid's death. But he said he couldn't promise anything.

When Will finally arrived at the conference room of Sherman's law firm to take Dr. Reichstad's deposition, he was surprised to find that J-Fox Sherman was still in New York. Sherman had one of his associates sitting in for him.

Reichstad looked rested, well-tailored, and confident.

Will immediately inquired of Reichstad's lawyer when they would be producing the 7QA fragment in accordance with Judge Kaye's order.

"Immediately after our hearing with Judge Kaye on Monday," the associate lawyer replied. "If your defense has not already gone down in flames as a result of Judge Kaye's ruling on our Summary-Judgment motion, then we will produce it that same afternoon. However, we expect that Judge Kaye will be finding in our favor on both issues—reckless conduct by MacCameron, and the lack of truth in his published article. And when that happens, then your request to inspect the 7QA fragment will obviously be moot, and we will be under no compulsion to produce it at all."

Will knew that if Riechstad's lawyers achieved a total victory on Monday, the original fragment would not have to see the light of day. In fact, Reichstad might conceivably never permit anyone outside his own, tightly controlled staff of experts to ever scientifically examine the 7QA fragment.

After Dr. Reichstad had been sworn in by the court reporter, Will questioned him about the various written allegations he had made in his lawsuit against MacCameron. Reichstad handled himself with ease.

Next Will asked him about the alleged damage to his professional reputation he claimed had been caused by MacCameron's article. Reichstad's response showed that he had been immaculately prepared by his lawyers, and that he was well aware of the presence of the court video camera.

"My reputation among my peers and colleagues was, for a period of time, devastated," Reichstad recounted. He described a gathering held at one of the Harvard faculty's homes shortly after MacCameron's article was published, a reception to honor his discovery of the 7QA fragment. Reichstad told how he had been humiliated.

"I was there with my professional colleagues—my academic peers—and when they raised their glasses to toast me..." Reichstad said, his voice trembling with drama and emotion, "there was a voice raised from a corner of the room...it sent chills down my spine, and it literally broke my heart."

"What did the voice say?" Will asked.

"The voice shouted out, 'Murderer! Murderer!'"

"And then another voice yelled out against me also."

"What did that voice say?"

"Well," Reichstad continued, his voice quiet and intense, and putting his hand to his forehead as if to soothe some blinding psychic pain, "that other voice said 'Fraud!' That's exactly what that other person said. 'Fraud!'"

"There I was," Reichstad concluded, "with a glass in my hand, being toasted for the greatest biblical archaeology discovery of all time—and right then and there, I am called a murderer and a fraud in front of my family, my friends, and my colleagues."

"Do you contend that my client, Reverend Angus MacCameron, had anything to do with your being embarrassed at this party?" Will asked.

"I certainly do! The article in that miserable little right-wing magazine, *Digging for Truth*, had come out the week before. In that article your client accused me, in essence, of being a murderer and a professional fraud. Of course I blame your client for my humiliation. My wife burst into tears. We left the party and drove home in silence. I have never been so embarrassed in all of my long career as a scholar and a scientist."

"Do you deny having any personal knowledge about the death of Harim Azid—or Dr. Richard Hunter?" Will asked pointedly.

"Of course I have no such knowledge!" Reichstad bellowed. "Don't be absurd!"

"Did you conspire with any person, anywhere, at anytime, to kill Harim Azid or Richard Hunter?" Will asked, looking straight into Reichstad's face.

"Your question is so degrading and so stupid it doesn't deserve a response," Reichstad said with a look of utter disgust.

"That's where you are wrong," Will countered. "When you filed a legal document in a federal court called a Complaint, instituting a lawsuit against my client, accusing my client of lying about you and being reckless in his publication of that article, and then demanding that my client pay you money—a huge amount of money—as a matter of fact, basically asking my client to pay to you the equivalent of the annual budget of a small island republic—then you put yourself into a position in which you must answer my questions, Dr. Reichstad. That's the way the law works. Now please answer my question."

With that, Will had the court reporter read the full question back again.

Reichstad had a smirk on his face when he finally answered.

"The answer to that question is this: I am absolutely, one-hundred-percent not guilty of what your client is accusing me of."

"And do you deny that your obtaining of the 7QA fragment—and your evaluation of it—and your published interpretation of it—were, and are, well below the standards of the average expert in biblical textual antiquities?" Will asked, and then turned to the lawyer from Sherman's firm and said he knew it was a multiple and compound question, and he would be glad to divide it up for Reichstad to more easily answer.

The junior attorney smiled and said that wasn't necessary. He knew Reichstad could handle "even the poorly formed questions that you are trying to throw at him."

Reichstad leaned forward onto the conference table and looked at Will Chambers. "What kind of man are you, Mr. Chambers, questioning my work as a scholar? What could you possibly know about the years of painstaking work I've done in my field?"

"Apparently," Will said, turning to the junior partner, "your client is incapable of answering my 'poorly formed questions,' judging by his last response. Would you like to instruct him to answer the question—or shall I?"

"Do give Mr. Chambers an answer, Dr. Reichstad," the associate said, "so we can all go home and start our weekend."

Reichstad folded his hands on the table, and spoke slowly, punctuating each word: "I deny that any of my work regarding 7QA was below the standards in my field. Furthermore, I will tell you right now, Mr. Chambers, that my work on the 7QA fragment is among the finest work ever known in the field of biblical textual antiquities."

Will paused a moment. He was astounded at Albert Reichstad's capacity for self-aggrandizement. Then Will led him into the final series of questions.

"Was your interpretation of the 7QA fragment motivated by a desire to deal a devastating blow—to bring an end—to conservative Christian scholarship on the issue of the resurrection?"

"Of course not!"

"Do you consider such conservative Christian scholarship—and let's define that term as the school of thought that holds that, in the original manuscript text, all of the Gospel stories reliably recounted a bodily resurrection of Jesus—do you consider such conservative Christian scholars to have been—well, how should I put this...have you ever considered such conservative Christian scholars to be on the level of 'cavemen' who haven't learned the secrets of fire, or the wheel?"

Reichstad laughed. Then there was silence.

"Absolutely not. I do not reach my conclusions because of my dislike of conservative Christian scholarship. I reach my conclusions based on the scientific method."

"So you would deny any kind of 'theological agenda' in trying to disprove the resurrection of Jesus of Nazareth?" Will inquired.

"I certainly deny that. I absolutely deny that."

"One hundred percent, absolutely deny it?" Will followed up with a wry smile.

"Yes. One hundred percent, absolutely," Reichstad said with finality and gusto.

"Doctor," Will concluded, "tell me every book and paper you have authored on the subject of Jesus of Nazareth."

"Counsel," Reichstad's attorney interrupted, "you already have, as an exhibit in this deposition, Dr. Reichstad's professional curriculum vitae. His long-form résumé. All of his published works are listed right there in front of you."

"Is that true?" Will asked Reichstad. "Are they all listed right here?"

"Yes." Reichstad responded with a sigh. "Everything is listed there," and he pointed to the papers on the conference table.

"Are you sure you haven't forgotten anything?"

"Yes, I am sure. Everything I have written about Jesus of Nazareth is listed on my curriculum vitae, which you have right in front of you," Reichstad answered with irritation in his voice.

"And you are as sure of that as you are of, well, the fact that you were not involved in the deaths of Azid and Hunter? As sure of that as you are of the fact that you have not committed scientific fraud?"

"Yes. As sure," Reichstad replied, and glanced at his lawyer as if he were searching for reassurance of some kind.

When the deposition was over, Will extended his hand to Reichstad, who merely sniffed and turned, and walked away.

When Will Chambers got into his Corvette in the parking structure he opened his briefcase, and pulled out the slender little book of Reichstad's that MacCameron had brought to their last meeting. He opened it up and re-read the book's prologue once more. Then he closed it, put it back in his briefcase, and started back toward Monroeville.

49

BY THE TIME WILL ENTERED MONROEVILLE it was dark, and the streetlights were on. He planned to stop by the Robert E. Lee Motel first and pick up his belongings, check out, and bid that place a fond, and final, adieu. With the money from Billy Joe Highlighter's church paying some of Will's legal fees, he had been able to rent a small apartment.

Will stopped at the lobby to pay for his stay and encountered the usual stout, expressionless desk clerk there. After Will had paid his bill the man reached down under the desk with some effort and pulled something out. It was a folded piece of paper.

"You received a message today," he said in his extra-coarse sandpaper voice, handing the note to Will.

When Will opened it up, he saw a communication that had apparently been printed in the desk clerk's own writing.

> Will—
>
> See you in court on Monday. I'll be in the audience section cheering you on.
>
> Jacki

As Will smiled and stuffed the note in his pocket the desk clerk asked him simply, "Girlfriend?"

"No, just a friend," Will replied.

"Nice to have friends like that," the desk clerk commented, thrusting his hands in the pockets of the gray sweatpants that were stretched over his wide waist.

"Yes. It sure is."

"You a lawyer?"

"Yes. I'm Will Chambers," he said extending his hand out to the other man.

"Vernon Dithers," the clerk said, shaking his hand.

"Well," Will said as he lifted his suitcase and swung his suit hanger over his shoulder, "it was good to meet you, Vernon. And thanks for giving me the message." He loaded up his Corvette so he could head over to his office.

He wanted to pick up some other parts of the *Reichstad vs. MacCameron* file and take them home with him for the weekend. "Home" was now the small apartment he had found a few blocks down from his office. He would stay there until he was able to finish his dispute with the insurance company.

Down deep Will wondered if there was any way he was going to be able to remove himself as a suspect in the arson without divulging the identity of the public defender he had met in New York that day. And until he resolved that question to the satisfaction of the insurance company, they would not pay off his fire loss.

Sitting in his car, Will took a minute to call the Public Defender's Office in New York. He figured he'd just leave a voice mail for his informant there, asking him to call back the following week. To Will's surprise, one of the lawyers, who was working late, answered the phone. But when Will asked for the voice mail of his contact, he heard something that made his heart sink.

"Sorry, he's no longer with the office here. Took a job overseas, I think. I'm not sure."

"You have no idea where he went?"

"No. I'm afraid not."

"He didn't tell me anything about this," Will said with a tinge of desperation in his voice.

"I think it happened kind of suddenly—all in the last week or so."

"How do you suggest that I contact him? It's very important."

"Well, you can contact our personnel director on Monday. But I do know that, as a matter of policy, they don't give out forwarding addresses of former employees."

After hanging up Will thought that the only thing he could do would be to break his promise of anonymity and lead the fire investigators to the public defender's office in New York. Surely, the personnel director would give the forwarding address information to law-enforcement officers.

The problem with that plan, however, was that if the investigators did track the lawyer down, Will had no assurance whether he would tell them the truth. What if he denied having met with Will at all that day? If that happened, Will Chambers would be notched up from a suspect to "prime suspect."

Further, what if his job change had had something to do with the fact that he had divulged classified information to Will? What if the man had been "relocated," as with the witness protection program? What if he could never be found?

It certainly seemed foolhardy to invite the fire investigators to try to track down his New York informant unless Will could contact him first. But now that looked impossible.

Driving over to the office, Will tried to forget about the arson issue. He tried to refocus on how he would allocate his time over the weekend to prepare for the Monday-morning court hearing before Judge Kaye.

He tallied off the parts of the file he would need in his argument against Sherman's Summary-Judgment motion. He also wanted to pick up the Bible on his desk and take it to the apartment with him. Will had read the four Gospels through in their entirety, and he had just finished a first reading of the book of Acts.

MacCameron had suggested that Will be conversant with Acts because it was the immediate historical successor to the Gospel accounts. Will had learned that it recorded the events after the resurrection of Jesus, starting with his departure from Earth and then going on to the founding of the first-century church. Now he wanted to read the book through a second time during his evenings alone in his apartment.

As Will approached the front of his law office building, the thought flicked through his mind that he might telephone Fiona on Saturday when he took a break in his work. Then he recalled their last conversation. He considered that to have been a complete and final "Dear John" sendoff. No, he would not call her. Though he had powerful feelings for her, none of that could matter anymore. If he truly had respect for Fiona, then he must honor her resolve that there could be nothing between them.

Will noticed, as he parked his car across from his office, that there was a man leaning against the front of the old, red-brick building, just to the left of the front door. He was dark-complexioned, possibly Middle Eastern, and he was reading a newspaper.

Just down the street, perhaps thirty feet away, there was a white, windowless van. Another dark-complexioned man was there, at the van's back. He was looking down at his keys, appearing to be busy.

As Will started across the street he felt uneasy about entering through the front door. There was something odd about these two men, though he could not put his finger on it. He decided to cross the street at a diagonal and head to the alley that ran along the side of the building. He could loop around the side of the building and enter through the back door.

While walking down the alley between his building and the next one, Will glanced in the side mirror of a car parked along the alley. Adrenaline shot through him as he saw the two men walking rapidly, shoulder to shoulder, after him.

Will ducked into the side doorway at his right. He grabbed the door handle and pulled hard, but it was locked. He turned and saw that the two men were now at a full run in his direction.

Will ran down the alley and turned the corner. One of the cleaning staff was coming out of the rear door of the next-door building, lugging a floor polisher. Will frantically squeezed past him and ran full speed down the hallway to the front entrance. He planned to cross the street to his convertible and take off. He knew that the van would be no match for his Corvette.

But the front door was locked. Will looked for a release but found none. He heard loud voices and yelling at the back as his two pursuers forced their way past the custodian, and into the building after him.

Will ran up the stairs to the second floor, two steps at a time. He could hear one of the men yelling in a foreign language as he came up the steps after him.

At the top, Will looked in both directions. He saw a fire escape to the right at the end of the hallway. He decided to go for it, and sprinted down to the door marked "Fire Exit" without looking back. The alarm started sounding as he smashed the lock, swung the door open, and started noisily scampering down the metal fire escape stairs that zigzagged toward the ground. He leaped down the last four steps.

Running hard and breathless now, he was heading for the street at the front of the building. The alley was clear. Only fifty feet or so to cross the street, leap into his car, and jam it into gear. Nothing to it. In thirty seconds he would be roaring down the street, with those guys, whoever they were, standing in the trail of his exhaust.

As Will reached the end of the alley he quickly glanced behind him, but saw no one following.

Then he got a very bad feeling.

His brain flashed a warning to stop short before he reached the corner, but his legs were unable to respond quickly enough.

A pair of arms reached out and clotheslined Will at the neck. Will fell to the ground with the man going down on top of him. Will smashed his fist into his face, crunching his nose. The man was shouting something in his language—and then there was a second pair of arms from the other side, wrestling him back down to the ground. Both men were yelling excitedly in an unrecognizable tongue, then the second man stuck something sharp into Will's neck.

Will felt the needle prick. As the man depressed the syringe, Will saw a brilliant flash of light that consumed everything. And then, in the brilliance of that light, he fell into unconsciousness.

There was a vision. Two rows of men, carrying guns, facing each other as if in a military ceremony. Off in the distance, beyond the rows of what might have been soldiers, and through an arched gate, there was an incandescent, glowing light. The light was getting closer. Out of it came a man in a robe. His robe was white—whiter even than the brilliant light around him. The man in the white robe was walking down between the rows of men, toward Will.

He spoke.

"Will Chambers, why do you struggle against the truth?"

"Who are you?"

The man in the white robe reached his hand toward Will and answered.

"I am..."

When he spoke those words, the men with the guns were thrown down to the ground, as if they were toy soldiers.

"I am the One you are searching for."

"Am I dreaming?" Will asked, barely able to speak.

"Is this a dream?" Will asked again, trembling in the presence of something so overpowering that—if it were not for the ocean of calm in the robed man's voice, a voice that sounded as if it could still the rushing of a thousand waters—Will feared his heart might stop in his chest.

Will regained consciousness, coming to the awareness of a rushing, roaring noise all around him. He had no idea how long he had been out. His head felt as though it were splitting.

Then he became aware that, even though he was awake, he was in darkness. Will felt some rough material wrapped around his head, covering his eyes. His hands were tied behind his back, and he was lying on his side, on a hard surface. He seemed to be floating—up, and then down, then up again.

Just below the edges of the blindfold Will caught a glimpse of the riveted metal floorboards he was lying on. As he struggled to sit upright he heard a man near him yell, and then he felt a blow to the side of his head that knocked him down. As he hit the floor, his blindfold loosened and he saw a man in a seat in front of him, seated at the controls—of a helicopter.

Will lay quiet, still groggy and confused. He heard the men talking back and forth in a language he couldn't recognize. While he lay there he tried to connect the bizarre events he was starting to remember.

He had been chased, and caught. But where was that? And he remembered having a dream.

Struggling to think, Will recalled that he had been pursued near his office. Two men. A van. He had been caught, and something had been stuck in his neck. He must have been given a drug.

Where was he being taken? He was sure he was being kidnapped. What did these men want with him? What was the reason behind it?

Then something hard and cold was put underneath his blindfold, between his eyes. He recognized a gun barrel, and heard the click as the hammer was pulled back. One of the men was laughing.

The gun barrel moved from between his eyes to the middle of his forehead. Then the laughing stopped.

Now there was no more thought about reasons, no more wondering about answers. There was only the reality of the gun at his head. Only Will's belief that he was now just seconds from death.

Will was praying silently, feeling the gun barrel pressed against his forehead, hearing only the roar of the helicopter's engine above him.

"God, please help me. I think this is the end."

50

IN HIS OFFICE AT THE STATE BUILDING, Department Undersecretary Kenneth Sharptin received a call. When he picked up the phone he heard the familiar digital voice requesting that he dial a specific number. He did so immediately.

In his research center in Maryland, Dr. Albert Reichstad received the same call, heard the same familiar computer voice, dialed the same number out, and became part of a three-way teleconference.

The third party led the conference.

"Dr. Reichstad, enlighten us about the status of your case. You are going to court on Monday morning are you not?"

"Yes. Sherman's firm is arguing our motion for a Summary Judgment."

"And you will prevail?"

"Sherman tells me our chances are excellent."

"I don't care about 'excellent' chances. Chance and probability, to me, are meaningless. Before the event, they are empty guesses. After the event, it is too late for such things to do any good. I prefer certainty. I'm sure you know that by now."

"Sherman is a typical lawyer that way, I'm afraid," Reichstad explained. "He says he can't guarantee the results. But he feels very certain that we will win both of the issues we are going after. And if we win *both* issues, we will not need to turn over the 7QA fragment at all."

"And if you don't win *both* issues on Monday?"

"Then we have to turn over 7QA for their inspection that same afternoon."

"That is exactly what I was trying to avoid," the third party said.

"It's not the end of the world if another set of experts has to inspect 7QA. Though I've fought off the rest of the academic world up to now, I really thought it was going to happen eventually," Reichstad continued. "But this way, if we *have to*, then we produce it to MacCameron's two experts. I would much rather submit 7QA to those 'experts': Dr. Giovanni—this disgruntled former nun—and the other one, that materials engineer who has never dealt with antiquities before. Better those two, who have to comply with all our court-ordered restrictions, than the whole of the archaeological world.

"Then after the analysis, we can tell the whole world we have permitted 7QA to be examined by 'outside experts.' That will shut the mouths of the critics who have been complaining that I've kept it all to myself. And even if MacCameron's people disagree with my conclusions about the fragment, we can still bury them in terms of public opinion. I mean, just look at their lack of credentials, and their lack of world-class credibility compared to me and my group."

"It sounds like win–win to me," Sharptin commented.

"Mr. Sharptin, I'm glad you see eye-to-eye with Dr. Reichstad on that," the third party said, "but I am still not satisfied that it gives us the kind of control I want over the big picture. I really don't want to see your case go to trial. I know you were going to have Sherman talk settlement with attorney Chambers."

"He tried," Reichstad said, "but he wasn't successful."

"Not surprisingly," the third party replied. "Which is exactly why I thought that Chambers was going to be a problem in the first place. Which is why I'm going to have to take matters into my own hands regarding the quixotic Mr. Chambers."

"Can I just point out that I am very uncomfortable with this conversation right now?" Sharptin interjected.

"Would you like to be more uncomfortable?" the third party shot back. "How would you like your name to be taken off the top of the shortlist for the vice-presidential slot?"

"Yes, I understand. But I need some assurance of my chances," Sharptin replied.

"Then let me reassure you again," the third party said. "If you can simply adapt to playing the ultimate game of hardball—if we all play our parts, you, Kenneth, will be the vice-presidential selection on the ticket."

Then the third party focused back on Dr. Reichstad.

"Do you still think you can use this lawsuit to get the remaining information we need?"

"Yes," Reichstad responded eagerly. "As you know, we have already had our experts analyze the recorded message that Richard Hunter left for

MacCameron. Chambers just produced it to us a few days ago. That was one of the benefits of our lawsuit, you see. I left you an encrypted e-mail on that, with the exact wording of the message, together with my attempts to decode his reference to the 'resurrection order.'"

"I have reviewed that, and we are already taking steps to follow that up. We are taking a direct operations approach."

"May I also join Kenneth in saying," Reichstad added, " that 'direct operations' in this have never been my idea—nor my preference. I have never been a man of violence."

"I really get a kick out of you, Reichstad," the third party said. "Do I need to tell you your own business? Do I need to repeat the great history lesson of Middle Eastern archaeology? Now, you remember the key to understanding the Egyptian hieroglyphics? All of those magnificent records—right there in front of the world—but the human race couldn't read them. We didn't have the code. Somehow the human race needed to build a bridge of knowledge between the ancient Egyptians and the modern world. Then comes Napoleon Bonaparte."

"Yes," Reichstad interrupted, "I'm very familiar with the story..."

"But you haven't learned the point of the story," the third party said. "Napoleon wages a silly, useless military campaign, starting in France and extending all the way into Egypt. It costs the lives of thousands of his troops. Napoleon gains little strategic or military benefit from all that blood—all that violence. But what did he discover while in Egypt? The Rosetta Stone. The archaeological find that would open up for us the meaning of all the other ancient hieroglyphics. How many treasures beneath the sand have owed their discovery to blood shed upon the sand? That even has a bit of a biblical flair to it, don't you think? The shedding of blood that, in turn, leads to truth."

"When do we get past this 7QA issue—and on to the second phase?" Sharptin asked.

"Hopefully," the third party explained, "after we get a victory in court on Dr. Reichstad's case, we can lift the media blackout. We can hit the press—starting with the *Washington Herald,* of course. Spread the word around the world that the 7QA discovery has been upheld by a federal court in Washington, D.C. Then we move into the second phase."

"And what if Reichstad is not successful in court?" Sharptin asked.

"I have contingency plans for everything," the third party added. "I want the second phase to be implemented, regardless."

"How soon after the election?" Sharptin asked.

"We'll talk, you and I, about that," the third party answered. "You know, I have a few more ideas to build some more bridges between East and West. After the election, there is the traditional Christmas tree–lighting ceremony. I thought there ought to be some kind of joint celebration for the Christians and the Muslims—maybe something about the annual pilgrimage to Mecca, you know, just like everybody coming to the Bethlehem stable to see Jesus. It could all happen at the same time, right there on the front lawn of the White House. What do you think?"

"Sounds inspirational," Sharptin replied.

"Of course," the third party responded. "I'm an inspired person."

51

THE OCEAN WAS CALM AS THE HUGE Portuguese freighter cut its engines and dropped anchor off the coast of Newfoundland. From the air, it looked like any other shipping vessel. Just below the water line, however, it was carrying a small five-person, submarine attached to its hull, in the event that a quick escape was needed for its passengers.

The lookout in the tower was peering through his binoculars when he spotted the approaching helicopter, off in the distance. A radio announcement crackled throughout the vessel. Soon the helicopter was hovering near the lookout. He waved to the pilot and his passenger.

With little crosswind, the helicopter landed with ease. The two men jumped out and greeted the lookout, who now was on the deck helping them tie down.

"Where's the cargo?" the lookout asked the pilot and his passenger.

"Back in the helicopter," one of them answered, and then they laughed.

The lookout slung a short-barreled automatic over his shoulder, and clumbed into the helicopter.

He looked at the figure of Will Chambers, lying on the floor slumped to his side.

"So, what are we going to do with him? Throw the body over the side?" the lookout said loudly to his compatriots, this time in English, and laughed again.

"Feed the body to the hungry sharks?" he added again in a loud voice, still in English.

The lookout unstrapped his machine gun and held it in his right hand. Then he bent down to take a look.

"Get up, American infidel!"

Will stirred, then struggled up to a sitting position.

The lookout pulled him up by one of his arms, which were still tied behind him, and pushed him out of the helicopter, across the deck, and then down the metal stairs that led to the hold.

Once they were below deck Will was shoved into a small cabin. In that room there was another man, a guard, who was standing and holding a machine gun. Next to him was another man, sitting in a comfortable chair.

The lookout grabbed Will by his hair and forced him down to a kneeling position.

"I am going to take your blindfold off, American infidel. You may not speak until you are spoken to. Do you understand?" the lookout shouted into Will's ear. Will nodded.

Then his blindfold was taken off, as he remained kneeling with his hands tied behind his back.

There was a round porthole in the cabin, and the light streaming into the ship's cramped cabin through that window was painfully bright to Will, who had been blindfolded for nearly twelve hours.

Will squinted through the glare. To his left, by the window, he noticed an Arab-appearing man holding a machine gun. He looked to his right and saw the man who had apparently brought him there—also armed.

Then, as his eyes began to adjust to the light, he looked straight ahead, and saw a man sitting directly in front of him.

Still squinting a little, Will looked at the man in the chair. This man was wearing a black turban and a brown robe. His beard was long and black, reaching down to the middle of his chest. He was wearing tinted sunglasses. The man removed them, revealing eyes that were dark, that seemed lifeless. His face was gaunt and furrowed. This man said nothing at first. But as Will observed him he knew the face was familiar. He had seen this man before. On the cover of a news magazine—perhaps on the covers of several magazines. On television news reports.

Then Will Chambers realized that he was in the presence of the most hunted and feared terrorist in the world.

He was kneeling in front of Abdul el Alibahd.

There was more silence. Then Alibahd began coughing violently and took out a handkerchief—he continued gagging, and then he coughed something into the handkerchief. After another minute of silence, Alibahd, having struggled to catch his breath, began to speak.

"Do you know why you are here?"

"No."

"I will tell you. You are here because you are going to..." Alibahd searched for the words, "...going to run an *errand* for me. You are my errand man. Now, do you have questions for me? Abdul el Alibahd will answer them."

Will thought for a minute. Then he asked a question.

"Did you kill Clarence—my dog? And burn down my house?"

Alibahd gave Will a quizzical look. The gunman to his right bent over and explained something in a low voice.

"I did not kill your dog," Alibahd said. "I don't trifle with dogs. I bring down the nations. I strike terror into the hearts of the murderous oppressors. And I kill those who are enemies of Islam. I kill to show the world that the enemies of Allah are as nothing."

Then Alibahd paused and smiled broadly, revealing stained teeth. He continued and said, "The only dogs I kill are the kind that wear shoes, and business suits, and work on Wall Street."

With that, his two armed guards burst into laughter, and raised their guns over their heads and waved them. Will's stomach churned, knowing that he was sitting a foot away from the barbarian who had slaughtered innocent people in front of the New York Stock Exchange.

"So you want to know about your house? You want to know about your dog? Then you should talk to the Great Satan! He is the one who did that. We don't bother with setting fires and shooting dogs. That is the coward's work of the Great Satan."

"Who is the 'Great Satan'?" Will asked.

"You will meet him. And you will deliver to him a message from me. Because I, Abdul el Alibahd, will give you, the little errand man, a message."

Then Alibahd leaned forward to stare Will in the eye. As he did, Will suddenly understood that he was not going to die—at least not right then. This terrorist had some strange job for him to do. And until the "errand" was run, he was apparently of some value to Alibahd.

"You must go immediately to the house of the Great Satan. And then tell him my message."

"Why me?" Will asked.

"Because he knows you, Mr. Chambers. He knows who you are. And he knows me. And when you show up at his house, and you give him my message, then he will know that this message truly came from me, Abdul el Alibahd. Now here is the message.

"You will tell him that I know he is the Great Satan. I know of the agreement he is making with OPEC, and what he wants to do together with Saudi Petrol Company. Tell him I also know he is no true follower of Allah. I know how he tries to play the harlot between the Christian infidels and the believers of Islam, to destroy the purity of Islam. If he does not withdraw all of his evil plans, my followers will visit him in the night. First they will kill his bodyguards. And then they will come to him with their long, sharp knives. And all night they will cut him apart, piece by piece, while he still lives. And the last thing they will cut out of him will be his heart. And then they will bring his heart to me."

Will was feeling faint after hours without food. "Am I supposed to recite this message exactly?"

"Yes," Alibahd responded. Then he handed Will a script of the message he had expounded.

"We did this on our laptop computer. We all have laptop computers. And we are on the Web. We are part of e-commerce. We are high-tech. Now, Mr. Chambers, memorize what is on this paper."

As one of the guards reached over to pull Will to his feet, Alibahd motioned for him to wait.

"You must deliver this message. Because if you don't, I know where to find those you love. I know where they live. My followers will seek them out, and they will die very bad deaths. There is a girl. A black-haired girl. A singer. You care for her. And her father. And her sick mother. And you have an uncle and an aunt, in..."

One of the gunmen whispered in his ear.

"...in North Carolina. We will find them all, and it will be most unhappy for them."

"One more question," Will asked, before being led away. "What happens to me after I deliver the message to this 'Great Satan'? Will I be free then?"

"You will be free to go, and if you survive you can tell the press, tell the FBI, tell anyone, that you met with Abdul el Alibahd—that Abdul el Alibahd can catch anyone he wants, but they still cannot catch him!" the terrorist responded. And then, after a moment's reflection, he added, "but, I think when the Great Satan hears your message, he will be angry, and he will have his men kill you then, anyway!"

At that, all three of the men started laughing. Alibahd laughed until he began coughing and choking, and then he covered his mouth with the handkerchief. As Will Chambers was led out of the ship's cabin he could hear Alibahd back in the room, still gagging and gasping for air.

"Just keep choking," Will muttered under his breath as they shoved him up the metal stairs.

52

NIGHT WOULD SOON FALL ON THE LAS VEGAS STRIP. The shimmering, glittering arcades of neon of casinos and hotels bathed the streets with otherworldly light. The pale moon was out, even though the sun had not fully set, and the desert was spectacular with color.

Fifteen miles outside of Las Vegas, in the Nevada desert, the attendant running the dilapidated "Last Chance Gas & Go" mart was watching television from the cracked leather seat of his wooden swivel chair.

From somewhere above him, the attendant heard a roaring noise. He turned in his chair, looking through the front door that had been jammed open for ventilation, and saw the dust swirling around outside by the single gas pump.

He turned down the television as the roar got louder. The dust and sand outside were now swirling like a miniature cyclone.

As he ran to the door the roaring was growing distant. He looked out onto the highway that passed in front of his gas station. He saw Will Chambers, lying facedown on the shoulder of the road.

Will slowly and stiffly rose to his feet. His suit and shirt were covered with dust. His tie, which had been loosened at the collar, was now dangling from his neck like a Boy Scout's kerchief. There was a bruise on his left cheekbone.

The attendant scampered across the road to Will, and then looked up at the sky at a helicopter that was disappearing.

"You g-g-got here from that helicopter?" the man asked in a stutter.

Will brushed himself off, and shook the sand out of his hair. "Yeah, that's right. I thought I'd just drop in," Will said, momentarily feeling a sense of exuberance at being free from his captors.

The attendant was still staring at Will as he made his way into the little convenience store.

"Do you have anything to drink that's cold? Anything to eat? Any sandwiches? I'm starving," Will said as he looked around the little store.

"Soda and b-b-beer is over there. I used to be able to make chili dogs on the r-r-...the rotisserie here, but it ain't working no more."

After riffling through his pockets Will pulled out some dollar bills and laid them on the table. Then he limped over to the cooler and pulled out two sodas, and grabbed a handful of candy bars and a few bags of corn curls.

There was a wooden chair with a little desktop by the door; it looked like it had once belonged in a school building. Will sat down in the chair with his load of junk food and started eating, intermittently taking large gulps from the soda can.

"Where am I?" Will asked.

The attendant looked at him quizzically for a few seconds.

"Nevada. Just outside V-V-Vegas."

Will polished off all of the corn curls, the candy bars, and the two sodas while the attendant watched.

Then the attendant cautiously asked, "You ain't with *him,* are you?"

"Who?"

"Him," the attendant repeated, and then pointed across the road to what looked like an entrance to someone's property. To the side of the entrance, there was a white stone pillar that had the words "Private Property—No Trespassing" printed on it in gold letters highlighted with black. The road beyond the sign seemed to disappear into the desert hills.

"What's that lead to?"

"That belongs to *him.* Ain't you ever heard of *U-t-t-topia?* That's where that road goes."

"Utopia?"

"Yeah. That's what they c-c-c-call the c-c-castle of Warren Mullburn. One of the world's richest men. You ain't with him?"

"No," Will replied. "But I think I'm supposed to pay him a visit."

"He's a mean one. His g-g-goons—his bodyguards, they sometimes come here for gas. Push me around. Make fun of my stutter. Just 'cause I stutter don't mean that I'm d-d-d-dumb."

"I'm sorry," Will said.

"I don't think he likes having neighbors. There's something real b-b-bad about him. The county cops don't like him neither. They've told me. I'd like to see him get what's coming to him—j-j-just once."

Will thought back to Abdul el Alibahd's parting words to him on the freighter. He knew he had no choice but to deliver the terrorist's message to Mullburn. It was clear now that the billionaire was the "Great Satan" of

Alibahd's rantings. But it was also clear that Mullburn was a dangerous man. If an international terrorist like Alibahd thought Mullburn had killer instincts, Will wasn't going to argue the point.

Somehow, Will had to deliver Alibahd's threat to Warren Mullburn and then get out alive. Will thrust his hand in his jacket pocket. He fingered the black felt-tipped pen that was still there.

"Where's your bathroom?" Will asked.

The attendant motioned to the outside of the building. Will took the key and disappeared.

After Will had cleaned himself up and was through in the men's room, he came around to the door again.

"Hey! You're going to have to check that bathroom right away!" Will yelled through the entrance.

Then he quickly crossed the highway and started up the desert road marked by the sign, "Private Property—No Trespassing."

53

WILL HAD BEEN WALKING FOR ABOUT FIVE MINUTES in the dusky half-light of sunset, along the road that wound through the brush and barren desert hills. Then he heard the sound of a vehicle approaching. A tan Land Rover topped a small hill in the distance, approaching fast with headlights and spotlights on.

When the vehicle was nearly even with Will, it skidded to a stop, sending small stones and sand flying.

Two burly men, in matching golf shirts and tan pants, and wearing ultra-light headsets, got out. One of the men grabbed Will and threw him to the ground.

"You are trespassing, mister!" he yelled, frisking Will while he was lying in the dirt.

"I have to see Warren Mullburn."

"Nobody sees Mr. Mullburn."

"I'm going to see him," Will said starting to get up. "I have a message for him."

"Yeah, I bet," the other man said. "So give us the message, and then get off this property in thirty seconds or we start shooting."

Will noticed that they both had Western-style handguns in holsters at their sides.

"I'll give this message directly to Warren Mullburn. And if he doesn't get it from me right now, I think he will be very upset. And if that happens, I have a feeling that you guys are going to end up being a meal—you know, for the desert animals that come out at night."

The two looked at each other, then one of them spoke into his headset. He reached around and grabbed Will's wallet out of his pocket, carried it over to the carlight, and flipped it open to his driver's license.

"Will Chambers," he said to his remote contact.

There was a pause.

"Yes—he's right here in front of me. Yes, I'm sure."

Another pause.

"No. He's on foot."

A few more seconds.

"No. He's alone. I don't know. Maybe he hitchhiked."

The man listened and nodded, and then he told Will to sit in the front seat of the Land Rover. While he drove, his partner sat behind Will. They sped up the dirt road for several miles, bumping and jostling, and occasionally jolting so hard it made Will's teeth chatter.

The unpaved road intersected with a paved one further into the desert, and after a few minutes on the paved drive they approached a large gate with a guardhouse. The driver stopped. The guard nodded to him and then they continued on for a couple more miles until, over the crest of a hill populated with only cactus and tumbleweeds, the road dipped down, and Will could see it.

Under the stars that were beginning to appear, "Utopia" shone forth, like a small lighted city below in the valley.

As they got closer, Will could see it was a complex of ornate white stone buildings that were connected with red brick walkways and lighted paths. The buildings were interconnected, and resembled the steps of some modern pyramid—like a mammoth, ascending temple of white stone terraced into the desert cliffs. Off in the distance he could hear music playing and voices laughing.

The Land Rover pulled up into a circle drive and stopped. He saw a Ferrari and and Rolls Royce parked to the side. There was a wall of glass in the front of the central building, with the word "Utopia" lettered in huge black-and-gold script across it. There were cascading fountains everywhere and hanging gardens of desert plants. Several peacocks ambled through the grounds, screeching now and then.

The two guards escorted Will toward the glass wall, which separated as they approached. Will entered a vast portico, with trees growing through holes in the terra cotta floor and up through openings in the roof. He was told to be seated on a couch. The two men stayed standing.

After about ten minutes, a tanned man in a bathrobe, accompanied by two muscular bodyguards, one of them a big blond, came striding into the portico.

The man in the bathrobe looked vaguely familiar. Will thought he might have seen him in a late-night TV infomercial years back. Will noticed that his hair was damp and his feet were leaving wet prints on the floor.

"I am Warren Mullburn," the man in the bathrobe said. "And you, sir, interrupted my evening swim. I do twenty laps. Olympic-size pool."

"Shucks, I forgot to bring my swimsuit," Will said, standing up.

"What do you want? Make it quick."

"I have a message for you."

"Who are you?"

"You know who I am," Will replied.

"Oh, yes. My assistant called ahead and told me. He said your name is Will Chambers."

"Mr. Mullburn, the fact is that you already knew who I was. That is why I was picked to deliver this message to you."

"Message? From who?"

"Abdul el Alibahd."

"You're insane," Mullburn laughed contemptuously.

"Am I? Perhaps you ought to hear what he has to say."

At that, Mullburn waved away the two men who had picked up Will on the road. They turned and left, leaving only Will, Mullburn, and the two bodyguards.

"Let's hear it," Mullburn barked.

Will paused. For a moment, he summoned up the mental image of Audra—making her hair, her features, her presence as real as he could. Then he recited what he had been told to memorize on the freighter.

> I, Abdul el Alibahd, the obedient of Allah, know that you are the Great Satan. I know of the agreement you are making with OPEC, and what you wish to do with Saudi Petrol Company. I also know that you, Warren Mullburn, are no true follower of Allah. I know how you try to play the harlot between the Christian infidels and the believers of Islam, and try to destroy the purity of Islam. If you do not withdraw all of your evil plans, my followers will visit you in the night. First they will kill your bodyguards. And then they will come to you with their long, sharp, knives. And all night they will cut you apart, piece by piece, while you still live. And the last thing they will cut out of you will be your heart. And then they will bring your heart to me, Abdul el Alibahd, for I am the avenger of Islam, the leader of the Great Jihad.

When Will had finished speaking, he saw that Mullburn's face was scarlet with rage.

Mullburn walked up to Will until he was so close that Will could feel his breath.

"Who told you this?"

"I already explained. Abdul el Alibahd."

"Why would he pick you? An alcoholic lawyer with a failed career who goes around chasing the memory of his dead wife—why would he pick *you* to come here to tell that to *me?*"

"Because you have been tracking me. Because you must have a really big stake in the lawsuit that Dr. Albert Reichstad brought against my client," Will responded firmly. "Because you know all about the deaths of Harim Azid and Dr. Richard Hunter—you're probably the one that planned them. Because you're involved in dirty deals with Kenneth Sharptin and OPEC. Because, even if Alibahd thinks you are the 'Great Satan'—you know what? I don't agree. You're not the 'Great Satan.' You and this Alibahd creep both work for Satan, but only as middle-level employees. You're nothing more than a demonic bureaucrat.

"And most of all, I'm here because you killed my dog and burned down my house. I wanted to see what kind of sick puppy would really do something like that."

Mullburn glanced quickly over at the big blond bodyguard, then looked back at Will. Mullburn managed a crooked smile.

"Well. You have quite a vivid imagination, Mr. Chambers. It was interesting to meet you. But I'm afraid that you and I will not be seeing each other again."

Then he turned to the big blond bodyguard and said, "Bruda, see Mr. Chambers out, won't you? I wouldn't want him to disappear in the desert at night. It can be dangerous out there."

Bruda Weilder walked up in back of Will and spoke to him from behind as Mullburn disappeared.

"Mr. Chambers, how would you like some new religion?"

"Actually, the old-time religion is beginning to look better every day," Will replied softly.

"Too bad," Weilder said, and then he put something hard against the back of Will's head. It felt like a gun barrel. "'Cause, when we get into the desert, I'm going to fill your brains with some really powerful karma." With that, Weilder and his partner snickered.

Suddenly there was a noise of engines outside, along with the sound of tire screeches echoing off the buildings.

One of the guards ran in and said something to the other bodyguard in a low voice. Weilder quickly disappeared, and a moment later four uniformed police officers strode into the portico area.

"Warren Mullburn?" asked the one in front, as the other three scanned the scene.

"No," Will replied, "I think he's enjoying his Olympic-size pool."

"Do you know anything about this?" the officer demanded, holding up a piece of tan paper towel with writing on it. Will smiled as he recognized his message:

HELP! I'VE BEEN KIDNAPPED! THIS IS NO JOKE. I'M AT THE MULLBURN "UTOPIA." SEND THE POLICE NOW!

Just then Warren Mullburn breezed into the room, still in his bathrobe.

"I wrote that," Will Chambers said, nodding toward the paper-towel note.

"Are you saying that Mr. Mullburn here is kidnapping you?"

"Certainly not," Will responded. "I'm not being kidnapped, am I, Mr. Mullburn?"

Mullburn smiled through a tight grin. "Of course not."

"Would you like to explain this note?" the police officer asked Will.

"I will be glad to," Will replied, "but if you don't mind, why don't we talk in one of your squad cars?" Then Will looked at his watch. It was Sunday night, midnight, East-Coast time. The court hearing before Judge Kaye would begin in nine hours.

"I've got a plane to try to catch," Will added.

54

JUDGE JEREMIAH KAYE SWEPT INTO THE COURTROOM of the U.S. District Court in Washington, D.C., his robe flowing, and he perched himself behind the mahogany judge's bench. His reading glasses were perched on the top of his head. His white hair was slightly unkempt, and a shock of hair hung down over his left eyebrow. His pale, wrinkled face was set in his characteristic early-morning smile—an expression whose good nature was subject to change depending on the level of good faith, cooperation, and intelligence of the attorneys who were to come before him on that day's docket.

With the Great Seal of the United States behind him on the wall, Judge Kaye leaned over to his deputy clerk and whispered something. She said something back, and after they had both had a chuckle, the judge turned to the courtroom.

"Case number 01 CV 767, *Reichstad vs. MacCameron and* Digging for Truth *Magazine,"* the court clerk called out.

J-Fox Sherman was at the counsel table with two of his associate attorneys. Dr. Reichstad sat at the end of their table.

At the opposite counsel table, Reverend Angus MacCameron was sitting alone. There was an empty chair next to him where Will Chambers should have been sitting.

Sherman rose to his feet.

"Jay Foxley Sherman, counsel for the plaintiff, your honor. We are ready to proceed. I do note the absence, however, of opposing counsel, Mr. Will Chambers."

"Reverend MacCameron, where's your attorney?" the judge asked.

"I am not entirely sure, your honor," MacCameron answered. "I am certain he will be here directly."

"Uh-oh," the judge said, looking over at his clerk. "This is not a good way to start out a Monday. Not a good way to start my docket at all. Here I came into this courtroom, having spent my weekend reading the voluminous briefs filed by both sides in this case. Prepared to listen to argument this morning—ready to decide the theological mysteries of the ages—I guess that's what this case is about, right? Somebody's going to be asking me to take sides on no less a question than the resurrection of Jesus of Nazareth—isn't that what's behind all of this?" With that, the judge smiled.

"Not really, your honor. Not even close." Sherman was smiling confidently.

"I was just pulling your leg a little, Mr. Sherman," the judge remarked. "I do understand the legal issues here. But it does raise the question—"

That was when Will Chambers strode quickly through the swinging doors in the back of the courtroom, accidentally banging them loudly.

Will noticed Jacki Johnson sitting in the audience section, and he darted over to her and whispered, "Jacki, give me a legal pad, will you?"

She tossed a yellow legal pad to him. Will grabbed it and walked quickly up to the counsel's table, carrying nothing but the pad of paper in his hand.

Judge Kaye carefully studied him.

"You're a mess, Mr. Chambers!" the judge exclaimed. "Look at you!"

Will's crumpled suit had several obvious grease spots, and the right knee of his pants leg was torn. Although he had gallantly tried to comb his hair in the airplane bathroom, his long tangled mane of hair sported several cowlicks. His white shirt had a few slightly cleaned-up bloodstains on it, and one of the buttons on his shirt collar was missing, causing one side of the collar to stick out slightly. His bruised face bore the stubble of having not been shaved all weekend.

J-Fox Sherman smirked and quipped to the judge, "Your honor, Mr. Chambers has obviously taken up a new legal specialty—homeless law!"

Sherman's associates burst into laughter.

Judge Kaye was not amused.

"Thank you, Mr. Sherman. Your compassion for the underprivileged in our society is a real comfort to the court."

Then the judge turned back to Will.

"What happened, counsel? Did you get mugged on the way over here?"

"In a manner of speaking, Your Honor."

"Right here, near the courthouse?"

"No, Your Honor. It's rather complicated. The FBI is looking into it."

And with that, Will glanced over at Dr. Reichstad, who looked away.

Judge Kaye, who had been a Deputy Director of the CIA twenty years ago, before his appointment to the federal bench, had heard enough to have his curiosity aroused.

"Well, I hope the Bureau gets to the bottom of this for you, whatever happened," the judge commented.

Then, collecting his thoughts, the judge resumed his statement to counsel.

"What I was saying before you stepped in, Mr. Chambers, was that the religious overtones make this an interesting case—but they are somewhat beside the point, considering the narrow legal issues I'll be deciding today. Nevertheless, for what it's worth, I will point out that my father was a rabbi. I know nothing in my background that would require me to recuse myself from hearing this case; I believe I can judge it fairly and dispassionately. But if either counsel wants to address my having been trained in the Torah as a young man, and my background in Judaism, I will not hold it against you. Either of you want me to remove myself from hearing this case?"

J-Fox Sherman was beaming. He shook his head "no."

"I have no concerns in that regard, Your Honor," Will seconded.

With that, Judge Kaye leaned back in his chair as Sherman walked to the lectern located directly in front of the bench and then began launching into his argument outlining why judgment should be entered against Angus MacCameron for having recklessly defamed and libeled Dr. Albert Reichstad.

Sherman's argument was methodical and brilliant. He laid out the facts in excruciating detail. He read out loud, with appropriate sarcasm, the portions of MacCameron's article that were the subject of the lawsuit.

"Your Honor," Sherman argued, "upon what basis could any *reasonable* man ever write, as the defendant MacCameron did in fact write, that my client, a world-famous scholar in biblical antiquities, was 'either lying, or he has committed scientific malpractice' regarding his writings about 7QA? Even further—and even worse—what reasonable, lucid, or *sane* person would ever dare to write that my esteemed client had anything whatsoever to do with the death of that antiquities dealer, or Dr. Richard Hunter? MacCameron's lawyer has failed, in his response to our motion, to show this court any credible evidence demonstrating why the defendant was *not reckless* in making those outrageous allegations against Dr. Reichstad. He points to no investigation undertaken by MacCameron to verify the accuracy of what he was about to publish to the world. That's because MacCameron did *no factual investigation* when he wrote this inflammatory pack of lies against Dr. Reichstad. His only basis for what he wrote was apparently a hearsay conversation with Dr. Hunter—mysteriously and conveniently incapable of being verified because Dr. Hunter is now dead."

Judge Kaye interrupted him.

"What about the tape-recorded message from Hunter—isn't that some kind of basis for MacCameron to have reached the conclusions he did in his article?"

"Clearly not, Your Honor," Sherman quickly responded. "The message on the answering machine was Hunter's obscure reference to his obvious paranoid delusions that he was being followed; but he doesn't say by whom. Further, there is no proof that the fragments he refers to in his message had any identity with the 7QA fragment."

"So," Judge Kaye interjected, "you do agree with Mr. Chambers, who has argued in his brief that when the message was analyzed the reference was to 'fragments'—more than one?"

Sherman glanced over at Reichstad, who was staring ahead blankly.

"Yes, Your Honor, our experts listened to the tape—as did Mr. Chambers'—and, for what it's worth, we agree that it was probably a reference to 'fragments.' But that point is irrelevant in any event. There is nothing, absolutely nothing, that connects Hunter's 'fragments'—even assuming they actually existed—to the 7QA fragment obtained by Dr. Reichstad."

"Do you agree," Judge Kaye asked, "that I must rule on the *recklessness* issue separately from the issue of whether, in hindsight, MacCameron's allegations actually ended up to be the *truth?* Aren't those two distinct and separate questions?"

"They are distinct—but related," Sherman answered. "We believe that MacCameron has produced no evidence thus far in this case that creates an issue of fact as to whether his outrageous and defamatory allegations are actually true. This court must rule in our favor. This court must find, as a matter of law, that Reverend MacCameron, undoubtedly fueled by his fanatical religious beliefs, viciously, recklessly, and falsely defamed and libeled my client. No jury trial is required on those issues. The only thing for a jury to decide, after this court awards judgment for Dr. Reichstad today, is what figure they want to put next to the dollar sign on the verdict form—where it says, 'What sum of money do you find will reasonably compensate Dr. Reichstad for the false and defamatory statements published by Angus MacCameron?'"

Sherman concluded by adding, with a confident smile, "And I would suggest, Your Honor, that the court have some calculators on hand for the jury's use—the kind that have room for lots of zeroes."

Will walked up to the podium with no notes. He smiled and thanked the judge for his attentive and astute questions during Sherman's argument. He first argued why the judge should *not* rule on whether MacCameron was reckless in making his accusations against Reichstad. Will recited from memory the legal cases Jacki had researched for him—court cases that stressed that a trial judge ought to refrain, whenever possible, from trying to make decisions in place of the jury, where such decisions hinge on the state of mind of a party to a lawsuit. Those kind of issues, Will submitted, "are usually appropriate to be made by *the jury* after hearing all the facts, and all of the evidence—after a full jury trial—not here, in a hearing before trial."

But Judge Kaye appeared impatient with that argument, interrupting Will and asking, "Then why do the Federal Rules of Civil Procedure specifically give me the power to grant judgment for Mr. Sherman's client here? Can you show me one, credible, concrete fact that indicates a reasonable basis for MacCameron's obviously defamatory article? I admit, most state-of-mind issues, like the recklessness issue here, are best left for the jury to decide at trial. But sometimes, Mr. Chambers, someone writes something that is so outrageous and so damaging, with no basis whatsoever in fact, that the court has no alternative but to find at this stage of the case, as a matter of law, that the element of recklessness has been proven beyond any doubt by the plaintiff."

Will attempted to continue, but was interrupted again by the judge.

"Really, counsel, what was the basis for those allegations against Dr. Reichstad that your client published, anyway? Aside from the conversation he had with Hunter at the Between the Arches Café—and, as a side note, I've eaten at that restaurant on some of my visits to Jerusalem. But anyway, aside from that conversation—and that strange answering-machine message—on what did MacCameron base his published accusations against Reichstad? A dream? A vision? Was he motivated by an upset stomach caused by an undigested bit of beef, to bring in something from Dickens' *Christmas Carol?* Really, Mr. Chambers, what other evidence of any kind did he have before he let loose with that diatribe against this world-famous scholar?"

"The truth, Your Honor. Reverend MacCameron saw the truth—and then published what he saw," Will Chambers replied.

"Does he have special eyes? Can he see things differently than the rest of us? Does he have X-ray vision? Is your client Superman?"

"No," Will responded, smiling. "But he does see things differently. He views the world through a glass—as we all do. For most of us that glass is dark and the light is imperfectly reflected. But Reverend MacCameron views the world through a particular glass—through the prism of the Bible. He believes that Dr. Reichstad's conclusions about 7QA are false—but not just false. Diabolically false.

"Mr. Sherman ridicules Reverend MacCameron's beliefs. But I do not. I do not presume to possess the knowledge—or the arrogance—that would cause me to ridicule a magnificent written record that is two thousand years old. A written record, as it were, printed with the blood of those who all died horrible deaths for a specific belief—a belief that what they saw following the death and burial of Jesus of Nazareth defied the laws of the natural world, and changed their lives forever.

"We have not yet had the chance, as the court knows, to examine 7QA in its original form. But I believe that if we are permitted to do so, we will find that 7QA is only one part of a larger fragment. Where are the other parts of that fragment? And what will they say when the jigsaw puzzle is put together? What message will they bring to us out of the dust and the desert sands of two thousand years of oblivion? If Your Honor permits us to go to trial on the issue of *truth* as a defense, then those are the very questions we will address—and that the jury will, in its collective wisdom—be able to answer."

Judge Kaye rocked back and forth in his black judge's chair.

"And exactly what is the truth here, Mr. Chambers?"

Will paused, and in a quiet voice he answered.

"Interestingly, that is the same question that Pontius Pilate put to Jesus in the Praetorium in Jerusalem, Your Honor. He asked that very same question of Jesus, within the great arches of that Roman hallway. But then, Pilate turned and left prematurely—oblivious, perhaps, to the answer. I am sure that this court will be much more judicious than that. I am confident that Your Honor will permit us to go to trial—at least on the issue of truth. For all his indiscretion, Pilate did let the people decide. That's all we ask here—a trial. And then, let the people in the jury decide."

Judge Kaye was expressionless. His rocking in the chair ceased.

"Let's adjourn for fifteen minutes. I want to review my notes. Then I will come back into court and give you my decision."

"All rise!" the court bailiff shouted.

Everyone in the courtroom rose to their feet as Judge Kaye took the reading glasses off the top of his head and walked down from the bench, then disappeared through the door to his private chambers. The strained silence through the courtroom was palpable as the door behind the judge slowly closed shut.

55

THE GEARS IN WILL'S MIND WERE STILL WHIRLING at high speed as he walked back to his counsel's table. He felt someone touch his shoulder. It was his client.

"Will, my boy," Angus MacCameron said with a furrowed brow, "are you alright? Who accosted you?"

"Accosted? You know, Angus, that word doesn't begin to describe my last forty-eight hours. But, miraculously, I am fine. Thanks for asking," Will responded.

MacCameron had a large manila envelope in his hand. His face suddenly broke into a beaming smile as he waved the envelope in front of Will.

"You will never guess what I have here!" MacCameron exclaimed. "Praise God, this is the beginning of the end for Reichstad's lies."

"What is it?"

MacCameron put the envelope in front of Will, who noticed the airmail markings on it. Then he noticed the sender's name: Judith Hunter—and a London address.

"Dr. Hunter's sister?"

"Precisely. God's timing is brilliant, don't you think?"

"Yes, but what is this about? Is it something we don't want Sherman to get wind of? Perhaps we should step outside the courtroom."

MacCameron agreed, and he and Will made their way out to the lobby and over to a corner where there was a bench.

"Okay, go ahead," said Will.

"Judith sent a short note. Saying that she thinks often about my friendship with her late brother. How hard his murder has been on her, the poor dear. And then, at the very end of the note, she hits the jackpot!"

"Jackpot?"

"She writes that, since his death, she had not done much with the flat where she and Richard had lived. But recently she decided to move into a smaller flat, because she's now living alone. She hired some men to come in and move her furniture. As they are moving the living room sofa, they see an envelope on the floor where Richard must have put it. It was addressed to me in the United States. He obviously intended to mail it to me, but was murdered first.

"So Judith simply took the envelope, put it in another envelope, and mailed the whole thing to me. I received it in the mail on Saturday. I was so ecstatic that I immediately called your office, but you weren't there. I tried to contact you at your apartment, but you weren't there either."

"I was tied up over the weekend," Will said with a wry smile. "So, what was in the envelope Hunter had addressed to you?"

"7QB!" MacCameron cried out, so loudly that several people who had been talking on the other side of the lobby stopped their conversation and stared over at Will's client.

"Just a minute—*7QB?"* Will asked.

"The very thing. There it was, tucked inside a little plastic baggie inside a plastic zip bag, and that inside a padded envelope. No note from Richard. He must have been in a hurry. He must have known they were closing in on him."

"What does it say? What's on the fragment? Does it match with the edges of 7QA? Was it part of the same piece?"

"Well," MacCameron continued, "I couldn't reach you—I hope this was all right—but I knew where Dr. Giovanni's office was and that she had agreed to testify as our expert. So I took this 7QB fragment over to her, to see if she could verify my initial reading of its language."

"And?"

MacCameron pulled out a piece of paper. It had the 7QA wording on the left side—and then, on the right side, the translation by Dr. Giovanni, of the Greek words of 7QB.

"I took a copy of the actual-size photograph I have of 7QA from Reichstad's magazine, and cut around the edge of that fragment," MacCameron continued. "Then Dr. Giovanni and I simply lined up the edge of 7QB with the edge of 7QA and they seemed to match perfectly! Of course, you will need to have the materials engineer examine it to make absolutely certain the edges were, at one time, joined. But when we joined them together, this is the message we saw created." He handed the paper to Will.

{7QA}

AND THE BODY

OF JESUS OF NAZARETH {7QB}

WAS LAID IN THE TOMB // *AT THE EAST GATE OF STEPHEN*

THEY DESIRED TO ANOINT IT // *THAT DAY*

BUT COULD NOT RETURN TO PREPARE THE BODY

THE BODY REMAINS IN THAT TOMB TO THIS DAY

MacCameron was studying Will's reaction to the translation. Will handed the piece of paper back and turned to his client.

"Do you know what this means?"

"Of course!" MacCameron answered. "It is proof that Richard Hunter's fragments were part of 7QA. Which means that Reichstad unquestionably came into possession of the fragment—which we know now *is* 7QA— that had belonged to Hunter and Azid before their deaths. Furthermore, 7QB is strong support for the fact that there may be a *third* fragment. There is still a 7QC fragment out there that must match up with the right hand edge of 7QA, and the top edge of 7QB."

"I can't argue with you, Angus," Will said. "But there is a huge down side to this 7QB fragment coming into your hands." And with that Will put his finger on the words of the 7QB translation—"AT THE EAST GATE OF STEPHEN."

"Do you know where that is?"

"Certainly," MacCameron answered. "That is one of the ancient gates of the old city of Jerusalem, along the wall that faces the Mount of Olives. It's also called 'the Lion's Gate.' But it is really known as the spot where they think that Stephen, the first Christian martyr, was stoned to death."

"The same one as in the book of Acts?" Will asked.

"My boy, you are getting to be a Bible scholar!"

"Are you familiar with any tombs there?"

"Well, I did some thinking about that over the weekend. Actually, there is an old Arab cemetery located in that spot today. It's just to the side of an eastern gate into the old city. But I don't know of any ancient tombs ever excavated there."

"Well," Will countered, "you are about to see an excavation there, and it's going to grab the attention of the entire world."

"Oh?" MacCameron replied, "how do you know that?"

"Because what you have shown me, here, is new evidence. When the judge comes back in, I will have to advise him about it, as well as Sherman and Reichstad. When Reichstad sees what 7QB says, watch him scramble to get over to Israel and start digging."

"Well, I have thought about that," MacCameron said. "But I know that if they find some tomb there, it certainly won't contain the body of the Lord Jesus. The Word of God is sure, certain, and perfectly clear about that!"

"I wish I had your faith," Will said. "The way I see it, we are about to play right into Reichstad's hands. I think this may have been the real reason that he sued you in the first place. To use you like a dog that brings the newspaper to his master—the way Clarence used to do it for me. To use you to locate 7QB, and then fetch it back to him. And with 7QB he gets the location of the occupied tomb of Jesus of Nazareth—which would be Reichstad's ultimate trump card to demolish the idea of the resurrection forever."

Will glanced at his watch. "We'd better get back in there. I'd rather not make another late entrance today."

Shortly after Will and his client had reached their table, the door of Judge Kaye's chambers swung open and the judge mounted the bench.

"All rise!" the clerk shouted out.

Judge Kaye waited until everyone in the courtroom was seated, and then he began speaking. He initially described the legal standards that apply to a judge's decision on a motion for Summary Judgment. The purpose, he pointed out, was to spare the effort of a full-blown jury trial in those exceptional cases where there is no real dispute about the underlying facts, and where the law is clear enough to permit the court to rule on the case in advance of the trial.

"On the issue of recklessness," Judge Kaye began—Chambers, Sherman, and their clients stopped breathing—"I find that defendant Reverend Angus MacCameron has *failed* to point to any adequate facts that could have served as a reasonable basis for his extreme accusations against Dr. Albert Reichstad, the plaintiff. I find that he showed a reckless disregard for whether his allegations against Dr. Reichstad were, or were not, accurate and truthful. There is no need for a jury trial on that issue because I find that there is no material dispute on the facts—and those facts, and the law, all point in favor of the plaintiff Dr. Reichstad, and against Reverend MacCameron."

Will heard Reichstad clap his hands together in joy at the other counsel table. Will glanced over and his eyes met the eyes of J-Fox Sherman. Sherman was gloating.

"On the second issue of the defense of truth," the judge continued, "while I find the poetic argument of Mr. Chambers to be enticing, and eloquent, I do not find it to be persuasive on this second issue."

It was at that point that Will began thinking that Sherman's motion against him for attorney's fees in the amount of $245,000 just might be granted.

"On that issue of the defense of truth," Judge Kaye said as he went on, and then paused for just a few seconds—seconds that seemed like hours to the watching lawyers and their clients—"I find as follows: While the facts are not really in dispute, the inferences that this court could draw from those facts *are* conflicting. Mr. Chambers, the cases you cited in your brief are somewhat persuasive on that issue. The fact is, the court could draw two separate and contradictory conclusions from the same set of facts. One conclusion is that Dr. Reichstad had nothing to do with the two deaths at issue and that he was exemplary in his interpretation of the meaning of the 7QA fragment; the other conclusion is that Dr. Reichstad may have had some 'connection,' no matter how remote, with those deaths, and further, that he either knew, or should have known, that his interpretation of the 7QA fragment was not scientifically sound and reasonable. I cannot, at this stage of the case, decide where the truth lies. Mr. Chambers—you will get your jury trial on the issue of truth. Jury trial will commence exactly one week from today."

Will attempted to rise to address the issue of the newly discovered 7QB fragment, but Sherman beat him to his feet.

"Your Honor, what about my motion for attorney's fees against Mr. Chambers for having wasted our time in making us litigate this totally meritless issue of recklessness? Now that we have prevailed on that issue, we would respectfully request every single dime of the attorney's fees that we have sought against Mr. Chambers."

"Really, Mr. Sherman, you didn't think I would grant that kind of motion in a case like this, did you? Your motion is denied, Mr. Sherman."

"Well, Your Honor, I would really urge you to—" Sherman tried to counter.

"Is this microphone working?" Judge Kaye said to his clerk, who was attempting not to smile. "I could swear that the attorneys in this courtroom can't hear me when I give a ruling. Mr. Sherman, this isn't the Harvard debating club. The way it works in a courtroom is that you lawyers are supposed to argue *before* the judge makes his ruling—not *afterwards*. When I make a ruling, your job is to smile, nod politely, and sit down."

"Your Honor," Will said, "I do have some procedural matters to bring to the attention of the court regarding the upcoming jury trial."

Judge Kaye nodded to Will to proceed and then leaned back in this chair.

Will described for the court how the 7QB fragment had just come into the possession of his client.

"Where is that 7QB fragment right now?" the judge asked.

"Reverend MacCameron has it right here with him, in the courtroom today."

There was a movement on the other side of the courtroom, and Will became aware that Albert Reichstad was walking in front of the judge's bench, heading over to him and his client.

"Your Honor, pardon me, but I would like to address the court as the plaintiff in this case. I do believe that you must order MacCameron to show that fragment to me immediately!"

By the time Reichstad had finished his words to the judge, he had made his way over to MacCameron's place at the defense table and was grabbing for the envelope.

With his eyes fixed on Dr. Reichstad, Judge Kaye bellowed, "You, sir, have a lawyer. Who is a highly skilled, and—I am assuming—a highly paid one. Get back to your seat next to your lawyer and let him do the talking. That's what you are paying him for."

Reichstad lingered for a few seconds in front of Will's table, his hand poised over the envelope.

"Now, Dr. Reichstad!" the judge yelled, his microphone shrieking with feedback.

As Reichstad walked back to his place next to J-Fox Sherman, who was struggling to hide his astonishment at his client's conduct, Will gestured to make a final point.

"Your Honor, we anticipate that the court will order us to produce what we have called the 7QB fragment to opposing counsel and his client."

"You have read my mind, counsel," Judge Kaye responded.

Sherman was back on his feet.

"We object, Your Honor, to any reference to this alleged fragment as being '7QB.' That is prejudicial to our case," Sherman pointed out. "That reference assumes that it is connected in some way with 7QA. And we vehemently deny that it is."

"Your Honor, how would he know that—until they examine it?" Will shot back.

"Okay. This is a tempest in a teapot," Judge Kaye said with finality. "This court is not going to be prejudiced by calling it 7QB. And if you think the jury will be prejudiced, then at trial we can refer to it as the 'X fragment,' unless someone else has a better idea. Now, when can you get this fragment to Mr. Sherman's experts?"

"This afternoon," Will explained, "we had planned to receive 7QA from the plaintiff's side. So at the same time, we will hand off 7QB to them. But we would ask that the court impose the same highly restrictive conditions on their examination of our fragment as they demanded for our examination of their fragment."

"Fair enough. So ordered," the judge said.

"I assume that this will require us to reschedule the trial date," Sherman broke in, in his best voice of reason and calm. "There is no way that we can now be prepared for trial in a week, in light of this new evidence."

"You assume wrong, Mr. Sherman. This trial date has been set for some time. You yourself pressed for the earliest possible date. We accommodated you. The trial date for next week stays. You and your experts will have to hustle a little, that's all, in examining this new fragment. And Mr. Sherman, you just may have to cancel your luncheon at the White House, or whatever it is that you had planned for this week. This trial comes first."

Then Judge Kaye turned to Will Chambers.

"And you, Mr. Chambers. You need to get a shave and a new suit."

As the judge rose and left the bench, the courtroom rose with him.

Will turned to his client.

"From now until the end of your jury trial—this is when the fur really starts flying," Will said.

"And I was just thinking of Exodus chapter 14, verse 13," MacCameron replied.

"What's that?"

"Moses and the Israelites were at the edge of the Red Sea. The Egyptian army, with their chariots and spears, was about to catch up to them, and it looked like they would all be slaughtered," MacCameron explained with a smile. "But this is what Moses told the people of God." And then he recited the verse from memory:

> Do not fear! Stand by and see the salvation of the LORD which He will accomplish for you today.

From the other side of the courtroom there came the sounds of J-Fox Sherman and his associate attorneys snapping shut their oversized briefcases and gathering their black trial notebooks.

Will looked at his client and said, "I think I hear the Egyptians coming."

56

THE DIRECTOR OF THE ISRAELI ANTIQUITIES AUTHORITY was at his desk, wishing he did not have to take the telephone call. He looked down at the red blinking light on his telephone. His secretary buzzed in to him and reminded him that Undersecretary Kenneth Sharptin of the U.S. Department of State was still waiting on the telephone, and was tired of being kept on hold. The Director had been expecting this call and knew that it required him to exercise extraordinary diplomacy—a daunting task because he would have to disguise his outrage at the State Department's meddling in the internal affairs of Israel.

He grasped the handset, punched the button, and in his warmest and most winning way, began to exchange pleasantries with Sharptin. Yes, the Director told Sharptin, he understood the importance of the call. And he explained that he understood perfectly well that if Undersecretary Sharptin had placed the call himself, it must be a matter of great urgency.

"So, Dr. Reichstad has contacted you?" Sharptin asked.

"Yes," the Director said. "I spoke to him just a few hours ago."

"Yet I understand that you were not fully cooperative with his request?"

"To the contrary," the Director explained, "I was as cooperative as I could be, under the circumstances. But Dr. Reichstad was asking for the *immediate* issuance of a permit for an unprecedented excavation along the walls of Old Jerusalem. These permits take time. I am always amused at the attitude of some American researchers. They must think that, because Israel is the land of Bible miracles, our government agencies can perform supernatural feats. Moses may have parted the Red Sea—but I wonder if his task would have been harder if he had to cut through Israeli red tape."

"I didn't call to get a taste of your Jerusalem humor," Sharptin responded bitingly. "I called to make sure that the permit would be issued *immediately*."

"Mr. Undersecretary, I can assure you we will place a very high priority on this request. As you know, however, I am required by our legal procedures to submit this request for archaeological excavation to our licensing committee for approval. That takes time. Now, Dr. Reichstad and his research center are certainly recognized experts. So the issue of scientific qualifications will not be a problem. But there *is* the issue of—well, how can I put this?—let's just call it 'religious geopolitics.'"

"That is why I am calling. I am speaking for the United States government when I say that if Israel wants America as a continued ally, then your absolute cooperation will be expected in this excavation. It is just that simple."

"Mr. Sharptin, you are forcing me to be blunt. So I will be blunt. This is an unprecedented insult—an incredible intrusion by your government, into the internal affairs of the sovereign state of Israel. I know the history of pressure that has been applied to our tiny little country. I am fully aware of the inroads that a past President made into our internal election process and the pressure from your nation for us to comply with Palestinian demands for land, and for the creation of a Palestinian state. But this ploy—this form of diplomatic coercion—is outrageous! I suggest that if you want us to give priority to this permit, then the U.S. Department of State should follow normal diplomatic channels."

"We've tried. Your ambassador has been stalling. Your prime minister won't take my telephone calls. So I am warning you—if you do not handle this excavation request posthaste, and get it approved *this week,* I will exercise every bit of my influence among the nations of the world, and among antiquities scholars everywhere, to demand your resignation and to embarrass your nation. And make no mistake—my influence is considerable."

"This week? That is going to be very difficult. Maybe impossible," the Director responded.

"Dr. Reichstad is engaged in some court hearings in the U.S. next week. We would like the excavation permit to be approved this week, and digging to start over the weekend *before* Dr. Reichstad has to be in court."

"Yes. The 7QA fragment lawsuit against Angus MacCameron," the Director noted. "The trial starts on Monday, doesn't it? Before Judge Jeremiah Kaye."

There was a pause before Sharptin continued.

"It sounds like you know a lot about that case. I would be interested in hearing what you know."

"Oh, Mr. Sharptin, let's not be naïve. There were some ham-handed attempts to keep the publicity down on that case. But the nation of Israel has a history of gathering intelligence about those things that have an impact on our land, our people, or our future. Just check your Bible. It goes all the way back to Joshua and Caleb."

"I want this permit for Dr. Reichstad *this week*. And further, I want a waiver of the procedures regarding ancient burial sites. Your own supreme court ruled in 1992 that burial sites can be excavated."

"That's true," the Director acknowledged. "But we are also bound by the guidelines issued by our attorney general in 1994. If Dr. Reichstad finds a tomb—that can be excavated as an antiquity. But if they find a corpse in that tomb—well, that is very different. The corpse has to be turned over—at the site of the tomb—to the Ministry of Religious Affairs for reburial. If the corpse is of Jewish descent, then it must be buried in accordance with Jewish law, in a Jewish cemetery."

"If Reichstad finds a corpse—and I am betting he will—then he is taking that corpse out of that tomb, and back to his lab for examination," Sharptin stated pointedly.

"That is not going to happen, Mr. Undersecretary. You are not going to goose-step your way into our internal, domestic laws, and demand that we waive them for your pleasure. Besides, while I know that you spent some time over here in your past diplomatic days, I don't think you can possibly imagine what is going to happen with this kind of dig."

"Do you know who you are talking to?" Sharptin sputtered in a controlled rage.

But the Director kept talking through the undersecretary's tantrum.

"First there will be the reaction of the Palestinians. The eastern, St. Stephen's Gate entrance to the Old City of Jerusalem is right next to a Muslim cemetery. We will be lucky if there aren't full-scale riots over the dig because of that fact alone. And because it is near the Temple Mount, some Palestinian anarchists are going to think that this excavation is just a ploy to start tunneling under the Dome of the Rock and the Al Aqsa Mosque, and they will want to start a war. Don't you remember the history of riots on the Temple Mount?

"Then there are the ultra-orthodox Jews—our own people. They will object to any digging next to the wall of Jerusalem—and they will want absolute adherence to the laws regarding Jewish corpses. We have had demonstrations, riots, and violence over other burial sites in the past. We've had the grave markers of deceased archaeologists desecrated. But nothing like this. You have no idea what kind of nuclear bomb this tomb excavation will become.

"And I know what Reichstad is looking for. What if he finds a corpse and says it is *the* Jesus of Nazareth? The apocalyptic groups who want to usher in the End-of-Days violence are going to have a field day with that one. We will have to make that tomb excavation a full-scale military zone."

There was another pause. Then Sharptin concluded the conversation.

"I look forward to the permit being issued this week. On behalf of the United States, I want to thank you for what I am sure will be your full and complete cooperation."

After the Director hung up the receiver he rubbed his forehead. He looked up at the ceiling fan for a moment. Then he called to his secretary. "Get the chairman of the Licensing Committee on the line in ten minutes."

Then he opened his desk and pulled out a little personal notebook of telephone numbers. Under "M" he looked up the word "Mossad," the name of the Israeli intelligence and espionage service. Under that listing he found the name of an old friend. Next to it was his telephone number.

The Director quickly called that number, and waited for his friend to pick up.

When he heard the voice on the other end, he said, "Nathan, this is Jacob over at the IAA calling. We've got a situation here. A permit request for a highly unusual burial excavation. U.S. Department of State is really putting the pressure on. This thing is an international time-bomb. We could use your help."

The voice on the other end said, "I keep telling the agency I'm supposed to be in retirement. You know, I am just starting to make some real money in my little art and antiquities shop." The voice laughed.

"Come on," the Director responded, "why do you get to retire so young? What are you, fifty-three? Besides, you know that spies never really retire—especially in Israel."

"So, how do I fit into this 'situation' of yours?"

"Well," the Director explained, "we've got Professor Reichstad, the researcher who revealed the 7QA fragment. He's got the backing of the State Department, and he wants to dig up an area where he thinks there is a first-century tomb located. First problem—the site is at the eastern gate, right there at the old Jerusalem wall. And if they uncover the tomb of an ancient Jew—well, you know what that means! The ultra-orthodox will fight to the death over that. And then there is the second little problem—he is proposing to dig right next to a Muslim cemetery. And of course the whole thing is within view of the Temple Mount. That's begging for riots.

And then there is this other little problem—he is going after this burial site because he thinks that is where he can locate the corpse of Jesus and lay waste two thousand years of Christian belief in the resurrection."

After a pause, the Director asked, "So, what do you think?"

"What you are describing—this is not exactly what I would call a 'situation,' my friend," the voice answered.

"Oh? Then what would you call it?"

"I think I would call it—Armageddon."

57

IN THE AFTERNOON, FOLLOWING THE COURT hearing before Judge Kaye, frantic phone calls were made between Will Chambers and his experts, J-Fox Sherman and his experts, and Judge Kaye's court.

By the terms of the judge's order, each group of experts were not only to be given access to both fragments, but they also were to be witnesses to the scientific examination by the opposing side at a "neutral site." The hot issue was the location of the proper "neutral site."

Judge Kaye had his clerk call a friend at Johns Hopkins University in Baltimore. The University hastily agreed to make a large laboratory available for several days. It was big enough to house several researchers simultaneously, as well as their equipment. The University officials agreed to pledge absolute secrecy to the project. Sherman insisted on that, and Judge Kaye ordered it.

By the end of the day, Reichstad and two of the scientists from his research center, together with Dr. Giovanni and Bill Kenwood, who was Will's materials engineer, were finally gathered together at the lab room in Baltimore.

An armored car with four armed security guards accompanied Reichstad's delivery of the 7QA fragment. The tiny piece of papyrus was enclosed inside a bullet-proof, vacuum-tight, barometrically controlled glass case.

Angus MacCameron showed up at the laboratory with the 7QB fragment, but with a great deal less technological sophistication. He carried it in a little plastic zip bag, inside a tattered mailing envelope.

The experts all agreed to work in shifts—from seven o'clock until two in the morning for the first shift, and from two until nine in the morning for the second shift. Bill Kenwood would work the first shift for the defense side, with Dr. Giovanni taking over on the second watch for her examination. Everyone brought cots, sleeping bags, and Thermoses, most of which contained black coffee. Dr. Giovanni brought packets of "stress-relieving" herbal tea.

Will stopped by the office for a few hours that night, and received a few calls from Dr. Giovanni about Bill Kenwood's progress. It was great news, although not unexpected.

Kenwood had done a preliminary microscopic examination of the right edge of 7QA and the left edge of 7QB. There seemed to be no question in his mind that 7QB had originally been part of 7QA; that they had been joined exactly where MacCameron and Giovanni had guessed. Further, it appeared that a modern, fairly sharp cutting tool (either a razor blade or an artist's blade) had been used to score the surface of the fragment. The fragment had then been torn at the scores into *three* pieces, yielding an irregular appearance at the torn edges. It was Kenwood's opinion that 7QA and 7QB were two of those three pieces because, when 7QA and 7QB were fitted together, it left an irregular vacant space in the upper right quarter.

Now there was no doubt: There had to be a third piece—7QC—still out there somewhere.

Will relayed the news by telephone to Jacki Johnson, who was working on the case every night from her home. Will thanked her again for the legal research she did that had been so influential in Judge Kaye's decision. A little after midnight, Will collapsed into bed at his apartment.

The next morning Will was about to leave for the day when his doorbell rang. He was greeted at the door by two FBI agents. They said they had been contacted by law enforcement agents in Nevada. They wanted to talk with Will about his alleged encounter with Abdul el Alibahd. Will had been half expecting them.

Sunday night, when Will was being taken away from Mullburn's "Utopia" by the squad of police officers, two of them had told him they would drive him to a cab stand along the Strip so he could catch a cab to the airport. On the way in, however, Will had sounded them out, giving them a few cautious details about his weekend with Alibahd's terrorists. He had assumed that the officers would stick him squarely into the category shared by bigfoot hunters and the people who complain of being medically probed by space aliens. But when the name of Warren Mullburn was implicated, their eyes had brightened up with interest.

The officers had called ahead to the airport, asked them to delay the last "red-eye" flight to Washington, D.C., and then gunned their squad car to the airport with lights flashing. As Will had jumped out of the car, the senior officer had said he would be contacting the regional office of the FBI.

It was nearly noon when the agents finished their interview with Will in his apartment. They suggested that a security detail be assigned to him, since he was now a material witness to Alibahd's own implied confession. Alibhad's words "the only dogs I kill are the kind that wear shoes, and business suits, and work on Wall Street," were the clincher in tying him to the Wall Street bombing. This time, Will quickly agreed to the safety measures. As the two agents left they said they would also be calling the investigators about the fire at Generals' Hill.

That last comment gave Will some renewed hope that he might be cleared, once and for all, as a suspect in his house fire. But just a few hours after that, it became a full-blown reality.

Will was back at his office, poring over the MacCameron file, when he heard someone in the lobby. He glanced around the corner and couldn't believe it.

Fiona was standing there, her cheeks flushed, and a huge, dimpled grin across her face. She was holding a small box in her hands.

"Do I have a present for you!" she exclaimed.

"What are you doing here?" Will asked, confused in his delight at seeing her.

"I've been turning my condo upside-down, rummaging through garbage cans, looking under my bed, tearing my closets apart looking for it—"

"Looking for what?" Will interrupted.

"...my attic, my storage space, my briefcase. I looked everywhere. I said to myself, *Fiona, there is no way that this dear man is going to jail for this arson charge when he is obviously innocent. This is not going to happen. After everything he has done for your Da, you are not going to let this happen.*"

As Will was looking Fiona in the eyes, his problems with the fire marshal's office seemed strangely far removed.

"So, I found it!" Fiona exclaimed.

"What?"

"The box. The box that came with the crystal Statue of Liberty you gave me. I knew we had to prove you had been in New York that day. The name of the shop in New York was on the box. So I called them up. I gave the people at the shop the date that you had been up there. They faxed me a receipt for the purchase of the statue. When I described you, the girl who was the sales clerk says she even remembers you being there."

"How did you describe me?"

"I'm not telling!" she said laughing.

"Fiona, I don't know what to say. This is incredible. You are so kind."

"The salesgirl's name and telephone number are on the fax with the sales slip." And then she added, "Isn't God good?"

"Well...there may be something to that," Will said.

"Of course there is!" Then she put her hand on his and said, "And Da told me about you being attacked, kidnapped, and your life being threatened. I can't begin to imagine what you've been through. There is no way I can thank you for the risks that you have taken—and for being my father's advocate, and his friend, through all of this."

"Coming from you, that means more than you will ever know," Will replied. For a moment there was an awkward silence as they merely smiled and nodded to each other.

"Please let me know if there is anything I can do to help you with Da's legal case."

"Oh—how is your mother?"

"Bless her heart, every day is a struggle. Everyday she slips away from us a little. But we thank God for every minute we have with her."

Then Fiona said goodbye and left the office with a little wave. As soon as Fiona was gone Will faxed a copy of the sales receipt to the fire marshal's office, along with a letter inviting them to contact the sales clerk to verify his presence in New York earlier on the day of the fire, and alerting them to the FBI's anticipated involvement in exonerating him.

Forty-eight hours later, Will received a call from the chief arson investigator. His message was terse, but hugely welcome. "You're cleared on the fire investigation. You are no longer a suspect. Your insurance company tells us they will be in touch with you to arrange payment for your fire loss."

After weeks of feeling like a man swimming under ice in the dead of winter, looking for an opening, Will was finally reaching the air.

Soon the insurance proceeds would be made available to him. The insurance company would start reimbursing him for his temporary housing costs. And he was cleared, finally, of the ridiculous but horrible suspicion that he had burned down his own house, and then killed his own beloved Clarence to make the whole thing look like someone else had done it.

Will also felt better about the Reichstad lawsuit. Jacki was a skilled lawyer, and the value of her help on the case was immeasurable. Just as important, Will liked the feeling of working again with his former associate and friend. Will was also beginning to be more optimistic about the outcome of the case. Bill Kenwood's conclusions that 7QA and 7QB had been parts of the same fragment upped the chances that 7QA was one of the fragments possessed by Richard Hunter before his death. It also supported MacCameron's allegations in his magazine article that Reichstad was scientifically sloppy in rushing to judgment about the meaning of 7QA without having all of the other evidence in front of him.

On the other hand, Dr. Giovanni's findings about 7QA and 7QB were less than stellar. She called Will the next morning after her examination of the fragments.

Yes, she affirmed that she could testify that Riechstand was unprofessional in rendering opinions about 7QA when it should have been obvious to him there were critical parts of the fragment which had been torn away—and which were still missing when he published his findings.

However, while Giovanni *did* believe that 7QB had been part of 7QA before Azid had torn it apart, the wording of 7QB actually *supported* Reichstad's conclusions on the essential point. Taken together, 7QA and 7QB did seem to unequivocally support Reichstad's opinion that Jesus was still buried somewhere, and that he did not rise from the grave on the third day. In fact, 7QB seemed to give a description of the actual place of Jesus' tomb—a location completely different than either the Garden Tomb, or the tomb at the Church of the Holy Sepulchre, the two possible sites of the place of Jesus' burial according to traditional Christian thought.

All in all, Will thought that the chances of clearing Angus MacCameron at trial from any liability for damages due to defamation or libel were now about fifty-fifty. Still, those odds were a lot better than where they had been at the beginning of the case.

As for the bizarre turn of events involving Alibahd and his band of oceangoing terrorists, and the threatening encounter with Warren Mullburn, Will now felt safer, knowing that he was under twenty-four-hour FBI protection.

Occasionally he found himself wandering over to the window to make sure the black, unmarked SUV with the agents was still outside his building. Will was checking on his security team when he received a call from Tiny Heftland.

Tiny had been able to talk with the Israeli police about the death of Harim Azid in Bethlehem. They said that the Palestinian police in Bethlehem had bungled the investigation. Further, the Israelis had seen clear, though subtle, evidence that Azid had been tortured. They noted small electrical burns around several of his body cavities. None of that information had made its way into the report filed by the Palestinian police.

Even more importantly, Tiny said the Israeli police had bent over backwards in promising cooperation when they learned that he was working for Will Chambers on the Reichstad lawsuit.

"Say, do you have some kind of pull over there in Israel?" Tiny asked.

"None whatsoever," Will said, wondering over their eagerness to help.

"But here's the icing on the cake," Tiny added excitedly. "The government over there is willing to *voluntarily* fly to the U.S. the two Israeli police officers who were at the scene of Azid's death, so they can appear at the trial. You simply have to agree to reimburse Israel for the transportation costs."

Will quickly cross-checked their names against the names Tiny had given him earlier—the ones he'd listed as potential trial witnesses in his written disclosures filed at the time of their pretrial hearing. They matched. Failure to disclose them would likely have resulted in Judge Kaye barring their testimony.

"There's one more mystery witness," Will said to his investigator. "According to the police, there is a wandering desert Bedouin out there somewhere by the name of Muhammad el Juma, a member of the Taamireh tribe. He's the guy MacCameron said that Hunter had mentioned. He found the original fragment in the cave near the Dead Sea. Amazingly, his family carried this thing around the desert for some fifty years. Something happened to make him decide to sell it to Azid, who was some kind of shirt-tail relative of his. Then he seemed to disappear off the face of the earth. I don't know what he would have to say. But I'm sure this Bedouin could be a key witness. Up to now I thought that locating him would be impossible. However, I hear you telling me that the Israelis are anxious to help—for whatever reason—and so, well, I'm thinking about something."

"What?" Tiny asked.

"Is your passport up to date?"

"Sure."

"I want you to go over to Jerusalem and meet with the head of the Israeli police. Explain who we are searching for—and why. See if, between the police and any of your old contacts, you can't locate this guy."

"Well, there's another possibility," Tiny said.

"What's that?"

"We might be too late. Maybe the bad guys got to this Bedouin. Maybe he's sleeping the big sleep."

"Well," Will responded, "then we had better know that too."

After Will hung up with Tiny he called Angus MacCameron. Fiona answered and said he was napping, but she would wake him. After a few minutes he came to the phone.

"Angus, this is Will. When was the last contact you had with Judith Hunter, Richard Hunter's sister, over in England?"

"Just her note to me, along with 7QB."

"How about with the British Museum?"

"Oh my," MacCameron replied, pausing to think, "a long time ago. I contacted them after Richard's death. And then again, after Reichstad published his findings about 7QA in his archaeology journal."

"What did you ask them?"

"Just whether they knew about any written antiquities that Hunter might have been working on at the time of his death—and if so, where they might be."

"What did they say?"

"They didn't have a clue. Hunter never talked to them about it. He showed up unexpectedly in London one day, fresh from Jerusalem. Did some work in his office. Then left and flew right back to Jerusalem. According to his secretary, he said he was going back to his field office to 'fetch one last thing.' Of course, he never returned. As soon as he got back to Jerusalem, he was murdered. Will, I believe he was returning for 7QA, which he must have hidden back there. But as soon as he returned and located it, he was attacked. That's why Reichstad only got his hands on 7QA. I think Hunter had already taken 7QB back to London, and planned to have his sister mail it to me if he felt threatened. Then he left it under the sofa, where it stayed until she discovered it."

"So what did he do with the missing third piece—7QC?" Will asked.

"I think," MacCameron said, "he took both 7QB and 7QC with him to London. He left 7QB in his sister's flat. His sister had subleased the apartment from a friend and had it listed under her friend's name—I believe that is why Reichstad's people didn't know to go there and ransack it."

"And 7QC?"

"His message was clear—he was leaving me a clue that it was at the British Museum. The Museum carefully checked his office after his death, but found nothing. It has to be somewhere else at the Museum."

"Why don't you make a follow-up telephone call to the people you know the best at the British Museum. Just ask around. See if anything has jogged their memories. Ask about other places Hunter may have kept any of his papers or files."

MacCameron said he would do it, and then he invited Will over for dinner on Sunday evening, the night before the opening of the trial. Fiona would cook. MacCameron promised to play a little "squeeze-box" music after dinner.

Will accepted immediately.

Then MacCameron added, with a little wry humor, "And we will huddle together like the Christians in the Catacombs—singing one last hymn, and steeling ourselves for the ordeal—when Reichstad and Sherman, and the

Court, take us by the scruff of the neck, and throw us gloriously to the lions!"

In the background, Will could hear Fiona laughing and telling her father to stop being so sarcastic, and then saying: "Don't forget, Da, you have the Lord. And, I might add, your own personal gladiator!"

Somewhere in a quiet spot deep inside him, Will Chambers wished he didn't have to wait five days to join them.

58

THE NEXT FEW DAYS, WILL FOLLOWED a familiar pattern. His career as a trial lawyer had taught him to prepare meticulously before every trial. He delegated the non-fact-specific legal research to Jacki. She was to put together their proposed Jury Instructions and Jury Verdict form, as well as a Trial Brief to the court on the general legal issues of the case from the defense standpoint. Will would prepare a shorter Trial Brief on the admissibility of documents, as well as responses to anticipated objections by Sherman to the evidence they would be presenting.

Will created a master log that summarized all of the evidence from all of the witnesses, and cross-indexed forty-three separate issues and sub-issues, assigning a code number to each issue and sub-issue, and then giving the location in the massive file where the evidence could be found supporting it.

It took from morning until midnight of one day to assemble the dozen big black trial notebooks that contained the entirety of Will's defense to Reichstad's suit.

Then it took another day-and-a-half for him and Jacki to assemble the notebooks that contained the sequenced, tabbed exhibits that would be handed to the judge, opposing counsel, and the jury, on the first day of the trial. Now that he had FBI protection, Will permitted Jacki to travel down to his office to help him.

The third and fourth days Will finished the outline of cross-examination questions and direct-examination questions for each witness that he had been compiling throughout the case, and questions for prospective jurors during jury selection.

The last thing he did was to outline his opening statement, and begin a rough sketch of what he anticipated as his closing statement.

The pattern of trial preparation fit him like an old pair of sneakers. He had gone through this procedure hundreds of times before. Yet on *this* case—with these people—and more particularly, with *these* profound issues at stake, his exacting preparation didn't seem to be enough. Will wasn't sure what else he needed, but he knew in his gut that there was something else. What was he missing?

On Sunday evening he drove over to MacCameron's home. Perhaps it was the stress of the upcoming trial. Or maybe the joy of an odd friendship with these super-zealous Christians who had, in a strange way, become a kind of family for him. But whatever it was, Will felt a special eagerness as he walked up and knocked at the door. When Reverend MacCameron and Fiona greeted him at the door, Will gave a good-natured laugh. MacCameron was outfitted in the full tartan of the clan Cameron. Fiona was decked out in a red tartan dress, and shoes with buckles. As she stood in the door for a moment, with her dark hair cascading down, with the blush on her cheeks, with her sparkling eyes, her beauty nearly punched the wind right out of his stomach.

"Why do I feel like I just stepped over the magic bridge into the land of Brigadoon?" Will quipped as he entered the apartment with an arrangement of flowers.

As soon as he was inside Will asked if he could see Helen MacCameron. They led him into her bedroom. He noticed that a woman who appeared to be a nurse was sitting next to her.

There was a glimmer of a smile on Helen's pale face beneath her oxygen mask when Will stepped in and touched her hand. Helen glanced over to the nurse, and the nurse bent over to her, lifted the mask up, and put her ear close to Helen's pale lips.

"She wants to know why you aren't wearing your kilt."

Will smiled, and explained that he had knobby knees. Besides, how could he possibly compete with a real Scot like Angus MacCameron, who looked so dashing in his clan outfit?

"You must be the Robbie she has been expecting," the nurse continued.

"No, I'm Will Chambers."

"Oh, she's been talking about her son—Robbie. A lawyer. She was expecting him tonight."

Will had not heard either MacCameron or Fiona mention that there was another member of the family. He turned to ask MacCameron about it, but the older man put his finger to his lips and said, "I think I'm going to leave the bedroom door open all the way. I think Helen would like to hear the sounds of friendly voices, and the music. We want her to be part of this."

As they stepped into the kitchen MacCameron took Will aside.

"Before Fiona was born, my dear wife had a miscarriage when she was eight months pregnant. It was a terrible loss to both of us. But I think it was particularly hard on Helen. As it turned out, it was a boy. We were going to name him Robert."

"Oh, I'm sorry," Will said.

"No need. She must see something in you—something that shows her what Robbie would have been like if he had lived and grown up. She seems to be living more and more in the past now. The doctors told us that the cancer has reached her brain."

Fiona walked into the kitchen and kissed her father on the cheek, then wrapped her arms around him and held him for a long time.

MacCameron wiped his eyes and brightened up. He said dinner was ready.

Will was informed that this was a "modified" Scottish dinner. Scottish salmon appetizers were brought out first, and homemade soda bread. There was mutton stew and beef roast (American—they couldn't find Highlands beef in Washington, D.C.). But the blood pudding was genuine. Will took a taste—but pushed it away discreetly while Fiona and her father laughed.

After dinner they went into the parlor and MacCameron brought out his accordion. He commenced to play several old Scottish tunes. When he got to some of the livelier music, he managed to coax Fiona, despite her protestations, into doing some of the dances he had taught her as a girl. Then Fiona sang a few songs in Gaelic, in a lilting voice so sweet that it seemed, to Will, to emanate wholly from another time, and another dimension.

The last song Angus MacCameron played was a slow, haunting melody called "Dark Island." Fiona accompanied him on a slightly out-of-tune piano in the corner.

Then Fiona offered to clean up and do the dishes while MacCameron and Will sat on the couch together and talked about the case.

"I accessed the *Jerusalem Post* on my computer earlier today, the minute I got home from church," MacCameron explained. "An article mentions that a permit has just been issued for an excavation in the vicinity of the St. Stephen's Gate entrance to the Old City, right along the wall. The permit was issued to Albert Reichstad and his team."

"He didn't waste any time, did he?" Will added.

"He must have filed an application with the Israeli Antiquities Authority earlier this week, as soon as he had translated the St. Stephen's Gate reference in the 7QB fragment. Will, this is unheard of—a permit for this kind of controversial dig being approved in just a matter of days! Somehow, Reichstad must have either applied incredible pressure on the IAA, or else he has an inside connection. In any event, we have to get to that excavation site—we have to be eyewitnesses to Reichstad's activities there." MacCameron's voice was rising in intensity.

"Da, please don't get all riled up," Fiona said, peeking around the corner from the kitchen.

"Angus," Will said, trying to calm his client, "we have a trial starting tomorrow. That has to be our priority. Besides, Reichstad has to be there in the courtroom with us. He is not going to be over in Jerusalem. And knowing him, he won't let his assistants start any significant work without him. He is going to want to be right there when the digging starts—so he can grab the headlines and get the credit."

"Yes, that is a good point. But didn't you say that the trial is only going for three days next week—Monday through Wednesday?"

"That's right. Judge Kaye has a judicial conference on Thursday and Friday. We will be off those two days—then we reconvene the following Monday."

"Then that is when Reichstad is going to start digging. He will leave immediately after court on Wednesday, fly out in the evening—and land in Jerusalem with at least three days to commence the excavation. I'm sure that, before he even gets there, his assistants will have done an electronic sweep of areas around that gate. As I recall it, there is a small rise just to the right of the gate entrance. They will try to get a fix on anything that looks like a burial site there."

"How?"

"Reichstad will have all of the sophisticated hardware. They have these little portable geophysical radar systems—about the size of a large laptop computer. They can detect the presence of burial locations, walls, almost anything underneath the surface of the ground. Will, I can't tell you how important it is that we plan on being there in Jerusalem when he starts digging. If we are not, he can come back into court the following week and say anything he wants about his excavation—he can say that he found a corpse with a name-tag on it, a name-tag that says 'I'm Jesus, the son of Mary, and I didn't rise from the grave,' and we won't be able to refute it!"

"I understand. But there's another issue," Will said, recalling his assignment to his client. "Did you call the British Museum?"

"Oh—why yes. They have no idea where Richard may have kept any other records and papers. But I did find out one other very important fact."

"Oh?"

"They had a break-in at the Museum a few weeks ago. Sometime *after* we disclosed the tape of Richard's answering-machine message to Reichstad and his lawyers."

"So?"

"Vandals, they said, ransacked the office of one of their researchers. A night watchman showed up, but they got away. And what do you think his last name was—the researcher whose office was burglarized?"

"What?"

"*Lazarus*. The office belonged to Isaac Lazarus."

Will thought for a minute. Then he cried out, "'Lazarus come forth!'"

"Exactly! The other side must have assumed, as I did, that the 'resurrection order' that Hunter was leaving as a clue in his message had to do with the Lazarus story in the Gospel of John. Therefore, they broke into Dr. Lazarus's office, thinking they could find 7QC before we did."

"Did they take anything from the office?"

"The Museum didn't think so. But I did get their preliminary approval for the two of us to search through Lazarus's office in order to locate any papers belonging to Hunter. And Richard's sister has been very kind. She was his last of kin and has already given me permission to locate and keep any of the papers or effects we find dealing with his discovery of his fragments in Jerusalem. Hunter's last will and testament actually bequeathed to me fifty percent of the value of any of his recent discoveries, and of his writings over the last ten years of his life. Can you imagine that?"

Will smiled at MacCameron's good fortune.

"When can we get over there?" MacCameron asked.

"To London?"

"Yes!"

"Angus, you've got me trotting all over the world. Let's put in a day or two of the trial this week. Then we'll talk."

"I'm going to book two tickets for us from D.C. to London, leaving Wednesday night. We have got to try to locate 7QC before the end of the trial. And then, if we have time, we will fly from London to Jerusalem, observe what Reichstad is doing at the excavation site, and then fly back for the rest of the trial next week."

"Are you trying to put your lawyer in a body bag?" Will asked with a wry smile.

"Isn't it exhilarating—*digging for truth?*" MacCameron exclaimed.

Fiona came into the room and joined them. She reminded her father that he needed to get his rest for the trial. But MacCameron said he wasn't sleepy. Besides, he added, after Will left he wanted to spend some time alone with his wife.

Before Will left, Angus MacCameron placed his hand on Will's head and prayed a blessing on him, asking for "God's power and wisdom" to guide him in the trial. And then he prayed that Will would, in God's own timing, open his heart to the resurrected Christ.

Fiona walked Will to his car outside, gave him a quick hug, and thanked him for coming.

When Will finally returned home to his apartment that night he realized that, in his busyness he had failed to check for Saturday's mail in his mailbox. He shoved his hand inside and pulled out a single envelope. It was from his uncle, Bull Chambers.

Inside the envelope there was a color copy of a photograph—and on it, Bull Chambers had written something. After Will had studied it, he laughed a loud belly laugh.

The photograph showed Will struggling to hold up the huge marlin he had caught that day on the ocean with his uncle. But Bull had drawn an arrow pointing to the marlin and then written: "J-Fox Sherman—your next trophy catch!"

Will was still chuckling as he locked the door behind him and headed for bed.

59

THE JURY TRIAL WAS SET TO BEGIN THAT MORNING at 10:00 A.M. in the U.S. District Court building in Washington, D.C. From its front steps, which face Constitution Avenue, to the left and upward the dome of the U.S. Capitol is visible in the distance. Farther still, just across the street from the Capitol, are the white marbled steps and columns of the U.S. Supreme Court building.

But the third branch of government—symbolized by the White House—is geographically removed in this triangulation of government power. Set apart, blocks away from the other two branches, the White House is bounded by trees, by guardhouses, and—at the behest of a recent President—by huge concrete pillars along its frontage on Pennsylvania Avenue—a monument to the threat of terrorism without.

But this morning, the White House rested comfortably secure from any threats of anarchy and violence from without. Within, the President was having a pleasant breakfast with Undersecretary of the Department of State Kenneth Sharptin. The shortlist of the three possible running mates was being winnowed, and sifted, and narrowed. Very soon, only one name would remain.

Billionaire Warren Mullburn had pledged his full financial support—and the recruiting of thousands of "unpaid" volunteers—to aid a presidential ticket, as long as it bore the name of Kenneth Sharptin as vice-presidential candidate. Mullburn already had in the works the construction of a lobbying organization that would fund its own massive, multimillion-dollar television ads in favor of a ticket coupling the President with Sharptin as V-P.

As Will Chambers trudged up to the front steps of the federal courthouse, wheeling a cart full of notebooks and file boxes for the *Reichstad vs.*

MacCameron case, he thought back on the history of that building. Here was the place where President Richard Nixon had been laid low by the decision of a single federal judge during the Watergate investigation. This same building was the locus of legal battles between the branches of government, grappling like titans of stone for mastery of decision-making—mastery of money—or the mastery of power.

But this was also the building where workaday grand jurors from the District—the unemployed, the hourly laborers, the civil servants—had considered, weighed, and sifted the conduct of President William Jefferson Clinton.

Here, in this architecture of freedom, even the lowly and the nameless were empowered to judge the powerful.

Will nodded hello to the security guards and bailiffs as he made his way through the metal detector and passed box after box through the X-ray machine. Judge Kaye had asked that legal counsel meet with him in his chambers at 9:30 to discuss preliminaries, and Will was a few minutes ahead of schedule. But J-Fox Sherman was already there ahead of him. He was surrounded by two legal associates, his personal paralegal, and a law clerk, all with laptop computers, freshly scrubbed faces, and steel-stiff postures.

Judge Kaye explained that each side would have three "peremptory strikes" for the jury—each party had the right to exclude three jurors for virtually any reason. He also explained his pattern for taking breaks—one mid-morning, one mid-afternoon, and lunches exactly one hour and fifteen minutes long.

Lastly, the judge indicated that he would be conducting the trial in "bifurcated" fashion. The evidence relating to Reichstad's damages—the injury to his reputation, and his "mental anguish"—would be reserved for the second stage of the case. That evidence would only be heard if Reichstad prevailed—and MacCameron lost—on the single question involving "liability." That question to the jury was this: "Did Reverend Angus MacCameron, in the subject article concerning Dr. Albert Reichstad, publish allegations which were substantially truthful?"

A "yes" verdict meant that the trial was over and MacCameron had won. A "no" verdict would require MacCameron to pay the hundreds of thousands—perhaps even millions—of dollars in damages that the jury would then determine in the second phase of the case.

"Bifurcation" is usually considered an advantage to the defense, since juries hearing evidence on a plaintiff's damages sometimes become more sympathetic toward the plaintiff on other issues in the case. But here, Judge

Kaye's decision was no sign of partiality toward Will's side of the case. The judge simply preferred that procedure in all of the damage lawsuits that came before him.

When Will and the other lawyers left Judge Kaye's chambers and entered the courtroom, one half of the benches in the audience section were filled with prospective jurors. On the other side, Will noticed Angus MacCameron sitting with Fiona.

Behind them was a round, familiar face. It was Brother Billy Joe Highlighter, flanked by elders of his church. As Will would learn at break, they were there in the courtroom to be a "spiritual presence for the truth."

Dr. Reichstad, and several of his research associates, were in the front row.

In the last row in the back, in the far corner, Jack Hornby sat with his arms stretched along the back of the bench, a look of subtle amusement on his face.

Jury selection in the case took all morning, and into the afternoon. Will struck from the jury an official with Atheists International and a disgruntled government scientist who had sued a co-worker (unsuccessfully) for having defamed his professional reputation. Lastly, he removed from the jury a pastor from a denomination called the Universalist Sanctuary of Light, which maintained that Jesus never rose from the dead, and whose members religiously followed the writings of Warren Mullburn, whom they considered a "prophet" of evolutionary theology.

J-Fox Sherman struck the wife of a Baptist minister, a YMCA leader (presumably because he also taught Sunday school at his church), and the director of a black gospel choir.

When the jury had finally been selected, Will felt that his client still might get a fair trial—though considering the jury he was left with, perhaps not in *his* lifetime, and perhaps not in *that* courtroom. It was at such times that Will Chambers the trial lawyer was reminded that human justice must invariably have a human face and a human heart.

If justice were to be meted out in the case of *Dr. Albert Reichstad vs. Angus MacCameron and* Digging for Truth *Magazine,* then something extraordinary would have to happen.

There were six jurors and one alternate juror: a chemistry professor who had "no use for most religion"; a bored-looking postal worker; an accountant from the General Service Agency, who said he feared "fundamentalists" because they "blow up buildings"; a grade-school teacher; a construction contractor; an anthropology teacher in a local high school, who said she had read and appreciated some of the writings of Dr. Reichstad, but boldly proclaimed that it would not affect her ability to be impartial; and lastly, a bouncer in a dance club.

After a break, Sherman and Will gave their opening statements.

Sherman was winsome, casual, detailed, and persuasive. He promised the jury that they would see evidence of three types that would compel a finding of "no" to the jury question.

First, he explained, the jury would behold the professional credibility of Dr. Reichstad. Sherman stretched out his arms—like a male "Lady Justice." A catalogue of Reichstad's world-class accomplishments tripped off Sherman's tongue: his awards, his published works, his multiple degrees from prestigious institutions, and the documentary film being made on his life by The Smithsonian Institution. As he listed Reichstad's qualifications, Sherman's outstretched right arm slowly lowered under the invisible weight of his client's professional prowess. Then he described the sparse and erratic career of Angus MacCameron. But as he listed MacCameron's qualifications, his outstretched left arm never moved, as if to say, "The defendant, ladies and gentlemen of the jury, is not only a lightweight, he is a featherweight."

Secondly, Sherman pointed out that when MacCameron wrote his article he had no proof whatsoever that a) Reichstad's opinions about 7QA were scientifically unfounded, or b) that Reichstad was in any way "connected" to the deaths of Azid and Hunter. He urged the jury to listen closely only to the evidence—and to reject any "speculations and fantasies which might be the product of a religious extremist like MacCameron."

Lastly, he pointed out that "right here, in this courtroom, you are about to see the unveiling of one of the world's most important discoveries about the real Jesus of Nazareth; and that unveiling will show the absolute falsity of Mr. MacCameron's lies against Dr. Reichstad." Then Sherman described the 7QB fragment, which, he asserted, actually corroborated the 7QA fragment—as well as Reichstad's interpretation of it. According to Sherman, 7QB actually mentioned the St. Stephen's Gate location of the very tomb—hitherto unknown—that Sherman declared passionately, "must obviously still, to this day, contain the body of Jesus, the world's greatest moral teacher, but who was certainly no resurrected godlike creature."

Sherman sat down, and Will rose to his feet and walked to the lectern in front of the jury box. He had no notes in front of him. The contours and lines of his opening statement had not just been memorized—they had been consumed into the fibers of his thinking and feeling about this case.

Then Will stepped away from the lectern, and began to speak.

"Ladies and gentlemen. You are to be the judges of 'truth' in this case. Not because Mr. Sherman or his client, or I or my client, have decided that it will be so. But because a free system of government has summoned you; called you from your everyday tasks to come here—to this place, at this time—to render a judgment about 'truth.' There is no greater task in a free nation than this.

"The facts will show that Reverend Angus MacCameron wrote a scathing article against Dr. Reichstad. And it was scathing. But the facts will show that he spoke the truth when he wrote what he did. When he stated that Dr. Reichstad's opinions about the 7QA fragment were seriously flawed, and perhaps even fraudulent. Much is at stake with Dr. Reichstad's opinions about this tiny, ancient piece of papyrus. For if he is correct, then we may be witnessing the death of Christianity as a religion.

"If Dr. Reichstad is wrong, then Reverend MacCameron has helped to expose where the real lie rests—because the lie is not with the article in his little magazine. To the contrary, the evidence will conclusively show that the lie rests squarely on the head of a world-renowned scientist who, for reasons yet to be explored in this case, is trying to sell to the world a hoax of unearthly proportions."

Then Will paced over to the center of the courtroom where, on a display easel, there was a greatly enlarged photograph of 7QA fitted together with 7QB. Will told the jury that in the upper right corner there was a missing fragment. But this missing "X fragment" completed the all-important first and second sentences of 7QA. Without "7QC," as Will called it, the 7QA fragment seemed, when considered just by itself, to be describing the corpse of Jesus of Nazareth, and suggesting that his body never left the tomb.

He urged them to consider that Dr. Reichstad had made no search for 7QB. That Angus MacCameron was the one who, in fact, finally produced it; and that 7QC was still out there somewhere in some hidden corner of the world. Without 7QC, the missing fragment, Will said, his voice becoming passionate, Dr. Reichstad had merely shown a part of a face, and then declared it to be a portrait. Displayed to the world a patch, and declared it to be a garment.

"If we commissioned a great artist to paint a full portrait, but received only half a face—and one ear, one eye, only part of the mouth—wouldn't we declare that painter to be inept?" Will asked the jury.

"If we pay a tailor to sew a suit, but it has only one sleeve, wouldn't we say that the tailor was a fraud?" he added.

Will continued by telling the jury that the evidence would show how Reverend MacCameron knew that a half-truth is much more dangerous than a full-blown lie. So he published the truth about 7QA and Dr. Reichstad in his magazine.

"The evidence will show that Dr. Reichstad mysteriously turned up in possession of 7QA immediately following the deaths of Dr. Hunter and Mr. Azid, both of whom previously had had possession of 7QA," Will stated. "Therefore, Angus MacCameron told the truth when he said that Reichstad was somehow 'connected' to their deaths."

Will continued. "Of course all of us—myself included—fear and distrust the forthright tellers of truth. We shrink back from those who dare to tell us *all* of the truth, because it may strike too close—it may mirror to us a sight we do not wish to see. So if you wish to throw stones at the prophet of truth—then have at my client. He is right here. And he makes an easy target. Or, you can do something else. You can realize your extraordinary opportunity to do a great and noble thing. You can do something quite rare in this unfair world. You can shed the light. You can do justice. You can let your verdict speak the truth."

The instant that Will ended his opening statement, attorney Sherman leaped to his feet and asked for a "side-bar" conference with the judge. Judge Kaye looked at his watch, and decided to release the jury for the day.

After the last jury member filed out of the courtroom, the judge entertained Sherman's argument.

"Mr. Chambers seems to have confused an opening statement—which is only to include a summary of the evidence that will be presented—with closing argument," Sherman snarled. "His so-called 'opening statement' was replete with argument, Your Honor. I move that his entire opening statement be stricken, and that the jury be admonished to disregard every word of his opening."

Judge Kaye turned to Will for his response.

"Your Honor, if Mr. Sherman had an objection, he should have raised it *during* the opening statement, at the exact moment when it occurred. Instead, Mr. Sherman hedged his bets and waited until I finished my entire opening statement to lodge his objection. By waiting, he waived his objection."

J-Fox Sherman jumped to his feet to respond, but the judge motioned to him to sit down.

"I don't need to hear any more. This isn't rocket science. Mr. Chambers' opening clearly had some improper argument, although I think it was somewhat responsive to some of the improper argument *you*, Mr. Sherman, included in *your* opening. But regardless, Mr. Sherman, you waited too long to object. Your objection and motion are denied. Gentlemen, I will see you tomorrow morning."

Sherman, unruffled, gave Will a confident smile as both sides packed up for the day. His motion had simply been a minor skirmish. Tomorrow, the ground war at Omaha Beach would begin.

60

THE FOLLOWING MORNING, WILL PULLED INTO the courthouse, tired but confident. He had worked on the case until three A.M., poring over his cross-examination notes, and reviewing the points made by Sherman in his opening statement. Much like a military conflict, a trial takes on a fluid, ever-changing topography. Despite exacting preparation, and voluminous discovery, and disclosure of facts by both sides, the real face of the battle never becomes evident until the trial itself. Will Chambers knew that the visage of a case—its character and essence—only becomes clear when the background and personality of the jury is known, and the opening strategy of the opponent is disclosed. With that information now in hand, Will had begun his usual exhausting routine of resurveying the prospective battleground of the case, all over again, in preparation for each day.

At the start of the second day, Sherman's first witness was Dr. Kurt Jorgenson, an associate in Reichstad's research center. Jorgenson was an expert in ancient papyrus fragments, especially those of Middle Eastern origin.

Under Sherman's friendly, casual questioning, the scientist gave a lively but highly detailed description of what papyrus was, producing several large diagrams and photographs as he talked.

Jorgenson described papyrus as a plant found in Egypt, parts of Ethiopia, and—notably—in the Jordan River valley in Israel. In ancient times the plant was used to create a form of writing paper; this was done by slicing it into thin layers, and then placing other layers of material crosswise over it. These strips were then moistened, pressed, and stretched out to dry, Finally, the sheets were scraped to a smooth finish with a sharp object, and fashioned into rolls. He then gave a long history of the different uses of papyrus by ancient peoples, including the Egyptians, the Romans, the Greeks, and the first-century Jews in "ancient Palestine," his nomenclature for the regions of the Middle East, and particularly that region centering at Jerusalem.

Most juries find such technical testimony—particularly at the very opening of the case—to be dry, dull, and occasionally confusing. In this case, however, Will noticed that every member of the jury was attentive, and some members were even transfixed during Jorgenson's testimony.

Then Jorgenson moved into his involvement in the 7QA analysis. He described how, at Dr. Reichstad's request, he had become part of the team of experts to evaluate the tiny papyrus fragment.

Sherman had anticipated Will Chamber's main theory of defense, and had decided to meet it head on.

"Now, you were aware that the 7QA fragment had an irregular shape?"

"Yes, that was very obvious during my examination."

"Is that unusual when it comes to fragments of documents two thousand years old?"

"Oh, not at all," Jorgenson noted confidently. "In fact, almost all such fragments tend to be partially destroyed, frayed, disintegrated, torn, water-stained, you name it and they come that way. Our job is to reconstruct, in a scientifically valid way, what the fragment looked like, and what it said, in its original form. In this case, it was obvious that 7QA was torn along the edges. That was not unique. That happens very often."

"So the fact that 7QA was ripped or torn—how would that have affected Dr. Reichstad's ability to reach conclusive findings about it?"

"It would have no effect. Let me make a comparison," Jorgenson offered, with a smile. "When the boy comes in to school and says 'Teacher, I finished my paper, and it was wonderful and I deserve an A-plus, but I can't show it to you because my dog ate it,' we all view that very suspiciously. But in the study of ancient papyrus writings—sometimes parts of a fragment *really have been eaten by dogs*. Why, I can even tell you stories about ancient fragments that were chewed up by wild hyenas!"

The jury smiled at this, and a few members laughed along with Dr. Jorgenson.

Sherman then had his expert witness recount the process of matching 7QA with 7QB, and Jorgenson described his confidence that they were, originally, part of the same piece of papyrus. Finally the scholar addressed the big issue in the case.

"I believe, unequivocally, that the quality of the 7QA and 7QB fragments are outstanding. Further, that they spell out, in the Koine Greek language, the facts surrounding the burial of a male individual known as Jesus of Nazareth, together with the fact that this particular corpse was not removed from the tomb—and therefore certainly did not stand up and walk out three days later. Lastly, I firmly believe that this fragment was written around the time of the death of Jesus, and that it was written in the area of Jerusalem by someone who purports to be an eyewitness. It is near-perfect evidence, historically and archaeologically, of the nonresurrection of Jesus."

"And your conclusions confirm Dr. Reichstad's published conclusions about 7QA?"

"Absolutely."

"Did you expect some religious/cultural backlash to your 7QA discovery?"

"Of course. But nothing like what Angus MacCameron published. That was just plain shocking."

"Was Dr. Reichstad guilty of either deception, or scientific malpractice—as MacCameron wrote—regarding his findings on the 7QA fragment?"

"Absolutely not. MacCameron's allegations about Dr. Reichstad were—and are—totally unfounded. And Dr. Reichstad's conclusions about 7QA are absolutely correct."

Sherman rested his direct examination. He sat down at his counsel table full of smiling legal associates and a radiant client.

Will walked to the podium, introduced himself to the witness with a smile, and then began his cross-examination with a seemingly minor point.

"You said that it is not unusual at all for a fragment to be torn along the edges like the 7QA fragment was. Do you remember that?"

"I'm not sure that is what I actually said."

"Well," Will said, "I have it right here in my notes. You said, and I quote, that it 'happens very often' in the case of ancient fragments. Now, do you want me to have the court reporter read back your testimony?"

"Not necessary," Jorgenson noted confidently, "I will accept your statement as accurate."

"So, tell me, how many other ancient papyrus fragments have you examined in your professional experience?"

"Oh my, hundreds—thousands—I suppose."

"And how many had irregular edges, and showed evidence of having been torn by something?"

"Many. Many. Too many to count."

"Now you agree with me, that 7QA, when examined microscopically, is shown to have been scored with a hard, metallic, sharp instrument—probably a razor blade or a artist's-type blade—and then torn along the scores?"

"Yes, that would appear to be the case."

"Scored with the kind of blade that is tempered steel?"

"Probably."

"The kind of blade that is found only in the twentieth or twenty-first century?"

"Oh, I might argue a little with your dating—but—yes, it was scored with a blade of recent origin."

"So tell me, Doctor, exactly how many ancient fragments have you rendered *conclusive opinions* upon, when their edges show signs of having been removed from another fragment with the use of a modern knife?"

Sherman was on his feet objecting, but Judge Kaye overruled him.

Jorgenson was deep in thought, and said he had forgotten the question and wanted it re-read.

After the court reporter had finished reading the question, Jorgenson tried to avoid the answer.

"I really don't understand the question," Jorgenson replied. "It doesn't make any sense."

"Then let's see what you don't understand," Will responded firmly. "Do you know what 'ancient fragments' are?"

"Of course."

"Do you know what I mean by 'conclusive opinions'?"

"I suppose."

"How about my reference to the 'edges' of a fragment having shown signs of having been 'removed from another fragment'—any problem understanding that?"

"Well, now you're being a little ridiculous," Jorgenson responded, feeling the noose starting to tighten.

"Perhaps you were thrown by my use of the unusual phrase 'modern knife'—do you have a problem understanding what a 'modern knife' is?"

Jorgenson paused. His smile was gone. There was a mild look of contempt on his face.

"I don't know."

"Is it a fact that the *only* ancient fragment about which you were willing to render a conclusive opinion regarding its origin and its meaning, when the edges of such a fragment show that it was in fact tampered with and torn apart by someone very recently—the *only* case of such a thing, is the 7QA fragment? Is that correct?"

"I don't know what you mean by 'tampered with.'"

"Well," Will continued, "what if an antiquities dealer by the name of Azid in Bethlehem, Israel, takes an ancient fragment, for whatever reason, and uses a modern knife to score it and then tears it into three smaller pieces, and sells you only one of the pieces. Would you consider that 'tampered with'?"

"I suppose I would."

"Would that be a reliable way to conduct your scientific evaluation—to base it on a piece of papyrus that had been tampered with?"

"7QA was *not* tampered with."

"But it had been removed from the rest of the fragment?"

"Yes."

"With the use of a modern knife—by someone who had the fragment before Dr. Reichstad did?"

"Yes."

"You don't call that 'tampered with'?"

There was a pause.

"I don't know."

"Let's change gears, Doctor. How important is 'context' in the matter of evaluating the meaning of an ancient fragment?"

"Define 'context,'" Jorgenson shot back.

"Well, let's define it the same way you used it last month in the *Journal of Ancient West Asian Archaeology*, where you wrote, and I quote, 'The physical context of an ancient papyrus fragment is always essential in order to fully understand it.'"

"Yes. I wrote that. And I agree with what I wrote."

"Is the best 'context' for understanding an ancient fragment always a complete fragment; one that is of superior quality in its written characters, and bears no evidence of missing pieces?"

"Yes, that is optimal."

"Have you ever, in your career, been forced to withhold final conclusions about an ancient fragment because the context was incomplete? Such as poor quality of the written characters, or too much destruction by the natural elements, or the absence of too much of the adjacent writing?"

"Yes, quite often."

"But you *did not* withhold your final conclusions *here*. You did not withhold your absolute confidence in the validity of Dr. Reichstad's opinions—even though at the time you didn't have 7QB, and certainly did not have the still-missing 'X fragment'—and even though you and Dr. Reichstad knew that the other missing pieces that had been torn away might still be out there somewhere?"

"Yes, Dr. Reichstad and I felt we could still make absolute and final conclusions about 7QA."

"Then let's evaluate why that is, Doctor."

Now Will moved away from the podium slightly so he could stand directly in front of the witness.

"Is it a fact that you, and Dr. Reichstad, are both members of an organization called 'Jesus Quest for the 21st Century'?"

"Yes, that's right. A very esteemed and forward-thinking group of New Testament and antiquities scholars."

"About thirty-nine different scholars?"

"Yes, that sounds about right."

"You are familiar with their writings?"

"Yes. I consider them my colleagues."

"How many have ever written or published any professional article that expresses even the most theoretical belief in the possibility that Jesus of Nazareth may have been physically resurrected?"

"I have not memorized their writings."

"I have them all right here, in several notebooks," Will said. "Do you wish to have me go through them, one by one?"

Judge Kaye interrupted, "Oh pray no, Mr. Chambers, let's not do that."

Then the judge turned toward Dr. Jorgenson and addressed the witness directly, leaning back in his large chair and scratching the top of his head as he spoke.

"Doctor, I notice in your credentials that you still do some university teaching. I trust that when your students ask you a question you give them a more direct answer than you are doing right now. Just answer the question. Do you know whether any of the members of this organization of which you are a member believe in the physical resurrection of Jesus of Nazareth?"

"Your Honor, we all, as members of this group of scholars, have pledged ourselves to absolute scientific integrity. How could we do that and still cling to the very medieval notion that a man three days dead in the grave suddenly gets up and walks out of his tomb?"

"I think you have answered the question," Judge Kaye concluded, and he nodded to Will Chambers to continue.

"Are you employed by Dr. Reichstad's research center?"

"Yes."

"Do you know what the going salary rate is, in America, for experts in papyrology, with your experience and background?"

"I have a pretty good idea."

"Are you being paid more than the average?"

"If I can speak frankly, my credentials are better than most scholars in my field. Therefore, I ought to be paid more."

"Do you consider yourself three times as good as other scholars?"

"Oh, hardly."

"Yet you get a salary from Dr. Reichstad that is three times the average for a scholar with your background and experience?"

Now Sherman was up with an impassioned objection. "This expert's salary has nothing to do with this case."

"I agree, Mr. Chambers," the judge said, "unless you lay some other foundation."

Will turned to the witness.

"Were you expected to be here testifying for Dr. Reichstad as part of your employment?"

"You might say that."

"Are you being paid a separate fee?"

"No."

"It's just considered part of your salary?"

"Yes."

"Is your yearly salary about $500,000?"

Sherman shrieked out his objection again.

"Overruled," the judge barked out. "Now this is a different ballgame."

"$500,000?"

"That's correct."

"And you have stock options in the research center, which recently became a publicly traded corporation?"

"Yes. Yes. That's right. This is still America. Land of opportunity."

"And your stock options are worth perhaps another $500,000?"

"Yes. I guess that is right."

Will now walked back to the podium to collect his notes. Jorgenson relaxed a bit, thinking the questioning was over.

"Oh, one other matter. Just a technical point, I suppose."

"Yes," Jorgenson replied with a manufactured smile.

"Exactly how much would your stock be worth if Dr. Reichstad were to lose this case, and the jury were to find that he committed scientific malpractice—or even worse—scientific fraud? How much would your stock options be worth then?"

Sherman popped up again with an objection that the question asked for "pure speculation."

The judge permitted the answer, "if the expert could venture an opinion."

"I suppose the stock might go down."

"Go down?" Will said with his voice rising. "Wouldn't it sink like the Titanic? Wouldn't it disintegrate like the exploding Hindenburg? Wouldn't your stock option be something akin to a very poorly forged copy of the Mona Lisa?"

"Is that a question, or merely an attempt at creativity, Mr. Chambers?" the judge asked. "I think it is the latter. So, rephrase it."

"If Dr. Reichstad's opinions about 7QA are shown to be fraudulent, or recklessly unfounded, as Reverend MacCameron has written, then your stock options become worthless, is that correct?"

There was silence as Dr. Jorgenson glared back.

"That is probably so," he replied, "but I am not too worried about that happening."

"Because you did your job well today? You came here and supported your boss, Dr. Reichstad, who pays your salary?"

"Yes, I support Dr. Reichstad."

"Because you came here and protected your stock options?"

"That's not why I came here."

"Because you came here to support the Jesus Quest for the 21st Century in their agenda to disprove the physical resurrection of Jesus?"

"I support that position. I am not ashamed to declare that."

"Does every person educated in biblical archaeology have the right to take a position, one way or the other, on the issue of whether the evidence supports the resurrection of Jesus?"

"Of course."

"But you deny to my client, Reverend Angus MacCameron, that exact same right?"

There was a pause, and Jorgenson shifted a little in his chair. At first he parted his lips to answer, but nothing came out.

After a full thirty seconds of silence, Will turned and began walking back to his counsel table.

"That's all right, Dr. Jorgenson," Will said in conclusion, "we'll let the jury answer that one."

61

THE SECOND WITNESS CALLED BY SHERMAN was Dr. Victor Beady. He was also an associate at Reichstad's research center. His testimony took up the afternoon.

Beady's evidence centered on his particular area of expertise—carbon-dating of ancient objects. He gave a convincing and impressive description of the concept of carbon-dating, both in general and in regard to the technique he had applied to date the 7QA and 7QB fragments as "definitely first century—and likely during the time period proximate to the death of Jesus, a religious figure who is reported to have lived in ancient Palestine."

"Radiocarbon-dating," as Beady referred to it, was based on the observation that the remains of organisms that were once alive (plants, animals, people) all contain C-14 (radiocarbon), which is absorbed into the tissues of organisms during their lifetimes. Because that element is both radioactive and unstable, he explained, and because it "decays away at a known rate," then at the death of that organism, the radiocarbon decay begins—at an ever-declining rate. By measuring the amount of radiocarbon left in a sample and assuming the rate of decay as a given, he further explained, one can extrapolate to obtain the date when the original sample was still part of a living organism.

In this case, he continued, from a radiocarbon-dating standpoint, the two fragments must be "from approximately the years 30 to 90 C.E.—'Common Era'—a designation that has replaced the traditional but religiously offensive 'A.D.'"

Then Beady left the realm of radiocarbon-dating and spoke on the basis of his credentials as a historian of antiquities. He testified that the 30 to 90 C.E. estimate for the origin of the fragments could be further refined down to the years between 30 to 68. He was able to do this, he assured the jury, because of what he and other scholars of history knew about the events of ancient Palestine in the year 68.

It was in that year that the Jewish desert religious community at Qumran had abandoned their dwellings by the Dead Sea because of the invasion of the Roman Tenth Legion. They had left behind their library of scrolls, stored in nearby caves—the so-called Dead Sea scrolls.

All this historical background, Beady went on to say, was very consistent with the information that Dr. Reichstad had published, and with what Reichstad and he had personally discussed, about the source of the fragment—that it had been in cave 7 at Qumran, stuck to the bottom of a jar, and was then found by an unknown Bedouin boy, who, after many years, had sold it to Azid, the antiquities dealer.

Beady concluded his testimony by indicating that Dr. Reichstad's conclusions about the date of the 7QA fragment—and the origin of the fragment being the Jerusalem area, and that the fact that it would likely have been written shortly after the time of the death of Jesus of Nazareth—were all undoubtedly correct.

As Sherman concluded his direct examination of Beady, Will listened carefully. He waited, expecting something more in Beady's final conclusions. Beady was fully qualified to have given a broader opinion about Reichstad's interpretation about the *meaning* of 7QA. But he didn't do that. And Sherman did not ask him to. Will knew that sometimes what is *not* said in court is sometimes more important than what *is* said.

But there was something else. Beady had been cautious in his testimony. Unlike Jorgenson, he had not made wide, sweeping statements of support for Reichstad and disdain for MacCameron. His testimony was clearly cut with square corners. Beady had been likeable and confident in front of the jury—but what he had had to say had been carefully controlled and limited. Dr. Victor Beady seemed to be a man who knew that the case had opened up some dangerous pitfalls. He, for one, apparently did not want to walk too close to the edge.

As Will walked up to the podium for his cross-examination he felt certain of one other thing. Beady had really done very little damage in his testimony. Most of it related to the *dating* of the 7QA and 7QB fragments. But MacCameron was not disputing these conclusions. So, while Will was prepared to challenge several technical points in Beady's arguments about the accuracy of his radiocarbon-dating procedure, he decided to let that go. He would just hit on a few essential points.

On cross-examination Beady readily admitted, without dispute, that he was earning the same half-million dollars a year at the research center as

Jorgenson was. And he quickly conceded that he had the same half-million-dollar stock interest in the center that Jorgenson did.

He also admitted his active participation in the Jesus Quest for the 21st Century group—and that the group was singularly opposed to the traditional idea of the bodily resurrection of Jesus Christ.

Will concluded his examination of Beady with a final line of questioning. His questions came from something Beady had said in his direct testimony, about the "jar" in the cave where 7QA had come from.

"Dr. Beady, you said that 7QA came from a 'jar.' Right?"

"Yes. That's right."

"Did Dr. Reichstad tell you that?"

"He had to. He obtained the fragment. And then at some point he must have told me that it had been kept in a jar in the cave before its discovery by the Bedouin, who then sold it to Harim Azid, who then sold it to Dr. Reichstad."

"So Dr. Reichstad told you that 7QA came from a jar in cave 7."

"Counsel, that is not too remarkable. Many of the Dead Sea scrolls and fragments in those caves had been kept in jars."

"But you said that Dr. Reichstad told you that 7QA had been 'stuck to the bottom of a jar' in cave 7. Right?"

"That's right."

Then, for some reason Will recalled a rather silly reference that Tiny Heftland had made to him once about Reichstad's research building. He smiled a little as he concluded his cross-examination.

"One last thing, Doctor. Would you describe the security system at Dr. Reichstad's research center as 'world-class,' perhaps 'state of the art'?"

"Yes. It is very sophisticated."

Will could see that Beady was growing slightly uncomfortable.

"Other than the 7QA evaluations that have gone on there at that building, are there any other 'secret experiments' going on—maybe down in the basement—that would require military-style remote sensors all over the grounds of the building?"

Will heard a noise off to the side of the courtroom. Dr. Beady's eyes widened as if he had just been punched in the solar plexus. Will glanced over, and saw Reichstad gesturing urgently to the witness—but Sherman had grabbed his arm and restrained him.

"Objection!" Sherman shouted. "Irrelevant. Immaterial. Prejudicial. And asking for confidential, secret, and/or proprietary information about Dr. Reichstad's research center."

Will agreed to withdraw his question. But as he walked back to his counsel table he knew that he had just hit a trip wire with Albert Reichstad. Perhaps Tiny had been correct. Maybe 7QA was not the only thing that Reichstad had up his sleeve.

Perhaps, he mused, he had really stumbled across the Frankenstein castle after all.

62

WILL CHAMBERS KNEW THAT CONDUCTING the ideological warfare of a jury trial required the litigator to constantly reassess the field of combat. To calculate the casualties; to observe the movements of the opposing troops; to anticipate the strategy of the other side before their bombs start raining down destruction.

But he also understood that a trial lawyer needed to practice the skill of a tightrope walker. As is the case with the man way up there on the high-wire, the success or failure of the balancing act in a jury trial is often *felt* before it is actually *seen*.

At the commencement of the trial, Will had determined that the odds would be stacked against him. In such situations his strategy was to force a break in the case—to change the feeling in the atmosphere. To gain absolute mastery over the physics of the high wire—because failure to do so could only mean to experience the desperate falling sensation of defeat.

As Will sat down at the counsel table on the third day he knew that Albert Reichstad would be the next, and last, witness for the plaintiff's case. J-Fox Sherman had originally listed a dozen witnesses. But for some reason, at the last moment he had announced that he would call only three—and his client was the last.

Originally Will had listed Bill Kenwood, his materials engineer, to testify that 7QA and 7QB had been scored by a sharp, metallic instrument of recent origin and then torn apart. But now he did not need to call him. Both parties, after their weeklong examination of the two fragments before the trial, had agreed on the findings that Kenwood would have presented. Now, it was an established fact in the case that 7QA had originally been attached to 7QB and that they had only recently been torn apart.

Dr. Giovanni was bound to do a fine job in her testimony, but Will knew that she could not carry the day alone. His client, Angus MacCameron, was an honest and forthright man, but he was not going to make a good witness. In particular, Will noticed that Angus had grown quieter during the trial, and by the end of yesterday's testimony had no longer been writing notes on his notepad. In fact, he looked more haggard and exhausted than Will had ever seen him before.

Will also had scheduled the testimony of the two Israeli police officers. But they could only show that "Tony" Azid's death was by an act of murder, rather than suicide. They could not *directly* link his death to Reichstad.

Ultimately, the case was about credibility. Who was the jury going to believe—Reichstad or MacCameron? In that department Will had a plan to expose Reichstad's lack of truthfulness. But it depended on Sherman or Reichstad making the right kind of mistake, in the right kind of way. Sherman was unlikely to trip up. Will's only hope was that Reichstad's own penchant for self-aggrandizement would compel him to walk into the silent trap. Will could only watch and wait.

As Dr. Albert Reichstad stood at the witness chair, raised his right hand, and swore to tell the truth—the whole truth—Will knew that his cross-examination of this witness would probably be the turning point—the hand-to-hand combat that could sway the course of battle over to MacCameron's side.

As Sherman began his direct examination of his client, Will noticed something out of the corner of his eye. Angus MacCameron had pushed something over to Will on the counsel table. They were two airline tickets. One for MacCameron, and one for him. Will noticed that it had them departing at 7:45 that night for London, out of Reagan National Airport.

Will glanced over at Angus who, though pale, was grinning. He obviously still believed that they could find the missing 7QC fragment somewhere at the British Museum even now, at the eleventh hour, in the middle of the jury trial.

How could his client still hold onto that hope? Was it that Angus MacCameron was the most blindly optimistic client Will Chambers had ever had? Or was there another explanation? Was this just one more example of MacCameron's maddeningly persistent faith in a God of both ultimate truth and personal familiarity? *What would it be like to have that kind of faith?* Will wondered silently.

63

After Sherman had finished taking Reichstad through his extensive professional credentials, he continued his direct examination by having his client relate his discovery of the 7QA fragment. Reichstad spoke slowly and confidently from the witness stand. As he talked, he turned and addressed the jury directly, as if they were one of his groups of adoring students at Harvard.

Will had read every article that Reichstad had ever written about the discovery of 7QA, and had traced every media quote he'd ever given on the subject. Reichstad had always been cleverly vague about how he had come into possession of the fragment.

Now, as Reichstad was testifying, he effortlessly recited the exact same information he had previously disclosed on that subject, sometimes using descriptions verbatim from his writings and media interviews.

Reichstad testified that he had been in Jerusalem, leading an archaeological conference, when he received a phone call from Azid to come over to Bethlehem and look at an ancient fragment. He said he had indeed met with Azid, but couldn't recall the exact day. There had been a free day in the conference, and perhaps that was when he had traveled to Bethlehem, but he wasn't sure. He had immediately concluded that the writing on this fragment, 7QA, referred to the burial of Jesus, and that it looked, at least at first blush, quite authentic, though he obviously had not been able to date it on the spot. Yet the Koine Greek inscription on the fragment had raised his expectations that this might just be a find of monumental proportions.

According to Reichstad, Tony Azid had told him that he bought the ancient papyrus writing from a Bedouin, some type of relative. The Bedouin said he had found it decades before, as a boy, in what was now known as cave 7 at Qumran, near the Dead Sea. The Bedouin had kept it for many years until deciding, for some reason, to finally sell it to Azid.

Azid, as Reichstad explained it, had agreed to accept $50,000 for the fragment. Reichstad left, and later wired the money directly into Azid's account. One of his "assistants" had actually picked up the fragment and brought it back to Reichstad by the end of the conference later that week.

"I am afraid that I can't recall the name of the assistant who picked up 7QA and brought it to me," Reichstad explained. "We have looked, but can't find any records on who it was. It was someone who was only working with me as temporary staff during the conference. He was a local Arab man, I think."

"Why didn't you use one of your own personal research assistants to pick up this potentially important fragment from Azid?" Sherman asked, anticipating one of Will's cross-examination questions.

"Well, that was my preference. But, unfortunately, all of my personal research assistants had their hands full during the conference we were hosting."

Then Reichstad was asked to explain his testing and evaluation of the fragment. He gave a smooth, carefully rehearsed description of his findings.

"This was clearly the most authentic, most historiographically and archaeologically profound document ever discovered on the subject of the burial of Jesus of Nazareth. It clearly showed that a person who was a contemporary of Jesus, who was a witness to his burial, was also a witness to the fact that his body was not resurrected—but indeed was—and is to this day most likely—still in that tomb. The examination I conducted was thorough, and was in keeping with the highest possible standards of science and scholarship. To date, except for Angus MacCameron's wild and unsupported libel against me, no scholarship has dared to question the competency, or the integrity of my conclusions."

Then Sherman led him into the article written by MacCameron.

"When did you first learn of the article by the defendant, which attacked you and your conclusions about 7QA?"

Reichstad lowered his head dramatically, and asked if he might take a sip of water. The judge and Sherman both nodded. He drank from the glass next to the witness chair. Then he sighed and stroked his eyebrow, a gesture apparently designed to disclose the inner pain of recalling what he was about to describe.

Will was riveted to Reichstad's testimony as he described the party hosted by his colleagues and friends in honor of his discovery of the 7QA fragment. Reichstad said it was at that party that he first learned the real details of MacCameron's "libelous" article against him.

Sherman was about to lead him quickly off that point and onto another, but Reichstad plowed ahead, describing in dramatic detail the "humiliating and shocking experience" of hearing his own friends and associates yelling "murderer," and "fraud," to his face, and in the presence of his wife.

There was a quick side-glance from Sherman toward Will's counsel table. Sherman anticipated a loud objection from his opponent as Reichstad's unprompted testimony about the details of what was actually said at the party violated Judge Kaye's order of bifurcation—an order which clearly prohibited at this stage of the case, any mention of evidence for damages, or testimony relating to injury to reputation or emotional suffering.

But no objection came. Will only sat silently. His face gave no hint of the fact that he was preparing the trap that would shut on Reichstad.

Sherman moved quickly to his final line of questioning.

"Did you have any 'connection' whatsoever with the deaths of Harim Azid or Dr. Richard Hunter?"

"Absolutely not. That is a preposterous allegation by that man, MacCameron, and it is absolutely false."

With that, J-Fox Sherman rested.

64

WILL CHAMBERS BEGAN HIS CROSS-EXAMINATION of Reichstad as he was still walking from his counsel table over toward the podium. Reichstad watched him, smiling confidently.

The large photographic blowup of the 7QA and 7QB fragments was on the easel in the middle of the courtroom. On another easel, a large display bore the fragments' message translated from the Greek:

{7QA}

AND THE BODY

OF JESUS OF NAZARETH {7QB}

WAS LAID IN THE TOMB // *AT THE EAST GATE OF STEPHEN*

THEY DESIRED TO ANOINT IT // *THAT DAY*

BUT COULD NOT RETURN TO PREPARE THE BODY

THE BODY REMAINS IN THAT TOMB TO THIS DAY

Will took a little laser pointer and indicated the word "JESUS" in the second line. "Now Dr. Reichstad, let's talk about the Greek language of 7QA and 7QB. In the Greek of that day—and I believe in modern Greek—the *endings* of words would reveal the grammatical structure of the sentence?"

"That is a rather crude way of putting it," Reichstad answered.

"Well, as an example: In English, the word 'Jesus' appears the same whether it is used as the object or the subject—or whether we are talking about the 'possessive' phrase 'of Jesus,' or referring to something happening 'to Jesus,' or someone being 'with Jesus.' In each case, in English, the word 'Jesus' would stay the same—but we would add things called prepositions, as separate words, to show how we are referring to 'Jesus' in the sentence?"

"I suppose that is one very rough, unpolished way to explain that."

"Well, then let's polish it up, by all means. In the Greek version of 7QA over there the word 'Jesus' ends with the Greek letter called 'upsilon,' something that looks a little like the letter 'U,' right?"

"Very good, Mr. Chambers. I see you checked out a book on New Testament Greek from the local library," Reichstad commented sarcastically. "Yes, that is correct."

"But," Will continued, "in the Greek, unlike the English, the *way* a word is being used in a sentence is reflected in the endings of the word itself, right?"

"Yes. That is very basic first- or second-lesson Greek."

"And if, in 7QA, 'Jesus' were the subject of the sentence; if the sentence said that 'Jesus' was in fact doing something, then the ending of the word 'Jesus' in 7QA would be different, would it not? The word 'Jesus' would look just like it does here on this enlarged photo of 7QA, except that it would end with one additional letter—the Greek letter 'sigma' which, at the end of a word, looks like an English 'S.' Correct?"

"Yes," Reichstad noted, with a sigh.

"Now let us assume, for a moment, that there is a missing fragment with more writing—in the upper right-hand corner, just to the right of the first two lines of 7QA and just above 7QB. And for the sake of argument, let's assume that the words after the end of the first line of 7QA that our 'X' fragment supplies are the words 'OF A FRIEND.' Now, that would create something that would look like this..." And with that, Will placed a small placard with those words in the spot where the missing X fragment would go.

{7QA} {X fragment}

AND THE BODY// **OF A FRIEND**

OF JESUS OF NAZARETH {7QB}

WAS LAID IN THE TOMB // *AT THE EAST GATE OF STEPHEN*

THEY DESIRED TO ANOINT IT // *THAT DAY*

BUT COULD NOT RETURN TO PREPARE THE BODY

THE BODY REMAINS IN THAT TOMB TO THIS DAY

"Now, do you agree with me that the ending of the word 'Jesus' would be exactly the same in my example, using my hypothetical idea of what the X fragment might contain, as the ending of the word 'Jesus' appears now in 7QA?"

Reichstad shifted a bit in his chair.

"In other words," Will continued, "my hypothetical idea of what the X fragment might contain is *consistent* with the Greek grammar of 7QA?"

"Yes, that's correct. But perfectly meaningless. We don't have the 'X fragment' as you call it. In fact, if the upper right corner of this piece were ever found, I firmly believe that it would contain no writing of any kind."

"You are sure of that?"

"Yes. Because, 7QA and 7QB make perfect grammatical sense, as they are right now, without any additional speculations on some unknown, hypothetical 'X fragment.'"

"Well, with all due respect, Doctor, you thought that 7QA made perfect grammatical sense too, before Angus MacCameron came up with 7QB. And you were wrong in that respect, correct?"

"No. 7QA made perfect grammatical sense alone. Now, with 7QB it makes even more sense."

"And until we find the third missing fragment—call it the 'X' fragment, or 7QC, or whatever you want—until we place that last part of the puzzle into this picture we are never going to be absolutely sure about the full meaning of this ancient piece of writing—isn't that correct?"

"You never have absolute certainty in science. But I am confident that there is no further writing that is missing from this piece."

"You would place all of your professional integrity behind that statement?"

"I certainly would."

Having placed Reichstad's credibility squarely in his sights, Will got ready to squeeze the trigger.

"I listened carefully to your testimony," Will noted casually, "regarding what you knew about the origins of the 7QA fragment. Where it came from. Cave 7. The Bedouin. Your contact with Azid. I took very good notes. Now my question is this—are there any more facts you can add about the way that the fragment had been preserved in cave 7 when the Bedouin found it?"

"No, Mr. Chambers. I was very complete in my testimony. I've given the jury—and you—a description of everything I know."

"Everything?"

"Yes, that is what I said."

"I was just interested, then, in the *jar.*"

"Oh?"

"Yes. The *jar.*"

"What jar?"

"The jar in which the 7QA-7QB fragment was stored for some two thousand years. Until one day the Bedouin, as a young boy, found it. In cave number 7 at Qumran. That jar."

"Well, it is a good assumption that it was kept in a jar."

"How do you know that?"

"Because many of the fragments of the Dead Sea scrolls were likewise found in earthen jars."

"But you never said anything in your testimony here today about knowing that the fragments *in this case* had been stored in a jar."

"Well, that was certainly understood..."

"By who? By you?"

"I always assumed that fact."

"And therefore you omitted that fact in your testimony—because you simply assumed it?"

"I don't know what you are getting at, Mr. Chambers."

"Simply this: I have read every paper and article you ever authored about the 7QA fragment. *Not one of them* ever mentions that the fragment had been stored in a jar. Not one. You do agree with that?"

"Oh, I don't know, Mr. Chambers. You have seen how many professional scholarly articles I have authored in my career. I can't possibly recall every detail just because you want me to."

"I have them right here—organized in my notebooks by date and by source. I would be glad to spend all day going through them with you, Dr. Reichstad. Is that going to be necessary?"

Judge Kaye came to life again, and broke in. "No, we are not going to do that, are we, Dr. Reichstad? Let's cut to the chase. Why don't you just tell us—do you recall ever writing about the fragment being found in a *jar* by the Bedouin?"

"Not that I can recall, no."

"Thank you," Will added. "But beyond even that—you *never,* at any time, *ever* wrote that fact that the 7QA fragment had been stuck to the bottom of a jar?"

"I suppose that's true, though I don't think it is at all important to this case—one way or another."

"Oh, but it is," Will responded. "Dr. Beady testified earlier, quite clearly, that you and he had discussed that the papyrus fragment was discovered by the Bedouin, *stuck to the bottom of a jar.* Now is that a fact? Is that what Azid told you shortly before his death?"

"I don't recall."

"Do you know why Dr. Beady—one of your trusted research associates—would make that up?"

"Certainly not."

"Any reason to believe that Dr. Beady lied about that?"

"No, not in the least."

"But you do recall ever telling him that?"

"No, I don't."

"The most important archaeological discovery about Jesus of Nazareth in the history of the world—according to you—but you can't recall whether it was found in a jar or, if it was, whether it had been stuck to the bottom and had to be pried loose by the Bedouin?"

"I can't recall ever hearing those things from Azid or anyone else. But in any event, I really don't see the point."

"Let me help you there," Will said more intensely. "Would you agree that if you came by this 7QA fragment in an honorable way from Mr. Azid, and Mr. Azid told you the details of how the fragment was originally found—that is, stuck to the bottom of an ancient jar—would it be reasonable to expect that you would have published that information in one or more of your many writings about 7QA?"

"Perhaps."

"But if you came by 7QA from Mr. Azid in a *dishonorable* way—and if Mr. Azid was in fact tortured before his death and gave up all the details he knew about 7QA while electricity was being shot into every orifice of his broken body, then perhaps you would be very hesitant to share such details, would you not?"

"This is preposterous! Where do you get those bizarre ideas, Mr. Chambers? From the grocery-store tabloids?"

"No," Will responded calmly. "From the two members of the Israeli police who are scheduled to testify for the defense next week. That's where I get those ideas."

Reichstad made an unsuccessful attempt to dismiss Will's comment by smiling at the jury. But he could only manage a twisted smirk.

"Dr. Reichstad, let's at least leave this matter this way: One of your own witnesses, who is a trusted scientific associate, has testified under oath that you told him about 7QA being stuck to the bottom of a jar; you, on the other hand, deny even knowing about that. Would you agree that we have a mystery on our hands, then?"

"You have it backwards, Mr. Chambers. Angus MacCameron is the one who believes in mysteries, not me. I believe in facts."

"Well then, let's talk about another mystery. The mystery of the humiliating party. Do you recall testifying earlier today about your friends and colleagues yelling 'murderer,' and 'fraud,' at you as a result of reading the MacCameron article?"

At that point J-Fox Sherman leaped up to object. Judge Kaye motioned to both attorneys to come up to the bench, outside of the hearing of the jury.

"Your Honor, Mr. Chambers is way out of bounds," Sherman sputtered. "You bifurcated this trial. No testimony is supposed to come out at this stage of the case about humiliation to Dr. Reichstad, or damage to his reputation."

"But your own client opened the door to that issue, Mr. Sherman," Will shot back at the opposing attorney. "He went on, in great detail, about that party and what was said. That door ought to swing both ways."

"Look, Jay," the judge responded, "your client swung that door wide open. I am sure you advised him about my bifurcation order. And then he chose to violate it. Mr. Chambers wants to capitalize on this. That's called trial strategy. Objection overruled. But Mr. Chambers—don't go too far with this."

When both attorneys had resumed their positions, Will continued.

"About the party. There was some drinking?"

"Yes."

"Everyone having a good time?"

"Until the comments about the MacCameron article came up. And then I was humiliated."

"Dr. Reichstad, I want you to listen very carefully to my next question. Here it is: When your friends cried out 'murderer,' and 'fraud,' were they, as well as you, all laughing and making merry about it—making it into a joke?"

"Absolutely not. I was devastated. Mortified."

"Was Kathleen Aberscombe there that night, at that party?"

"Yes," Reichstad said.

"If she were here—would she agree with your recollection of the party? Or would she agree with how I have characterized the party?"

"She would agree with me. But she isn't here," Reichstad declared. "I happen to know that she is in Turkey, with her husband."

"No, Dr. Reichstad, she is not. I would represent to you that her husband fell ill. Her trip was delayed. And I was able to serve her with a subpoena, to come and testify next week when the defense puts on its case. And I know what she is going to say, because I have a sworn affidavit from her." Will lifted up a typed document in his right hand.

Sherman jumped to his feet again, but Judge Kaye cut him off.

"I'm not making decisions about defense witnesses right now," the judge said firmly. "I have looked at Mr. Chambers' witness list for this first phase of the trial—and Mrs. Aberscombe's name is not on it. On the other hand, I'm sure she was not listed in *this* phase of the case because Mr. Chambers assumed that Dr. Reichstad would not violate my bifurcation order by talking about the details of that party at Harvard. So Mr. Sherman, sit down. And Mr. Chambers, please get to the point."

Will Chambers looked into Reichstad's eyes. They both knew the same thing. It was a roll of the dice. If the judge ultimately prevented Aberscombe from testifying in the defense case, Reichstad could say anything he wanted to about the party, without fear of being contradicted. But if Aberscombe did testify, not only would the jury see him as a liar—but he also might be facing a criminal perjury prosecution.

Will pressed in. "Was there, in fact, great laughter and joking and merriment when the words 'murderer' and 'fraud' were uttered at that party?"

"Someone may have been laughing."

"Several people?"

"Perhaps."

"Almost everyone?"

"I didn't count noses."

"Did your wife begin laughing so heartily that tears welled up in her eyes?"

"I think she may have had too much to drink."

"In fact, there were gales of laughter at that party as you and your scholarly friends made fun of my client—Reverend Angus MacCameron?"

"Angus MacCameron deserves ridicule from the scholars of the world—he took that chance when he decided to write that ridiculous article against me."

"But you think the article—and the allegations—were ridiculous?"

"Absolutely!"

"As did your friends at that party?"

"Anybody with scientific sophistication believes MacCameron is a joke."

"Including all your friends at that party?"

Reichstad leaned back in the witness chair. He smirked slightly and rotated his head and his neck, as if he were relieving a cramp.

"We were joking—yes. It was a party."

"So then—you lied, under oath, when in your deposition you testified in these exact words," and with that Will Chambers read from the transcript of Reichstad's deposition:

> There was a voice raised from a corner of the room...it sent chills down my spine, and it literally broke my heart...
>
> The voice shouted out, 'Murderer! Murderer!'...
>
> That other voice said 'fraud!'"

"I did not lie!" Reichstad shouted out.

"Was that statement that I just read from your deposition—was it the whole truth, and nothing but the truth, so help you God?" And with that, Will lifted up the affidavit from Kathleen Aberscrombe and displayed it prominently in front of Reichstad.

"Maybe my deposition testimony was not entirely accurate in all its details," Reichstad finally responded. "I had gotten very little sleep. You were badgering me. I may have made mistakes. I had been very busy with a complicated research project before coming to the deposition."

"A 'complicated research project'? In other words, you become more of a liar the busier you get—is that what you are saying?"

Sherman howled out an objection, but Judge Kaye beat him to the punch.

"That's enough! Mr. Chambers, I've given you plenty of rope. But you are getting perilously close to hanging yourself—and your client. That question is ordered stricken. The jury will disregard it."

Will nodded, apologized to the court, and then positioned himself directly across from Reichstad and smiled at him as he launched into his next cross-examination attack.

"When you testified under oath at your deposition, you said that you had identified for me every single book that you had ever authored. Were you being truthful?"

"Of course. Don't be insulting."

"Did you list for me a little book you authored called *A New Quest for Jesus?*"

"I'm not sure."

Will showed Reichstad a copy of his typed curriculum vitae that had been given to Will at the deposition. Reichstad's lawyers had represented that the résumé, drafted by Reichstad, contained all of his professional credentials and publications.

Reichstad glanced at the document for a moment.

"Apparently I inadvertently omitted that book from my résumé."

"Was it merely inadvertent?"

"Yes, naturally."

"Not intentional?"

"No!" Reichstad responded with irritation.

"You know who Warren Mullburn is?"

Reichstad studied Will Chambers for a moment before he responded. He straightened up a little in the witness chair, squaring his shoulders and trying to look bored and uninterested in the questions.

"Do you know who he is?" Will repeated.

"Of course. Most of the civilized world has heard of Mr. Mullburn. He is quite famous. Books. Screenplays for science-fiction movies. The world's third richest man. Inventor of various geological devices for the discovery of oil. And on and on."

"But you know him better than most. You have met with him."

"Perhaps."

"Your research center, in fact, has been funded by millions of dollars from one of his subsidiary corporations. You would admit that?"

"What does that have to do with this case, Mr. Chambers? I object."

J-Fox Sherman leaped up and joined in his client's objection.

The judge asked where the questioning was going.

Will Chambers gave three simple words—concise enough to let Judge Kaye understand the legal justification, but without tipping off the witness. Will simply said, "Motive for bias."

"Overruled," the judge barked.

"Has your research center received millions of dollars of funding from one of Mr. Mullburn's corporations?"

"Yes. He believes in the advancement of science."

"Does he also believe in gaining a share of Saudi Petrol Company, Saudi Arabia's leading oil company, and one of the largest oil interests in the world?"

"He is in the oil business. Why not?"

"Well, for one thing, OPEC has never permitted Western nations to participate in OPEC meetings; and Saudi Petrol Company has never permitted shared ownership with a Western corporate interest. Are you aware of that?"

"I do read the financial pages. So I suppose I knew that."

"Is it a fact that you reported your progress on the 7QA discovery to Mr. Mullburn?"

"Yes. He is a controlling shareholder of our research venture. That is entirely appropriate."

"And Mr. Mullburn was pleased that you had concluded that 7QA disproved the bodily resurrection of Jesus Christ?"

"Well, he felt that my interpretations would open up new human understanding."

"Mr. Mullburn was pleased—because he had announced his conversion to Islam shortly before meeting with Muslim religious leaders in Vienna, Austria, and the Muslims reject the divinity of Jesus—reject him as the Son of God. Correct?"

Now Reichstad was taking more and more time between his answers. He searched Will Chambers' face in some kind of psychic effort to divine where Will had learned so much about his partnership with Mullburn.

"As a convert to Islam, I suppose he felt gratitude that we had finally disproved that Jesus was one with God, theologically."

"And the Islamic leaders in the oil-producing countries—those clerics who exert indirect influence within OPEC—they would have been particularly pleased with the fact that Mr. Mullburn's well-financed research center, the one that you operate, had supported a major element of the Islamic faith—that Jesus was a human prophet, not a divine Son of God. Correct?"

"Fine. Yes. Everyone here would probably agree with that. That proves nothing."

"And in addition to being helped by Warren Mullburn, you have also benefited from the assistance of Kenneth Sharptin, Undersecretary of the Department of State, who along with Mr. Mullburn has encouraged the 7QA project?"

Judge Kaye jumped in as he saw the scope of the case now broadening to include the Executive Branch.

"How far are you taking this, Mr. Chambers? Are you asserting some kind of concerted agreement among a high-level State Department official, an oil magnate, and Dr. Reichstad regarding this papyrus fragment?"

"It is my position, Your Honor, that both Kenneth Sharptin and Warren Mullburn provided my client's opponent with an opportunity, and a motive, to misinterpret, and exploit, the incomplete nature of the 7QA fragment."

After a few seconds of silence, Judge Kaye looked at Will and said, "You are on very thin ice. I don't want to hear any half-baked conspiracy theory against a high-ranking State Department official that you cannot absolutely prove. You have been warned."

Will quickly glanced toward the rear of the courtroom. Jack Hornby was still sitting in his favorite perch at the back. But now he was leaning forward on the bench in front of him; his eyes were trained on Will.

As Will turned back to Reichstad, and continued his questioning, his voice was slow, deliberate, and powerful, as it filled the courtroom.

"Is it a fact that you obtained help from Undersecretary Kenneth Sharptin? And by help I mean this: that he used his considerable diplomatic power to obtain special permission from the Israeli government—the Israeli Antiquities Authority to be precise—to enable you to dig along the St. Stephen's Gate wall of Old Jerusalem in an effort to locate the tomb whose location is mentioned in 7QB?"

"Is this really necessary?" Reichstad said in a pleading voice to the judge.

"Answer the question!" Judge Kaye commanded.

"Yes. The State Department was of some assistance in getting that permission for me and my research team. As a matter of fact, we are ready to start digging any day now."

"You would agree that such a dig is most extraordinary?"

"Certainly. We expect to find nothing less than the remains of Jesus of Nazareth. I would say that the word 'extraordinary' is barely adequate."

"And for permission for such a dig along the old wall of Jerusalem to be granted within just a week or two of the request by you—that also is extraordinary?"

"Of course. That is obvious."

"And the dig will take place right next to a Muslim cemetery, and just a short way from the Temple Mount area, where mosques are located that are held sacred by the followers of Islam."

"All that is true, yes. Yes."

"All of that makes this proposed dig of yours politically and religiously sensitive to say the very least—making it even more extraordinary that permission was granted so very quickly. Wouldn't you agree?"

"This is such a waste of time. I have admitted how extraordinary it all is. So what?"

"Well, it all seems to come down to this: Undersecretary Sharptin must have placed *extraordinary* diplomatic pressure on the Israeli authorities to get permission so quickly for your excavation. Is that the fact—or not?"

"I don't know. I am not an expert in foreign relations."

"But you have attended a number of functions, meetings, and conferences sponsored by the State Department since the 7QA discovery, correct?"

"Yes. As well as those sponsored by a hundred other organizations and agencies."

"I'm just concerned with the State Department functions. Just those. At those, the Undersecretary was present, and he praised your 7QA interpretation as something that boosted the Administration's 'cultural reconciliation' policy in bringing together the Islamic East and the Christian West?"

"For peace. It is all for peace. Peace among mankind. The way you say it, you make it sound very sinister, Mr. Chambers."

"Perhaps. Maybe I've gotten carried away. When we think of one of the world's richest men, owner of the world's fifth-largest oil interest, funding a religious antiquities project that will disprove the divinity of Jesus at the same time he is courting OPEC and Islamic leaders in an effort to join the OPEC oil monopoly—when we think of the Undersecretary of the State Department praising that very same religious antiquities project and bending over backwards to arm-twist Israel into giving you special permission for the excavation that you expect will disprove the resurrection of Jesus forever—which looks for all the world like a massive public-relations gimmick for the Administration's 'cultural reconciliation' project to bring the Islamic East in closer harmony with America. When you think of all of that—all those little pieces, like a jigsaw puzzle on a card table, all fitting together that way—doesn't that look sinister to you?"

"Only a paranoid conspiratorialist would think that it is sinister."

"Then am I being paranoid in suggesting that, in addition to whatever other financial benefits you have received from Warren Mullburn—and apart from the special benefits you have received from Undersecretary Sharptin—and even apart from becoming a world-renowned scholar whose picture is on the cover of magazines around the globe, and on the prime-time talk shows, as the man who debunked Jesus. Apart from all of that, is it paranoid to suggest that deep down, you really wanted to interpret 7QA the way you did because of your disdain for traditional Christianity, and for conservative Christian Bible scholarship?"

"That is the most absurd thing you have said today—and you have said some very absurd things in this case! I am a scholar in my field. I am a scientist. I have no agenda except for the truth. Unlike your client, who uses his medieval religious beliefs to obscure and distort the truth."

"*Are* you here for the truth, Dr. Reichstad?"

"I am here for the truth, and you know it."

"Have you given us the truth today—the truth under oath?"

"Yes. Again you make me repeat myself. Yes. I have told the truth under oath. Yes, I have."

"You have said 'yes' three times—so I guess you really mean it. So then you told the truth at your deposition—also under oath—when you also denied having any theological agenda behind your interpretation of the 7QA fragment?"

"Yes. Yes. I told the truth then too."

"And you told the truth at that deposition when you denied ever having considered 'conservative Christian scholars' to be on the level of 'cavemen' who haven't learned the secrets of fire, or the wheel?"

Reichstad was growing weary of Will Chambers. He glanced over at J-Fox Sherman for some help; but Sherman had long since decided that if he persisted in more questionable objections he would risk alienating the jury. Sherman quickly shot a glance at them to measure their reaction. They were all wide-eyed and solemn. During the silence the bouncer at the dance club cleared his throat loudly, and then leaned the side of his face on his hand as he slowly swiveled in his chair and stared at Dr. Reichstad.

"Did you tell the truth in that regard—in denying that you had any agenda against conservative Christian Bible scholars?"

"Yes, I did. Right. I told the truth. Correct. Anything else you want to bore the jury with, Mr. Chambers?" Reichstad snapped back.

"Well, just one more matter—and I'll try not to put the jury to sleep with this one. In fact—if any of us are getting sleepy, I think these last few questions will be a wake-up call for all of us in this case, Dr. Reichstad."

At that point, Will walked quickly over to his table and, from beneath a file, he pulled a slim little book. He held it high in his right hand as he walked back to the podium.

"I am holding in my right hand a copy of *A New Quest for Jesus*. This is your book?"

"It is one of my books. One of my older books. I've written many books—frankly, I thought this one was out of print."

"But it is the *only* book that you failed to disclose to me at your deposition, right?"

"Oversight. Little slip-up. That's all."

"I am going to read the prologue to this book—a prologue authored by you," and as Will said that, he handed the book to Dr. Reichstad. "Read along with me, and make sure that as I read it to the jury I have read the words accurately. Your words. Your book."

Will took a photocopied page of the prologue from his counsel table and began reading it loudly and slowly. While he did, Reichstad's eyes were flitting back and forth between the book in his hands and J-Fox Sherman, who was grimacing.

Will was emphasizing key words as he read.

> While you will find that this book, in its quest for a new idea about who Jesus was, is eminently scientific, I must confess my own *personal agenda* in writing it. The world has, for too long, been plagued with the poorly reasoned writings and teachings of those who desperately hang on to outdated notions of Jesus as the "resurrected Lord." This book will, I hope, convince the reader that the *conservative and fundamentalist Christian scholarship* on the issue of the resurrection of Jesus is much like the thinking of the *Neanderthal cavemen, before they had discovered the secrets of fire, or of the wheel.* Soon, I hope, the world will begin to reject their dangerous and misleading mythology about Jesus.

Will looked at Reichstad, who was now holding the book by his fingertips, as if it were contaminated—as if its pages were covered with bubonic plague.

"Were those *your* words, written in *your* book?"

Reichstad dangled the little book from his fingertips. His face bore a look of disgust and disdain.

"Yes. My words. My book. All right. That is correct. All right? Anything else? Anything else here, Mr. Chambers? Anything else you want to dig up against me? Anything else?"

These last words were voiced by Reichstad at just below a shout, with his body thrust forward in the witness chair. He had nearly risen to his feet.

"No further questions," Will said quietly. And he walked over to the witness stand and reached out his hand so Reichstad could give the little book back to him.

Reichstad held the book out, but just beyond Will's grasp, letting it fall to the floor with a small bang.

Will reached down and picked the book up, and looked into the eyes of Dr. Reichstad, then turned to cross back to his table. As he did, he felt the sensation a high-wire artist might feel when the act has been performed, the risk faced, and the only thing left to do is make the quick walk, one foot in front of the other, back to safety.

65

THE JET WAS SOMEWHERE OVER the Atlantic Ocean, winging through the blackness of the night. In the seat next to Will Chambers, Angus MacCameron was sleeping soundly and exhaustedly. Most of the passengers had turned off their reading lights and were dozing. But Will could not sleep. His mind was racing. And he was troubled.

He couldn't keep from venturing back to the trial, and the cross-examination questions and the answers. The judge's interjections and rulings. The look on the jury's faces as they had filed out of the courtroom that afternoon, not to resume their seats until the following Monday. The cross-examination of Reichstad. And the sound of Reichstad's little book hitting the floor. He had the feeling that the tide of battle had changed. Slightly, yes—but it had changed in their favor.

But instead of feeling satisfied with the progress of the trial Will was in turmoil. Somehow the trial, its outcome, and winning and losing were no longer the issue. Now that the legal flurry had subsided for a few days, Will, in the quiet, rushing darkness of the jet, was reflecting on the gnawing emptiness within. And on the cold, glacial dissatisfaction he felt with his life.

Of course he was aware how he was finally coming to terms with Audra's death. And how his abrupt termination from the law firm, his problems with alcohol, the destruction of his home, and the possibility of criminal arson charges had all, somehow, been weathered. He had even survived a bizarre encounter with an international terrorist—followed by his brush with Warren Mullburn, which had been equally bizarre, and just as dangerous.

And Will was even at peace, in a strange way, with the fact that the delightful and gracious Fiona, who seemed to be so full of life, laughter, and tender decency, could never be more than a friend. Though he was tired of loneliness—tired down to the depths of his heart—that was really not what troubled him most. What tortured him was the hunger in his soul. A longing. A quiet voice that could not be stilled. Not a threatening voice—or a nagging one. But a persistent calling. Like a parent who calls an errant child back to dinner. Or a father who calls for a son to join him down at the pier for a fishing trip; like a voice echoing off the lake. It was a strangely familiar voice that was calling. A little like the memory of a reunion, long forgotten. Why did he resist it, even fear it? Why would he not respond to a call that came to him in a way that sounded, and felt, so much like family?

God, it seemed, was closing in. Will knew that he had to make a serious decision about what he really believed. Something would have to be done. The call had to be answered or refused.

Angus MacCameron slept nearly the entire flight. Will nodded off in only small fitful, and interrupted, episodes.

When the jet landed at Heathrow Airport, the two collected their bags and scurried to the subway. The "Underground" was the quickest way into central London and the Bloomsbury District, where the British Museum was located.

MacCameron had called ahead to secure permission to search the office of Dr. Lazarus, who was still out of town on an expedition in the sub-Sahara.

The two of them hurried up the steps of the Museum, and walked through the main entrance of the yawning portico, entering between the mammoth, scroll-topped columns of stone that dwarfed them as if they were ants.

They introduced themselves to the security guard in the cavernous main lobby. He placed a phone call, then asked them to wait.

After a few minutes they were approached by the assistant administrator of the Museum, a thin, middle-aged woman in a drab suit. They showed their identification, and she proceeded to lead them through the hallways, and upstairs, to the office of Dr. Lazarus. They were accompanied by one of the security guards, who, the administrator indicated, would have to be present during their review of the files in the office. As they walked, the administrator shared a little history of the British Museum—which only she seemed to find interesting.

"Now I know," she explained in her crisp British accent, much like a schoolteacher might lecture a grade-school class, "that you are trying to locate some of Dr. Hunter's missing artifacts. I know you've come a far way.

I know you are rather excited about finding them. But I should caution you that the museum here is not like something that people see on the telly, or in the cinema. We don't have mysterious antiquities lying about, gathering dust and cobwebs in forgotten corners or hidden back rooms. We are a very modern and scientific operation. I should be quite surprised if you find the misplaced object that you are searching for."

"Have you ever misplaced any antiquities here at the Museum?" Will asked.

The administrator giggled a bit. "Well, not antiquities—but there was this one incident. Oh my, it caused an absolute frenzy! Five human heads were found—I think they were dried-out heads of South African Khoisan bushmen. Someone found them in a cardboard box, in a back room of the Natural History Museum, back about ten years. Can you imagine! Apparently the heads had been brought here from the field in the mid-1800s. They were prepared by an archivist and put away and apparently forgotten for more than a hundred years! South Africa demanded the return of the heads so they could be buried. But of course the Museum felt otherwise. It nearly caused an international incident. Well, here we are."

The administrator opened the office door of Dr. Lazarus's office and turned on the lights.

"Good hunting," she said, and with a "cheerio," she left.

Will and MacCameron spent nearly six hours searching Lazarus's file cabinets for any evidence of documents, or files, from Dr. Hunter. But they found nothing. MacCameron looked pale, and had to sit down frequently to rest.

Will was beginning to feel as if this idea of flying all the way across the Atlantic just to search for the elusive 7QC fragment had been a disastrous waste of time. They had no assurance it still existed. All they had was the cryptic message from Hunter that *seemed* to indicate that it might be in the British Museum somewhere. Will was tired, and knew that he still had work to do to prepare for the next week's session of the trial.

"Look here," MacCameron said, trying to muster some enthusiasm. "Let's try to take Hunter at his word. Maybe the fragment was never in Lazarus's office after all. Maybe the people who broke into his office did not find it there either."

"Angus, where does that leave us? I think we are at a dead-end."

"If we take Hunter's message *literally*, he said 'the next time you come to the *halls* of the British Museum...' I think that means that we should comb the *halls* for clues."

Will felt himself getting angry and frustrated. For an instant, he wanted to force his client to face the grim reality. He was fed up with the expedition.

"One hour," Will said. "We walk the halls for one hour. And then we go out for dinner. I'll even buy. Then we check into our hotel rooms for the night. Tomorrow we fly back."

They started to look through the hallways of the administrative wing. MacCameron was walking more slowly than usual, and stopped to take sips of water at the water coolers.

"Actually," MacCameron told him as they walked the halls, "I have booked us on a flight tomorrow to Jerusalem. I believe that Reichstad is already a step ahead of us. I am sure he is already there, beginning excavation of the area at the St. Stephen's Gate."

There was silence between them for a while as they looked in vain around the Museum, being followed by the assigned security guard and occasionally dodging staff of the Museum. They were looking, but they did not know what they were looking for.

As they rounded a corner, Will wanted to start disputing MacCameron's plan for a side-trip to Israel. But he glanced at his watch and realized that the hour was almost up. Soon the two of them would be dining quietly, and then Will could talk some sense into his client.

Will glanced to his right for MacCameron, but he wasn't there. He looked back. Angus MacCameron had stopped in front of one of the staff doors. He had an amazed, bewildered, almost pained look on his face. His mouth was slightly open. But no words were coming out.

After a moment, he lifted his hand and pointed to the name over the door.

The nameplate said, "Dr. Lundgren Dedencrist—Department of Oriental Antiquities."

"So?" Will asked, not seeing the connection.

"This is it. This has to be it!" MacCameron cried out. "How could I have been so cloddish and stupid?"

But Will could still not see the significance of the name over the door.

"Will, boy. Reichstad must have told his goons to hit Dr. Lazarus's office because of Jesus' 'order' for Lazarus to come forth. They thought it was *that* kind of order. But they were wrong."

Will was nodding thoughtfully as he recalled how MacCameron and he had discussed that point previously.

"I still don't understand."

MacCameron was jabbing his index finger toward the name over the office door.

"But there is *another* kind of 'order,' isn't there? Tell me, Will, what is another meaning of the word 'order'?"

"Well," Will said, "there is the kind of 'order' that you get when there is a well-organized state of something. Like a 'well-ordered' society. Like that?"

"Stop thinking like a lawyer! There is another kind of 'order.'"

Will was getting tired of playing twenty questions.

"Well, there is—oh, I don't know—maybe 'order' in the way it is used in baseball. The 'order' of the line-up. Batting order."

"Exactly!" MacCameron cried out. "The batting order! Oh, that's rich. Except in the Bible, the apostle Paul talks about an order much more important than a batting lineup. He gives us the 'resurrection order!' Don't you see?"

"No," Will replied.

"Richard Hunter, bless his heart—I don't know whether he ever finally believed in Jesus before his awful death. But one thing about my friend Richard—he knew his New Testament. Better than some pastors. That's what he meant by the 'resurrection order.' First Thessalonians, chapter four, verse sixteen. Paul talks about the resurrection." And with that Mac-Cameron pulled out his little pocket New Testament and started reading:

> For the Lord Himself will descend from heaven with a shout,
> with the voice of the archangel, and with the trumpet of God,
> and the dead in Christ will rise first.

"I tell you, that's the 'resurrection order' Hunter was talking about. He said, when I am in the *halls of the British Museum*, to remember my Bible, and to remember the *resurrection order*—in which the 'dead in Christ' rise first...'dead in Christ'...Dr. Ded-en-crist...Somewhere, on the other side of this door, just a few feet from where we are standing, lies the missing 7QC fragment. It's somewhere in the office of Dr. Dedencrist. I know it."

MacCameron needed to rest, so he asked that Will run down to the central administrative office and gain access to the office.

The assistant administrator was just leaving for the day when Will caught her and explained the urgent need to get into Dedencrist's office and search it.

She looked skeptical. "Dr. Dedencrist is currently somewhere in the hills of Mongolia, with a group of American explorers, looking for the burial site of Genghis Khan. I don't know how we can contact him to obtain permission."

"Does he have a cell phone that works internationally?"

"Well, he did leave some numbers. I can try. Heaven only knows where he actually is."

Will walked back to the locked door where MacCameron was sitting on a bench in the hallway, and explained the problem.

"I'm going to pray. Want to join me?" MacCameron asked.

Will somehow felt compelled to bow his head as Angus MacCameron, in labored but impassioned words, asked for the intervention of "our Most High King of the universe, our dearest heavenly Father," that he might make possible a connection between the British Museum and Dr. Dedencrist. By the end of the prayer, MacCameron was out of breath, and Will was beginning to have serious concerns about his client's condition.

Will offered to find some water for his client, and went down the hallway. After he had walked about twenty feet, he heard the fast paced clacking sound of a pair of high heels down the corridor. He turned and saw the assistant administrator approaching MacCameron. She spotted Will and shouted, very uncharacteristically, "Mr. Chambers! Quite extraordinary. Most unusual. I was able to get him on his cell phone on the very first try. Dr. Dedencrist gave me immediate approval for you to look for Dr. Hunter's things."

"Isn't that marvelous!" MacCameron said.

"And I think you should know what else he said."

"What is that?" Will asked as he quickly approached her.

"Dr. Hunter was tight on space in his offices. He was something of a pack-rat. Never tossed a thing away. He ended up keeping several filing cabinets of his with Dr. Dedencrist, who didn't mind because he had the extra space. So, there you are!"

She fished through her keys, and tried several that didn't fit.

Finally she found the right key, unlocked the door, and swung it open.

As she turned on the switch, the fluorescent lights buzzed, flickered, and then illuminated the room, as Will and MacCameron walked in.

66

THE ADMINISTRATOR TOLD THEM SHE WOULD BE back to check on them in about an hour, when they would have to leave for the day. She left, and the two began to scan the room.

It looked like what one would think of as the office of a museum staff member. Stacks of semi-organized papers and files were scattered over Dr. Dedencrist's desk and credenza. There was a table in the middle of the office, covered with maps and books. In one corner there was a computer on a small desk. Beyond the desk there was a row of windows that gave a panoramic view of the spires of the Royal Courts of Justice and the River Thames off in the distance, reflecting the sun that was setting over the city of London.

Against one wall of the office there were floor-to-ceiling bookshelves crammed with books.

On the other wall there was a row of four brown wooden file cabinets. Next to those there were three tan, metal file cabinets, with a small label on each drawer that simply read, "Dr R.H."

"This is it!" Will exclaimed. He told Angus MacCameron to sit down and rest in the leather armchair in the corner of the office while he went through the drawers.

First, Will did a quick inventory of the general contents of the three file cabinets. Not surprisingly, Hunter's files were arranged largely in general alphabetical order. There were hundreds of manila file folders with a variety of different-colored labels, most of them with handwritten titles.

"Didn't Hunter believe in storing information on computer?" Will asked, as he considered the number of files he had to scan. He was beginning to worry that they might run out of time before the administrator returned and told them to leave for the day.

"He was old-school—like me. He didn't trust storing a lot of information on a computer," MacCameron replied.

Will noticed that several categories nearly took up a full drawer each, like "JERUSALEM," "MAPS," "MONTHLY REPORTS," and "PENDING PROJECTS."

After a hurried scan of the labels of all of the files to see if anything directly relating to the 7QC fragment would jump out, Will had come up with nothing.

"I suppose it was too much to ask for, that Hunter would make it easy for us," Will said out loud to himself. He decided to hit "PENDING PROJECTS" first, as that would be a logical place for Hunter to have hidden the fragment. Will found budget projections, correspondence on planned excavations south of the Qumran, articles on some promising sites in Jordan to investigate, memos and notes, receipts for cash expenses that Hunter had incurred; but nothing even remotely connected to the ancient fragment he was looking for.

Next he dove into the "JERUSALEM" file—again thinking that it would be a *logical* location for the fragment, but found only letters, Museum conference agendas, memos from the Israeli Antiquities Authority, personal cards from friends in Jerusalem, newspaper and magazine articles about the Temple Mount, diagrams of various projects planned in the Kidron Valley, just outside the Old City area—but no 7QC. Will looked again at the papers in the file, then reached in and pulled out something that looked like parchment.

Will glanced at the paper, and then shook his head. "Dr. Hunter saved a menu from a Jerusalem restaurant," he said. "He hides the most important archaeological fragment of all time, but keeps a menu handy. Does anyone see anything funny about that?" Will said to the air.

"Try Bethlehem," MacCameron suggested from his leather chair, as he swabbed perspiration from his forehead.

"Yeah, that's right—that's where Azid's shop was located," Will said as he pulled open another file drawer. But when he located a thin folder with a "BETHLEHEM" label, he found it empty.

"There's nothing here," Will exclaimed. "You think he took it out of the file at the last moment and put it somewhere else?"

MacCameron said nothing, but simply shook his head.

Then Will thought about checking for "AZID." But there was no such file.

Finally Will decided to simply leaf through the files alphabetically. But the next time that he glanced at his watch, he realized that their hour in the office had already passed. Any minute their host would arrive and politely kick them out, and he had only gotten to the files bearing the label "MAPS." He flicked through the maps, diagrams, and charts, but nothing looked promising. The next categories were "MAPKON," "MIDRASH," "MITHRAS (ROMAN—2ND-5TH CENTURY)," "MITZVAH (see: PENTATEUCH)"—all of them looked unpromising.

The door to the office swung open and the assistant administrator appeared, putting on her raincoat.

"I'm afraid you will have to leave now, gentlemen. I hope you brought your umbrellas; there is a tiny bit of a drizzle outside. The security guard will escort you out."

She disappeared from the doorway, and the sound of her heels on the marble floor echoed away in the distance.

So, this is it, Will thought to himself. "Here we are with our backs to the Red Sea. The Egyptians come roaring down at us in their chariots. But the sea just doesn't part. Not this time. This time they grease their wheels with us."

Will glanced over at MacCameron, who was leaning back, his head resting against the high-backed chair. He seemed to be talking, mouthing words—but Will could hear nothing.

Looking back at the file drawer he had been working on, Will ran his eyes over the file tabs once more. Finally he closed the drawer, and walked away.

And that was when he was aware of the silent touch from somewhere in the dark—the invisible neuron firing, the minuscule current of a thought—sparked from the finger of someone or something. Was it something he had heard? Or had read somewhere? He turned and looked back at the file drawer he had just closed.

"Something there..." Will muttered. "Something in that drawer..."

He grabbed the metal handle, and yanked the drawer open with such force that the file cabinet rocked and banged against the wall.

Will madly ran his fingers over the tabs: "MAPS," "MAPKON," "MIDRASH," "MITHRAS (ROMAN—2ND-5TH CENTURY)," "MITZVAH (see: PENTATEUCH)."

"Greek," Will mumbled to himself. "The Greek for 'Mark.' The Greek name for the Gospel of Mark...it looks like...'MAPKON'...in the Greek, the 'P' makes the *sound* of an 'R,' so it sounds like 'Markon,' but it reads 'MAPKON'!" His thoughts were tumbling over themselves as he reached for the "MAPKON" file.

"Reichstad wrote that 7QA was the true original ending to the Gospel of Mark. But that wasn't really *his* idea," Will continued to himself now loudly. "He stole it—just like he stole 7QA. It was *Hunter's* idea...and Hunter told Azid...and that's where Reichstad got the idea...as well as the 7QA fragment." With that Will pulled from the folder its only contents, a large olive-green envelope, with the flourish of a magician pulling a rabbit out of a hat.

"This is it!" Will yelled, and quickly unwound the thread from the round tab on the outside flap.

He then pulled out the only thing within: a clear plastic zip bag. It contained an irregularly shaped and yellowish piece of material with the block letters of Greek writing.

Will ran to the large table that was cluttered with books and maps and papers. With his left arm, he cleared a corner in one sweep, sending books clattering to the floor and papers flying in the air.

He reached into his pocket and pulled out the photocopy of 7QA joined together with 7QB and laid it on the mahogany surface of the table. He placed the plastic bag with the fragment onto the upper right-hand corner of the photocopy, carefully lining up its lettering to the right of the top two lines of 7QA, and just above 7QB—exactly where MacCameron had always thought that 7QC belonged.

It was a perfect fit. The left-hand edge of this piece was an exact match with the right-hand edge of 7QA; and the bottom of this new fragment matched the top of 7QB. And the two lines of Greek letters matched perfectly with the top two lines of 7QA, apparently completing them.

"Just like a jigsaw puzzle on Aunt Georgia's card table!" Will exclaimed.

But Will suddenly realized that he had absolutely no idea what the two lines of Greek writing on this new fragment actually said.

He whirled around to Angus MacCameron.

Will felt as if the wind had been knocked out of his stomach.

MacCameron had slumped over to one side of the chair. His face, which was drained of all color, was grimaced in pain, and his right hand was balled up in a fist, held tight against his chest. Will rushed over.

MacCameron was drenched in sweat, and his skin was cold and clammy. Will heard him groaning—a low, quiet groan of intense suffering.

Will dashed to the door. He saw the security guard strolling down the hall toward him. "Get an ambulance! Now!" Will screamed out. "I think he's having a heart attack!"

67

In the hospital, Will stood at the telephone with the receiver at his ear. He dreaded making this phone call to Fiona.

She answered on the second ring. Will started explaining everything. He shared with her that her father had suffered a serious heart attack. He blamed himself—Angus had not been looking good the whole trip. He'd seemed tired and sick. Short of breath. Will knew the symptoms. His own father had died of a heart attack. Why in the world hadn't he been able to figure it out before it was too late for Angus MacCameron?

Will gave Fiona the name and location of the hospital, the necessary telephone numbers, and the name of the attending cardiologist. The doctor had found a blockage in one of the left coronary arteries. They had to stabilize his condition, and then would administer drugs in an attempt to dissolve the clot. If that didn't work, Angus would have to undergo surgery.

Fiona listened quietly, intensely, then quickly asked a series of questions. Was he expected to survive? She would immediately fly over to London and be with him. Was he conscious? Was he in great pain? Fiona said that she knew someone from her church who could stay in the house with her mother while she attended her father in England.

"You said that the heart attack happened just as you found the 7QC fragment?"

"Yes. Your father was right about finding it—he's been right about a lot of things. I didn't think we could locate it."

"Be careful with that little piece of papyrus. You have to continue the case next week—even though you will have to do it without him."

"I don't know how I can defend his case without his being there—without his testimony."

"You have to," Fiona pleaded. "Da knew what was at stake in this case. He believed in the cause he was fighting for. And he believed in you."

"Fiona, I'll do whatever I can," Will said.

"There is one more thing I know he would want you to do."

"Anything."

"You must still go to Jerusalem tomorrow. To be an eyewitness to whatever Reichstad finds in his excavation."

"I can't do that—I can't leave him alone," Will said, feeling torn.

"Please. Do this for my da. This is what he wants. Please do this. This is what he lived for—to vindicate the truth. You have to be his eyes and his ears at that wall in Jerusalem while Reichstad is digging. The Lord will take care of my father..."

There was a pause as Fiona's voice cracked and she began crying.

"The Lord will take care of him until I get there. I'm going to leave right now. I may be able to catch a plane out of D.C. within a few hours. But you *have* to be in Jerusalem for my father tomorrow. Now please tell my da I love him. Tell him I love him so very much. And that I will see him as soon as I can—within twenty-four hours. And Will..."

"Yes?"

"Please take care of yourself. I don't want anything to happen to you..." Fiona's voice cracked again, as they said goodbye to each other.

When Will was finally allowed into his room, Angus had IV tubes in both arms, as well as tubes in both nostrils. A heart monitor beeped next to him. The nurse told Will he could only have five minutes.

Will took Angus MacCameron's hand and squeezed it slightly to let him know that he was not alone.

MacCameron's eyelids fluttered, and he opened his eyes. After he had focused, the corner of his mouth rose slightly in a smile. Then he parted his lips to say something.

"Don't try to talk, Angus. Just listen. I spoke to Fiona. She's flying over to London immediately. She says to tell you she loves you very much."

"You...found...it," MacCameron said in a voice that was barely audible.

Will pulled the baggie with 7QC out of his pocket and held it up.

"No. *You* found it. You found it, Angus, with your stubborn faith."

MacCameron blinked a few times. Then he said something that Will could not hear. Will bent down close to listen.

"Bible..."

"Bible?" Will asked. Then he noticed the little pocket New Testament on the nightstand next to him. He picked it up and opened it to the place where the ribbon bookmark was placed. It was at chapter eight of the book of Romans.

"Read...thirty-eight..."

Will ran his finger down the page until it rested on verse thirty-eight. Then he read it out loud:

> For I am convinced that neither death, nor life, nor angels, nor principalities, nor things present, nor things to come, nor powers, nor height, nor depth, nor any other created thing, shall be able to separate us from the love of God, which is in Christ Jesus the Lord.

Then Angus MacCameron whispered something barely perceptible. But Will understood it perfectly.

"I'm ready for the Lord...are you?"

Will was still struggling for a response when the nurse came in and ushered him out of the room.

He grabbed a cup of coffee from the hospital cafeteria, and then found a phone. After dialing Tiny Heftland's number at his hotel in Jerusalem, Will got the hotel voice mail. He left a message for Tiny's room. He told him about Angus MacCameron, and their amazing discovery of what he decided, on the spur of the moment, to code-name the "laundry ticket." Will ended the message by explaining his plans to fly to Jerusalem the next day.

Rather than go directly to his hotel room, Will decided to wait for a while in the hospital lobby, just in case there was any change with Angus. He put his coffee down beside his chair and started to leaf through a magazine. It occurred to him that he ought to somehow copy the fragment.

Will's head jerked suddenly, and he realized he had been falling asleep. He rubbed his eyes. A few family members of patients were at the other side of the lobby. A man operating a floor-polishing machine was working down the hallway.

Deciding to try Tiny again, Will went over to the pay phone. This time Tiny answered.

"Hey—Will, my man! Wow. This is really bad news about MacCameron. Is he going to make it?"

"I hope so. You know that I'm flying into Israel tomorrow."

"Yeah. I'm sorry I'm going to miss you. We've got one last lead—some guy in Bethlehem who says that if we're willing to play a couple rounds of 'pitch the American greenback,' he will locate our Bedouin friend for us. I'm leaving for Bethlehem right away.

"Look, I'm glad you're coming here to Jerusalem. There's some unbelievably heavy stuff coming down."

"Like what? Reichstad?"

"Bingo. Reichstad's put up this huge astrodome tent thing around the whole site. Guys wearing spacesuit-looking things are going in and out of the tent with all kinds of high-tech equipment. They've already done some excavation. And the local folks are really starting to rock and roll. I mean rock-throwing. Gun battles by the wall. Israeli troops and Palestinian police shooting at each other. This is a major war zone here, buddy. The Mayor of Jerusalem is talking about shutting down the whole city—complete curfew—martial law. This is really getting berserk. I hope you can get into the city."

"Reichstad has already excavated?"

"Oh yeah. And man, do I have some news for you. Not good for your client's case, I guess."

"What did they find?"

"A tomb."

"Say again? I couldn't quite hear you. Did you say a tomb?"

"A tomb. Big time. The Israeli government, for some reason, is feeding me all this information about what Reichstad is doing over at the site. And the government folks are real anxious for you to get here. How they knew you were coming I can't tell you."

"So they've located a tomb..."

"Yeah," Tiny explained. "They locate the tomb with their gadgets. They start digging. They stop. They start again—I'm telling you, this whole thing is like Bible-times Mystery Theater—then they punch through with little remote cameras—you know the kind of really thin optical wires with a lighted video camera on the end? And they use their locator gadgets again. They detect something..."

"And what did they detect?" Will queried.

"Okay, right there, chief—right there you got a problem."

"What do you mean?"

"Well, they scan into the tomb..."

"Yeah? And what? What?"

"Will buddy, let me just say it this way...the tomb doesn't look empty."

68

THERE WAS VERY LITTLE CHANCE OF WILL'S catching much sleep on the 747 jet as he flew to Israel. Not that he couldn't use it. Between the trip from the U.S. to England, and the time changes, and his vigil at the hospital, followed by a dash to the airport for another flight to the Middle East, he hadn't had a solid hour of sleep for almost two days. But he had his homework to do—a little "light reading" before stepping into the midst of a battle zone in the most geopolitically explosive, religiously charged hot spot on the planet.

Before heading to the London airport, he had dashed over to a large, all-night bookstore near Picadilly Circus to pick up a couple of books about the history of Jerusalem. He wanted to take in as much information as he could about the St. Stephen's Gate area along the wall of the Old City part of Jerusalem. He wasn't sure what he was going to do once he landed. And of course, there was always the possibility that, because of the riots and unrest caused by Reichstad's excavation, he wouldn't be able to get anywhere near that portion of the city.

On the other hand, if Will *could* get close to the dig, he wanted to know something about the area he would be looking at. He had pledged to be Angus MacCameron's "eyes and ears." He was not going to break that promise.

In the waiting area of the airport in London Will had made a frantic call to Dr. Giovanni. It had suddenly dawned on him that he would need his main expert witness there in Jerusalem—right next to him—while he tried to monitor what Reichstad was doing. He left a message on her voice mail, but he had no idea whether she could—or would—drop everything to fly directly over to Israel, just to turn around and fly back less than two days later in order to be in court for the continuation of trial on Monday.

And then there was another reason he wanted Giovanni with him. Will was still carrying the little plastic bag containing 7QC in the pocket of his coat. MacCameron had been stricken with his heart attack before being able to interpret it. Despite schooling himself in the rudiments of Koine Greek for the trial, Will couldn't read it. Giovanni was his only hope. While in Jerusalem he wanted to transfer the fragment to her and get her evaluation.

As Will searched through the books he had picked up, he learned a great deal about the historical development of the Old City of Jerusalem, but only a few sketchy facts about the area at St. Stephen's Gate.

As Will had learned from MacCameron in one of their first meetings, the gate was the place where, just outside of the city proper, a Christian disciple named Stephen had been stoned to death for his bold proclamation of the gospel, not long after the crucifixion of Jesus.

But, as he read on, Will was bewildered at the maze of contradictions about this gate. He discovered that most historians had actually ascribed the place of Stephen's stoning not to St. Stephen's Gate, but to the *opposite* side of the Old City walls at a gate known in the modern era as the "Damascus Gate."

However it seemed to Will that, because 7QB specifically referred to the "East Gate of Stephen," then at least the mystery of which gate was the site of Stephen's stoning appeared to have been solved. After all, the writer of the fragment would certainly have been knowledgeable about a major event of his own time. So the gate at which Reichstad was digging, then, was *Stephen's Gate.*

But that didn't solve the question of *whose* tomb it was that Reichstad had unearthed by following the clue in the 7QB fragment. Reichstad was undoubtedly still pursuing his mission to prove that the tomb was the burial site of Jesus.

Perhaps the little 7QC fragment that Will carried in his pocket would end up providing the answer. Each time Will reflected on that, he found himself patting his pocket just to make sure that the plastic bag was still safely there.

From time to time his mind would wander back to Angus MacCameron, and the agony in his face as he had desperately grasped his chest. And then he thought about Angus at the hospital. "I'm ready for the Lord," he had said. When Will had heard that, his heart had seemed to burn within him. And it was strangely similar to what he had been reading on the plane about Stephen's death. His sources quoted the book of Acts: While Stephen was dying, he was still able to utter, "Lord Jesus, receive my spirit."

Will could only wonder, in awe, at such peace of soul in the face of impending death.

As he thought about Fiona rushing to her father's side, he also recalled how he wished he could have been with his own father in his final moments of life. Will's dad, by all accounts, had died in the early morning hours there in his newspaper office, completely alone. There had been no goodbyes. No final words, nor any closing of all that personal business of life between father and son. Only the absence. The loss. The missed opportunities.

Turning to the window that was next to him, Will clumsily tried to mutter a short prayer for Angus. Afterward, the only thing he was sure that he had said was the "Amen" at the end.

When the sun came up over the horizon, Will looked out of the jet and had his first glimpse of Israel. It appeared as a long brown strip of desert along the blue Mediterranean. As the plane approached the Tel Aviv airport, which was ringed with date trees and palms, he considered what a strange pilgrimage it was that had brought him there. What powerful force was it that had led him all the way to this ancient land?

The jet jolted as it touched down on the runway, and then it taxied to a halt on the tarmac. As he unbuckled himself, Will couldn't help but feel, despite whatever message there might be for the entire world from within that ancient burial site along the Jerusalem wall, that he was about to receive some profoundly personal message there also. Perhaps he was about to find out something about himself. Maybe even something about the very face of God—the inscrutable One—the "Ancient of Days."

69

As Will entered the airport lobby in Tel Aviv, he heard his name spoken from somewhere near.

Calling out his name was a man with thinning hair and a huge grin, and large navigator-type glasses.

"Mr. Chambers, we have been expecting you," he said, as he reached out and shook Will's hand with gusto. "Amnon Solomon. But you can call me 'Nony.' I'm the Assistant Director of the Israeli Antiquities Authority. How was your flight? You look tired. You need to get something to eat? We'll pick up something for you on the way to Jerusalem. Is this your first visit to Israel?"

Will was not expecting anyone to meet him, and was more than a little surprised.

Then, as they walked through the airport, Nony was joined by a tall, broad-shouldered man in a tailored leather jacket, with curly, jet-black hair and darkly-tanned, chiseled good looks.

"I'm Nathan Abrams," the other man said with a casual smile, "and it is wonderful to meet you, Will. I'm here to be a kind of guide for you. A driver. Show you around. Get you into places."

As they approached a black Mercedes parked in front of the airport, Will said, "I certainly appreciate your offer—but I don't expect to do much sightseeing while I'm here."

When he said that, Nony laughed a little, and Nathan gave Will a knowing look. "No, I don't expect you will," Nathan replied in his deep baritone voice. "But the Israeli government wants you to be comfortable, and well tended-to, while you do your very important business here. And, above all, they want you to be safe."

At that, Nathan and Nony glanced at each other in a way that told Will that there was more to Nathan's helpful assistance than met the eye.

Inside the car, and speeding toward Jerusalem, they asked Will about his law practice back in the States. And about American politics. Nony talked a little about his family. Nathan, who was doing the driving, was warm and friendly, but shared nothing about himself.

After a while Nathan began asking a few questions about Will's involvement in the Reichstad case. They were quickly followed up by a series of questions about Reichstad's research center in Maryland—and the need for its super security system—and what Will knew about any other projects that Reichstad and his staff might be working on.

Remembering what Tiny Heftland had said about the assistance he was getting from the Israeli government, Will told the two men everything he felt he could reveal.

After a thirty-minute drive, Nathan pointed to the hill they were climbing and said, "It's just over the horizon. Jerusalem."

He pulled the car over to the side of the road, reached into the glove compartment, and pulled out two identification tags. He handed one to Nony and one to Will.

"Where's yours?" Will asked.

Nony chuckled. "Oh, Nathan has his own ID. Besides, he does business with everybody. They all know him."

Nathan went to the back of the car and pulled something out. He reached through the window and handed them each a black flak jacket and a helmet.

"Put them on," Nathan said nonchalantly.

As he got in the car he reached under the seat, produced an Uzi machine gun, and laid it on the seat next to him.

It was at that point that Will began to understand that Nathan was more than a tour guide.

As they topped the hill, in the distance Will saw the crowded mass of stone buildings of Jerusalem and the burnished Dome of the Rock, all of it reflecting the bright sun like a city of gold.

"Look down there," Nathan said, pointing straight ahead in the distance. "The hill off to the left, that is the Mount of Olives. To the right, across from it, is the Old City section of Jerusalem. And down there closest to the northeastern corner of the wall of the Old City, that's Stephen's Gate—that's where we are headed."

Will squinted in the intense sunlight as he gazed out toward the city.

"Do you mean down there," Will said, pointing to the spot where Nathan had indicated, "down there where the smoke is rising up?"

Turning around with a grin and a little side nod of his head, Nony said, "Probably tear gas. It should be cleared out by the time we get there."

As they turned off of HaShalom and onto Sultan Suleiman Road so they could circle around the north end of the Old City, they ran into a tangle of traffic, beeping horns and hands waving out of cars, buses, and taxis. Up ahead they could see a military checkpoint had been created in the middle of the street, flanked by Israeli soldiers.

Nathan reached onto the floor of the car, pulled out a portable flashing police light, turned it on, and put it on the dashboard. Then he wheeled the Mercedes into the wrong side of traffic, dodging cars as he went, until he roared up to the checkpoint.

Two soldiers who could not have been older than nineteen or twenty ran up to the car, holding onto the machine guns that were strapped over their shoulders.

"Let me talk to your commanding officer," Nathan shouted out.

In a few seconds an older-looking man approached the car, bent down to the driver's side, and stared at Nathan.

As Nathan reached into his jacket pocket he announced, "I am reaching for identification..."

But the officer smiled, and waved it off, and said, "Nathan, how have you been?"

"Not bad. Business has been pretty good. New shop. Plenty of customers."

"It's pretty rough going up there," the officer said, looking beyond the checkpoint. "Do you want an escort?"

"No, thank you very much. I don't want to be a bigger target than I already am."

The soldiers opened the barricade to permit the Mercedes through, and the line of cars left behind them redoubled their horn-blasting. Nathan turned the car from Sultan Suleiman onto the road that ran parallel to the high, ancient Jerusalem wall to their right. Above, over the walled city, Will could see the golden Dome, rising up in the middle of the Temple Mount.

As they drove, Nony explained that the Stephen's Gate area was in a particularly volatile spot for an archaeological dig. Not only was it not very far from the Islam-controlled Mount, as well as right next to a Muslim cemetery, but it also butted up against a wall of the Old City in Jerusalem—considered the sacred property of Judaism.

"This is unusual—all of this violence and rioting. You know," Nony pointed out, "Israel is safer than New York City, or where you come from—Washington, D.C."

"Actually, Virginia," Will said, "but that's close enough."

"The conflict thus far near the Gate has been mostly between Jewish soldiers and the Palestinians," Nony commented. "We haven't seen any violence from the apocalyptic zealots—the ones that believe they can bring on Armageddon by armed conflict. But we have to be ready for anything."

As they wound along the road in a shallow valley, a garden area off to the left and the Old City wall on the right, they hit a bend in the road. Suddenly the valley and hills around them opened into what looked like the chaos of a battlefield.

A canister of tear gas was being lobbed by a soldier toward a group of fifty or sixty young male Palestinians who were running headlong toward the Mercedes. The frantic mob rushed toward them and began screaming, trying to get their faces near the windows.

"Fasten seatbelts," Nathan said casually. He pronounced the words with the calm of an airline pilot—one who knew more about the turbulence ahead than he wanted to share with the passengers.

70

As THEIR MERCEDES CONTINUED FORWARD, rocks started bouncing off its hood. "Oh no, and I just had a new paint job from the last set of dents," Nathan moaned.

Nathan slowed the car and tried to navigate it through the mob, but several men hopped onto the hood and started banging on the windows with their fists. Nathan did a quick zig-zag with the steering wheel, and the men on the hood slid off. Suddenly Will heard a loud crack near his head. He looked at the window next to him and saw a small chip in the glass. Then there was the crackling sound of gunfire off to his left, as Will spotted several Palestinians with handguns firing—and the approaching Israeli soldiers firing back.

As the soldiers converged on the Mercedes and surrounded it, the mob dispersed.

Will pointed to the chip in the glass next to his head.

"Bulletproof glass. Great stuff, huh?" Nathan responded, looking in his rearview mirror.

The soldiers walked alongside the car as it took one more curve in the road, and then Will could see the little alley that was their destination.

The small, short street that led up to Stephen's Gate cut through a hill. On top of both sides were tall, temporary metal barricades that acted as shields. Nathan stopped the car, got out, and chatted with the armed guards at the entrance of the street. Then he returned and told Will and Nony that they had to walk the rest of the way, about seventy-five yards, up to the Gate. Nathan explained that he now had to drive back to the airport to pick up someone else arriving from America.

"Nathan, one thing you haven't explained," Will commented. "You haven't told me how you knew I was coming. And why I'm getting this personal escort. Why the VIP treatment?"

"Well," Nathan explained in his deep voice, "here in Israel we survive on good information. Both to warn us of our enemies—and to help us welcome our friends."

Then Nathan shook Will's hand and said, "Whether you know it or not, you are one of the friends."

Will and Nony, dressed in their flak jackets and helmets, quickly exited the car and walked up the street that led directly to the Jerusalem wall. As they did, they were flanked by young Israeli soldiers who lined both sides of the narrow road, weapons slung over their shoulders. Will was squinting in the bright sunlight.

As Will shielded his eyes with his hands, he could see straight ahead, to the end of the row of soldiers. In the ancient wall that rose up about forty feet, there was a gateway made of yellow stone, which surrounded and towered above an arched entrance that led into crowded alleyways of the Old City within. To the right was a huge white inflated tent of some kind that reached almost to the top of the wall. Trucks, backhoes, and other pieces of digging equipment were parked around the outside. Dozens of people were milling around the entrance.

One man with rolled-up shirtsleeves and a clipboard walked briskly up to Will and Nony. He nodded to Nony, and then introduced himself to Will.

"I'm Saul Rosencrantz. I'm the official designee of the IAA at this project. Nony here is my boss. So I have to be on my good behavior. You fellows can take off the military gear. You're safe here."

As Will was led to the entrance of the tent, he looked over to his left, through the arched opening of Stephen's Gate, inside to the narrow street surrounded by shops and buildings.

"What's that, on the other side of Stephen's Gate?" Will asked, looking at the ancient arched gate.

"Oh, you would know that as the 'Via Dolorosa.' The street where they say Jesus was led to his crucifixion."

Saul ducked to enter the tent. But then he realized that Will was not with him, and turned around.

Will was still standing motionless at the same spot, slack-jawed, staring intensely at the winding Via Dolorosa through the archway.

"First time here?" Saul asked.

Will nodded. Saul smiled and put his hand on his shoulder, and said, "Time is short. A lot is going on inside. Come on."

Inside the tent Nony had scurried off somewhere, while Saul quickly, in a hushed tone, began describing to Will the group of dignitaries that were jammed inside. As Will looked around at the bazaar of men in head pieces, beards, and multicolored robes, he felt as if he had walked into an international religious convention.

"That's Cardinal Guido Veronni from the Vatican, and Fr. Anthony Barronette, Personal Emissary of the Pontiff. Over there is a representative of the Coptic Church of Ethiopia, and there, the designate of the Greek Orthodox Church. Some of the American Protestant groups are very upset that we didn't give them a chance to be here. But the problem was that this thing was thrown together so quickly there simply wasn't enough time. Not to be glib about this, but this is not an 'orthodox' type of burial excavation. Not by any means. I think you realize, Mr. Chambers, that, with all due respect, the U.S. State Department put incredible pressure on us to get this set up in record time."

Will heard some arguing to one side. He turned and saw an elderly man in a long gray beard, wearing a black fedora on his head, and a black coat and a shawl over his shoulders. He was flanked by a younger man in blue jeans and a yarmulke, whose long brown locks curled down the side of his head and who had a rifle slung over his shoulder. Those two were arguing with two others, apparently Muslim clerics—one with a short beard, black robe, and square white hat, and the other in a white robe that was wrapped, in one piece, around and over his head.

"That's Rabbi Micah Karinsky. He's arguing with the Islamic Mufti of Jerusalem and Sheik Ahammen Yessar. Those two are both with the Waqf, the Muslim trust that controls the Temple Mount. The Muslims are upset with the fact that the Rabbi insisted on bringing his own personal bodyguard into the tent."

Saul took Will to the midpoint of the tent, where a group of scientists and researchers had gathered around a large foldup table. The table was covered with computers, cables, and several video screens.

Beyond the table by a few feet was another adjoining compartment of the tent, but it was closed with a flap and a sign was posted that said, "No Entrance—Excavation in Progress."

Most of the researchers were crowded around one large monitor. The black-and-white image on the screen showed what looked like the interior of a rocky cave.

"Adam, this is Mr. Chambers from the United States," Saul said to the man at the controls of the video screen, who was wearing a headset and microphone. "Why don't you give us both a rundown of the status thus far?"

"Well," Adam explained, "we have a square closing stone to this tomb. Characteristic of first-century Herodian. The tomb itself has decorative features in keeping with some of the tombs we have found from the same time period—20 to 60 C.E. Time of Jesus, we are all convinced. Hard limestone, precise angles on the entrance, good aesthetic finish. Ornamentation. The owner of this tomb had some pocket change to spend. From what we can see from this position, it shows what I think is the standard first-century arrangement. Two, maybe three interior compartments. But we can't be sure until Reichstad gets inside with his camera guy. They say they are going to need another thirty or forty minutes before they are ready to go deep inside the tomb."

The researchers were all looking at their watches and milling around, making conversation that, though apparently largely in English, sounded like a foreign language to Will. Saul excused himself for a few minutes and disappeared.

Will found a folding chair to sit down on. As he did he patted his coat pocket and felt the outline of the plastic bag. Adam came over with a Styrofoam cup of coffee, and offered it to Will.

"It may be strong. We like it that way over here."

Will thanked him. "You're the lawyer?" Adam asked.

"Yes. And feeling a little out of my league here. I'm no religious expert. And I'm not an archaeologist."

"No, but you're a lawyer," Adam replied as he headed back to his video monitor. "That means you ought to feel right at home in this place. The Christian Gospels say that Jesus had some of his best arguments with lawyers, don't they?"

After finishing his coffee, Will leaned back and relaxed. He listened to the sound of the tent billowing in and out with the breeze. He hoped that Angus MacCameron was faring better. And he wondered what Fiona was doing right then.

While he gazed at the video screen, Will wondered where Jesus of Nazareth was in all of this. Here in a small, ancient corner of Jerusalem that had been turned into a war zone. Amid the high-tech equipment, and computers, and scientific knowledge of this bevy of experts—and in the middle of all of the disputing religious leaders and the government bureaucrats. Was Jesus going to be ultimately found—or lost—in such a place?

After more than an hour, Will was aware that everyone—scientists, religious representatives, Nony, and Saul—was gathering around the table with the video screen. Adam was talking on the headset. Reichstad and his camera assistant were about to enter the tomb.

There were several moments of silence while the crowd stood, shoulder-to-shoulder under the large white canopy.

Someone tapped Will on the arm. He turned and saw the familiar face of Dr. Mary Margaret Giovanni next to him. She was carrying a small metal suitcase. She adjusted her glasses and shook Will's hand, but said nothing at first.

Saul stepped over, and asked "What is your name?"

"This is Dr. Giovanni," Will answered. "She is my expert."

One of the younger scientists reached his hand over to Dr. Giovanni, and said in a hushed voice, "Are you the Dr. Giovanni who worked with the legendary Geza Vermes? And also at the École Biblique at one time?"

"Yes," Dr. Giovanni said. "That was a while ago."

"I'm honored to meet you," the young scientist said.

"I'm glad I got here in time," she said to Will. "A good-looking man at the airport escorted me personally. You must have some real connections. You know, it's scary out there. Rioting. Shooting. Where is 7QC?"

Will pulled the plastic bag out of his pocket and discreetly passed it over to her.

While the crowd was riveted to the video screen, she walked over to a corner, bent down to the ground, and snapped open her metal briefcase. She put on surgical gloves and pulled the fragment out with tweezers. Then she placed it between two glass plates, put plastic clamps at the edges, and locked the clamps.

Then she took out a small handheld microscope that looked like a tiny telescope, and stared through it for several minutes at the fragment under the glass. After that, Dr. Giovanni seemed to stare out into space, blankly. She then took a small pad of paper and rapidly scribbled some notes down on it. After looking through the microscope again, she placed it and the glass plates with the 7QC fragment into her briefcase and locked it.

Will was about to ask her what the 7QC fragment said, but Adam started talking into his headset.

"We are ready for entry into the tomb, ladies and gentlemen. The next voice you hear will be Dr. Reichstad's."

On the video screen, Will saw Reichstad in a white protective suit with a helmet that looked like it belonged on an astronaut. The cameraman was following right behind him. The floodlight mounted on the handheld video camera illuminated the area. The two men ducked into the opening, and Reichstad began to speak.

"The outer chamber here...is...as you see very typical...This is the 'loculi,' the outer chamber...and...the interior chamber...with arched shelves...over there...Against the wall is the 'ossuary,' the bone box...very typical of the time of Jesus...Now we are turning right into the interior chamber..."

For a moment Reichstad's body blocked the view of the camera. The crowd around the video monitor broke into intense chatter. Then suddenly all conversation stopped as Reichstad started speaking again.

"I am looking right at it...Here it is!...Oh—it's a perfect specimen... The corpse is covered with grave linens...Oh, this is fantastic! A corpse...It looks like a male judging by the proportion of the hips and shoulders... about five feet seven inches in height...incredibly well-preserved...Ladies and gentlemen...I give you...the body of Jesus of Nazareth!"

Reichstad moved out of the way and the camera zoomed in on the outline of the corpse.

"There is something on the ground next to the corpse, in the form of a circle of some kind...very fragile vegetation...I will speculate here...I will have to take very careful samples of this...I'm sure our botanists can confirm this...but I am guessing that what we have here is the 'crown of thorns' that must...must have been buried with the body of Jesus..."

The crowd of religious representatives exploded into an angry, dumbfounded, and confused cacophony of complaint and disputation.

"I can't hear Dr. Reichstad! I can't hear him with all this noise—" Adam shouted out. But the noise from the crowd subsided only slightly.

The only person who was stone quiet, and calm, was Dr. Giovanni. She moved through the crowd, elbowing her way to the screen.

"I want a close-up on the ossuary box," she ordered Adam.

"What?"

"A close-up on the bone box there in the corner."

"We would like a close-up of the ossuary box...yes...a close-up..." Adam said into his microphone.

The camera moved and focused on the stone-lidded box in the corner.

"Closer," Giovanni said.

The camera zoomed in.

"Closer and to the right a little, I want the full front and center..."

Once again the camera zoomed in.

Then Giovanni quickly scratched down some notes on her notepad.

"Thank you, that's all I needed," she said, and started walking away from the crowd at the video screen. She picked up her metal briefcase and nodded for Will to follow her.

"This process is now going to take some time...They are going to X-ray the corpse before doing anything else. My guess is that Reichstad will not be able to actually do much to this corpse until *after* our trial next week. It is all going to be a long and drawn-out process."

"Are you just going to leave? Now?" Will asked incredulously.

"We've got a plane to catch if we are going to be in court by Monday morning for your trial. You know, I am really jet-lagged," she said. "I really hustled to get over here."

Will was thunderstruck by her laissez-faire attitude.

"What about that?" Will asked, motioning over to the video screen.

"That?" Giovanni said. "No. Take it from me. No—that's *not* the corpse of Jesus of Nazareth."

And then she smiled, and started walking toward the entrance.

71

WILL CHAMBERS SAT AT THE DEFENSE COUNSEL table in the courtroom of Judge Jeremiah Kaye, waiting for the judge to enter for the continuation of the jury trial. As Will sat and pondered the events of the last few days, he fingered a coin in his right hand. He was thinking about Jerusalem. And something that Nathan had asked him.

After Nathan had dropped off Will and Dr. Giovanni at the airport in Tel Aviv, Will had reached through the window of the freshly dented black Mercedes and shaken his hand, thanking him for everything.

"Is there anything else you can tell me about yourself?" Will had asked.

Nathan had smiled and handed him a card that read, "Art & Artifacts—Nathan Goldwaithe, Proprietor," with an address and telephone in the Old City of Jerusalem. "This is all you need to know," he had said with a smile.

Then Nathan had reached in his pocket and pulled out a coin.

"I think I'd like to give this to you. Do you mind my asking—are you a Christian?"

Will had thought for a minute. Then he had said, "Let's just say, right now I'm standing at Stephen's Gate, looking through at the Via Dolorosa on the other side."

"Okay, my friend," Nathan had said laughing, "as a businessman I try to be sensitive to all my customers. And I get the feeling that you are going to be back here again. So here is a little sample—free of charge."

He had handed a small, dark coin to Will. After studying it for a few seconds Will had thought he could see the image of a face—a man with a beard—perhaps, but the image was indistinct.

"This is a coin from the Byzantine period, just a few hundred years after Jesus is said to have walked the streets of Jerusalem. But don't get too excited—it's really not that valuable. I've got a number of these. The unique thing about this coin is that it has one of the first images of Jesus that appeared on any coin."

Will had looked again at the visage on the coin. He had been able to see the long, bearded face, and the eyes, but the features had been rubbed down to what was now only a trace, a faint shadow of a likeness.

"It's been worn down, of course, over a millennium-and-a-half. So, you'll have to fill in the rest of the features, imagine how Jesus appeared, on your own."

After Will had reached back through the window to shake his hand again, Nathan had said, "Shalom," and sped off.

Will's mind snapped back to the present as the door of Judge Kaye's chambers suddenly opened and Judge Kaye entered with his clerk.

Everyone in the room stood up. The judge placed the thick court file on the judicial bench in front of him.

"Any preliminaries before I call the jury back in for this morning's testimony?"

Will glanced over at the empty seat next to him, where Angus MacCameron should have been sitting. When he had arrived back to his apartment from Jerusalem, he had called Fiona at the hospital in London. But MacCameron had not gotten better. In fact, he had suffered a stroke in the hospital and was in and out of consciousness.

Judge Kaye noticed the absence of Will's client.

"Mr. Chambers, is your client going to be joining us?"

"Your honor, Reverend MacCameron is seriously ill."

The judge paused for a second. Will was hoping that he would not press for any more information. If he did, Will would be required to disclose it.

"Well," the judge said, "give him our best, and we hope he can join us as soon as possible. Any objections, Mr. Sherman, to the defendant not being in the courtroom?"

Sherman was more than pleased for the defense case to proceed in the absence of the defendant himself. Dr. Reichstad sat expressionless next to him.

Will stood up and addressed one more preliminary matter. "Your Honor, I have a matter of great importance. I wish to give notice of the discovery of the missing fragment—7QC—just a few days ago in the British Museum."

Sherman leaped to his feet. Reichstad was standing next to him, trying to argue something in Sherman's ear.

"This is absolutely incredible, Your Honor!" Sherman exclaimed. "How can we possibly rebut this evidence after we have already rested our case?"

"Would you explain, Mr. Chambers, exactly how you came upon this 7QC fragment in the last few days?"

Will proceeded to explain in detail the search that he and MacCameron had conducted at the British Museum.

"What do you contend that this 7QC says? How does it affect the credibility of Dr. Reichstad's interpretation of 7QA?" Judge Kaye asked.

"It proves, conclusively, that what Reverend MacCameron said in his article about Dr. Reichstad was the truth, Your Honor. 7QC completely changes the meaning of the sentences in 7QA. I have a diagram here of what all three fragments say together, now that we have all the pieces."

Sherman howled out an objection that the court should not even *see*, let alone *consider* admitting such prejudicial evidence.

Judge Kaye quickly dispatched Sherman's objection and told Will to put up the chart.

Will placed on the easel the blow-up of all three pieces joined together. He also put up his translation diagram, which read this way:

{7QA} {7QC}

AND THE BODY// **OF THE DISCIPLE**

OF JESUS OF NAZARETH// **THE HONORABLE COUNSELOR**

{7QB}

WAS LAID IN THE TOMB // *AT THE EAST GATE OF STEPHEN*

THEY DESIRED TO ANOINT IT // *THAT DAY*

BUT COULD NOT RETURN TO PREPARE THE BODY

THE BODY REMAINS IN THAT TOMB TO THIS DAY

"Your Honor, we are prepared to show that all three fragments, when taken together, clearly refer, not to the burial of Jesus, but in fact to the burial of *Joseph of Arimathea,* a member of the religious ruling body called the Sanhedrin, and a secret follower of Jesus."

Dr. Reichstad stood up and in a commanding voice declared, "This interpretation is clearly a hoax. Besides, Your Honor, I can clearly think of a way that this is really describing Jesus as the 'honorable counselor' who was buried. So this changes nothing."

"Oh, there may be a hoax, Your Honor," Will countered, "but it does not lie with us. Dr. Giovanni is here to testify that the only reference in the Bible to an 'honorable counselor,' is a reference to Joseph of Arimathea in the

Gospel of Mark, chapter fifteen, verse forty-three. Another translation of the two Greek words in 7QC for 'honorable counselor' would be 'prominent member of the council.' It would be an utter absurdity to contend that Jesus was a member of the same religious council that condemned him to death!"

Sherman again rose to his feet, arguing that if this evidence of 7QC was going to come into the case, then Dr. Reichstad should be able to introduce the evidence of the discovery of the corpse of Jesus in the tomb at Stephen's Gate over the weekend, exactly where 7QB said it was.

But Will was unflustered.

"Your Honor, Dr. Giovanni and I were present at that excavation. She was a witness to an inscription on a stone ossuary. That is a bone box the Jewish people would use a year or more after the initial burial. They would return and deposit the bones in that box for permanent burial.

"There was an ossuary in that tomb. And this is the inscription that was clearly written on its front, in both Aramaic and Greek:

> **Joseph of Arimathea**
> **honorable counselor**
> **and**
> **disciple of the risen Lord Jesus**

"Your Honor, this tomb by Stephen's Gate that Dr. Reichstad has excavated is the *second tomb* of Joseph of Arimathea, and clearly contains *his* corpse. The bone box proves that. And all the fragments, when read logically and together, show that. The *first tomb* of Joseph was the one that was used for the burial of Jesus, and it is empty."

"We found proof of the crown of thorns next to the corpse!" Reichstad shot out.

"Of course," Will replied. "Joseph of Arimathea took possession of the body of Jesus after the crucifixion and made all the burial arrangements. It is logical that he also came into possession of the crown of thorns. And his friends obviously buried it with Joseph when he died, in honor of his loyalty to Jesus."

"This is exactly what I didn't want to happen," the judge shot out. "I am not going to turn this courtroom into a theological or archaeological discussion of last week's news. By the way," and with that the judge pulled out three newspapers and fanned them out for all to see, "three national newspapers all reported yesterday, on page one, the 'discovery of the corpse of Jesus of Nazareth.' Now we are going to have to deal with the issue of that publicity possibly tainting the jury. But before I rule, I think I am going to have to listen to Dr. Giovanni's testimony on all of these issues, in the exclusion of the jury."

As Will looked out into the courtroom to summon Dr. Giovanni to the witness stand, he noticed Jack Hornby sitting attentively.

But now, Jack had moved forward to the front row of benches, right behind Will Chambers' defense table.

72

AFTER DR. GIOVANNI'S TESTIMONY, Judge Kaye took a ten-minute break to consider his rulings. Giovanni had conducted herself brilliantly. The judge had been impressed with her credentials and her candor. She had described her evaluation of Dr. Reichstad's faulty methodology in making conclusive findings on 7QA under circumstances where it was, or should have been, clear to him that crucial parts of the fragment had recently been torn away. She also had showed how the configuration of the sentences in 7QA alone, while it made grammatical sense, was nevertheless questionable. She had reasoned that the obvious missing fragment had the potential of radically altering the complete meaning of those sentences.

Then Giovanni had described her observations at the excavation at Stephen's Gate. But Judge Kaye had asked one question that bothered Will.

The judge had asked, "Can you, Dr. Giovanni, still give us your opinions as they stood *prior* to seeing the 7QC fragment, and *prior* to seeing the burial site at Jerusalem? Are you able to do that?"

After a moment of reflection, Dr. Giovanni had indicated that she could still give her opinions as they had stood a week ago—if the Court were to instruct her to disregard and not mention the more recent developments.

After ten minutes exactly, Judge Kaye stepped back into the courtroom.

"Here is my ruling. No one is more keenly aware than I am of the importance of getting to the truth in any case—it is essential to the pursuit of justice.

"However, in this case I believe that Dr. Reichstad would be unfairly prejudiced for the defense if, at this late hour of the case, evidence of 7QC or evidence relating to the inscription on the ossuary box in that tomb were presented.

"But I also am ruling that Dr. Reichstad may *not* introduce evidence of his discovery of the corpse in that tomb in Jerusalem over the weekend. And the jury will be questioned on whether they were exposed to any prejudicial publicity or news reports about that discovery."

Will was stunned. Without Angus MacCameron to testify, and without being able to present all of the recent facts they had uncovered, it appeared that he had almost no chance of winning the lawsuit.

"Are you ready, Mr. Chambers," the judge asked, "to present Dr. Giovanni's testimony to the jury, consistent with the ruling that I have just made?"

But before Will could answer, he noticed that the judge's attention had been diverted by something going on at the back of the room. Will turned around.

There was Tiny Heftland, grinning as if he had just won the lottery. He was holding the door open with one hand and making a flourish with the other, like an impresario introducing the next act at a variety show.

Entering behind Tiny was an elderly man who looked like an Arab, dressed in a flowing white robe and carrying a tall, carved staff. A young boy was holding his hand and looking around wide-eyed as they walked into the courtroom.

"This trial is quickly becoming a three-ring circus," the judge remarked. "Mr. Chambers, can you explain this?"

"Your Honor, I will need a few minutes to confer with my investigator."

"Granted. I will be right here waiting for you."

Will walked up to Tiny and the elderly man.

"I struck gold, chief," Tiny said. "Will, meet Mr. Muhammad el Juma and his son Ahmed. The reason we couldn't locate him? Turns out that when he discovered that Tony Azid had been killed for the fragment—well, he took the money that Azid had paid him for it, and bought a little place in Bethlehem, and changed his name.

"Now, you might ask, how did Muhammad the desert king find out that Azid was murdered? Because *he is the one who found the body!* He had delivered the whole fragment, complete, to Azid, and Azid paid him like six or seven thousand dollars for it and says, if he resells it to a guy he is thinking about, he will give Muhammad a percentage. Azid confides that he is going to tear the piece into two or three parts in an effort to bump the price up."

"Did Azid say who he had in mind?"

"Yep, chief," Tiny replied excitedly. "Our own Dr. Hunter. So Muhammad packs up his tent and slips away into the night. But a week later, he decides to return to cousin Tony's shop to see how things are going with their mutual investment, and to see if Hunter is going to get the British Museum to pay out a bundle. As Muhammad is walking up to the shop, he sees this big blond dude walk out of the shop in a hurry, I mean the guy is leaving there in a sweat. Muhammad goes in and discovers that poor Azid had been done in. He gets the police. But the Palestinian police have jurisdiction, and they blow the investigation and call it a suicide."

"How about the blond guy?" Will asked.

"Oh, that's just perfect," Tiny continued. "Get this. When the Israeli police and I locate Muhammad they have him do a photo identification of some suspects. Guess who he ID's as the guy leaving the shop? A guy named Bruda Weilder. He was suspected of an arson and murder in Tel Aviv a few years back. Unfortunately they couldn't make it stick. He is also listed by Interpol as a suspect in crimes in Austria and West Germany. But the best thing is this: Weilder was—at the time of Azid's death—the personal bodyguard for Warren Mullburn. The Israelis tell me that now with Muhammad's testimony, they are going to reopen the Azid and the Hunter matters and charge this thug with double murder. They've already started to look for him."

Will turned and strode up to the front. "Your Honor, I would like to move that the court permit me to amend my witness list to add Mr. Muhammad el Juma. The relevance of his testimony—and the great lengths we went to, to try and locate him—will be spelled out in the preliminary testimony I would like to present, in the exclusion of the jury, from Mr. William Tinney Heftland, aka 'Tiny' Heftland."

Over Sherman's loud objections Judge Kaye permitted Tiny to testify for almost an hour regarding his search for Muhammad, how they had finally located him, and how the evidence he had would link 7QA, 7QB, and 7QC all together. Tiny explained how the Bedouin tribesman could also connect the death of Azid with Hunter's death, and lastly, could connect Mullburn's bodyguard to the deaths, during the same week that Reichstad—a beneficiary of Mullburn's financial support—had admitted coming into possession of 7QA.

Judge Kaye asked Tiny as many questions as Sherman and Will Chambers did. Sherman ferociously attacked Tiny's credibility by showing that he was a paid investigator for Will. That he was biased, that he had been unsuccessful in his prior federal and police employment. But Judge Kaye wasn't buying it.

When Tiny's testimony was finished, Judge Kaye leaned back in his chair. He would not, he said, retire to deliberate this one. He already knew how he was going to rule.

This was it. Will could feel it. He knew this was one of those moments that could turn a mere courtroom contest into a triumph of justice.

Judge Kaye leaned forward on his arms, which were crossed in front of him.

"Here is my ruling. Muhammad el Juma's testimony will be allowed. In order to be fair to Mr. Sherman's side, the new witness is to be made available to Mr. Sherman for a deposition this afternoon, if Mr. Sherman so desires. That way, Mr. Sherman, there will be no unfair surprises. You may ask him anything you want before we resume in the presence of jury tomorrow. Mr. Chambers, do you have an interpreter?"

Will looked back at Tiny, who nodded and pointed to a woman who had been standing next to the Bedouin and his son.

"All right. Then we will adjourn for the day. We will start right at nine o'clock in the morning, with the jury present, first with the testimony of Muhammad el Juma. After that, Mr. Chambers, you can recall Dr. Giovanni and present her testimony to the jury, and then that of the two Israeli police officers."

There was arguing somewhere in the courtroom. Suddenly, Will realized that it was coming from the opposing counsel's table. Dr. Reichstad was frantically yelling something at Sherman, and J-Fox Sherman was yelling back.

Judge Kaye gave them both a bewildered look.

"Do you have a problem that concerns this court, or may I adjourn this case for the day?" the judge asked.

After Sherman and Reichstad had conferred in only slightly quieter tones, Sherman walked slowly up to the podium.

"I have a motion, your honor."

"What kind of motion?"

"It is a motion that I feel I must make to accommodate my client, though I do so with great reluctance."

"What kind of motion? Spell it out!"

"We are moving for a voluntary dismissal of this lawsuit—which is the plaintiff's right, Your Honor."

"In the middle of a jury trial? *Now* you decide to dismiss your case?"

"Well, Your Honor, perhaps my client can explain..."

Reichstad hurried up to the podium.

"Your Honor. You said, yourself, that you have read the headlines. You know by now that I have achieved something far beyond what anyone has ever achieved in my field—I have located and revealed the body of Jesus of Nazareth. At this point I don't need the decision of a jury to vindicate me. The world has vindicated me. History will vindicate me. Besides,

MacCameron wouldn't be able to pay me whatever the jury might award anyway. I am trying to be a gentleman about this..."

"Gentleman?" Will shot back. "Your Honor, we object. We don't want a dismissal. We want justice. We want Angus MacCameron's reputation restored after the plaintiff has so wantonly smeared and defamed it in this courtroom."

"Mr. Chambers, I don't think I have any choice. I must permit plaintiff to voluntarily withdraw his lawsuit, even at this late hour."

"Then I want compensation for my client—and my attorney's fees to be paid by Dr. Reichstad and Mr. Sherman!" Will countered.

"On the basis of what?" Sherman shot back.

"On the basis of Rule 41 of the Federal Rules of Civil Procedure, and the ruling by the Court of Appeals of the D.C. Circuit in *Taragan vs. Eli Lilly and Company*," Will replied.

Sherman was speechless.

"How soon can you file a written request for me to consider, Mr. Chambers?"

"Within twenty-four hours."

"Mr. Sherman," the judge continued, "within forty-eight hours after you receive Mr. Chamber's written request for attorney's fees and other compensation for his client, you are to file your written response and any arguments you have as to why I should deny Mr. Chamber's request. I will then try to get my written decision out as rapidly as I can. This case is dismissed. Court adjourned. Clerk, discharge the jury. Tell them they can go home. Someone else, I guess, is going to have to solve the mystery of the ages—it's not going to be them."

73

The following day, Will, as promised, filed with the U.S. District Court of the District of Columbia, Judge Jeremiah Kaye presiding, a written request for Dr. Reichstad or his attorneys or both, to pay two separate sums of money.

First, Will demanded payment for his attorney's fees and the total costs of the defense of the case. After he had added up his hourly fees as well as those of Jacki Johnson—hundreds of those hours not yet billed to his stricken client—together with the costs of international travel, depositions, expert fees, long-distance charges, express deliveries, hotel rooms, and thousands of photocopies of documents, he came up with a substantial figure. He was asking that Reichstad and his lawyers pay MacCameron the sum of $596,843.74 for the legal fees and costs incurred by the defense in the case.

The second sum that Will demanded gave him particular pleasure. Although he wondered whether Judge Kaye would award a single penny for this category—because of its unusual nature—he put it in anyway. Will asked that the Court order Reichstad and his lawyers to pay the sum of $500,000 for the "inconvenience and stress caused to Reverend Angus MacCameron, and the defamation to his reputation."

The argument that Will made on this latter point was simple and logical: Reichstad and his swarm of legal sharks had done irrevocable damage to MacCameron's integrity and reputation in presenting their side of the case. By then prematurely dismissing their lawsuit before the defense had had its chance to vindicate MacCameron, they left, as Will put it in his brief to the Court, "an indelible stain on Reverend MacCameron's good name; they drew, for all the world to see, a grotesque caricature of my client, forever recorded in a court record; then promptly dismissed their lawsuit, thereby wrenching the pen out of our hands, and preventing us from ever adequately correcting their ugly and false picture of Reverend MacCameron."

A copy of Will's brief to the court and request for compensation was taken by courier to the offices of Kennelworth, Sherman, Abrams & Cantwell.

There was a time, not so long ago in the past, where Will Chambers would have personally delivered the papers to J-Fox Sherman himself just for the pleasure of seeing his expression. Just to tell him, eye to eye, that now the shoe was on the *other* foot; that now Sherman and his client were the ones who had to worry about whether they might soon be reaping the bitter harvest they had planted themselves. There was a time when Will would have done exactly that.

But that time was not now. Will was no longer that man—nor, it seemed, was he interested in taking that same road.

After the courier had picked up the written arguments to the judge, Will returned calls from a few new clients. In between those calls he connected with Fiona, who was still in London. He was saddened that the news about MacCameron had not changed. She said that the doctors had told her to "brace for the worst." Will asked her some questions, but mostly listened.

Fiona asked about the trial, and Will explained the strange turn of events—the eerie excavation at St. Stephen's Gate, and Dr. Giovanni's conclusion that the corpse found there was definitely that of Joseph of Arimathea; how Tiny had located Muhammad el Juma, and how Reichstad had withdrawn his own lawsuit rather than permit the truth to come out. And Will also explained to Fiona how, in a rare reversal, Reichstad, the complainant in a libel and defamation case, was now facing *their* demand for attorney's fees and compensation for damage to Angus's good name.

"Da would be so proud of you!" Fiona said. "How I wish he could have been there."

Will told her that Angus MacCameron was very fortunate to have a daughter like her. Fiona said this was a very lonely time for her, and could he please call her again that evening. She would be by her father's side in the hospital throughout the night and into the morning.

Will went out for some supper, then returned to work afterwards. As he locked up his Corvette in front of the old red-brick building that housed his office, the bells of St. Andrew's Church began ringing.

As the tolling of the great bells filled the air, Will froze in his tracks, next to his car. He looked over at the church, and its towering steeple. Then he quickly walked over to the entrance. He laid hold of one of the iron handles and swung open one of the thick doors.

Will stepped inside onto the worn-looking multi-colored stone of the vestibule. He saw a stairway to his left. He started walking up, then increased his pace. Soon he was running up to the second floor. From there, a very narrow set of stairs led upward in a dizzying spiral. Will ran up the cramped stairwell, around and then around again as it took him higher and higher. He glanced through the small side windows and, as he quickened his steps, the street, the office building, and the passersby down below, kept getting smaller.

Finally, several stories above the city of Monroeville, the staircase came up into a square, musty room with dark, warped wooden floorboards, and thick ropes dangling through an opening in the ceiling.

There was a thin young woman in the center of the room, with long brown hair that reached to the middle of her back. She looked straight at Will through the bell ropes, still hanging on to one of them. The woman was smiling, and then Will noticed something shiny at the collar of her sweatshirt.

As Will walked a little closer he saw that she was wearing a little baby's-feet pin—and then he recognized her face.

"You were there in court that day. You're the one who grabbed my arm."

"Yes," she said softly. "That was me."

"And you told me you would be praying for me."

"Yes. And I *have* been praying for you. You haven't remembered who I am, have you?"

Will struggled but only shook his head.

"I'm Kimberly. My father was the police chief. You were his lawyer, a long time ago. You won the case for him, when the department tried to suspend him from duty to force him to get help for his alcoholism."

"You were just a little girl then. Now I remember," Will replied. "I didn't mean to scare you by running up here like this. I really don't know why I'm here."

"Oh, but I do," she said gently. "I know exactly why you are here."

Will wanted to reply, but whatever words he had intended to speak became stuck in his throat.

"You see," she continued, "I sort of wished you would have lost that case for my Dad, then maybe things could have changed and he wouldn't have drunk himself to death. In the years after that, I would see your cases mentioned in the newspapers, or a magazine here or there. So I started praying, every day, that the Lord would lead you to become a defender of his truth—and a mighty advocate for his kingdom. I've been one of the bell-pullers here at St. Andrew's for a while, ever since I moved up here. Sometimes I've been up here at night, and the only light shining in that building across the street has been coming from your office. And I've been able to see you working at your desk. And I pray for you. So I figure that's why you're here, right?"

Turning away slightly, Will had no words to speak at first; all he could do was nod his head in agreement, and try to clear the catch that was in his throat.

The woman put her hands in her jeans and smiled an even broader smile.

Finally Will said, "Kimberly, I've got to go. There is something I have to do."

He went on. "Sometime I would like to come by, and we'll talk some more. You can get me caught up on how you and the rest of your family have been doing all these years."

As Will started down the stairs, he stopped and turned, and looked back at the woman standing amid the ropes.

"Thank you, Kimberly," he said, "from the bottom of my heart." Then he walked down the long spiral descent to the ground level.

Will crossed the street to his building and steadily climbed the stairs. He strode through the lobby and through the door into his office, where he then plucked the Byzantine coin given to him by Nathan out of its place in the glass box he had put it in on top of his desk. He studied it, and then sat down on the carpet with his back against his large mahogany desk, knees drawn up, the coin in his hand. Will looked hard at the semi-obscured, fifteen-hundred-year-old visage of Jesus that lay in his hand.

He was quiet for a long while, oblivious to the sounds of cars down on the street below, and the occasional noise from elsewhere in the building. Now he was intent on conducting only one piece of business. Nothing else, at that moment, seemed to matter very much.

Crossing his arms, he rested them on his knees and bowed his head against them. And with his eyes closed he walked into the silence of that moment. Time slowed. Will Chambers knew that in these quiet seconds of eternity he was to encounter the Person of God. The ever-watching and unseen face of the Everlasting One.

"God," he started out, "I don't know how to do this. I'm not much of a man. Lost. Confused. Busted dreams. And a broken heart. I have so many questions. And not many answers. But I've read your written record. And I know that Jesus is real—I know it. That he was killed on that cross for my sins. And for everybody's. That was the mission. That's why he came. Death couldn't hold him back—and the tomb couldn't either. Which means he really was your Son, after all."

Will thought for a second and then said, "I'm afraid I don't know what comes next. Tell me what I ought to do now. Just do what you have to do with my heart. Thanks for listening."

Then he added, "Amen."

"Praise!"

Will started at the shout. Opening his eyes and turning himself to the side, he heard it again.

"Praise!"

Hattie, the cleaning lady, was looking at him through the open door. She was standing in the lobby of his office, beaming.

"Praise God!" Hattie was exclaiming. She was sweeping the air grandly, back and forth with her hands, and doing a little jig with her feet.

"Lord, oh Lord! You went fishing and you caught yourself a lawyer today!"

Will started to get up to his feet, but Hattie walked in and admonished him boldly, wagging her index finger.

"Don't you get up from there. That's holy ground. Holy ground! You stay right there on that floor, Mr. Will Chambers."

Will complied, leaning back against the desk again, still seated on the carpet.

"I want you to know, now, I wasn't spying on you. I was just coming in to empty your wastepaper baskets," she continued. "But I must have been led here for a reason. Now, you don't want to be a wasted seed, do you?"

There was a puzzled look on Will's face. "That's bad, right?"

"Jesus says that the sown seed that gets swooped up by the birds, or gets scorched by the sun, or gets all choked off by the weeds—well, that seed is no good to nobody."

"Yes," Will said remembering, "I think I read that..."

"Do you have a church?"

"I don't think so."

"Now you ought to come down to my church; it's the one down by the river. Not five blocks from here. Mount of Olives Church of the Risen Savior. Brother Henry Bickford, Pastor. You come on down there any Sunday morning."

"I surely will," he said.

"And you bring a friend. That's our motto. 'The message is too good for just one.' You got someone to bring with you?"

"Yes," Will replied. "As a matter of fact, I think I do."

"You invite that person."

"I most assuredly will. I will be calling her tonight. I'll ask her to join me in coming to your church sometime."

"You do that, Mr. Chambers. God bless you real good now," she said as she left the office and closed the door.

Will could hear her singing "What a friend we have in Jesus..." as she pushed her cleaning cart down the hallway.

74

ONE WEEK LATER, AFTER SUNDOWN, when the street lamps along the cobblestone streets of Monroeville had just come on, Will was making a quick trip back to his office. It was a mild night. Some of the evening birds were still chirping, and there was a soft breeze blowing through the blossoms on the pear trees. He had forgotten his wallet and checkbook and was returning to the office to fetch them. As he got out of his car he paused a minute to enjoy the sweet evening air.

Then he entered the building, locking the tall oak front doors behind him, and walked up and the stairs to his darkened office and turned on the lights. He spotted his wallet and checkbook—on his desk, as he had thought. He was about to leave when the phone in the lobby rang. He thought about letting it go to voice mail, but instead picked up the receiver. Jacki Johnson was on the other end.

Her voice was excited and she was talking a mile a minute.

"I was just on the Internet—I saw something that indicated that Judge Kaye had just filed his decision...he's posted it on the Web...but I can't get through to read it."

The fax line started ringing in the copy room.

"Wait a minute," Will yelled, and he ran down the hallway.

After a few seconds the document started printing out. Will could see the letterhead of the U.S. District Court of the District of Columbia on it.

He ran back to the lobby and picked up the phone.

"Jacki—the court decision is just coming through the fax right now...hang on the line, and I'll tell you what the judge ruled as soon as I read it." Will put the receiver down and started to run back down the hallway, but the second phone line rang.

When Will picked it up he heard a woman's voice.

"Mr. Chambers, I am a reporter from the Affiliated Press Service. We have just received something in, a few minutes ago. I'm wondering if you could confirm Judge Kaye's ruling, and give us a statement—"

"Listen, could you hold on for a minute?" Will broke in. He put her on hold, and started back down the hall to the fax machine, but the third telephone line started ringing.

He grabbed it and asked that caller also to wait just a minute, and then put him on hold as well.

Before Will could start for the fax machine again, he heard someone yelling his name outside, down on the street.

Will ran over to the window and yanked it open. There, down on the street, was Jack Hornby.

Hornby was standing next to a television truck with a large satellite dish.

"Will Chambers! I need to talk to you!" Hornby yelled. "I really need the first interview here...after all I've done for you. So what do you say? Come on down here and unlock the door of this relic and let me in."

"What's going on?" Will shouted down.

"Reichstad versus MacCameron. That's what it is."

"I'm just getting the court's decision now on my fax, I haven't even read it yet!" Will yelled.

"You don't have to. I have it right here!" Hornby shouted back, waving a copy of the court's ruling in his hand. "Just give me the first crack at this story, and then after you talk to me, a *real* newsman, then you can do the standup interview for these TV clowns down here, alright?"

"So why did the *Herald* change their mind and decide to cover this?" Will asked, leaning out of the window.

"They didn't. I changed jobs. Congratulate me. I'm the new Washington, D.C., bureau chief for American Press International. Now go pull the court decision off your fax—just read the last page and then the footnote on page seven—that'll give you the box score. You can read the rest later."

Will sprinted down to the fax machine and pulled off the sheets of paper. He riffled through them and pulled out the last page and page seven, as Hornby had suggested.

Hornby was right. At the last page Judge Kaye summarized his ruling.

Regarding Reichstad and his attorneys having to pay MacCameron for the prejudice caused by their abrupt dismissal of the lawsuit, the court found Will's demand for half-a-million dollars "slightly excessive." Instead, the court ordered Reichstad to pay Angus MacCameron $400,000.

As for Will's attorney's fees and costs, and those of Jacki Johnson, the court granted the entire $596,843.74; this also to be paid personally by Dr. Reichstad.

J-Fox Sherman's law firm, however, had been mercifully let off the hook.

Then Will turned to page seven of the court's ruling and looked at the footnote. It read:

> Plaintiff Reichstad argues that he decided to dismiss his lawsuit in the middle of the jury trial because his recent discovery of an ancient corpse has 'vindicated' his claim to have disproved the bodily resurrection of Jesus of Nazareth—thus dispensing with the need for a jury verdict to clear his professional reputation.
>
> This argument the Court believes to be so incredible as to not be worthy of belief. MacCameron's expert, Dr. Giovanni, testified convincingly, as to the identity of the corpse found recently in Jerusalem, near St. Stephen's Gate, most likely being that of one Joseph of Arimathea, a follower of Jesus and the religious official who, according to the New Testament, was the prime mover behind the burial of Jesus.
>
> It would appear to this court that Dr. Reichstad's real motivation in dismissing his lawsuit when he did was to avoid the damaging—indeed, perhaps even indicting—testimony of Muhammad el Juma, a Bedouin tribesman who discovered the 7QA, 7QB, and 7QC fragments—and who could have linked Dr. Reichstad to the suspicious deaths of antiquities dealer Harim Azid and Dr. Richard Hunter.

Judge Kaye concluded the unusual footnote this way:

> The conclusion of this rather extraordinary legal action now ends the inquiry into the burial, and possible resurrection, of Jesus Christ—the most central tenet of the Christian religion. That question is left *unresolved*. But then, perhaps that is also fitting. It is better left decided within the chambers of the human heart, rather than the chambers of a court of law. So, as matters stand, this Court, at least, can venture no *official* opinion on that issue.

As Will started toward the door to go down and speak with Jack Hornby he remembered Jacki on hold. Her line was beeping at the front desk.

"Jacki," Will said, picking up the phone, "the court gave us almost everything we asked for. I can't talk right now. I'll call you back in thirty minutes.

But when I call you back, I'm going to make you an offer to come back to work for me, so be prepared to say yes!"

When Will got down to Jack Hornby on the sidewalk, the reporter was smiling one of his ironic smiles.

"I wanted to interview God on this one, like you once suggested, but he's not available. So I'll have to settle for you instead."

"Don't be so sure about that," Will replied. The bells of St. Andrew's were now beginning to toll from above them. "That may be him calling right now."

75

Seven Months Later

WASHINGTON, D.C., IS A CITY OF MANY SECRETS—but ultimately, secrets only poorly kept.

The word had begun to surface that a federal grand jury had been convened in the District regarding actions of Undersecretary Kenneth Sharptin—the subject matter was illegal campaign fund-raising, possible violation of several foreign relations laws, and influence-peddling and international bribery regarding Warren Mullburn's attempted entrée into OPEC. The federal prosecutors handling the grand jury were in possession of unique evidence that had been gathered by the FBI.

The FBI's agents had followed up on Will Chambers' strange story of his abduction by Abdul el Alibahd. Will's description of Alibahd's physical condition confirmed other information gathered by the CIA and military intelligence. The terrorist, it appeared, was dying, and his web of international criminal activity was expected to soon unravel; his organization, it was thought, would be retooled and continued by several of his lieutenants. But that would not happen. American military operatives were closing in on Alibahd and his group. Soon they would kill his bodyguards, and capture the man himself. Consumed by lung cancer, Alibahd would be carried away by Delta Force commandos on a stretcher—gasping for air, but finding none.

The FBI was also actively investigating the message Alibahd had delivered to Warren Mullburn through Will. Mullburn himself soon became their focus, as well as his cozy relationship with Kenneth Sharptin and his financing of Sharptin's bid for the vice-presidential slot. But the federal agents were astonished at the breadth and audacity of their apparent conspiracy: a joint effort to bribe their way into a foothold in OPEC's oil monopoly by using the currency of pro-Islamic American policies and leveraging increased U.S. military aid to the Arab nations.

All of that was more than sufficient, several times over, to short-circuit any possibility of Sharptin's running as the vice-presidential candidate. The public explanation given by the White House for Sharptin's name being dropped from the shortlist of running mates was that he needed to "spend more time with his family."

The real question was—what family? Sharptin's wife had moved out a year before, when she had learned of his various affairs.

One night, after Sharptin had learned that he had been targeted by the grand jury, and while his mistress slumbered beside him in the bedroom of his Old Town Alexandria townhouse, the Undersecretary slipped out of bed, put on his best bathrobe, and quietly walked down the plush, carpeted steps to his well-furnished den. He eased himself down onto the smooth luxury of his leather sofa. Then he popped the top off a small plastic bottle and poured the contents into the glass of liquor that was sitting in front of him on the glass coffee table.

There would be no hesitation. Kenneth Sharptin prided himself on being a man who knew how to make decisions. He looked at the glass for only a second before he swallowed the contents in a single gulp.

The next morning, following that fatal decision, his mistress would find his body sprawled out on the couch. She would grab her things and slip away, before the police—and the press—descended on the townhouse that was about to achieve fleeting celebrity status as the scene of the suicide of the Undersecretary of the U.S. Department of State.

By the time the news media started reporting Sharptin's suicide and the grand jury in progress, Warren Mullburn had already relocated his primary residence to a secret villa in Switzerland. To his extensive staff he had left the formidable task of clearing out his Nevada desert mansion. Fifteen moving vans and three auto-transport trucks were needed to contain the imported antique furniture he had collected from France, Austria, and Russia, some modern furnishings inspired by Frank Lloyd Wright, the Italian stone fountains, the eclectic mixture of original artwork ranging from Cézanne to Andy Warhol, the antiquities purchased from dealers around the world, the classic antique automobiles, and the large collection of the world's most expensive sports cars.

The last thing the staff did, before locking the doors to the sixty-five-million-dollar compound, was to drain the Olympic-size swimming pool.

Then the parade of moving vans and transports began rumbling past the property's "For Sale—By Appointment Only" sign and down the desert road on their route to the highway that led to Las Vegas, and points beyond. The convoy of trucks, bearing the spoils of Warren Mullburn the multinational corporate raider, snaked its way along, creating clouds of dust in the Nevada desert like a procession of some modern-day Genghis Khan.

Only this Genghis Khan had already skipped town.

The only trace of Mullburn's presence in the Nevada desert was the now-vacant collection of buildings known as "Utopia," and a decaying corpse that would be found months later in the nearby hills. The murdered body, identified as one Bruda Weilder, had been left to be preyed on by the beasts of the wilderness.

While his small army of agents and employees were moving his worldly goods, Warren Mullburn was on the telephone from Switzerland, talking to his attorneys. The subject was how to fend off a possible criminal indictment against him. The law firm was Kennelworth, Sherman, Abrams & Cantwell—the Washington, D.C., office.

However, the attorneys were worried about a potential conflict of interest in representing Mullburn because of the possibility that Dr. Albert Reichstad, also their client, might be named as a conspirator by the grand jury. That, of course, would be a shame—if not a tragedy—for the firm, as Mullburn was a high-profile client, and was certainly in a position to pay every penny of their high-profile legal fees.

But the decision of the attorneys in that firm about representing Mullburn became much easier when, about three A.M. that Sunday morning in Jerusalem, Reichstad would suddenly become indisposed from being the client of Kennelworth, Sherman, Abrams & Cantwell—or any other law firm for that matter.

Reichstad had been working through the night inside the excavation tent at the burial site at St. Stephen's Gate. His assistants had all left for the night and returned to their hotels. A disturbance farther down the eastern wall of the Old City had drawn all of the guards away from the area momentarily.

A man, carrying what looked a little like a black trombone case, was climbing the hill just above the Mount of Olives and the Garden of Gethsemane. He stopped at the spot where he could view St. Stephen's Gate and the great white tent of Dr. Reichstad.

The man opened the case, took out a lightweight missile launcher, and rapidly assembled it. Then he loaded in an armor-piercing missile, pointing it toward Reichstad's archaeological dig site, and looked through the sighting device until he had the center of the white tent perfectly lined up. When he squeezed the trigger the missile left a faint wisp of smoke behind it as it flew across the small valley that separated the Mount of Olives from the old wall at St. Stephen's Gate and slammed into the excavation area where Reichstad was in the process of using an X-ray machine to analyze the ancient corpse that was scheduled to be moved the following day.

After the explosion, very little of Dr. Reichstad—and nothing of the corpse—was left. Reichstad was able to be identified only because a few of his teeth were found at the scene of the missile hit.

News reports indicated that no suspects had yet been named by either the Israeli government or the Palestinian Authority. However, several media accounts speculated on whether "Christian fundamentalists" intent on preserving belief in the resurrection of Jesus could be linked to the murder of Dr. Reichstad and the destruction of the tomb at that archaeological site.

The Secretary General of the United Nations, a few days later, had the occasion to comment on the attack. He remarked that "it was time for all nations, peoples, and groups to renounce that kind of religious fanaticism that breeds violence." And then, while urging "Christian leaders around the world to exhort their flocks and congregations to be tolerant toward ideas that might challenge their own deeply held beliefs," the Secretary General suggested that it might be time to take concrete steps regarding religious extremism.

"Let our children and grandchildren," he continued, "see the twenty-first century as the time when all the people of the earth come together, through the United Nations, to prevent the spread of that species of religious fundamentalism that threatens global peace."

76

A WEEK AFTER REICHSTAD'S DEATH, following the memorial service for their murdered boss, Dr. Victor Beady and Dr. Curtis Jorgenson sat in Beady's car, a quarter of a mile down the road from their research center, and talked.

They were unaware of the van parked around the corner of the next crossroad, screened from them by some trees. The two occupants of the van were monitoring the conversation through a listening device that had been planted in Beady's car radio.

One of the men, listening intently through his headphones, was Nathan Goldwaithe, sometime member of the Israeli Mossad. The other man, who was sitting next to him in the back, adjusting the sound levels, was Caleb Meir, a fellow agent.

"This is ridiculous, conducting business in the car this way..." Jorgenson said while he fidgeted in the passenger seat.

"No, not at all. Mullburn has the whole building and grounds wired and bugged. There are remotely controlled video monitors everywhere," Beady reminded him.

"So what is the report? Have they named any suspects in the Reichstad thing?"

"Not that I know of. But I have read a few reports speculating that it may have been the work of 'Christian fundamentalists.' That's grand—and amusing, don't you think?"

"What is the plan...I need to know what our plan is..."

"Stop worrying. Take a Valium. We are now in the second phase. Nothing's changed. And this phase is much more airtight than the first part. Besides, when Reichstad filed that idiotic lawsuit against MacCameron he ended up destroying any chance we had to really exploit 7QA."

"Now that Reichstad is...he's gone...I'm beginning to wonder. Are you sure it was a good idea?"

"Of course. With Reichstad out of the way, and the corpse in that tomb blown to oblivion, who is to say who that corpse *really was?* All the data disappeared in the explosion. And now we can actually turn Reichstad into a martyr for the cause of scientific enlightenment, and get on with running this show *our way.*"

"But I've still got questions about out ability to pull off this second phase. That's why I wanted to talk. How can you be absolutely sure you can produce the results we want?"

"How? Because I'm the world's greatest expert in radiocarbon dating since W.F. Libby, who invented it—that's how."

"You may be sure about your carbon-dating, but what about your genetic manufacturing? Are you sure you can get our parchment and ink to test out to 700 B.C. a hundred times out of a hundred? If we're going to pull this off with a single fragment, it's got to reliably date older than all the existing Old Testament manuscripts."

"Why do you think I've been doing all this in the basement of that ugly, stuffy, windowless building? Of course I can do it. Now all we have to do is get in touch with the right people in Syria, or Iraq, or Iran. Can you imagine how much they'll be willing to pay us for our little Deuteronomy production—when we tell them that the inscription on it reads that God gave 'Israel' to the *Arabs,* through Ishmael?"

In the van, listening to the conversation, Nathan gave his partner a flinty look. They nodded to each other as they finished capturing it on tape. The next day they would return the rental van, destroy the audio equipment, and convert the final audiotape to a tiny electronic strip that would fit into the end of a fountain pen. Nathan would carry that fountain pen clipped inside the pocket of his leather sport coat as he boarded the airplane in New York. In less than forty-eight hours he hoped to share his information with ranking officials within the Mossad, a few trusted members of the Knesset—and perhaps even the prime minister of Israel.

77

BECAUSE IT WAS WARM THAT SUNDAY MORNING in Monroeville, the big windows of the Mount of Olives Church of the Risen Savior were cranked wide open. The gospel choir was singing and swinging and moving together like an undulating field of wheat. The sounds of their hymn, and the snare drum and electric guitars that accompanied them, floated across the river and could be heard on the other side where some boys were fishing by the shacks that dotted the bank.

Inside, Brother Henry Bickford, the pastor, strode up to the pulpit as the church rang with the sound of three hundred "Amens."

"We are pleased," he began, "to have a special guest, a brother with us this morning. Someone who had medical problems—very serious medical problems. To the very point of death!"

When the "Amens" died down, he continued.

"But the Lord healed him, and brought him here to us today. The *Lord,* who does all things perfectly...the *Lord,* who is from Everlasting...the *Lord* who takes the sting out of death and snatches victory out of the grave!"

The congregation exploded into a great, surging, joyful noise. Someone was shaking a tambourine.

As the pastor introduced him, Reverend Angus MacCameron slowly stood up, leaning on his cane, and waved to the smiling faces in the jammed church sanctuary.

MacCameron wore the face of a man who had come back from the grave, but whose heart was still lingering at another grave—and on the memory of the woman who had been called into eternity before he was.

While MacCameron had been struggling to survive a heart attack and a stroke, his wife, Helen, had quietly lost her long battle with lung cancer. Helen had been buried in a cemetery in northern Virginia in a simple ceremony, attended by Fiona Cameron, the members of her musical group, and a few friends of the MacCameron's from church. Will Chambers had been there. Angus MacCameron, because of his critical medical condition, had not.

However, there had seemed to be a powerful though invisible presence of Angus during the funeral. It was a palpable feeling as the casket of his beloved wife was lowered into the ground. Perhaps it was because of the bagpiper who played an old Scottish hymn at the graveside. Or perhaps it was simply that—as those near him knew—Angus was the kind of man who had always loved his wife more than life itself.

When Angus had regained consciousness and could be told that Helen had died, he had mourned his wife—and the fact that he had not had a chance to tell her goodbye. But then he had said, through his tears, "Now I will simply have to give my darling wife that 'goodbye' in glory, at the same time I give her my most magnificent 'hello.'"

After Angus had resumed his seat in a tall, ornate chair just behind the pulpit, Brother Bickford continued.

"Now, Brother MacCameron is going to deliver a message this morning called 'The Resurrection of Jesus—the Power and the Glory.' But first, we are going to be blessed again by our choir as they lift their voices to the Lord."

In the third row from the front was Hattie the cleaning lady, wearing her best white hat. She adjusted her reading glasses as she studied the church bulletin.

Sitting next to Hattie was Will Chambers. Will shifted his Bible to his hand that was nearest to Hattie, and reached his other one over to the slender, graceful hand that was resting next to him on the pew. He folded the fingers of his big hand around the woman's hand, enclosing it.

Fiona laughed quietly and removed Will's hand from hers, and whispered to him, "Da always taught me that it was *not* appropriate for a lady to hold hands with a man during church."

"Hands?" Will asked slyly.

"Yes," Fiona replied.

Then Will moved his little finger over and wrapped it around Fiona's little finger.

"Will!" Fiona said with another hushed laugh, "You are such a *lawyer*."

After the church service, Will and Fiona were going to drive to Generals' Hill. Will wanted to show her the construction that was going on at the site of his old house. Rather than trying to replicate the pre–Civil War mansion that had burned to the ground, he had decided on something else. He had always wanted to build a huge log house, the kind that had a massive stone fireplace and high, timbered ceilings.

Will Chambers was about to do exactly that.

The new home would be built, its walls raised, its roof established, on the scorched ground of the past. Will walked hand-in-hand with Fiona, as they looked upon the beginnings of construction on what had been a hill of desolation. Now, with Fiona at his side, and a peace that lay within like a calm ocean, Will knew that this was a place where old things had passed away. He also knew, just as surely, that for him all things were becoming new. The long night was over. Resurrection had begun.

About the Author

Craig Parshall is a highly successful lawyer from the Washington, D.C., area who specializes in cases involving civil liberties and religious freedom. He is also a frequent spokesperson for conservative values in mainstream and Christian media. Now, in *The Resurrection File,* he shows himself to be a gifted novelist.

THE CHAMBERS OF JUSTICE SERIES
by Craig Parshall

The Resurrection File

When Reverend Angus MacCameron asks attorney Will Chambers to defend him against accusations that could discredit the Gospels, Will's unbelieving heart says "run." But conspiracy and intrigue—and the presence of MacCameron's lovely and successful daughter, Fiona—draw him deep into the case... toward a destination he could never have imagined.

Custody of the State

Attorney Will Chambers reluctantly agrees to defend a young mother from Georgia and her farmer husband, suspected of committing the unthinkable against their own child. Encountering small-town secrets, big-time corruption, and a government system that's destroying the little family, Chambers himself is thrown into the custody of the state.

The Accused

Enjoying a Cancún honeymoon with his wife, Fiona, attorney Will Chambers is ambushed by two unexpected events: a terrorist kidnapping of a U.S. official...and the news that a link has been found to the previously unidentified murderer of Will's first wife. The kidnapping pulls him into the case of Marine colonel Caleb Marlowe. When treachery drags both Will and his client toward vengeance, they must ask—*Is forgiveness real?*

Missing Witness

A relaxing North Carolina vacation for attorney Will Chambers? Not likely. When Will investigates a local inheritance case, the long arm of the law reaches out of the distant past to cast a shadow over his client's life...and the life of his own family. As the attorney's legal battle uncovers corruption, piracy, the deadly grip of greed, and the haunting sins of a man's past, the true question must be faced—*Can a person ever really run away from God?*

The Last Judgment

A mysterious religious cult plans to spark an "Armageddon" in the Middle East. Suddenly, a huge explosion blasts the top of the Jerusalem Temple Mount into rubble, with hundreds of Muslim casualities. And attorney Will Chambers' client, Gilead Amahn, a convert to Christianity from Islam, becomes the prime suspect. In his harrowing pursuit of the truth, Will must face the greatest threat yet to his marriage, his family, and his faith, while cataclysmic events plunge the world closer to the Last Judgment.